AF444641

Jay Bell Books

Pride High : Book 4 – Green © 2024 Jay Bell

ISBN: 979-8-3305-4755-5

Cover art (Mindy, Diego and Ricky) by Cassy Fallon

THANK YOU!

These are the people I'd want to sit with at lunch. Because of their support—both emotional and financial—I'm able to write and release books publishers have no interest in that have gone on to change lives, including my own.

Joseph M Acosta ♥ Jake Allman ♥ Mark Andrews
Jeremy and Andy Bearberger ♥ Charles Azcona
Kevin Bowling-Swan ♥ Kevin van Breugel
Chris & Kai Burton ♥ Scott Caldwell ♥ Chadwyk
Cory Chamberlin ♥ Matthew Christian ♥ Conn
Andy Corvin ♥ Neil Courtney ♥ Troy D ♥ Jason Dittmer
Mark Edwards ♥ Julian/Ilona F. ♥ Shannon Farnsworth
Neil Ferman ♥ Tallian Fisher ♥ Zac Ford ♥ Jim Frier
Richie G. ♥ Sal Guenette ♥ Brian H ♥ Li H
Nick Hancock ♥ Keith Heathcote ♥ Paul Henriksen
Florian Heym ♥ Stephen Hurwitz ♥ Daniel Hutchinson
Xavier Ibarra ♥ Nathan Jackson ♥ Jason Jermyn
Leigh Juhlke ♥ Shaun King ♥ Ken Koyle ♥ Lisa Lieurance
Carol Molinari ♥ Chris Marcou ♥ Marc Martinez
Vince Marsters ♥ Peter Mawer ♥ Michael, Koda, & Kida
Olli N ♥ Olivier Ochin ♥ Jim & Gary Omaha ♥ Tim P.
Zara Park ♥ John Parkinson ♥ Brandon and Jared Reeves
Matthew Richards ♥ Ryan Riebeling ♥ Urban Andenius
Skeppstedt ♥ Stephen Shelton ♥ Lee Short ♥ Marc Shur
John Smeallie ♥ Somyos and Russell ♥ Bert Snyers
Heather Somma ♥ Muyang Song ♥ SonicPhil
David Spry ♥ Stephanie Sullivan ♥ Michael Swearingen
Skylar Sweeney ♥ Holly Trebing ♥ Stuart Turnbull
Bob Turnure ♥ Nick Vallina ♥ Mychel Vandover
Carlos Vela ♥ Peter VH ♥ Alan S. Villafana
Michael Wallace ♥ David Wood
Chris and Thea Woods ♥ JR Woods

Anthony Cullen, no longer able to deny his lifelong crush on his best friend Omar, finally accepts that he is gay. He gets his first real shot at love when he meets Cameron, a sweet guy from his school. Their relationship begins to attract attention, some of it unkind, so Anthony writes a coming out article for his school paper that the principal refuses to publish. Anthony distributes the article himself, receiving more backlash, but he's not done fighting yet. Or finished experimenting with his appearance.

Omar Jafari feels like all his dreams are coming true when he lands his first girlfriend, Silvia, and gets a job at Archie's Pizza Pie that supports his passion for cinematography. The cracks begin to show when he learns that Silvia kissed another girl while dating him. After searching his heart, Omar makes the difficult decision to break up with her. But only temporarily. As the summer begins, they promise to be friends with the intention of starting again someday.

Silvia Diaz has always tried to protect her undocumented parents. When her father is sent to the emergency room after a worksite accident, her family's future becomes uncertain. They consider moving to another state for a fresh start. Silvia shares the truth about her parents with her friends, leading to a job offer on Keisha's family farm where her father will be safe. When he accepts, the move is canceled, and Silvia is finally able to turn her attention to matters of love. Unfortunately for her, Omar wants out and Keisha has already met someone new.

Keisha Hart is certain that she's found her soulmate in Silvia, especially when they kiss and it's electric. But after receiving too many mixed signals, she decides her best option is to remain friends. That, and a new girl has caught Keisha's attention. Hope Song is athletic and mysterious, and sure seems interested. But it's hard to be certain when Hope's domineering twin sister Faith is always getting in their way. As the school year ends, she decides to find out if they have true potential together.

Ricky Nishikawa gets a rough start after moving to Kansas, especially when a hot bully named Diego begins to pick on him. After a failed suicide attempt on Ricky's part, they become close and begin to date. Even though he does his best to soften Diego's hard edges, they keep getting into trouble. When the police become involved, they plan to run away together until Ricky gets cold feet. His parents send him to another state to stay with his grandparents for the summer, but not before he sees Diego taken away by the police, their relationship seemingly in ruins.

Cameron Huxley has always compensated for his mother's drinking problem, doing his best to take care of her while his father is out of town. He finally confides in his boyfriend Anthony about the situation and puts his foot down with his mother. She agrees to attend a support group. His father, on the other hand, seems to be a lost cause as he distances himself from Cameron after learning that his son is gay. The devastating blow is softened somewhat by his adult friend Charles, who he discovers is married to a teacher at their school, Mr. Finnegan.

Mindy Beaumont goes on a date with the new guy in school, Troy Mitchell, who turns out to be a pushy jerk. She isn't pleased when he shows up in her theater group, along with his new girlfriend Faith Song, who is just as unkind. She takes comfort that Diego is there to balance things out. She begins to spend more time with him, helping Diego learn his lines for the play after he's suspended. She assumes her crush on him can only be unrequited until learning that he likes girls as well as boys. With his encouragement, Mindy conquers her stage fright, the newfound feelings inside her intensifying.

Diego Gomez has kept most people at arm's length since his father committed suicide and his mother became mentally unstable. Diego opens up to Ricky about his past and they begin to date. After taking another role in a school play, his life seems to be getting back on track until one of Troy's friends, Graham Fowler, antagonizes him. Diego retaliates by toilet-papering Graham's house… and starting a fire. When the police take this prank seriously, Diego is forced to leave town. At the last second, Ricky changes his mind about going with him, those old feelings of abandonment hitting Diego hard. He intends to flee to El Paso on his own, but after realizing that Ricky would be left to take the blame, he returns home and turns himself in. Diego is sentenced to a juvenile detention center for the summer, cut off completely from anyone who cares about him. Or so he thinks…

BOOK 4: GREEN

PRIDE HIGH

JAY BELL

CHAPTER 1
AUGUST 31ST, 1993

Lights twinkled below, like little stars fallen from the sky, as Ricky leaned his head against the acrylic window of the airplane. The last vestiges of the setting sun had set the horizon aglow with a blur of magenta, leaving just enough radiance to see the plains of Kansas. He was almost home. And yet his frustration only increased—as it had all summer—because they were still so far apart. Taxiing to the gate, an hour-long drive to the town of Pride, and then… a massive gulf that he was supposed to leap over somehow. So much stood between him and Diego. Thousands of miles, despite the illusion of nearness, because for the past three months, Ricky hadn't heard a single peep from his boyfriend.

Or perhaps, more accurately, his ex. Ricky wasn't sure. His stomach twisted up with anxiety. None of the letters he'd written to Diego had elicited a reply. Ricky had put everything into them that he could think of. Apologies. Long-winded explanations. Declarations of love. Promises to never make the same mistake again. Over and over again he'd tried, but to no avail. He wasn't even sure that Diego had received the letters. Maybe they had been read and thrown away by some cruel warden. Or whoever was in charge of the youth detention center.

His mouth went dry as he tried to envision Diego in such a dreadful place. Ricky had suffered countless nightmares over the summer. In them, he'd see inmates sneak up on Diego from behind with shivs and clenched fists. Ricky would always cry out, wanting to warn him, but Diego never heard or even looked in his direction. Ricky was powerless each time, only able to watch as some horrible fate befell the man he loved. He had even asked his friends—his voice shaking over the phone—if Diego was okay. He still remembered how long Mindy had paused before wordlessly handing the phone to Cameron, who had been ridiculously upbeat in his equally vague response. They were hiding something from him. Ricky was certain of that. And now he was about to find out what.

Except not really, because even once the wheels of the aircraft touched down, everything seemed to take an eternity. By the time he was allowed to unbuckle his seatbelt and stand up, the sky had grown dark. Considering how long the days still were, this was a ridiculously late flight. By design, no doubt, because tomorrow was his first day of school. His mother must have planned it that way when she booked his return trip. She had wanted to ensure he wouldn't have the opportunity to see Diego, both when forcing Ricky to stay with his grandparents for the summer, and when he returned home. The injustice of that made his blood boil. Oh well. He'd get his way soon enough. His mother wouldn't be able to keep them apart tomorrow!

Only one person had that power, and nobody could tell Diego what to do. He was the type of guy who would break out of jail, just to call Ricky from the closest pay phone to let him know that nothing had changed.

I love you, Ricky.

Diego had spoken those words like a promise. So why hadn't he done something? Even if he was locked up too tight to escape, he could have gotten a message to him through Mindy somehow, or an inmate who was released sooner than him. A letter or a collect call or even a freaking fax… Anything!

Ricky swallowed as he shuffled down the airplane aisle to disembark. Maybe his own words were to blame.

I'm scared. I want to go home.

That hadn't been the end of it. Diego came back to him, even though it led to his capture. And now? All the waiting and wondering was pure torture. Just a little longer. Then he would know the truth, for better or for worse. Ricky walked through the jet bridge and into Kansas City International Airport. He saw his parents waiting for him near the gate and felt hatred rise up in response. If he didn't need a ride, he'd turn his back and walk the hell away from them. Maybe he would anyway! Anthony could come pick him up instead. Or maybe Cameron. Ugh! Too late. His parents had rushed over to him.

"Riku!" Ami cried emotionally. He refused to think of her as his mother anymore. She would be Ami from now on, and his father would be Ken. He'd keep it cold and impersonal. Business only. "I missed you so much," she blubbered, wrapping her arms around him.

Ricky kept his own locked at his sides. That was the plan at least. The familiar comfort of his mother, from the way her body felt as she squeezed him close to her reassuring scent, broke down his defenses. Ricky felt his anger drain away, leaving him small and vulnerable as he whimpered in response.

"Oh, I missed you so much!" his mother said, planting a series of kisses in his hair and on his cheeks. "Let me look at you," she said, pulling back to do just that. "You've gotten so big! You're the spitting image of your father." She turned to Ken. "Isn't he?"

"He's very handsome," Ken said with a warm smile. "Welcome home, son."

Ricky was pulled into his arms next and gave up his plan to hold a grudge. He loved his parents too much. And it was obvious that they loved him. Even though they *had* ruined everything. Except that wasn't quite true. Sure, he could blame them for forbidding him to see Diego, and for calling the cops when he showed up on their doorstep, but if he was honest, even then he'd still had a choice. He should have grabbed Diego's hand and run for his car. They could have escaped together.

I'm scared. I want to go home.

Ricky tried to push the thought from his mind. Anger was useful in that regard. When he had a target to focus on, it meant he didn't have to look inward.

"How was the trip to Disneyland?" Ken asked. "I know what you said on the phone, but I want details. Did you make a list of the rides you went on, like I asked?"

"Yeah," Ricky said. "Grandpa didn't want to go on any of them, but Grandma did."

"She was in the Air Force," Ken said, putting an arm around Ricky as they waited in front of the baggage carousel. "I bet a roller coaster can't compete with shooting across the ocean in an F-15."

"She said the loop-de-loops are nothing compared to the g-forces of actually flying upside down," Ricky murmured without much enthusiasm. His grandma was cool, but there was a burning question he was dying to ask. Ricky clamped down on the urge. He didn't want to push his luck. Not yet anyway. So he made small talk with his parents while collecting his baggage and on the walk to the car, but when he was buckled up in the back seat, he couldn't take it anymore.

"Did I get any mail while I was gone?" he asked. "Like, letters from people I know?"

"I don't think so," Ami said.

"Oh. Did anyone call?"

His mother turned around to look at him in concern. "No. All your friends were aware that you'd be out of town. Why would they call?"

"I don't know." He licked dry lips. "I thought maybe Diego might have stopped by or something. Now that he's out, I mean."

"I'm afraid not." Ami faced forward again. "Have you eaten? Are you hungry?"

"Nothing at all?" Ricky pressed. "You would tell me, wouldn't you?"

His father's eyes met his in the rearview mirror. "We would tell you, son. Now answer your mother."

"I'm not hungry," Ricky said, slumping down in his seat, despite trying to keep his spirits up.

Diego was no fool. He knew that Ricky's parents didn't want them to be together. So of course he hadn't left a message with them. Although he also didn't give a shit what anyone thought, so it would've been possible. Ricky didn't bring up the subject again. The waiting and wondering continued, followed by restlessness when they pulled into a quaint town devoid of the usual sprawl of chain restaurants and strip malls. The businesses here were local, and often just as quirky as the brick road (red, not yellow) that was Main Street. Ricky's attention locked on to one of the bars in particular. He hoped to spot a Trans Am with mismatched panels parked outside and strained his neck to see into the interior, just in case a hunky guy in a leather jacket was kicking back a beer while playing darts. No luck either way.

He sighed and gave up the hunt, but only for now. Ricky tried to play it cool when they finally reached his house. He barely blinked an eye when his mother said, "You're home for the night. Okay?"

"Yeah. I'm tired from the flight anyway."

He hung out with his parents and ate when his mother insisted. Eventually he was able to go up to his room for some much-needed privacy. Ricky flicked on the light. He checked under the bed, where he'd once found Diego hiding, and then in the closet, but no luck. Ricky was alone. He grabbed the phone and dialed a number that he knew by heart. Diego's pager. He left his own number as the message and hung up. Ricky bit his nails, waiting for the phone to ring. He paced his room, threw himself on his bed, and bounced back out again a minute later to check the clock. Thirty grueling minutes. Diego never took that long to call him back. Maybe he was on his way over.

Ricky went downstairs, listening carefully to make sure his parents were occupied and wouldn't notice. Then he slipped out the front door and plopped down on the steps there, leaving enough room for someone to sit next to him. Just like when Diego had shown up out of the blue so that Ricky wouldn't take the fall for a stupid prank that had spiraled out of control. The details didn't matter to him. Not as much as the memories that filled his mind: Deciding to run away together, meeting Diego in a cave filled with candles, making love on a sleeping bag, the reassurance of being held afterward… Ricky had felt that they'd become one person, like they could never be parted again. And maybe they wouldn't have after beginning their new life together in El Paso, except—

I'm scared. I want to go home.

Ricky had chickened out. And bailed on someone who had been abandoned by his father, his best friends, and even his mother. The guilt was overwhelming. As was the growing certainty that Diego wasn't going to call him back. His car wouldn't roar down the street to whisk him away. Ricky had broken Diego's heart and ruined everything they'd had together. He sat there on the front stoop, listening to insects hum in the dying heat. Eventually the door behind him opened.

He looked over his shoulder and saw his father standing there with a surprised expression. "Did someone call me?" Ricky asked.

"Not that I know of," Ken replied.

"Did you hear my phone ring?"

"No." Ken quietly shut the door behind him. Then he sat next to Ricky on the stoop. He didn't say anything. Not at first. He simply stared up at the late August sky before sighing. "Your mother doesn't want you to see him."

Ricky swallowed. "I know."

"You're growing up so quickly," his father said, voice tinged with sorrow. "Which makes me feel old, but at the same time… I swear I was your age not that long ago. I remember how it felt."

"Did it hurt?" Ricky asked around the lump in his throat.

"Sometimes. But looking back, things were never as bad as they seemed in the moment."

Ricky shook his head. "You don't understand."

"No, *you* don't understand," Ken said, bumping shoulders with him playfully. "But you will. Someday."

A comfortable silence settled between them as they sat there taking in the night.

"You wouldn't believe how many chances your mother has given me," Ken said eventually, seemingly at random. "If this guy is the right one for you..." His father shrugged. Then he nodded to the heavens. "Otherwise, it's a great big universe. Do you know how many stars are in our galaxy alone? Even if you pare it down to those that could potentially have planets orbiting them—"

Ricky snorted. "I've heard the 'other fish in the sea' lecture before."

"Don't I at least get points for originality?" Ken asked with a wink. He stood and brushed himself off. "Wanna go inside and see what's on TV?"

"I'll be there soon," Ricky promised him.

His father lingered. "Are you okay?"

"Yeah. I'm all right."

And it was true. Even when the door shut behind him and he was alone again, because Ricky had faced worse. This time last year, he was a stranger in an unfamiliar town. He didn't have any friends then. All he'd had was the lingering heartbreak of a failed relationship in another city, another state. Tomorrow would be different. His new friends would welcome him home, and then... Well, he would find out one way or another and take it from there. But before he went inside, he closed his eyes and imagined a leather jacket creaking next to him, the faint smell of marijuana, and a deep rumbling voice that always sent goosebumps racing across his skin.

I love you, Ricky.

Anthony placed his palms on the bathroom counter and leaned over the sink, bringing his face closer to the mirror. The powder and base had been expertly applied—in his amateur opinion—every blemish and imperfection hidden beneath a subtle mask that moved with his face. He absolutely loved it!

His green eyes considered themselves briefly, the temptation to add liner ever-present, but he was too worried about blinding himself with the pencil. He'd have to ask Silvia to teach him. For now… His attention darted down to his lips, which felt naked. That was easy enough to fix.

Anthony opened a drawer, reaching toward the very back, where he wrapped his fingers around two small vials. One contained pink lip gloss that he sometimes applied in secrecy. The other was a tube of red lipstick he'd bought from a pharmacy. *"It's a gift,"* he had explained to a disinterested cashier. *"For someone else,"* he'd added, deepening his own embarrassment.

Which had felt so out of sync with all the progress he'd made. Anthony was gay and proud of it! That's why he had decided to debut his new look on this, the first day of school. He didn't want anyone to think that he'd been shamed back into the closet. Especially homophobic dickwads like Graham Fowler. Anthony would show them, beyond any shadow of a doubt, that he was defiantly queer. So why hadn't he put on the lipstick before, even in privacy? He took off the lid and twisted the bottom, a crimson slope rising up to meet him, as if eager for a kiss. Then he checked the mirror again. The pink dye in Anthony's hair was only present at the very tips. The rest was blond, since Cameron had always wanted to see it that way. Which wasn't a big deal, but if they weren't dating, Anthony would have asked his mother to color it for him.

He turned to the full-length mirror on the back of the bathroom door and smoothed down the three layers of loose-fitting shirts he wore. White was closest to his skin and then pink, like flesh and bone. The outermost shirt was black, matching his tight jeans. If he blurred his vision, the oversized shirts looked more like a short dress that obscured his figure, his legs wrapped in dark leggings. Solid red Vans on his feet completed the look, although not really, because he had planned for the lipstick to bring it all together. Then again, maybe he was already pushing his luck.

Anthony tossed the makeup into the drawer and slammed it shut, returning to his bedroom to collect his things. He noticed the poster of The Cure's lead singer that was taped to his closet door. The calm unwavering expression held a hint of judgment.

Possibly because of the bright red lipstick that Robert Smith always wore. Anthony could practically hear the man chastising him in a thick British accent.

"There's nothing to be afraid of, luv. It's just a wee bit of color."

"Exactly," Anthony replied. "It doesn't have to mean anything. I mean, *you're* straight. So are most glam rockers. Nobody accuses the guys in Poison of being gay and they are slathered in makeup."

Robert Smith simply stared in response. Anthony felt foolish, and not because he was talking to a poster. He wasn't worried that anyone would think he was gay. That was exactly the point! Wasn't it? Everyone knew already. So what did he have to lose?

Cameron.

Anthony frowned while stuffing his backpack with school supplies. He loved having a boyfriend, but it was limiting, in certain ways. Like having to worry if the other person found you attractive. Then again, the powder and base had been received well. Anthony had first worn it on one of their dates, and without being prompted, Cameron had told him how nice he looked. A smidge of color wouldn't make much difference. His eyes darted over to Robert Smith again, whose lips were like a splatter of blood on white porcelain. Maybe it was better to ease into such things.

Anthony returned to the bathroom, ripped open the drawer, and grabbed the pink lip gloss. He felt the same sensation he always did when putting it on, like he was stepping into cozy slippers after being on his feet all day. Speaking of which... He went to his bedroom and traded the red Vans for a pair of pink Chuck Taylors. There! The look was complete. He felt great. Now he just needed to hold on to that confidence while everyone around him reacted. Starting with his family.

His parents—both working late shifts this week—were lounging around the breakfast table. His older brother Mike had moved out last month. Anthony was the last bird in the nest, which meant that he had his mom and dad's full attention.

"Don't you look nice!" Dawn said, her eyes sparkling at him. "Is that lip gloss, hon?"

"Yeah," he replied, his attention darting over to his father.

"I don't get it," Joe said. "I thought gay guys dressed like bikers. Shouldn't you be trying to grow a handlebar mustache?"

Anthony laughed. "I think that was back in the seventies or something."

"So this is what," Joe pressed, "some sort of punk rock thing?"

Yes! Anthony leapt on the explanation. He loved it, especially since he was so into music. "That's right. I've gone punk."

"Stick it to the man!" Joe said, raising a fist in solidarity.

Anthony laughed, never expecting to hear those words from someone who worked for the fire department. "You *are* the man," he said when hugging his father.

Joe blinked. "That's a good thing, right?"

"Drink your coffee," Dawn said to her husband before receiving a hug of her own. "Have a nice first day, darling."

"Thanks, Mom."

Anthony noticed the time and hurried out the front door to his car. No more walking to school for him, or riding the bus on rainy days. He'd moved up in the world. Even though he always had to beg other people for gas money. Who wanted to work during the summer? Basically everyone he knew, it would seem, aside from Ricky who'd been in exile. Anthony was eager to see him again. But first, as if to undermine just how punk rock he actually was, he turned the ignition and an upbeat pop song began playing. Culture Club, to be specific.

Anthony had been thrilled to find the album in a cardboard box of 8-track tapes at the record store where Silvia worked, each marked down to fifty cents. Not that it helped clear the unwanted inventory. 8-tracks had fallen out of popularity in the early eighties, but hey, that was the joy of owning an older car. Anthony felt his nerves dissipate as Boy George serenaded him. Mostly because of the famous singer's appearance, which unapologetically blurred the line between genders. Anthony had become obsessed with him over the summer. And inspired. Oh god, was he really going to do this?

He checked his appearance in the rearview mirror and all doubt fell away. If there were consequences, so be it, because this felt right. At least until he pulled up to his best friend's house, turned down the music, and honked.

Omar came running out a few seconds later. If he had changed over the summer, it was difficult to tell. His black hair still flopped over one side of his forehead and covered all but his earlobes before cascading down the back of his neck. His dark eyes glimmered over a relentless smile as he dived into the passenger-side seat and tossed his backpack and skateboard in the rear.

"We're officially juniors, dude!" Omar crowed before doing a double take. "Whoa! You look hot!"

"You really think so?" Anthony asked, not hiding his insecurity.

"Hell yeah!" Omar's attention lingered on the lip gloss before his grin widened. "You're making me feel kinda gay."

Anthony laughed. "I love you," he said warmly.

"I love you too," Omar replied easily as they pulled out into the street. "Are you freaking excited or what? This year is going to be huge for us!"

"In what way?" Anthony asked.

"Uh, let's see. Prom is gonna happen. You've got a boyfriend and I've got a girlfriend, so even if we somehow manage not to have sex before then, it's basically guaranteed that we'll do it after the dance. Those are the rules. I mean, even if I'm not in the mood, I'll suck it up and do my sacred duty. And don't try to sidetrack me with stories about all the sex you've been having with Cameron. You know exactly what I mean." He repeatedly inserted a finger into his fist, just in case there was any doubt.

"We'll see," Anthony said. "Right now prom seems very far away."

"Nobody says we have to wait."

He felt a jolt of concern. "Are you and Whitney talking about…"

"Porking?" Omar finished for him. "Nah. She's hard to figure out. Whitney is like, I dunno, a free spirit or something."

Anthony felt relief, even though it shouldn't matter to him either way. On paper, he wanted Omar to get laid. His best friend was hot. Someone should be riding him like a bronco. But the possibility of that actually happening made him uneasy. Maybe because he preferred it when Omar had been dating Silvia. She was secretive about her feelings, but Anthony was certain that she still loved him. His best friend's first time should be with someone like her.

"The dude is crazy about you," Omar said, drawing him back

to the present. "Why else would he be waiting outside?"

The car slowed just as Anthony's pulse quickened. He pulled into his boyfriend's driveway and parked as Cameron ambled over. His skin was still bronze from three glorious months of sunshine. Cameron was a little broader and taller than when they'd first met, nicely filling out the blue polo shirt he wore. His tousled brown hair swept across his forehead, touching his left eyebrow, the rest neatly trimmed. He smiled when locking eyes with Anthony through the windshield.

"Oh yeah," Omar said while watching him approach. "You guys are totally gonna do it soon."

"Get in the back," Anthony said while fighting down a smile.

"All right."

Omar started climbing over the seats.

"You could get out first!" Anthony chastised, but he was laughing when Cameron opened the door. With a final push on Omar's shoes, he cleared the space between them.

"Hey," Cameron said with a dopey grin as he slid close.

"Hi," Anthony replied shyly.

Cameron's blue eyes had him pinned as he leaned close for a kiss, but before that could happen, he backed off suddenly. "Wait, are you wearing lipstick?"

"Lip gloss." Anthony tried to sound confident. "What do you think?"

"It's different," Cameron replied.

Different good or different bad? He didn't have a chance to ask because Cameron was leaning toward him again. Just like before, he changed his mind at the last second. "Will it get on my lips?"

Omar laughed from the back seat.

"What?" Cameron asked, glaring at him. "I've never kissed a girl before."

"I have," Omar said gleefully. "As in *multiple* girls."

"We know," Anthony said with an eyeroll that he hoped disguised his discomfort. Was the base and powder enough to hide the blood rushing to his face?

"So will it?" Cameron asked, his attention still on the back seat.

"If it doesn't stop me, dude," Omar replied, "then it shouldn't stop you."

Cameron shrugged and finally kissed Anthony, thank goodness. Although he noticed, when reversing out of the driveway, the way his boyfriend discreetly wiped his mouth on the back of his hand. No big deal. All part of the experience. Anthony was just as eager to check his own lips to see if they were still glossy enough.

"Hey," he said, addressing the rearview mirror, "speaking of your girlfriend, do we need to pick her up?"

"Nope. Whitney likes to walk, so she can commune with the trees along the way. I'm tellin' ya… Free spirit."

"I think you make a nice couple," Cameron said in approving tones.

Anthony remembered how relieved he'd seemed when learning that Omar was dating someone new. Which was understandable, but there was nothing to worry about. Anthony loved Cameron. Nobody could compete with that. Especially a straight guy who could never love him back. Not in the same way, at least.

Anthony turned the music back up and laughed when the others groaned. They were sick to death of hearing the same songs, but there weren't many options, and *Colour by Numbers* was a great album.

"It's a miracle," Omar said as they reached the school, intentionally referencing one of the song titles, "that I haven't lost my mind yet. Are there seriously no metal 8-track tapes?"

"I'll dig around next time I'm at the record store," Anthony promised as they got out.

"It'll suck not starting each day in journalism class together," Omar said, pulling out his camcorder to shoot footage of the school.

That was indeed a bummer. Having completed the course, their choices were to write for the newspaper or work on the yearbook, which were separate classes. They each felt strongly about which path they wanted to take, even though it wasn't the same one. So they had made a tough decision.

"At least we've got lunch to look forward to," Anthony replied.

"Yeah." Omar perked up, but not because of the reminder. He'd spotted someone. "There she is! I'll see you guys later."

He dropped his board to the ground and skated away.

"Alone at last," Cameron said before coming in for another kiss. His features were concerned when he pulled away. "I uh… better walk you to your first class."

Anthony shrugged. "Okay. Are you worried about something?"

"Yeah," Cameron admitted as they slowly made their way across the parking lot. "What about Graham and—" He looked Anthony over. "—everyone else."

"Oh *that*," he said casually. "They might call me names again and paint another bad word on my locker, but somehow, I think I'll survive."

Cameron didn't seem reassured.

"Who cares what small-minded people say or do," Anthony told him, his attention flicking in the direction Omar had disappeared in. "All that matters to me is what you guys think."

"Do you want my opinion?" Cameron asked, taking his hand to stop him.

Anthony swallowed and nodded. "Yeah. As long as it's the truth."

"I think you're beautiful." Cameron kissed him. He didn't stop either. Not for a long time, which made Anthony glad that he decided to bring the lip gloss with him, just in case it needed to be reapplied. If this kept up, he'd be burning through multiple tubes a week!

CHAPTER 2
SEPTEMBER 1ST, 1993

Cameron leaned against the doorframe of Anthony's first class while watching him get settled. His boyfriend noticed, seeming to get more and more embarrassed each time he checked and saw him still standing there. Cameron supposed he *was* behaving like a parent who had just dropped off their child at school, but he just loved Anthony so much and…

He finally turned away, letting a grimace appear on his face. He was worried. Last year had been bad enough. Anthony tended to play down the name calling, and he never brought up how Graham had punched him in the face, or the way he'd been ganged up on and knocked to the floor before Diego came to his rescue. Each of those attacks had happened here, inside the school, where they were supposed to be safe but obviously weren't. And now he'd shown up on the first day of junior year wearing makeup! What did Anthony think was going to happen? Cameron wasn't sure how to protect him from the inevitable backlash. He'd tried to kiss off all the lip gloss before they entered the building, hoping that would help. Cameron wiped his mouth and saw a shimmer of pink on his hand.

Anthony was going to get pulverized! But not if Cameron could help it. He would walk him to each class if need be. He was already jogging to make it to his own on time, the hallways slowly clearing. He pulled his schedule out of his back pocket and checked it again before reorienting and going down another hall. Finding the right door was easy, because someone was standing outside of it while glancing around. Ricky! Except the shrimpy little guy he'd been expecting had been replaced by someone much lankier with a shock of black hair that was parted on one side. He looked older. And handsome!

"Cameron!" Ricky cried.

A blur closed the distance and slammed into him. Cameron laughed in surprise and wrapped his arms around a body that was definitely taller. Ricky was holding on to him for dear life and didn't seem intent on letting go. Cameron closed his eyes, imagining a messy mop of hair and permanently askew glasses.

There was still a hint of that boy when they finally let go of each other, but he was quickly being replaced by a man with refined style. The glasses were new, the frames subtle and the lenses thinner, allowing sensitive dark eyes to stand out clearly as they moved over Cameron's body.

"Wow," Ricky said, pushing the glasses up on his nose. "You look great!"

"Have you checked the mirror lately?" Cameron asked. "You're like a different person. How many years were you gone? Ten? Twenty?"

"That's how it felt," Ricky croaked. "I missed you guys!"

"We missed you too." Why were they talking in plurals? Maybe because it was less awkward than saying outright how they felt. Which was silly, because Cameron wasn't shy about such things. "Me especially," he said. "I missed you the most."

Ricky smiled at this, but it was subdued. "That's probably true."

Oh crap. "I'm sure Diego missed you the most-est."

"I don't know," Ricky said. "I still haven't heard from him."

"You just got in last night, right?"

Ricky nodded when leading the way into the classroom. "I tried paging him, but he never called me back. Do you know if his number changed or something?"

"I don't, sorry." Cameron glanced around. The walls were lined with desks, a computer set up at each. Tables that sat two were in traditional rows in the middle of the room, but this was clearly going to a be a different experience than they were used to. "Hey, this looks neat!"

"Yeah!" Ricky said. "I was worried they'd have those horrible old computers we used in grade school and junior high. You know, the ones with the orange screens?"

"Ours were green," Cameron said with a laugh. "But yeah, whenever I tell people how fun computers are, you can tell they're thinking of those. So what do we have here?"

"Brand new 486s!"

"No kidding?" Cameron asked. "Are they multimedia?"

"I wish, but they *are* running Windows. Have you ever used that?"

He shook his head. "Only when messing around with display models at stores. This is exciting!"

They grinned at each other. Cameron earned enough money to pay for the long-distance calls, so over the summer, they had managed to stay in touch. As the school year neared, he had read the course catalog over the phone to Ricky, so he could pick his electives. When realizing that a new class had been added—Computer Sciences—they had about lost their minds, since it was one of their mutual hobbies. What was next, a course that focused on eating cereal while watching Saturday morning cartoons?

"This is going to be amazing," Cameron breathed.

"Yeah!" Ricky said. "I hope we get to—"

"Okay, everyone!" an adult voice interrupted. The teacher at the front of the room was an older man with scraggly gray hair that ringed a bald dome. His glasses were so thick that it was a miracle his pointed nose wasn't bent from the weight. "I'm sure we're all excited to get our hands on the new machines, but we won't always be working on them. Have a seat at the tables for now."

Cameron and Ricky glanced at each other before racing toward the nearest so they could sit together. The teacher took attendance and provided an overview of what they'd be learning, which included programming. That would be an interesting challenge! The atmosphere became thick with impatience as the hour wore on.

"All right," the teacher said, finally standing up at his desk. "Each of you will be assigned a computer to work on. You'll use the same machine each day. There aren't enough for everyone, so a few of you will have to share. Do I have any volunteers?"

Cameron's hand shot up at the same time that Ricky's did. The teacher nodded in approval. He walked them over to the computer they would be using and left them there so he could get the rest of the class set up.

"I wonder if they have any games installed," Ricky said, clicking the mouse while peering at the screen.

"If they do it'll be *The Oregon Trail*," Cameron replied.

Ricky laughed. "That or *Where in the World Is Carmen Sandiego?*"

Cameron grabbed the keyboard, since Ricky had opened up a word-processing application, and typed, *She's pooping in a bathroom stall!*

Ricky laughed like it was the funniest joke in the world, the joyous sound making it impossible not to smile. His adam's apple bobbed up and down in a neck that looked a little thicker and stronger.

"What?" he asked self-consciously when raising his glasses to wipe at his eyes.

Cameron realized that he'd been staring. "Nothing," he said quickly. "It's just amazing how much you've changed."

"I don't feel any different," Ricky said with a shrug.

"Really? You didn't wake up one morning and hit your head on the ceiling?"

Ricky laughed again. "I haven't gotten *that* much taller. You're still bigger than me." His eyes moved to the curve of Cameron's bicep.

"Okay, everyone!" the teacher said. "Let's start with some basics."

They listened dutifully to the lecture, and followed the instructions, but it wasn't anything they didn't already know, even with their limited experience using a graphical user interface. Cameron noticed Ricky's knee begin to bounce. It only stopped when he grabbed the keyboard.

Can I ask you something? Ricky typed into the word processor. After watching him nod, he added, *Did something bad happen to Diego?*

Cameron hesitated before reaching for the keyboard. *Mindy said he looked a little rough the first few times she saw him.* That's all it took to make Ricky's chin tremble, so he hastily typed, *But he seemed fine by the time he got out.*

Ricky swallowed and reached for the keyboard again. *Are you guys holding back? Did he say anything about hating me or never wanting to see me again?*

Cameron didn't make him wait. He started shaking his head while typing his response. *She never got to talk to Diego. It wasn't possible but—*

Ricky cut him off by minimizing the window, which confused Cameron until he heard the teacher's voice behind them. "You need to double-click the icon on the bottom left of the desktop to open the correct program," he instructed.

Ricky complied. They fell in line for the rest of class. Cameron couldn't help noticing how the same troubled expression kept returning to Ricky's face. It was still there when the bell finally rang. They stood and gathered up their things.

"Diego's going to be happy to see you," Cameron told him.

"Maybe." Ricky sighed and shook his head. "Who knows?"

"I do. You look amazing. And you're *you*." He laughed when Ricky scrunched up his face at this. "Trust me. Diego might do his grumpy 'I don't need anyone' act, but I don't envy his chances, because you're the most lovable guy I've ever met."

Ricky looked like he was on the verge of tears again, but then he smiled and slammed into him for another hug. Cameron wrapped his arms around him, wishing more than ever that he could keep the people he cared most about safe from harm.

Omar couldn't stop smiling. Junior year was off to a great start. He'd made sure to choose electives that should each be an easy "A" and had also hit the jackpot with his assigned lunch break. He'd be eating with both his best friend and his girlfriend each day. And um… also his ex. Omar looked across the table where Silvia and Anthony were sharing the contents of their sack lunches. He would've been over the moon to have seen that last year, and while he was happy about it now, it *was* a little awkward. He hadn't seen much of Silvia recently. For the past month or so, they'd mostly kept in touch through Anthony. Omar felt bad about that, because they'd promised to stay friends and to maybe try again. But then Whitney had happened. He glanced around for her, unsure where she'd gotten to, and noticed someone else.

"Hey, look who it is!" he said when getting to his feet. "My man, Ricky!"

Anthony stood up too. Pretty soon they were on either side of him, ruffling Ricky's hair and patting him on the back. The poor guy nearly dropped his tray. Omar looped an arm around his neck and guided him to the table.

"It's good to have you back," Anthony said warmly.

"Even though you *are* a lowly sophomore," Omar teased.

"What?" Ricky cried. "I thought only being a freshman was bad. You guys acted like sophomores were cool!"

"That was last year," Omar said dismissively. "What did we know? We were immature sophomores. It's baked into the name and everything."

"You're thinking of sophomoric," Anthony corrected, "but it's true. We're much more mature, so you should always do what we say."

Ricky rolled his eyes and laughed. "I'm not sure why I missed you guys."

They all settled down at the table, Ricky attempting to sit on Omar's right.

"Sorry, my dude," he said, "but that seat is reserved for my girlfriend."

Ricky looked to Silvia in confusion before remembering everything that he'd heard about while away. She didn't blush or squirm. Silvia was too damn cool for that sort of thing. She patted the empty space on the far side of her. "You're welcome to sit next to me."

Anthony shook his head and scooted down the bench toward her to make room. "I need my little brother close to me. Get over here!"

Ricky grinned and took a seat next to him. He nodded across the table. "Hi, David!"

"Hey," came the muted response.

Ricky began glancing around. Omar could guess why, so he started shaking his head in warning, not that it helped.

"Where's Dave?"

Omar grimaced at the same time that Anthony did. Like them, Dave and David had always been a package deal, best friends who were inseparable. Except quite a few things had changed over the summer.

"He's a traitor," David mumbled.

"A what?" Ricky asked in confusion.

"A traitor," Omar repeated for his friend. He jerked a thumb over his shoulder.

Ricky's brow furrowed in confusion until he saw what they'd already witnessed: Graham Fowler, sitting with a bunch of his stupid cronies, Dave right there in the middle of them.

Ricky was aghast. "Why would he sit with those jerks?"

David merely shrugged. He wasn't happy with this turn of events.

"Well you're still cool," Ricky said to him, picking up on the dour mood. "I really like your mustache."

David stroked it with a finger, summoning a smile. "Thanks! It finally got thick. I've been trying since junior high. Hey, I like your new glasses."

Omar narrowed his eyes. "Wait a minute, they *are* new!"

Ricky shrugged and quickly occupied himself with his food.

"Where did you get them?" Omar demanded. "I know you just flew into town last night. So unless you ordered them before you left and picked them up this morning…"

Ricky wore a guilty expression. "My old ones broke when I was out of town!"

"That's no excuse," Omar chastised. "You should have called my parents' store and given them your prescription. They could have mailed you a new pair."

Anthony snorted. "They're a different style. How would he have tried them on?"

Omar turned on his best friend. "Oh you're taking *his* side? Don't come crying to me the next time you stay the night and there's nothing to eat. My dad already gives me guilt trips for not having many friends who wear glasses." He turned his accusation on Ricky. "And now you do *this* to me?"

"*You* could always get a pair," Silvia said casually. "Instead of wearing contacts."

"You wear contacts?" David asked in surprise. "I didn't realize."

"Because he doesn't want anyone to," Anthony said, adding in a stage whisper, "It's a secret!"

"Not anymore," Omar said with a sigh. "That's what I get for letting a beautiful woman stare into my eyes."

The words had slipped out of their own accord, as they so often did. His gaze met Silvia's before they both hurriedly looked away again.

Ricky was staring at the empty space next to Omar, his expression confused. "Is Whitney absent today?"

"No, she's here somewhere," Omar said, glancing around. "She's sort of a—"

"Don't say it," Anthony interjected.

"—free spirit," Omar continued. "Like a soaring eagle."

That had become something of a running joke between them. Most of his time with Whitney was spent laughing. They had a lot of fun together. Where the hell was she anyway?

"Has anyone seen Diego today?" Ricky asked casually.

Everyone shook their heads.

Except for Silvia. "I had a class with him this morning."

"He's here?" Ricky asked in excitement. "I was starting to think that he skipped. Did he ask about me?"

"No," Silvia said.

Anthony nudged her discreetly.

"Although he did seem to be looking for someone," she added, before seeming to struggle within herself. "But I don't know if it was you."

"Silvia!" Anthony hissed.

"What?" she shot back. "I don't want him to think I'm a liar."

"I prefer the truth," Ricky assured her. "As you know."

What could have been a tense moment ended in laughter. They no longer seemed to hold a grudge against each other, even though she had once blackmailed Ricky into staying silent about the time she'd kissed Keisha, *while* still dating him. That had been the wedge which finally drove them apart. Omar had broken up with her. And she had broken up with him on a previous occasion, so it obviously wasn't meant to be. Too bad. Silvia was such a cool chick. Her eyes met his again, but he didn't feel the need to look away this time. Omar offered a sympathetic smile that she returned. He hoped that she, like him, mostly thought about how good it had been.

"Screeeeeee!"

He started laughing as a thin blond girl came running over with her arms spread wide. Whitney circled the table in this manner before finally plopping down next to him.

"The eagle has landed!" she declared. "What's going on, everyone?"

Her long hair had been trimmed to shoulder length, hints of her ears sticking out at the sides. Omar loved running his fingers through those wavy locks to reveal them fully. Was it weird to be attracted to someone's ears? If so, it wouldn't bother her, because Whitney was weird to the core. In a good way.

"Hey, girl!" she said, waving at Silvia happily. "Thanks again for your help."

"No problem," Silvia said without a shred of animosity.

Which kind of bugged him. Would it kill her to be a *little* jealous?

"I'm still singin' it!" Whitney said before doing karate chop motions in the air. "Es es es es! Ay ay ay ay! Ef ef ef ef! Ee ee ee ee!"

Omar shook his head in confusion. "What are you talking about?"

"Tee tee tee tee," Silvia replied. "Why why why why!"

"'Safety Dance!'" Anthony said with a grin.

Omar rolled his eyes. "I should have known. Music is your secret language."

"Whitney came into the store the other day," Silvia explained.

Whitney nodded enthusiastically. "I had to hear it again!"

"About five times in a row, in fact," Silvia said with good humor. She nudged Anthony. "Who's the artist?"

"Oh! I've got this one. Umm…" Anthony's brow crinkled in concentration before it stretched thin again. "Men Without Hats!"

"Anyway," Omar said as they high-fived each other. "I saved some fries for you, babe."

"Thank god," Whitney said. "I, am, *starving!*"

She dove in with both hands, happily humming under her breath while chewing and bobbing her head left and right. She was so adorable! Omar could spend all day just—

"Jessica!" Whitney cried suddenly. "Oh my god! I haven't seen you in ages!" Within seconds, she had leapt to her feet and run off again, clusters of fries still gripped in each hand.

"Is she coming back?" Anthony asked. Then he held up a palm to ward off his response. "Never mind. I know what you're going to say."

"I missed you guys so much," Ricky said with a grin. "Hey! Did I tell you that I went to Disneyland?"

They caught up for the remainder of lunch break, Omar eating the rest of the fries he'd been saving for Whitney. When the bell rang, he stood and held out his tray when he noticed Silvia gathering her trash, so she could place it on top. He always did the same thing for Anthony.

"Thanks," she said, and to his surprise, followed him to the trash cans.

"I appreciate you being so nice to Whitney," he told her. "I was kinda worried about how that would go."

"She's cool," Silvia said. "You should've seen her dancing around the store. You would have filmed it for sure."

"Nah," he said, his throat feeling raw. "There can only be one record store girl."

She smiled at the reference to a film he'd made of her and had watched countless times since. Including recently, because it still occupied a special place in his heart.

"You make a nice couple," Silvia said. "I'm happy for you. So if that's why you've been avoiding me…"

"No!" he said before he could stop himself.

And yet, he also couldn't tell her the real reason why. So he shuffled his feet while the tension seemed to increase between them.

Silvia was the first to look away, her eyebrows raising. "I'm going to say hi to Mindy," she said. "I'll see you around."

"Yeah," Omar said, watching her go with an ache of nostalgia. "See ya."

CHAPTER 3
SEPTEMBER 1ST, 1993

Mindy had her left knee on the cafeteria table and her right foot on the bench so she could see over the swarm of incoming students. Lunch was always the most stressful part of the first day, everyone scrambling to figure out where to sit and with whom. There were two separate lunch breaks and no method to ensure you'd end up sharing yours with a friend. Oh sure, everyone had their theories. Taking the same electives or submitting your enrollment papers simultaneously were the most popular, but she'd tried all of that and learned that it was mostly a crap shoot.

"Keisha!" she said, waving a hand in excitement.

A lithe black girl with a crew cut turned in a slow circle until spotting her. Then she sauntered over with a lopsided smile. "It's good to be wanted," Keisha said, setting her things on the table. "Who can we expect to join us for this little soiree? A certain mutual friend of ours?"

"I wish and so does she," Mindy said, crinkling her nose. "Silvia got stuck in the same lunch break with Omar. I saw her on my way in."

"Oh the irony," Keisha drawled. "And so soon after the divorce."

Mindy giggled. "Hopefully they can get along like my parents do."

"See anyone else we know?" Keisha asked in tones that were a little too casual. She seemed to be searching for someone in particular.

"Yuck!" Mindy quickly lowered herself. Troy Mitchell, the pushy jerk who had been her first kiss, had just walked into the cafeteria with the Song sisters flanking him. "Unfortunately I do."

Keisha followed her gaze, one of her fine eyebrows arching as a smile played about her lips.

Mindy stared, her attention divided between her friend and some of her worst enemies. "Oh my gosh," she gasped. "Which one of them is it?"

"I don't have the faintest idea what you mean," Keisha said dismissively.

The liar! Keisha had come out to her earlier in the year, and despite trusting her with that bombshell, refused to spill the beans on who she had the hots for. Aside from Silvia, of course.

"You know who my heart belongs to," Keisha said without prompting.

"I'm not sure that I do," Mindy said, intending to peer suspiciously at the Song sisters, but she became distracted when noticing someone familiar. "Cameron!" she squealed with glee.

He grinned and hustled over, giving her a hug and then Keisha too. He was the sweetest! Mindy had really bonded with him over the summer. She'd never had a close guy friend before, but she absolutely adored him.

"Are we going to eat outside like we planned?" he asked.

"Yeah!" Mindy surveyed the cafeteria and experienced a pang of disappointment when she failed to spot someone tall and brooding. "I guess it'll just be us. Let's go!"

Beyond the windows of the cafeteria was a walled-in courtyard, where she and Sylvia had often eaten in earlier years. Mindy led her friends to a corner where ivy climbed the brick, giving it the appearance of a fairy-tale setting.

"Have you seen Ricky yet?" Cameron asked. "Because I have."

"No!" Mindy exclaimed. They had talked about him so much during the summer that he felt like a beloved character from a TV show. On occasion they had called him together too. Mindy hadn't known Ricky all that well before the break but was eager to see him again. "How's he doing?"

"He got hot," Cameron said with a guffaw.

"Really?" Keisha asked. "The little guy who was always following Diego around?"

"Yup," Cameron confirmed. "He's still cute, but with an edge of hotness. If that makes sense."

"Nothing about love does," Keisha replied, "and that's just the way I like it."

"Oh yeah?" Mindy pried as they settled down on the concrete, sitting cross-legged and unpacking their lunches while facing each other. "How would you know?"

"I've had my share of experiences," Keisha answered.

"Any of them recent?" Mindy pressed.

Keisha's eyes flicked to Cameron and back again.

"He already knows," Mindy admitted. "I told him during the summer."

Keisha's jaw dropped. "You outed me?"

"He's gay!" Mindy said, gesturing at him like a showroom prize. "You're from the same tribe."

Keisha thought about it and shrugged. "As long as it stays between us."

"I told Anthony," Cameron said sheepishly. "He's my boyfriend! I had to."

Keisha sighed. "And he no doubt told Omar, who probably told everyone else."

"Omar can keep a secret," Mindy said. She didn't defend him often, but he'd behaved like a gentleman in the aftermath of his split with Silvia. "And um… He already knew. Remember? That's why they broke up."

"Anthony already knew when I told him," Cameron confessed.

"Wonderful," Keisha said with a wince. "Apparently it was the kiss heard 'round the world."

"And now it's ancient history," Mindy said, nibbling on a sandwich. "So who's lucky bachelorette number two?"

"Oh no!" Keisha said, shaking her head. "If anything, you've both just reminded me of the importance of discretion."

"Fine," Mindy said, intentionally sounding clipped. "We can do this the hard way. Just be aware that I always catch my man. Or in this case, my woman. *Your* woman."

"You might as well tell her now," Cameron said. "When it comes to gay people, Mindy is like a bloodhound."

"It's true," she said proudly. "I don't even have to try. They just flock to me."

The others laughed and continued joking around. They didn't have much catching up to do, since they'd seen each other during the summer. And would again later today in theater class. Although she was disappointed that Cameron wouldn't be joining them this year.

"What are we going to do without your amazing sets?" she complained when the topic came up.

"Sorry," Cameron said. "Anthony wanted us to have a class together, so he talked me into taking the same creative writing elective as him."

"Boooo!" Mindy said with a pout. "Don't you see enough of each other already?"

"Not really," he said with a dopey grin.

"What about the plays themselves?" Keisha asked. "Would you still be willing to work on those after school?"

"I don't have time. I got a job restoring furniture. Hey, speaking of which, how old is the farm that you live on? Because my boss says those are a great source of furniture and antiques."

Mindy checked the elegant gold watch that she'd gotten as a gift from her father on her sixteenth birthday. She had to look at it twice, because she's forgotten to take note of the time when admiring the fine details. They only had about ten more minutes before classes resumed. "I'll catch up with you guys later," she said while standing. "I have to um… take care of something."

They were already deep in conversation, thank goodness, or they might have noticed her blush. She had nothing to be ashamed of. Mindy simply felt a sense of responsibility for Diego, as she had all summer. That wasn't her idea. Ricky had *asked* her to stay in touch with him. And she'd managed to, even though it meant jumping through a few hoops. The youth detention center where he'd been locked up only allowed immediate family to visit, so she'd volunteered. Nothing about it had been easy. Mindy read to a room full of unruly boys for half an hour at a time, often suffering verbal abuse, but only at first. Diego took care of that. Her stomach lurched at the memory, because it was sweet, in a way, but also painful to witness. The first time she'd seen Diego, he'd had a nasty black eye. He was even more beaten up the next visit, but so were the guys who had given her the most lip. They'd kept their swollen mouths shut after that. Thankfully, as the summer went on, such incidents became less common. Diego had almost looked like his old self by the time she finished the book. Mindy still remembered looking up from the pages to find—without fail—his smoldering eyes locked onto hers, never wavering. She had wanted so badly to talk to him, to treat his wounds and take him somewhere safe where he couldn't be hurt anymore.

Mindy reached the doors that butterflied out to the parking lot. Diego used to eat alone out there. She left the building and searched for his car, struggling to remember what it looked like. Mindy had only seen it briefly when taking refuge inside it on a cold night, when she'd fled from the worst—and only—date of her life. Although she *had* seen it again some months later, when he'd shown her a trunk full of toilet paper. Which had seemed so funny at the time, but it was the same night he set fire to Graham Fowler's house. Even if it had been an accident. Of sorts.

The breath caught in her throat. There he was! Diego was leaning against the side of his car, his massive arms crossed over his chest. He was wearing a black sleeveless T-shirt and a pair of tight blue jeans, which suited him so much more than the horrible orange prison uniforms. He looked like his old self again. Especially when he noticed her, pushed away from the car, and walked over wearing a subtle smirk.

"Hey princess," he said, running his hand through his swept-back hair.

"Hi," she said, almost overwhelmed to be speaking to him again. Mindy had wanted to say so much over the summer, but now she found herself at a loss for words. So she hugged him instead.

Diego raised his arms to his sides and didn't lower them again until she let go, but that was all right. She felt the beating of his heart against her ear, which was reassuring. At least he was free now and would be okay.

"How have you been?" Diego asked after she stepped away and collected herself. "I hope you did something more fun this summer than reading to my dumb ass."

"You aren't dumb," she said. "But yes, that was a terrible place! Are you okay?"

Diego shrugged. "Wasn't my first time there and probably won't be my last. I'm all right."

But he hadn't been. She knew that from the note he had given her. The one she had carried with her like a talisman ever since, so she wouldn't forget how important it was to keep going back to that wretched place week after week.

"Forget about all that," he said, reading her face. "Tell me something fun you did."

"I got my lifeguard certification," she said proudly. "And I used it! I actually got paid for sitting around a swimming pool all day. Can you believe that?"

"Sounds like a good deal," Diego replied. "Of course, someday you'll have to give mouth-to-mouth to a guy who tastes like a triple cheeseburger. That's when you'll really earn your paycheck."

Mindy giggled. "I *did* have to dive in to help a little girl who got the wind knocked out of her. She jumped off the high dive and hit the water face first. It was painful to watch, but gratifying to use the skills I'd learned."

"Awesome," Diego said with an upward nod. "That's really cool."

She wanted to reach up and touch his thick lips where they had been bloody and split, just to make sure that he was truly healed. Instead her cheeks flushed. He must have noticed because a dimple appeared in his cheek when he smirked again. "What else did you get up to?" he asked.

"I went horseback riding with Keisha, out on her farm. Do you know Silvia? We all had a slumber party together. It was really fun. Oh! And I hung out with Cameron a lot. We stayed in touch with Ricky. Have you seen him yet?"

"Nah." Diego's eyes moved to the horizon and remained there. "Not yet."

"Oh. Me neither. I'm sure he'll be thrilled." The bell rang, sounding distant.

Diego's eyes sought out hers again. He tilted his head toward his car. "Wanna get out of here?"

"You mean skip?" she cried, already scandalized. "No way!"

He laughed. "You've gotta at least once. It's part of the experience."

"But not today," she said, gently swatting his arm as an excuse to touch him. "So um… What was it like? If you don't mind me asking."

He didn't need her to elaborate. Diego was quiet as they walked toward the school. "Like being in a war," he said, "except you're not sure if anyone is on the same side as you."

She wished she could take his hand. It wouldn't have to mean anything. Mindy simply wanted to give him the comfort that he'd been deprived of.

"And some other stuff happened," he added.

"Like what?" she asked.

"I don't know." He reached past her to open the door. "I'm still trying to figure everything out."

When would they have a chance to talk about it? Would it

be weird to invite him over to her house? They'd had so much fun there when she'd helped him rehearse lines for the play, after he'd been suspended. "Are you going to audition again this year?" she asked.

He shrugged his massive shoulders. "I dunno. Are you taking the theater elective?"

"Yes," she said. "I'll still be doing wardrobe."

"Or maybe you'll end up on stage again," he said with a sly smile.

She never would have made it up there without his encouragement. Or repeated the experience on a smaller scale, over and over in front of leering boys, if he hadn't needed her so much. She thought of the note again.

"Hey," Diego said, his hand brushing against Mindy's to get her attention. She stopped and looked up at him. "Thanks. For everything."

"I wish I could have done more," she said. "It's so mean that they wouldn't let you see any of your friends."

"Didn't bother me," Diego replied. "I don't have any."

"That's *not* true," she said. "I'm your friend. Aren't I?"

"Yeah," he admitted. "I guess you are."

"So there you go. And speaking of which, stop eating lunch outside all by yourself. Come sit with me and the others!"

He raised a critical eyebrow at the suggestion. "Who are we talking about exactly?"

"Keisha," Mindy said. "You know her, don't you?"

"Yeah. She's cool."

"Cameron has the same lunch break too."

"Huxley?" Diego said, sounding slightly more optimistic. "He's all right." The first eyebrow joined the other in a scowl. "What about his boyfriend?"

"Nope," Mindy said. "That's it. Just the three of us. But it could be four. Will you sit with us tomorrow? Please?"

Diego looked to the ceiling and groaned. But when his eyes returned to hers, they were sparkling. "Maybe."

"Really?"

"No promises."

"Well if you do, we sit outside in the courtyard. It's not so different from the parking lot really. Don't make me bring my friends to you. Because I will!"

Diego chuckled. "I'll see you around."

"Okay," Mindy said, wanting to hug him again. "Umm." She glanced around and pointed. "My locker is that way."

"Don't let me stop you," Diego replied.

She hurried down the hall, looking over her shoulder once. He was still watching her. When she reached her locker, Mindy unzipped her backpack so she could switch to the books she would need. That's when she noticed the folded note. Diego had dropped it at the end of one of her reading sessions, as the boys filed out of the room under the watchful gaze of a guard. He had done so casually, making it seem like an accident, until his eyes flicked to hers and away again. She'd told the guard it was hers when she picked it up and had waited until she was sitting in her car before unfolding and reading the note. Mindy had expected it to be a message for Ricky. Instead, in messy handwriting, it said,

You're the only thing keeping me sane. Thanks princess.

From that point on, she never struggled with motivation to show up and read to the inmates. Or if she was honest, to one person in particular, because she wasn't a saint. Mindy hadn't gone to that bleak place out of the goodness of her heart. But it *was* her heart that had led her there regardless. For other reasons.

Keisha bent over to touch the tips of her fingers to her toes. When she stood again, she swept her arms through the air with a flourish. To better stretch them, of course. And to impress anyone who might be looking. Although when she checked the entrance to the gym, Keisha still didn't see who she was waiting for. She remained attentive when continuing her routine, ignoring the excited chatter of the other students. Her vigilance was finally rewarded when someone with a mane of dark hair and an impressive chest strolled into the room, but sadly, he wasn't her type.

"Hey!" Omar said, walking over to join her. "This is cool! I've never been on the girls' side of the gym before."

Probably because a partition ran between it and the boys' side, where she could already hear shoes squeaking on the floor.

"Actually, that's not true," Omar said, placing his hands on his hips while surveying the scene with a satisfied grin. "I filmed some cheerleaders in here last year."

Keisha stopped working her neck from left to right and gave him her full attention. "What are you doing here now?"

"This is dance class, right?"

"Yes. Is this for the video yearbook? Where's your camcorder?"

"In my locker." Omar beamed at her. "I'm here to bust some moves."

"Really?" she asked, not hiding her surprise.

"Uh-huh." Omar was watching some freshmen attempt to pirouette. "I'm pretty good too, so I figured it would be easy." He looked at her while scratching the back of his head sheepishly. "And uh… I really need to up my grades."

"Cool," she said, deciding it wasn't so strange after all. Not after seeing someone like Diego Gomez shake his hips so skillfully during their production of *West Side Story*.

"Have you been in this class before?" he asked.

"Nope."

"Maybe we should have done this sooner." Omar leaned in close to speak in conspiring tones. "Looks like I'm the only guy. And you're a lesbian, so no matter who we end up dancing with, we're in for a good time." He nudged her. "Am I right?"

Keisha nudged him back. "Maybe. What exactly are you expecting from this class?"

Omar shrugged. "Today? Not much. We'll probably start with something easy, like slow dancing. I can already do a waltz. And a tango. I can give you some pointers if you need them."

"Much appreciated," Keisha said, barely managing to keep her amusement in check. Did he really think everyone would be dancing in pairs, like they were practicing for prom? Although she shouldn't judge. Her own reason for being here was far from innocent.

A pair of twins entered the gym. When one of them noticed her and perked up, Keisha's heart rolled gleefully down a hill covered in dewy green grass.

"Uh oh," Omar said loudly to attract their attention. "Here comes trouble."

The Song sisters walked side-by-side toward them, making it easy to spot their differences. Both were lean and athletic, with fine features and dark straight hair. Faith's was longer, her expression ever-critical. Hope wore her hair in a short bob. She had an air of perpetual patience that came from being around someone as domineering as her sister, because Faith could be a real pit bull.

"Are you going to film us again?" she asked Omar.

"Nope! I'm here to dance!"

"Hey," Hope said before biting her lower lip.

"Hey yourself," Keisha replied with a self-assured smirk that was all façade, because her insides were going wild.

"So are you gay now too?" Faith demanded.

Keisha tore her attention away from Hope, relieved that the question wasn't directed at her.

"Huh?" Omar said. "No. What makes you think that?"

"Because you're in a class that boys don't take," Faith said, continuing to grill him. "And all your other friends are gay. Aren't they?"

"Not *all* of them," Omar spluttered. "Who cares either way?"

Faith shrugged, her dark eyes considering Keisha briefly before she addressed Omar again. "Are you still dating that girl?"

"Nah. We broke up."

Faith seemed to reconsider him. "So you're single?"

Keisha noticed the way that Hope tensed up.

"Nope. I'm dating Whitney Brannigan-Habersham. Isn't that a crazy name?"

Faith sighed, as if disappointed, and not because she was interested. Faith was dating Troy. And for some reason, it bothered her that Hope was still single. Faith looked around the room as if searching for other options before grunting. "I hope this class is fun."

"It will be," Hope said, her gaze settling on Keisha briefly. "I'm sure of it."

The teacher entered the room, clapping her hands and gesturing for them all to come near. She had frizzy gray hair and was wiry like a yoga instructor. "Welcome everyone," she said. "My name is Mrs. Fiscus. I see some familiar faces this year. And a few new ones too. I'm sure you're eager to get started, but first, we'll need to go over some basics. Starting with what you'll wear during this class. You'll want light flexible clothing, all in black please."

"That's exactly my style," Omar said from next to Keisha.

"Short-sleeved shirts," the teacher continued, "and tights or leggings for the pants."

"Wait, what?" Omar murmured.

The teacher didn't hear him. "Athletic shorts are fine during practice, but not when we have an official performance at a pep rally or during a special event, like a football game."

"What's she talking about?" Omar whispered.

Keisha shrugged innocently, certain that he would transfer out before the end of the week.

"For today, I'd like to lead you through the stretching exercises that we'll begin each period with. If you were in this class previously, feel free to help the others with their form."

One of the freshmen smiled at Omar. He turned a panicked expression on Keisha. "What does she mean tights? And football games?"

"Maybe she expects us to do the foxtrot during halftime," she replied drolly. "Just remember that easy A."

"Right, right," Omar said.

They spread out into rows. Hope tried to stand next to her, until Faith grabbed her hand and yanked her toward the front. That became sweet torture as they stretched and strained. Keisha normally prided herself on her synchronization, but her movements now were intentionally delayed. Especially when Hope put her palms flat on the floor, her face appearing upside down between her spread legs. She smiled at Keisha, who bent over while laughing.

They tended to have fun together, even though it was always fleeting. Keisha's summer had begun with a frustrating revival of a hopeless crush. Silvia was finally single, which could have paved the way for them to explore their potential together, if she wasn't so hung up on Omar. Keisha had tried to convince herself that she was fine with being friends, but the feelings had swollen, like a ship taking on water. Just when it seemed like she would sink to the ocean floor, she'd bumped into a lifeboat. Or more accurately, a group of teenage girls wearing slinky shorts and tight-fitting T-shirts. Keisha had been walking down Main Street when she ran into Hope and the group she played soccer with. They'd stopped to chat, the rest of the team hustling along the sidewalk like a burning fuse. Hope was clearly glad to see her but just as obligated to catch up with her friends. That's when she'd thrown Keisha a lifeline.

"We play every Wednesday," Hope had said.

"At that park over there?" Keisha had asked, pointing at it until she saw a nod. "That's funny. I like to read in that park.

Usually on Wednesdays. Maybe we'll see each other next time."

Hope had bit her bottom lip—as she was prone to do—before nodding and racing off to catch up with her friends. And so it went. Keisha would show up early enough to wish her luck, watch her on the field while holding a book that she made little progress on, and they'd talk after or sometimes during the game. Which never lasted long before prior commitments stole Hope away from her again, but she walked away from each encounter having learned something new. Hope wanted to be a coach, for instance, and was allergic to cats. She hated crying in front of other people despite loving sad movies. Each tidbit was a piece of a jigsaw puzzle that Keisha was slowly putting together to form a complete picture, but there was plenty more she wanted to know. So when the start of the school year neared, she'd asked if Hope would be joining the theater group and learned that Faith had insisted they try this class next, making Keisha's course selection effortless. And here they were. At the end of the first of many hours they'd be spending together.

"What the hell?" Omar said when the bell rang. "I'm so confused! What does stretching have to do with dancing? I mean, my parents never do it, and you should see their moves."

"Just remember to bring a fresh pair of tights tomorrow," Keisha said before walking over to join Hope. Who was with her chaperone of a sister, so she adopted a new strategy and tried engaging with them both.

"What did y'all think?" Keisha asked. "Is this what you've been looking for? I know you've blown through gymnastics and cheerleading already. And you danced with us in the theater group. How does this compare?"

"We'll see," Faith said. "Stretching is boring. I didn't break a sweat."

"I liked it," Hope said, her smile demure. "I think it'll be fun."

"When we get to the first routine," Keisha said, "maybe we can practice together and pull ahead of the others. We'll work up a sweat like you want and lead the rest of the class toward greatness."

She figured that would appeal to Faith's ambitious nature, and more importantly, Hope's desire to coach.

"We'll see," Faith said, taking her sister's hand and leading her away.

Hope glanced over her shoulder with a wince of apology as they went.

Keisha smiled to assure her that it was all right. And it most certainly was, because if there's one thing she enjoyed, it was a challenge.

CHAPTER 4
SEPTEMBER 1ST, 1993

Diego felt like an idiot when walking to his second elective of the day. Unlike the Spanish class he'd enrolled in, what possible use could it have? Once he opened his own auto repair shop down in El Paso, he'd need to be more fluent in Spanish than he already was, since a lot of his customers wouldn't speak English. Or have a lot of money, so maybe it wasn't the best business model, but that was fine with him. Diego didn't have any interest in fixing some rich guy's Jaguar. He only wanted to deal with real people who owned normal cars, because that's who he was too. Fucking real! So why had he signed up for a class where a bunch of kids got together to play make-believe? Ridiculous!

And yet, the people in the theater group were kind of cool. Diego had felt welcome around them. They acted like he was good at what he did and didn't seem fake like the characters they played. Hell, most of them never made it on stage. Not to perform. They seemed happy to have a place where they actually fit in, even if that meant they had to sew some dopey curtains or paint a wooden cactus and weird shit like that. Diego realized he was walking faster, eager to return to that sense of belonging, before he reminded himself that nothing stayed the same.

By now, they'd all have heard that he was a serial arsonist. Didn't matter that he'd only lit some toilet paper on fire after TPing a couple of trees. If he'd really wanted to burn down Graham's house, Diego would have gotten the job done. Nothing would be left but a pile of ashes. Instead the house's exterior had merely gotten singed, but that didn't matter to people. Nor did the facts. Just like Omar's stupid garage that Diego had supposedly torched years ago, history was not only written by the victors, but spread far and wide to ensure the losing side could never win. No matter how hard you tried.

He reached the auditorium door and braced himself for the fearful gazes and hissed whispers that awaited him on the other side. Nothing he hadn't dealt with previously. Ricky, on the other hand… Diego was surprised to have gotten this far into the day without seeing him. That might be about to change.

Ricky had written endless letters over the summer, many of them outlining various plans on how they could be together. Including taking the theater elective. Diego had imagined doing exactly that, along with countless other scenarios, since it was the only way to immunize himself against the future. If he felt a small hand take his right now and turned around to see dark wet eyes staring up at him in sympathy and need… That would be tough to resist. But only if he was taken off guard. So while locked in a shitty institution, he had made himself picture all the different ways Ricky might try to force his way back into his life, even though it was torture. Such as lunch break, which had seemed the most likely opportunity for him to show up, but then—

"Diego!"

The voice cut straight to his heart, despite all the precautions he'd taken. When he saw the figure running down the hall toward him, Diego was struck by how much Ricky had changed. The mop of black hair was styled now, parted on one side. His arms and legs were lankier. Even his face had matured. Which was a timely reminder that nothing stayed the same. If he needed further proof of that, Ricky slowed and stopped when they were still six feet apart. He never would have done that before. Ricky would've slammed into him, grabbed hold, and refused to let go. But he too must have sensed that they'd parted ways three months ago in a manner that transcended the physical.

"I missed you," Ricky said, his voice sounding vulnerable, because a question was hidden in that statement.

He wanted to know if Diego had missed him too. Which of course he had, but feeling that kind of thing was a luxury he hadn't been able to afford when locked up with a bunch of psychopaths.

Ricky swallowed at his lack of a response and tried again. "Can we talk?"

The bell rang. He brushed past Ricky, and annoyingly, it fucking hurt. So what had been the point in imagining this moment so often? His plan hadn't worked. Diego felt like someone had dropkicked his heart anyway. Goddamn it! He was so lost in thought that he made it into the auditorium without being truly aware of his surroundings.

"There he is!"

"Told you he'd join this year."

"So cool!"

Diego glanced around in confusion, including behind him, but Ricky was nowhere to be seen. They were talking about him!

"Hey," he said with an upward nod at a couple of guys who'd run the lights in the previous play.

They looked at each other, as if needing guidance for how to respond before saying "Hey!" in unison.

Diego cast his gaze across the rows of seats, which were only occupied toward the stage. Although quite a few people were standing while talking. Keisha was one of them. She nodded in his direction, Diego close enough to read her lips when she said, "Look who's here."

Mindy turned around in her seat. Then her jaw dropped. He laughed, despite everything he was feeling inside. That's how it had gone all summer. He'd been in a hopeless place and she had shown up, like a delicate flower bursting through the concrete. So of course some asshole immediately tried to stomp on her. Diego had put a stop to that, mostly for his own satisfaction, because Mindy was strong. She'd kept coming back, week after week, no matter how bleak the surroundings or how abusive the audience. She had sat there in front of angry fucked-up guys—including himself—and read a goddamn book. She must have felt like a piece of meat under all those sexually frustrated stares. Her flower didn't wilt though. Not one bit. Mindy only seemed to grow taller and more beautiful with each visit.

Diego realized he was smiling. Which felt weird, so he stopped. She didn't. Mindy kept beaming at him.

"Okay everyone," Ms. Deville said, walking to the front of the stage. "Let's get started." Her attention moved to the back of the room. "Hurry up! I run a tight ship. Don't be late to my class."

He glanced over his shoulder. Ricky had finally arrived, his eyes red around the edges. Diego shrugged off the sympathy that was nipping at him and chose a seat at the end of the row, a tiny dark-skinned girl sitting on his left. No one else would be able to sit next to him unless… Ricky settled down across the aisle from Diego, shooting furtive glances in his direction.

"For the first day," Ms. Deville said from a position of authority on the stage, "I always like to explain what to expect from this class before giving you a chance to do the same."

Diego listened half-heartedly. In his peripheral vision, he

was aware of Ricky's stare. Rather than pretend he didn't notice, Diego turned his head and looked right at him. Better to get this out of the way now. For both their sakes. He was struck again by how much Ricky had changed, although his apologetic expression was familiar. Diego had seen it during the painful drive home from the failed trip to El Paso. Ricky had kept saying how sorry he was. Just not enough to actually go through with it. And it pissed him off, because they could have taken the whole damn world by storm!

He realized he was scowling. Ricky swallowed, his eyes wavering, like he was going to cry right then and there. This was a bad idea. Getting to see Mindy's reaction had been worth it, but Diego wouldn't show up after today. What was the point?

"Okay," Ms. Deville said. "I'd like to hear from you now. One by one. Please introduce yourself and share what motivated you to take this class."

Oh boy. Maybe he should walk out right now. Although he *was* curious to hear what other people said.

"Hey y'all! My name is Keisha Hart. I enrolled in this class as a freshman because my best friend said it would be easy for us to hang out and gossip. I took two acting parts the first year but figured out quick that I prefer working on the production as a whole. Last year I focused on choreography. This year I'm hoping to become stage manager. All I can say is, if you're new, stick around. There's plenty of variety. You'll find where you fit in soon enough."

Keisha sat, the person next to her springing up. "Hi! My name is Mindy Beaumont. I'm the one who wanted to gossip. As it turns out, you'll be *way* too busy for that. Unless you're sitting in my makeup chair, where I do love dishing the dirt, so I wasn't completely wrong."

Diego snorted. The others laughed.

"I also do wardrobe," Mindy continued. "At a certain age, you're supposed to stop playing with dolls, but this is the next best thing. Actually, it's even better. I can't wait to work with everyone again!"

"Me neither!" a blond girl said, hopping to her feet to give Mindy a high-five. "My name is Whitney Brannigan-Habersham. Try saying that three times fast. No really!"

A chorus of jumbled syllables was the response.

"It's not actually hard to say," Whitney said. "I just think it's fun. Like this class! Last year I got to be a princess who moved into a castle with some sort of crazy werewolf. Oh! And I got to sing and dance with a street gang. I can't believe this is part of school. It's hilarious!"

And so it went for most of the hour, Diego paying close attention, since many of the speakers had been kind and supportive to him last year, despite him being a stranger to the group. Before he knew it, his turn had come.

"Hey," Diego said, standing up. "I'm here because— Oh wait. My name is Diego. As in Gomez Auto Repair. That's not a weird hyphenated last name. It's the family business."

There was a rumble of laughter, but not at his expense.

"I starred in a couple of plays last year—" he began again, only to be interrupted by applause. "You guys are cool," he said when they quieted down. "That's the main reason I'm here. And also because…" He sought out Mindy. "I had a really shitty summer, but someone went out of their way to make me happy. I figured it would make her happy if I signed up for this class. So yeah… Here I am."

Mindy was blushing, but she seemed pleased.

He sat down satisfied until he heard a voice to his right.

"My name is Ricky Nishikawa and umm…" Diego glanced over just in time to see a trembling chin. "I think I'm here for the wrong reason."

Ricky rushed down the aisle and out the door, leaving a confused silence in his wake.

"I've got this!" Mindy said. She shot to her feet and hurried after him.

Diego sighed. This isn't how he'd wanted things to play out. He remembered returning to school after a shitty summer years ago and the way his so-called best friends had walked away, leaving him to wonder what went wrong instead of having the decency to tell him to his face. He wouldn't do that to Ricky. Time for a do-over.

When the bell rang not long after, he left the auditorium. Mindy was farther down the hall, talking to Ricky who noticed him first, his face creasing in pain. Mindy followed his gaze before walking over.

"You really need to talk to him," she said, placing a hand

on one of Diego's crossed forearms. "He was a mess the entire summer. It was heartbreaking."

"Yeah, okay," he replied.

Mindy's eyes were pleading with him. "Be gentle."

"I'll be honest," Diego countered. "See you tomorrow."

"At lunch!" Mindy raced off before he could say otherwise.

His gaze moved down the hall, where Ricky was watching him sullenly. Diego walked in his direction, Ricky looking more hopeful with each step. This was going to suck.

"Hey," Diego said, leaving it at that.

"Can we talk?" Ricky asked.

"We already are."

Ricky swallowed. "I'm really sorry."

Diego sighed wearily. "Are you?"

"Yes!"

"Uh-huh. So you wish you were in El Paso right now?"

Ricky shook his head. "What?"

"You said you were sorry," Diego growled. "Prove it! We'll do it all over again. I'll drive you out to Candle Cave. We'll get my money, I'll fuck you, and then we'll hit the road. Right now. Let's go!"

Ricky hugged himself and leaned against the row of lockers for support.

"Well?" Diego barked. "What's it gonna be?"

"I don't want to," Ricky said.

"Why not?" Diego demanded. "Be honest. You know I can take it."

Ricky opened his mouth. Then he closed it before trying again. "I guess because…"

"Yeah?"

Ricky swallowed "I wouldn't feel safe."

"I *never* feel safe" Diego snarled, his stomach twisting up with the truth. "I've been on that road for years when you… you haven't even left your goddamn bedroom! But you will. Someday you'll look around and realize that you aren't safe and never were. Then it'll click. But I hope you're an old man by then, because you have a good life. Your parents are both alive and sane. You get to go home to a nice cozy house each night. I envy you, but there's no turning back for me. I don't get to go home again. I'm on a one-way trip. So you did the right thing. All I can do is drag you down with me, but I won't, because it would ruin you just like—"

His voice strangled to a halt, which pissed him off.

"There's nothing wrong with you," Ricky said.

Diego grimaced. "You know I hate well-meaning bullshit."

"You're not fucked up!" Ricky cried. "Sometimes I feel like you're the only one who *isn't* crazy. That's why I love you!"

"No!" Diego slammed his palm against the locker near Ricky's head and left it there. "You do *not* get to say one thing and do another. Not to me."

Ricky jutted out his chin. "So I have to do exactly what you want, or it means I don't love you?"

Diego leaned close, bringing their faces together to make him understand. "I would have marched straight through the gates of Hell if it's what you needed. In fact, that's exactly what I did."

"What about now?" Ricky asked, his eyes catching fire. "If you still love me, what about what I need right now?"

Diego clenched his jaw, his eyes moving hungrily to Ricky's defiant mouth.

"A-*hem!*"

They turned their heads in unison. Principal Preckwinkle, a short woman with a mess of blond curls, adjusted her glasses with a frown of disapproval. "I hope we can avoid a repeat of last year's indiscretions," she snapped. "I went out of my way to ensure that you wouldn't share any of the same classes. Must I also assign someone to escort each of you through the halls?"

"See what I mean?" Diego said, turning to Ricky. "I'll only drag you down with me."

He pushed away from the lockers and winked at Principal Preckwinkle before sauntering in the opposite direction. She obviously hadn't tried hard enough to keep them apart, unless Ricky had shown up in that class when he was supposed to be in another. She probably wouldn't notice or care. Preckwinkle was more interested in taking him down. Diego wished she would get it over with and expel him already. That way he wouldn't have to suffer the humiliation of being a sophomore, when he was supposed to be a junior. He wouldn't have to see Ricky again, or figure out if he was going to sit with Mindy at lunch tomorrow, or take a role in another dumb school play. He could work on cars all day in peace and quiet. Nobody would bother him anymore. He'd be free.

Disconnected.

Alone.

So why had he shown up today? How come he hadn't moved to El Paso? Nobody was stopping him. Diego thought of his mother. And of Mindy and how people in the theater group had actually clapped for him, like he'd done something good for once. What if Ricky was right? Maybe running away was a bad idea. Fuck! Diego stopped and turned around, but the hallway behind him was empty.

The first day of her political career and Silvia already felt like throwing in the towel. Mostly due to the company she was forced to keep. She continued to doodle in her notebook, her head tilted downward, even when checking the corner of the room to collect embarrassing details. Troy Mitchell was standing next to Faith Song's desk, where she sat on the surface while slowly making out with him. And it was so gross! Not just because he was a sleazeball who couldn't keep his hands to himself. At times it was hard to look away, because Silvia could swear she saw his tongue moving around in Faith's cheek, like she was sucking on a leech. Disgusting! She couldn't wait to tell Mindy all about it.

Silvia wasn't feeling much chemistry with the rest of the class either. She had expected to be surrounded by bookish people who humbled her with their knowledge of government policies. Instead a group of girls near her were excitedly debating prom themes. The only other person she knew here was Dave, who she had met at a couple of parties last year. When she'd said hello to him, his response was muted before he took a seat next to Troy and Faith. Her attention returned to the couple in the corner. Troy was making *"mmm"* noises like Faith tasted good. So gross!

Mindy had dodged a bullet. Silvia had been fortunate too, because Omar was a great kisser. She thought of the way he'd always pull back to smile at her, his eyes alight like she was the most beautiful woman in the world. She missed that. No… She missed *him.* Yes they saw each other on occasion, usually with other people around, but it wasn't the same as being together in his bedroom or out at the lake while fishing.

"You! Get off that desk." A heavy-set black woman had just marched in, her finger pointing at Troy before swinging to the far side of the room. "And you, go sit over there. Don't give me that look! I'm the vice-principal!"

"But—" Troy said.

"I told you where to sit. Now *move!*"

Troy slunk to his corner.

"Okay then," the woman said, standing in front of the teacher's desk. "Most of you don't know me yet, but as you just heard, I'm your new vice principal, LaVern Freemont. Even though teaching falls outside of my regular duties, I felt it was important to establish this class. How your country is governed will color your entire lives, and it's crucial to understand the inner workings now, so that you can prevent your voice from being diminished in the future. High school, as you'll discover, is a microcosm of the world you'll enter into as adults. You're here to prepare yourselves. I'm here to guide you."

"Umm." A girl to Silvia's left raised her hand. "Vice Principal Freemont?"

"LaVern will do. Otherwise we'll be here all day."

"Oh. I think I might be in the wrong class. I thought we were going to plan the pep rallies and dances."

"You will," the vice principal replied. "The student council, much like the United States government, has limited—albeit important—roles to play in the lives of its people. Let's go over them, one by one."

Silvia perked up. This was more like it! She stopped doodling and started taking real notes. A lot had changed since this time last year. She had gone from not wanting to be noticed to... well, she still wasn't eager for public scrutiny. Mostly because of her undocumented parents, although she didn't worry about them as much lately. Not in the same way. Both of her parents were working for Keisha's family now, out on Hartland Farms. That meant driving away from Pride in the morning and returning each evening to a trailer park on the edge of town where they lived, reducing the likelihood of them being pulled over. Her parents were working for good people who wouldn't try to exploit them because of their immigration status. Silvia's mother had, until the end of June, been employed as a maid at a cheap hotel. Her boss had never been timely when doling out paychecks. When her mother raised the issue with him, he had suggested that sleeping with him might help. That was the final straw. Her mother had quit. Now she went to work with her husband each day, so it was a happy ending. For them. And for now.

All it took was losing their jobs and they'd be back to square one. Silvia's family wasn't the only one dealing with these issues. She wanted to find a way to help and needed to decide on a career, so while smoking weed in the woods by her trailer, it had dawned on her that politics might be the answer. Not in the "hey, vote for me and I'll make all your problems disappear" type of way. She was more interested in the people behind the scenes who created the rules instead of breaking them. By changing the system, Silvia could protect her family while helping countless others in the same situation.

"None of you are elected officials yet," LaVern said. "Tomorrow we will go over the student council positions and their parallels with the American political system. For now..." She glanced at the clock, her timing impeccable, because the bell rang. "Congratulations on surviving your first day back at school."

The classroom cleared out to the sound of discontented grumbles, although Sylvia noticed a few people like herself who seemed more awake than when the class first started. Two of them even remained behind to talk to the vice-principal.

Silvia was too eager to get outside to the warmth and sunshine. She stopped by her locker first, almost expecting a camcorder to be shoved in her face while an over-enthusiastic guy raved about how great everything was going to be. She lingered for a moment, just in case, before leaving the building and unlocking her bike. She rode a short distance to the wooded lot next to the school and dismounted. Silvia guided her bike along a narrow path until she was deep enough into the trees that she wouldn't be spotted easily. After glancing around to be sure, she dug around in her backpack and pulled out an old tin that used to contain mints. The only thing inside now was a joint that she'd rolled earlier and a book of matches. Silvia lit up, and unlike the current president, she most definitely inhaled. The smoke carried a hint of menthol, infused by her choice of container. Maybe she should keep some actual mints in there to enhance the effect. And to use afterwards so a customer wouldn't smell the pot on her breath. She only took a couple hits, since she needed to clock in, but it was enough that everything felt good. From the breeze on her skin to the sounds of the leaves rustling in the branches above, she became aware of the beauty of the world. Who needed a goofy guy to film such things for her? *Le sigh*. Silvia pushed her bike toward the street. She had just reached the sidewalk when she noticed someone standing there, peering into the trees.

"Oh," Ricky said. "Sorry. I thought I smelled weed and thought Diego might be in there."

"You got one out of two right," Silvia said. "Wanna get high?"

Ricky shook his head. "I've tried. It's not my thing."

"Cool. Welcome back, by the way. I don't remember if I said that at lunch."

"Thanks." Ricky peered at the trees again with a troubled expression.

"I didn't notice anyone else in there," Silvia told him. "I'm guessing you never found Diego?"

"I did," he replied tersely.

"How'd it go?"

Ricky's voice sounded hoarse when he responded. "Do you know what it's like to spend three months wishing you could be with someone, only to find out that they want nothing to do with you?"

"Yes."

He blinked in surprise. "You do?"

"More or less," she said. "Just before you left town, Omar broke up with me. He said he wanted to start over as friends and take things slow. Which was fine, but I thought we'd get back together before too long. Imagine my surprise when, while at work, I happen to see him walking down the sidewalk with Whitney Arm-and-Hammer-Baking-Soda. Or whatever her name is."

Ricky snorted and laughed.

Silvia joined him. "She seems nice. And it's not like I can complain. I had my chance and blew it."

Ricky winced. "Sorry about that. I kind of ruined everything for you."

She shook her head. "It's not your fault."

"Yeah it is. If I had promised to keep a secret, then you wouldn't have blackmailed me, and Omar wouldn't have gotten so upset."

"*I'm* the one who kissed Keisha!" Silvia said. "And the one who kept secrets from him. I only have myself to blame."

Ricky sighed. "I know the feeling."

She eyed him a moment. "I have to get to work," she said, "but if you're heading that way, we could keep talking."

"Sure! Can I ride on your handlebars?"

Silvia chuckled at the visual image. She was definitely feeling that weed! "You've gotten a little too big for that," she said as they began walking. "So anyway, what happened when you saw Diego today?"

Ricky rolled his eyes. "He lectured me about how he's from the wrong side of the tracks and that I should stay away."

"Classic," Silvia said. "And very hot."

"It is," Ricky replied. "I shouldn't joke about it though, because I really hurt his feelings. I don't think he'll ever forgive me. Diego is the type to hold a grudge. I tried getting him to be friends with Anthony and Omar again, but it didn't work. And their feud started *years* ago! If he's still mad at them after all this time…"

"That's rough," Silvia said in sympathy. "I'm sorry it didn't work out, but I'm sure you'll find someone new. Maybe we should put personal ads in the school newspaper. That's not really a thing, but they'd be fun to write."

Ricky was staring at her incredulously. "I'm not giving up! Are you?"

Silvia shrugged. "Omar is dating someone else now."

"So? That doesn't mean you've already lost. It's possible to have feelings for more than one person at a time. You know that."

She certainly did, but the girl Silvia had the hots for was chasing down a different lead.

"Diego has been abandoned by people his entire life," Ricky continued. "He thinks I'm one of them, but I'm going to prove him wrong. You shouldn't give up on Omar either. He's a really great guy."

"And funny," Silvia said longingly. "And sweet. And handsome."

"*And* he's got a big you-know-what," Ricky said with a naughty grin.

Silvia laughed. "That's right, we've both slept with him!"

"Did you guys ever go all the way?"

Silvia shook her head. "I wasn't ready. I wish I could have

met him this year instead, but then, I'm not sure if I would have changed this much. Not without meeting him first. Omar was good for me."

"I feel the same way about Diego," Ricky said, "even though he's convinced the opposite is true. So is it a deal?"

"What?"

"Are we going to get them back?" Ricky took off his glasses to polish them. "We could come up with plans and help each other out."

She thought about how good it would feel to spend a lazy Sunday afternoon fishing with Omar again. "Okay. Why not? We should at least try."

"Yes!" Ricky said, grinning when he returned his glasses to his nose. "This is going to be great!"

Silvia matched his expression. "I know someone who can help us. He understands Omar better than most people. Diego too, I bet, since he's been their best friend."

"You mean Anthony?"

Silvia nodded. "He's stopping by the record store soon. Cameron will probably show up too. Come hang out with us."

"Awesome!" Ricky glanced at her bike. "You know, I bet I actually could fit on the handlebars."

Silvia laughed and swung a leg over it to get seated. "Let's find out!"

CHAPTER 5

Cameron clenched the sheets as Anthony's head bobbed up and down. The lights in his bedroom were low, their favorite mixtape drowning out his moans. They listened to it so much when making love that just hearing the songs was enough to turn Cameron on. In fact, the last time he'd gone shopping at the mall, he'd gotten a boner when New Order began playing over the department store speakers. Too bad Anthony hadn't been with him at the time, or they could have snuck into a changing room and—

"I'm getting close," he gasped. Cameron released the sheets and wove his fingers between mostly blond hair as Anthony's head began to bob faster. "Actually," he grunted. "I wanna finish on top. Roll over."

Anthony happily complied. Once his boyfriend was on his back, head resting against a pillow, Cameron put his knees to either side of Anthony's chest so he could do the work himself.

"Look at me," he said while thrusting.

Green eyes met his, eager and affectionate. Cameron's entire body tensed.

Anthony swallowed greedily, not willing to let him go when he tried to pull away. Eventually he had to, because it felt a little *too* good. Cameron laughed before stretching out and lowering himself on Anthony for a kiss.

"That was incredible," he breathed.

"I liked it too," Anthony said with a satisfied smirk.

Cameron kissed him again. Then he pushed himself up. "All right. Take off your clothes."

Anthony blanched at the suggestion. "Why?"

"Uh, that's usually how these things work." Cameron glanced down pointedly. He was nude. Anthony was still dressed. He hadn't even taken off his shoes.

"Sure," Anthony said with a shrug, "but I lose all interest in sex after I come so…"

"But you didn't."

"Right. I'm thinking of you."

"Well stop," Cameron said, rolling off him and tugging at his shirts, plural, because Anthony always wore at least two these days, one of them long-sleeved. "I wanna see you naked. And make you lose all interest in sex."

Anthony took his hand and squeezed it. "I'm okay. Really," he added when Cameron opened his mouth to protest.

Not wanting to force anything, he snuggled up to him and draped a leg across his body. Anthony seemed to relax, so Cameron let his hand wander, his index and middle fingers becoming a little man that walked across Anthony's stomach and up his chest to tickle his chin. Anthony laughed, grabbing the little man like King Kong, but only to kiss him. Once his hand was released, Cameron used it to stroke Anthony's cheek, which felt different than it used to. Because of the makeup. It wasn't caked on by any means, but it also wasn't the natural sheen of Anthony's skin. Which he was beginning to miss.

"I wanna show you something," Cameron said.

"Time for round two?" Anthony asked.

"No. This is even better."

He got out of bed, pulling on his boyfriend's hand so he would follow. Cameron led them to the bedroom door.

"If we're going for a walk," Anthony said, "you might want to get dressed."

"It's a very short walk," Cameron told him. He opened the door and stuck his head out to make sure the coast was clear. Then he darted across the hall while dragging Anthony after him. Once they were safely locked in the bathroom, he let go, opened a drawer, and took out a washcloth. He wet it down with warm water and raised it.

Anthony blocked him with an arm when the washcloth neared his face. "What are you doing?"

"Trust me," Cameron said, trying again.

His boyfriend went rigid as he gently wiped one of his cheeks clean. "You don't need to wear makeup," he said, gesturing to the mirror so Anthony would look at himself. "I like your natural skin, and your lips are already pink. You're handsome."

"I *like* wearing makeup," Anthony said, barely glancing at the mirror.

"How come?"

"Do I need a reason?"

Cameron shrugged. He tossed the washcloth in the sink and

considered his boyfriend before trying a more direct approach. "I'm worried that you have body image issues."

Anthony's face became drawn. "What?"

Cameron tugged on one his sleeves. "You dressed like this the whole summer. No matter how hot it was outside."

"So what?" Anthony snapped, yanking his arm away.

"So look at us!" Cameron pointed at the mirror. He was naked, his sun-kissed skin only getting paler when reaching his hips. The guy next to him was fully dressed, like he'd barged into the bathroom by accident. "Do we look like a couple who just had sex?" he pressed. "Half the time you don't want me to do anything to you."

"I'm really sorry about that," Anthony huffed. "From now on, I'll take off my clothes as soon as I get here. Except for my collar, of course, and the chain attached to it, since apparently I'm your dog."

He stomped from the room. Cameron followed him after a moment of surprise until Anthony disappeared down the stairs. Cameron swore under his breath and rushed back to his bedroom to get dressed. Then he took the stairs two at a time on his way down.

"Everything okay?" his mother called from the living room.

"Yes!" he lied before ripping open the front door.

What the hell was going on?

The driveway was empty except for the station wagon that he shared with his mom. Cameron almost went back inside for the keys before he remembered that Anthony had walked over. They'd met halfway. Cameron had kissed him, feeling and tasting the lip gloss even in the dark. He didn't mind the makeup exactly. But he also wasn't fond of it. None of that mattered at the moment. Cameron took off running down the street. He saw a tall shadowy figure on the sidewalk ahead and sprinted to reach him.

"Hey!" he panted, grabbing Anthony's hand. "Wait up!"

His boyfriend turned around—expression wounded—and watched silently as Cameron caught his breath.

"What's going on?" he managed at last.

"You tell me," Anthony retorted.

Cameron's stomach sank. He thought about how, earlier today, a couple of guys had noticed Anthony and had called him a fag. They'd been walking down the hall together, Cameron as good as invisible, despite being right next to him. Even when he took his boyfriend's hand, the guys remained focused on Anthony, laughing and doing a prissy exaggeration of his body language. Their second day of school and the bullying had already begun. Cameron was certain that wouldn't be the end of it. *Everyone* noticed Anthony now. He was a moving target.

"I'm scared," Cameron admitted. "I don't want something bad to happen to you."

"That wasn't a concern when we decided to come out," Anthony replied. "Why is it now?"

"I've always worried about you," Cameron said with a swallow. "Even then. And yeah, especially now, because you stand out. You're tall and…"

Anthony hugged himself protectively. "Just say it."

He had a softness to him. And it was beautiful. But the world wasn't always kind to beautiful things.

"What if you dressed differently at school?" Cameron tried. "Afterwards you could go home, or come back to my place, and put on whatever you want. Including makeup."

"I can't believe you're saying this," Anthony said, shaking his head. "People are going to hate me no matter what. And yeah, it sucks, but nothing I can do will change that. So at the very least, I should be able to be—" His voice strangled to a halt. Anthony shook his head, clenching his eyes shut, but tears slipped free anyway. "I'm sick of worrying what everyone else will think. You especially!"

He turned and ran, his long legs carrying him away faster than Cameron could follow. He was too shocked to give chase anyway. Instead he stood there in stunned silence while wondering what went wrong.

Mindy was pleased with her ragtag bunch of lunch-break buddies. Diego had joined them yesterday and gotten along great with Keisha and Cameron, which wasn't a surprise, since they'd all spent time together during their sophomore year plays. Best of all, Diego had picked up two of the heavy stone benches and placed them across from each other in her favorite corner by the ivy. Now they could face each other while eating instead of sitting on the concrete. Each bench was only big enough to hold two. She was seated next to Cameron, who was carefully unpacking his lunch on the napkin he'd spread over his lap. This involved a variety of small Tupperware containers.

Diego cocked an eyebrow. "What is that?" he asked.

Cameron glanced up. "Chicken salad. I don't like it as a sandwich, because the bread gets soggy, so I use celery stalks like spoons." He demonstrated. "See?"

Diego snorted. "Did your mom pack that for you, Huxley?"

"No," Cameron replied. "I did."

"I hope your mother *didn't* pack yours," Keisha murmured, nodding at the sandwich Diego held. A stack of lunch meat was trapped between two slices of generic white bread. "Did you use the entire package of bologna?"

"I like my protein," Diego grunted.

"So do I," Cameron said. "Wanna try?"

Diego shrugged. "Yeah, all right."

Mindy laughed as she watched him wrap a big paw around a stalk of celery laden with chicken salad and begin gnawing.

"Who packed yours, princess?" Diego said with a scowl that she didn't take personally. "Your royal servants?"

"Basically, yes," Mindy said shamelessly. "My dad has packed mine my entire life." She nibbled delicately on a carrot stick, taking deliberately tiny bites until she noticed him fight off a smile. She could tell because a dimple always appeared in his cheek.

"My older brother packs mine," Keisha said, lifting a slice of bread to inspect the contents of her sandwich. "Ham and cheese. Again. Still, I shouldn't complain. He has to pack them for all the kids in my family. That's on his list of chores. My favorite is when he's feeling lazy and gives me money for a hot lunch instead."

"I love a hot lunch," Mindy said longingly.

"I can buy you lunch," Diego offered.

"Why don't you buy your own?" she asked in confusion.

"Because they don't serve it out in the parking lot." He shrugged. "Bringing my own is a habit."

"I don't like the food here," Cameron interjected. "Although you know what sounds good? Chocolate milk."

"Ooh!" Keisha breathed. "I haven't had one of those in ages."

"For real," Cameron said. "It's been years for me."

Conversation moved on to other topics, but toward the end of the break, it circled back around.

"I can't stop thinking about chocolate milk," Mindy admitted.

"Me neither," Diego said, leaning to the side to take out a money clip. "If someone else wants to get it, I'll pay."

Keisha and Cameron raised their hands at the same time. Then they laughed and went inside the building together, leaving her alone with Diego. Mindy pressed her lips together, but only to stop herself from smiling.

"So," Diego said, moving to the center of the bench. His strong hands gripped the edges as he leaned back. The tight maroon T-shirt he wore looked good against his bronze skin.

"So," Mindy repeated when it became clear that he didn't intend to say anything more.

Diego smirked, his russet eyes shining. "What's next for us?"

The air felt thin in her lungs, but she still managed to squeak out, "Next?"

"Well," he said. "First it was *West Side Story*."

The play she had helped him rehearse for. Mindy had always liked Diego, but until he got suspended, they had never really spent much time together.

"And then it was *Lord of the Flies*," he continued.

The book she had read to him while he was in the juvenile detention center. Mindy was glad that meant so much to him. Of everything that had happened over the summer, she thought of those moments the most.

"So where do we go from here?" Diego asked.

What about Ricky? Those were the words she needed to say, but her mouth wouldn't cooperate. Was he asking her on a date? Oh god… Mindy could feel a flush begin to spread that worked its way up to her cheeks. *What about Ricky?* Just say it! "Umm…" she managed.

"I mean, it's up to you," Diego said, "since you'd be the one reading."

"Huh?" Mindy blinked. *"Ooh!"*

He was talking about the books she had read to him. Back when they were rehearsing *West Side Story*, Diego hadn't been convinced of the plot, so she'd read the novelization to him. Now her cheeks were positively burning, but there was nothing she could do about it.

"You all right?" Diego asked, having noticed.

"Mm-hm!" she said, nodding rapidly.

"So what do you think?" he pressed.

"You *do* know that you can get books on tape," Mindy said to him. "You don't have to rely on me."

"I like listening to you read," he said easily. "But if it's a pain in the ass—"

"No! Not at all. I like it too." Mindy tittered nervously. She'd come awfully close to embarrassing herself. "I umm… I usually read romance novels."

Diego made a face. "I guess beggars can't be choosers."

"I read other things too. Do you like fantasy novels?"

"You mean wizards and stuff?" Diego shrugged.

"Why don't we go to the library and pick out something together?"

His gaze moved to the building—giving her the tiniest fraction of a second to gasp in air—before returning to her again. "You mean here?"

"No," Mindy said. "Although we could. The librarians here try, but there's way too much censorship. I was thinking the public library."

Diego seemed to think about it before nodding. "Yeah, okay."

The others returned before they could make plans. Which was a relief, because she had wanted to suggest they go to the library on the weekend, when they'd have nothing but time to spend together. Would that be so wrong? She wasn't sure, but even chocolate milk couldn't soothe her troubled soul as she remained haunted by one very important question.

What about Ricky?

Anthony was sitting in the same classroom that journalism had taken place in last year, which was also used for the creative writing elective. The tables here sat two, which was great, because it meant he could share one with his boyfriend. Cameron was on his left and seemed tense, like he had during the ride to school this morning. They hadn't spoken since their argument last night, and with Omar chattering nonstop from the back seat—or sometimes leaning forward to practically join them in the front—there wasn't the opportunity to say much to each other. Cameron had kissed Anthony before they went inside, but not as passionately as the previous two days. Maybe because Omar had stuck around, Cameron's jaw clenching all the while. Due to the lack of privacy? Or because Anthony had worn just as much makeup today?

"So what do people mean when they say you should begin with the second chapter," Mr. Finnegan said from the front of the room, "and is that good advice?"

Their teacher was a handsome guy with silver hair and pale gray eyes. His wife defied gender. Charles wore makeup, dresses, and wigs, despite using male pronouns. Had that ever been an issue between them? Did they argue about it in the beginning? Probably not. By the time Charles met Mr. Finnegan, he had already found himself. Anthony felt half-baked by comparison. Like a work in progress. Which would be exciting to explore if he wasn't afraid of losing Cameron. So of course Anthony had yelled at him before storming off, like an idiot who was trying to make his worst fears come true.

He swallowed and turned to a blank page in his composition book.

I'm really sorry, he wrote. *I shouldn't have freaked out last night.* He nudged the book toward Cameron, who read it and started scribbling before passing the book back to him.

I'm the one who's sorry! I was only trying to make you feel good about yourself, but I messed it all up. You're beautiful! I love you just the way you are.

Anthony's stomach sank, because he didn't feel the same way about himself. He wasn't satisfied with his appearance or who he was. Not because he had self-esteem issues. The makeup wasn't to hide who he was. Putting it on felt more like revealing something new. He reread what his boyfriend had written, his attention lingering on "just the way you are." Some things were easier to write down rather than say aloud. Maybe this was a good time to ask.

Do you want me to stop wearing makeup?

He watched Cameron carefully when passing the composition book back to him. A battle played out on his boyfriend's face before he hunched over to write his response.

I want you to be safe. And happy.

That was nice. But it didn't really answer the question, so he tried again.

Do you still find me attractive when I do?

Anthony couldn't bear to watch this time. He focused on the

front of the class, not really hearing or seeing much of anything. His heart pounded while he waited. This might hurt. The composition book slid across the table toward him.

Yes. But I don't think you need it. Like at all, so I don't get why you take the risk.

Anthony stared long and hard at that *yes* and felt like crying tears of relief. Cameron kept glancing at him, as if expecting a response. Anthony was happy to leave it at that. Exploring the issue any deeper would be too complicated. He wasn't sure if he could explain what was happening to him. Only one word came to mind. A name, actually.

Charles.

Were they the same? Is that who Anthony wanted to be like? He honestly wasn't sure.

Cameron lost patience and took control of the composition book again.

Do whatever makes you happy, he wrote. *I'll protect you.*

Anthony felt his insides flutter. He took the book back and began drawing hearts around their conversation, making Cameron laugh. They smiled at each other. Everything was going to be okay.

They stood when the bell rang, but they didn't make it far.

"Mr. Cullen, Mr. Huxley," their teacher said. "I'd like a word with you both."

Their smiles weren't returned as they approached Mr. Finnegan. The older man watched the remaining students file out of the classroom before clearing his throat. "I feel the need to reiterate how important it is to me—crucial even—to keep my professional and private lives separate."

"Yeah, of course!" Cameron said instantly.

Mr. Finnegan didn't relax. "Even something as simple as passing notes back and forth puts me in an awkward position. If it had been anyone else, I would have said something. And I will next time. Please don't take advantage of my friendship again."

"We weren't!" Anthony said. "Yes, we were passing notes, but not because we thought you'd let us get away with it. We didn't want you to notice at all."

That was the honest truth, but it wasn't enough. Mr. Finnegan turned his attention to Cameron. "What inspired you to take this class?"

"Oh!" Cameron was clearly caught off guard. "I uh…"

"Thought it would be a nice way to spend time together?" Mr. Finnegan suggested. "I don't expect every student to feel passionate about the subjects I teach. Especially when a parent chooses for them. But you *can* get something good out of this class, no matter your initial motivations. To do so, you'll need to pay attention. Do I make myself clear?"

"Yes, sir," Cameron said respectfully.

"Thank you. You'd better get to your next class. I need a bit more time with Anthony."

Cameron hastily withdrew.

"Sorry," Anthony said when they were alone.

"I remember how you're feeling now," Mr. Finnegan assured him, "but it's important that you in particular get the maximum benefit out of this class. You have more natural talent and untapped potential than any student I've had in recent years. I'm eager to see where this course takes you. Let your love for Cameron *inspire* you, rather than distract you. At least while you're in these hallowed halls. What happens outside of school is nobody's business. That's where I'll be your friend. While we're here, I can only be your teacher."

Anthony nodded his understanding. "I won't make the same mistake again," he promised. "Thank you for being so cool about it all."

"You'd better run along," Mr. Finnegan said with a twinkle in his eye. "I'll see you next week, if not sooner."

Anthony hurried to the hall and was surprised to find his boyfriend waiting for him.

"What are you still doing here?" he asked with a laugh.

"Walking you to your next class," Cameron replied.

"Which is in the opposite direction of yours. You'll be late."

"I don't care."

"You should. That's exactly what Mr. Finnegan was trying to tell us. What if your teacher asks *him* why you were late?"

Cameron shrugged, a smile tugging at his cheek. "Then we better start running."

Anthony laughed and pushed him playfully. "Would you get out of here? I'll be fine."

"Okay," Cameron said. "Just promise me that we'll go to our tree after school."

In a vacant field stood a lone willow. That's where they'd shared their first kiss and—shielded behind the curtain of its drooping branches—so much more.

"I want to reconnect with you," Cameron added innocently.

"Uh-huh," Anthony replied. "I'm starting to think you've got a fetish for trees."

"Wood gives me wood," his boyfriend said when leaning close.

Anthony placed his palms on the strong chest to keep him at bay. "After school," he said.

"At our tree?" Cameron asked sweetly.

"Yeah," Anthony replied, resisting a lovesick sigh. "At our tree."

CHAPTER 6
SEPTEMBER 3ᴿᴰ, 1993

Keisha spun, her arms held before her in a circle, before she landed and carefully stretched. The ballet classes she had taken as a child were long behind her, so it was a poor pirouette, but it felt good to do something more advanced. Her efforts caught the attention of the girl who kept watching her in the mirrors that had been rolled out into the gymnasium. In the world that was reflected back at her, a smile played about Hope's lips before she bent over to touch the tip of one foot while the other raised gracefully behind her to provide a counterbalance.

"Stay in sync with the others," the teacher called, having noticed these antics. "If you've already mastered a move, your role is twice as crucial, since you can lead by demonstration."

Keisha rolled her eyes playfully, as if to say, *"This is too easy."*

Hope smirked in response, as if she agreed.

Despite never having much time to talk, they'd found their own way of communicating. Although life kept getting in the way. Like when Omar stumbled into her a minute later, nearly knocking them both over.

"You all right there?" Keisha asked while helping him catch his balance.

"Yeah," Omar replied. "I think I'm getting the hang of it."

He was full of surprises. Keisha was certain that he'd bail on the class after realizing what it actually entailed, but he'd shown up today wearing black tights and a big grin, like he was proud of what the skin-tight pants revealed. And to be fair, she did notice quite a few of the girls checking him out. Hope wasn't one of them. She didn't seem the slightest bit interested in Omar. Their eyes met again in the mirror, Keisha experiencing a jolt of excitement, as she often did. They had chemistry. Or was she deluding herself again? Except she hadn't been wrong about Silvia. Keisha had only made the mistake of going after someone whose heart was already taken.

The class continued working on the same small segment of a larger routine. To an outside observer, they probably resembled an aerobics workout video that kept repeating the same five seconds. Once they mastered each segment—or got the general hang of it—they would move on to the next bit. Keisha enjoyed the exertion, always feeling centered when focusing so intently on her body. She was determined to impress her audience of one, because it was all too easy to forget that anyone else was—

"Whoops!" Omar said, barreling into her again.

"Stop flinging your arms around," Keisha told him. "You're throwing your own weight off."

She gave him some quick pointers, mostly for her own sake. But when she saw Hope biting her bottom lip while watching them in the mirror, Keisha knew she'd scored points. Probably because of the coaching aspect, more than the charitable nature of her actions, although she could work with that. Keisha had coaching experience, of a sort. She could coach Hope on coaching.

"All right," Mrs. Fiscus said, clapping to get their attention. "We only have ten minutes left. Let's put it all together and see what you learned in your first week. From the top!"

They ran through the entire routine, and while it was far from synchronized, at the end of it there were surprised expressions and gleeful laughs. All except Faith, who seemed irritated.

"That was so cool!" Omar cried happily from next to her. "I really tried to control each motion, like you said. I think this is going to make me a better skater. I'll be like… disciplined or whatever."

"Very nice," Keisha said. "Now how about you do me a favor?"

"Yeah, all right," Omar said, signing the contract without bothering to read the fine print.

"I need you to run interference," Keisha said, nodding toward the Song sisters. "When the bell rings, go up to Faith and start talking about the video yearbook. Tell her she was the highlight of the last one and ask if she'd be willing to do something special this year."

Omar made a face. "How come?"

"Why do you think?" Keisha asked dryly.

Omar glanced at the Song sisters before grinning. "They're hot, huh? I can't blame you. I mean, they're twins! Can you imagine the possibilities?" He tugged at the front of his tights self-consciously. "Actually, we better change the subject. So um… You want me to be your wingman?"

"Just make sure you keep Faith busy," Keisha told him.

"We still have time!" Mrs. Fiscus shouted. "From the top again!"

They ran through the routine twice more, her attention repeatedly flicking to Hope. Watching her contort her exceedingly flexible body was bringing all sorts of positions and possibilities to mind.

"Great job!" Mrs. Fiscus said while applauding. "Look at what you managed to do in just three days! I hope to see you all here next week, because we're just getting started."

Their classmates were already moving toward the lockers. Omar wouldn't be able to follow, since the changing room for the boys was on the other side.

"Actually," Keisha hissed after sidling up to him. "Can you do it now?"

Omar shrugged. "Sure!"

Keisha accompanied him as he walked toward the Song sisters.

"Faith!" Omar called out as they neared. "You were killin' it! We've gotta talk about you doing something special for the video yearbook. People were losing their mind over that crazy routine you did last time."

"Really?" Faith asked, sounding interested.

She'd swallowed the hook. Omar just needed to keep her on the line. Keisha tilted her head toward the locker rooms before continuing on her way. Hope noticed and followed. Keisha braced herself, certain that Faith would call out and tell her sister to wait.

"I'm thinking like a big halftime show," she heard Omar say from behind them. "It'll be *huge*!"

Bless the boy! Keisha reached the locker room door and slipped inside. Hope kept pace with her. She didn't ask why Keisha moved past the rows of lockers until she reached one at the back that was unoccupied. Once they had turned to face each other, it felt monumental, because they were finally alone. Sort of. Keisha could hear burbling voices as lockers squeaked open and slammed shut, but they weren't standing on a busy sidewalk or being scrutinized by an overbearing sister.

"Hey," Keisha said casually.

"Hi," Hope replied, biting her bottom lip again.

They eyed each other while smiling. Hope *couldn't* be straight. The potential practically crackled in the air between them, but the window was already closing. No matter how good a job Omar did, the bell would ring soon. Keisha needed more than just a stolen moment here and there to figure this out.

"What's a gal have to do to get you alone?" she asked. "You aren't Siamese twins." Keisha feigned uncertainty before peeking around the lockers. "Wait, *are* you?"

Hope laughed and pulled on her arm, as if worried Keisha would be spotted. "Faith is going on a date with Troy this weekend," she said, her hand lingering before it slid off Keisha's arm.

"Please tell me she doesn't plan on making you tag along."

Hope made a face. "Why do you think she's always trying to find me a boyfriend?"

"I honestly don't know," Keisha replied, "but I'd love to talk about it."

"Saturday night," Hope said. "Where should we meet?"

"That depends on what you like to eat. I'm partial to barbecue myself." She noticed the way Hope pulled back at the suggestion. "Wait, are you vegetarian? Because there's a great place on Main Street we can try instead."

Hope shook her head. "You know the park where I play soccer?"

Keisha pretended to think about it. "I believe so."

Hope laughed again. "Eight o'clock. Okay?"

"Sure," Keisha said. "I'll be there."

"Good." Hope smiled shyly before she turned and went down the aisle, so she wouldn't have to return the same way. Keisha counted under her breath before backtracking. She noticed Faith enter the locker room while looking flustered. Keisha decided to help Omar whenever and however he needed from now on, because he made a damn fine wingman. The results couldn't be argued with: After a long summer of waiting and wanting, she was finally going to solve the mystery of Hope Song!

Ricky felt jittery during theater class, which was no different than the previous couple of days. The two hundred pounds of Latino muscle sitting across the aisle from him sure didn't help. Being this close to Diego and yet separated by an invisible gulf was sheer torture. At least he had a plan today, but if they kept sitting there while debating which play they should produce next, Ricky wouldn't get a chance to enact it. Not with the teacher keeping tabs on everyone.

"*Our Town* is supposed to be a good play," a young guy suggested. "Or at least, it's famous, so it's probably good. I guess."

"A sparkling recommendation," Ms. Deville said drolly. "Keep in mind that every production will encounter its share of issues, but those obstacles will seem much smaller for a play you actually feel passionate about. What story *moves* you?"

"*Lord of the Flies* is cool," Diego said, exchanging a look with Mindy.

Ricky noticed the way she blushed and felt uneasy.

"That *is* a very relatable story," Ms. Deville said in approval, "and a compelling scenario. No matter the age of the audience, it's captivating to imagine how one would react if stranded on an island, especially under such circumstances."

"Isn't that book about British school boys?" someone asked dubiously. "There aren't any roles for women."

"So we make it about American teenagers instead," Diego grumped. "We always change stuff to be better, right?"

"Yes!" Whitney said. "I love how we put our own mark on everything." She pantomimed using a branding iron, even making a hissing sound. "I want to play the monster this time!"

"There is no monster," someone else said.

"Yeah there is," Diego shot back. "That's the entire point. I'll play Jack Merridew."

"That isn't how these things work," Ms. Deville said patiently. "Every role is open to audition."

"Do whatever you want," Diego said, crossing his arms over his chest. "We all know it's the perfect role for me."

Ricky swallowed. The plot and characters were still fresh on his mind, since they had read the novel last year in English class. Jack Merridew was the antagonist of the story. The worst of all the kids. A murderous jerk. Is that really how Diego saw himself?

The discussion moved on to set design, making him wish Cameron was still part of this class. Ricky could use the moral support. He was starting to feel glum when the teacher told them to come up with a short list of options to present to her on Monday. Finally! They were kind-of sort-of free!

Ricky stood and walked over to Mindy. "Do you have a second?"

"Sure!" she said cheerfully. "What's going on?"

He glanced over his shoulder, to make sure Diego wasn't sneaking up on him. If only. "Do you have any leather jackets left over from the last play?"

"Yes! It gets cold in here, doesn't it?"

"A little, yeah," he said, chuckling nervously.

She led him backstage to racks of clothes and a table filled with makeup. "Do you care how it looks?" Mindy asked, already shifting through the options. "Or are you going for maximum warmth?"

"Actually, I'm hoping to dress up like Diego."

Mindy paused before glancing over her shoulder. "So brown leather or more the general style?"

"Both," Ricky said sheepishly. "I'm trying to win him back."

Mindy pressed her lips together before asking, "By dressing like him?"

"Yeah. I know it sounds dumb but…"

It was the best plan he had come up with. Ricky needed to talk to Dr. Sharma, the therapist he used to see. She always knew what to do, but when he asked his mom when his next session was, she'd seemed surprised that he was interested. "I'm not sure what the point would be," Ami had responded, "considering how much trouble you still managed to get yourself into." So when teaming up with Silvia, he had tried to channel Dr. Sharma's wisdom, for both their benefit. He'd imagined her listening patiently to his woes before saying something sage-like such as, *Only those who flow like water can pass through the cracks of a stone.* In other words, Ricky couldn't force his way past Diego's defenses, so he planned on disarming him with humor instead.

"He always takes everything so seriously," Ricky tried to explain. "And he thinks that we're too different to be together so… I don't suppose you know what he puts in his hair?"

Mindy studied him a moment. Then she smiled. "I'll see what I can do."

She continued her search until she found a woman's jacket that would be a little tight. That was perfect, because the one Diego had inherited from his dad was too small for him. But he sure made it work! Mindy asked him to sit and began running her fingers through Ricky's hair.

"I have some styling mousse that should do the trick," she suggested.

"I trust you," Ricky assured her, before wondering if that was really true. He knew that Diego and Mindy had grown close over the summer. Even before then, he'd wondered if something was going on between them. "Have you been hanging out with Diego much lately?" he asked casually.

"Not really," Mindy replied. "We have the same lunch break, so I see him then."

He'd heard about that from Cameron. Diego used to eat by himself in his car. Ricky was glad that had changed, even though it did little to soothe his concerns.

"Does he ever talk about me?" he pressed.

Mindy was quiet, her expression determined, like she was digging deep to find an example that would support what he wanted to hear.

"Never mind," Ricky said with a sigh. "I know how he is."

Diego wasn't forthcoming with his feelings. Not the deep-down personal stuff, like what he'd gone through when losing his dad. Ricky was probably a taboo subject now. Another former association that Diego would rather forget. He could go ahead and try, but Ricky wouldn't make it easy for him.

"There!" Mindy said, taking a step back and beaming in satisfaction.

She held up a mirror for him to see. Ricky's hair was swept back and glistening slightly from the styling product.

"Yeah!" he said in excitement. "I wonder if this is what he uses."

"I don't think so," Mindy said. "Whatever he puts in his hair feels different."

Ricky scowled at this. "How would you know?"

"Because I had to mess his hair up to turn him into the Beast."

"Of course. Sorry."

"No, keep that expression!" Mindy said. "He always looks so grumpy. Also, you need to cuff your jeans."

"Oh yeah!" Ricky lifted his legs to do just that. Then he stood and glowered, trying to make his voice sound deeper. "What do you think?"

"Cross your arms over your chest," Mindy said. "Yeah, like that but up higher. Perfect!"

He checked himself in the full-length mirror and was impressed. He didn't have Diego's massive bulk, but the intent was clear enough.

Ricky let his posture relax again. "You sure know him well," he said. "Mannerisms and all."

"That's part of what I do," Mindy replied easily. "I'm sure he'll get a kick out of this. Are you going to show him now?"

Ricky studied her. Why would Mindy go to these lengths to help him if she was after his man? He really could trust her. "I'm going to wait until after school."

The bell rang.

"That was fun," Mindy said while collecting her things. "Good luck, Ricky! I hope it all goes well."

Gosh she was nice! Ricky felt indebted to her for the way she had helped Diego, although that gratitude was laced with envy. He thanked Mindy for her help and lingered behind until the auditorium had cleared, not wanting Diego to see him just yet. Once the coast was clear, he amused himself by puffing up his chest and marching down the hall. Ricky couldn't be certain, but he thought a few freshmen might have shied away from him in fear.

He got a few startled looks when arriving at his final class of the day. No wonder Diego dressed like this! Ricky felt undeniably cool. And okay, sure, he heard some snickering as well, but he decided to get into the act and pretend not to care. He was *way* too aloof to be touched by other people's opinions!

If only that were true. When sixth period ended, he literally ran to the parking lot to get there before Diego did. Ricky leaned against the Trans Am, at first to catch his breath, and then because that's exactly where we wanted to be. He crossed his arms over his chest, just like Mindy showed him, and glared at the entrance to the school.

Diego showed up not long after, noticed him standing there, and slowed.

"How's it goin'?" Ricky asked, making his voice artificially deep as he jerked his head upward.

Diego stared a second longer. Then a deep rumble escaped his throat as his shoulders began to shake. Ricky saw the broad smile, along with the dimples that always appeared in his cheeks, and felt like he'd been given a second chance. It had worked!

"What are you doing?" Diego asked, sauntering over to him.

"Figured it was time for a new look, that's all," Ricky grumbled before coughing and reverting to his normal voice. "Ouch! How do you talk like that?"

Diego shrugged. "It just comes naturally to me."

"I thought this could be our new thing," Ricky said, smiling at him. "Will you dress up like me tomorrow?"

"Nah. I'm not that cool," Diego said without a trace of irony. But he *had* to be kidding. Right? "Besides, now that you've shown me how hot I look, Friday nights are never gonna be the same." He made a pumping motion with his hand.

Ricky did his best not to salivate. "Or those nights could go back to how they used to be," he said. "I know you think we're too different. You're wrong. This isn't me, obviously," he said, pulling on the leather jacket's lapels, "but we both know what it feels like to be abandoned. You lost your friends, I lost the first guy I ever loved. And I know what it's like to be an outsider. I didn't feel like I fit in here until I met you."

"Ricky…" Diego said, starting to bristle.

"I know what you're going to say. My dad is still alive. But we've both been touched by suicide, right? We're different, and yet there's still enough to connect us. Otherwise we never would have gotten as far as we did. You have to admit that at least."

To his surprise, Diego nodded. "Yeah. We're human beings who more or less feel things the same way. That's where it stops. Our lives couldn't be more different, Ricky. Sharing mine with you was a big fucking mistake. If we do that again, it'll end in disaster."

"Keeping me out will be worse. I'm not happy without you, Diego. Weren't you happier with me? I felt like we made each other's lives better." He swallowed. "You literally gave me something to live for."

Diego shook his head. "Don't rewrite history to suit your own needs. Your friends showing up at the hospital after you tried to kill yourself, *that's* what gave you something to live for. I was only the piece of shit bully who pushed you toward the brink."

Ricky took a step toward him. "That's not true. I swear!"

"It couldn't have helped." Diego leaned against the car and looked him over with a smirk. "You're ridiculous."

Ricky shrugged. "I wanted to see you smile. Totally worth it."

Diego took a deep breath. "Listen, you know I'm not the type to beat around the bush. Me and you? It's not happening. No matter how many stunts you pull. I shouldn't have tried being with anyone again. It never works. I do just fine on my own."

"*We* were doing just fine," Ricky said, wanting desperately to take one of his big strong hands. "We just got unlucky, that's all."

Diego sighed. "I set someone's house on fire. Yeah, it was only toilet paper hanging from a tree, but I'm not an idiot. I knew what would happen. I *wanted* it to spread. Which it did. And then you got caught in the crossfire. It had nothing to do with luck, Ricky. I made a stupid mistake. One in a long line."

"So let's try again and be more careful."

Diego's cinnamon eyes moved across the parking lot to the wooded acres where things had first gotten interesting between them. At the time, Ricky had been driven by lust. And yes, the beefy body and smoldering eyes still made his dick twitch, but now the physical attraction was infused with love. Ricky couldn't envision a future where he wasn't a part of Diego's life. No matter how many sacrifices he had to make.

"Can't we at least be friends?" he pleaded.

Diego pushed away from the car and looked him over again. "Is that why you got all dressed up like me? Because you want to be my little buddy and nothing more?"

"No," Ricky admitted.

"Then there ya go."

"Do you miss me?" he asked, knowing that he could count on Diego to be honest. Even if he wouldn't like the answer.

"Yeah," Diego said hoarsely. "I miss you."

"Are you okay?" he pressed.

Diego shook his head. "I don't know." He took a deep breath, as if he was going to say more. Then he sighed. "I've got places I need to be."

"Okay," Ricky said, stepping away from the car.

Diego took the keys out of his pocket. The hand-made Frankenstein head still dangled from them. Ricky had given it to him as a Christmas gift. Then they'd built a snowman together. His chin began to tremble with the memory until he steeled himself. "I'm not giving up on you," he said.

"You should," Diego replied. "I did a long time ago."

Ricky watched him get into the Trans Am. He placed a hand on the roof fondly and stepped back before the car tore out of the parking lot. Ricky felt like giving chase. And he would, in a different way, to prove his love. Diego had said a lot of things, but none of them mattered more than one last glimmering beacon of hope.

I miss you.

CHAPTER 7
SEPTEMBER 3RD, 1993

Omar swung the camcorder back and forth, unsure where to settle, because being in a girl's bedroom was awesome. What a great way to end the first week of school! He panned across a shelf full of random knickknacks, such as a tiny flocked teddy bear and a little unicorn made of twisted glass. Oh sure, his sister had similar things in her room, but she didn't really count as a girl. And besides, Whitney was more like a woman. And he was her boyfriend! So freaking cool! He pointed the camcorder at Whitney, but she never stayed in place for long, so he only captured a blond blur that was soon drowned out by backlighting. Omar gave up and stopped peering through the viewfinder.

"I just love fresh air," Whitney said while opening the window. "Don't you?"

"Yeah," Omar replied. "That's like my favorite kind of air."

"Me too!" Whitney cried. She raised the screen before hanging her upper body outside.

"Easy now!" he said, coming up behind her and grabbing her hips. Which sounded sexy, but in reality, they were on the second floor of her house, and he didn't want her to end up as a pancake covered in strawberry syrup. Actually, that would be a funny sketch. They could somehow fake her falling out and cut to a shot of a pancake on the ground. He shared this idea with Whitney, who turned around and laughed.

"That's hilarious!" she said. "We could do the same thing with other people, except have them turn into different kinds of food."

"Like spaghetti?" he asked, weighing the idea.

"I was thinking a tuna salad sandwich," Whitney replied.

"That doesn't make sense."

She blinked in confusion. "Does it have to?"

"I guess not," he said with a shrug.

She was so weird! His summer had gotten much cooler when she showed up. Omar had been out at the park with Anthony, trying to teach his best friend to skate, but he tended to give up after he fell down a few times.

"I prefer to watch," Anthony had said, making the strained face he always did when trying not to check him out. So of course Omar took off his shirt. Anthony was so horny for him. And it was rad, because there could be no greater compliment.

Anthony had sat near a halfpipe while Omar did his best to gain air and do tricks. That's when they'd heard cawing. Or more accurately, eagle screeches. They'd gone to investigate together, following the sound to one of those bowls that resemble an empty swimming pool, and saw Whitney running around with her arms spread wide, like she intended to take flight. Omar had grinned and positioned his board on the edge before dropping in to join her. They had swooped around each other like some sort of strange dance.

Or mating ritual, because that's when it all began. Omar had offered the pink skateboard to Whitney, since Anthony didn't use it for anything but a place to sit. He'd pushed her around on it while she tried to keep her balance. Getting to touch her shoulders had already been exciting. When she'd hugged him before they'd said goodbye, Whitney didn't let go. They sort of swayed back and forth for a while first. Anthony had rolled his eyes while watching this, his face pure agony when Omar asked Whitney if she wanted to meet again the next day for another lesson.

"I thought you and Silvia were going to get back together," Anthony said once she had gone.

"Hey, I'm back on the market," Omar had replied. "Let's see who the highest bidder is."

He'd only been talking shit. Flirting was fun. And yeah, he'd been legit interested in spending more time around Whitney, but he hadn't expected to hit it off like they did. She showed up at the skatepark the next day. Anthony had plans with Cameron, so they'd been alone. The weather was perfect. They spent most of the time laughing while Omar showed her the ropes. Then it got serious. Whitney had kissed him without any warning. Omar had been hooked ever since, because it felt so good. And easy! Silvia always made him work for it. As far as he was concerned, the thrill of the chase was overrated. Having a girl who was crazy about you and wasn't afraid to show it was great for his self-esteem. He really liked her too.

Back in the present, Whitney abandoned the window to

squat next to a large cage. A pair of guinea pigs were inside. She made little cooing noises at them that the animals responded to. Omar thought it was cute, so he resumed filming. "What are their names?" he asked.

"Hardy and Costello," Whitney replied.

Omar made a face. "I think you're getting your comedy duos mixed up."

"But they're both fat," she replied sullenly. "I love my chubby little boys. If I changed their names, I'd have to put one of them on a diet."

How could he argue with that? While she was occupied with giving them a treat, he continued the tour of her room. This was the first time he'd been here. Most of their relationship took place under the open sky. Omar thought briefly of fishing with Silvia and felt all kinds of complicated things, so he tried to focus on the now. He lowered the camera again.

"Hey, what are all these magazines?" he asked. Two rows of bookshelves were stuffed full of them.

"Those are my Nat Geos," Whitney said. "My favorite magazine."

"Really?" Omar said, not hiding his surprise. *"National Geographic*? Isn't that kind of boring?"

"No way!" Whitney leapt up to join him. "Those are like a guide to the entire world. I want to see it all. Look!" She took a random copy off the shelf, her eyes filling with delight when she saw the cover, which she then held up. "Dinosaurs!" she said, her jaw falling open briefly. "How cool is that?"

"Pretty damn cool," he admitted, grabbing a random issue. The cover was zoomed in on a face painted in white, a pair of chopsticks placing some sort of food between stark red lips. "The prodigious soybean?" he read aloud before making a face. "That's not cool. I'm not even sure what it means."

"I love eating soybeans," Whitney said, taking the magazine from him. "Tofu is great." She held the magazine over her face like a mask. "I would *love* to go to Japan."

"Japan is definitely cool," he said, grinning as she tilted her head back and forth. "I wonder if Ricky has ever been. He's Japanese."

"Oh my god!" Whitney lowered the magazine, revealing fresh excitement. "You know what we should do?"

He shook his head. "What?"

"Throw a welcome home party for Ricky!"

"Yeah! I bet he'd love that. When should we do it?"

"Tomorrow," Whitney said, returning the magazine to the shelf. "Oh my gosh, there's so much to plan. This is going to be fun!"

"Like, *tomorrow* tomorrow?" Omar asked her. "Is that enough time?"

"For sure," Whitney said. "All we have to do is call people."

"Yeah, but we also need a place."

"We can have it here. My parents won't mind."

"Okay," Omar said with a shrug. She was so different from Silvia. Whitney seemed to live in the moment. "I guess we should start calling people. Ricky especially. It'll be weird if he can't make it."

"He'll be there," she replied, not seeming worried about it. "You know what I want to do?"

He watched her tiptoe theatrically to the bedroom door so she could lock it.

"What?" he asked, licking dry lips.

Whitney grinned at him. "I wanna press my boobs to your chest!"

"For real? Should I take off my shirt first or— Oh!"

She had already pulled the T-shirt over her head, revealing a turquoise bra that cupped two perky breasts. This hit the ground a second later.

"Damn!" Omar said, feeling a little dizzy as he quickly unshouldered his camcorder and tore off his shirt. "Okay. Let's do this!"

Whitney bounded over to him, pressing warm flesh against his own before giggling with delight. He grinned back at her. The summer had been nice, but if this kept up, junior year was going to be ridiculously epic!

Diego was replacing the brake pads on an eighty-seven Ford Mustang when he felt the pager on his hip begin to vibrate. He angled the screen without unclipping it and saw a number so familiar he couldn't forget it. Because he would have already, if that was an option.

"Omar," he grumbled under his breath.

Diego didn't know what his former friend wanted, but he wasn't in a hurry to find out. He took his time cleaning the guide pins and tightening the caliper bolts. Then curiosity got the better of him. "Put the tires back on and take it off the rack," he told one of the mechanics his mother had hired. "Then you can go home."

The guy got a pinched expression, like he did whenever Diego gave him orders. He probably wasn't used to having a teenage boss, but he better get used to it, or he could go wait in the unemployment line. Diego retreated to his father's old office, which mercifully, hadn't changed while he was away. He sat behind the massive desk in an old chair whose cracked leather had tufts of stuffing sticking out, but he wasn't interested in replacing it. This place was sacred. The last remaining vestiges of his father. Besides himself, of course. Diego soaked in the atmosphere, careful about which memories he allowed himself to linger on. When he felt fortified against the outside world, he dialed Omar's number.

"What do you want?" he said as soon as he heard the line click.

"Diego!" Omar said, sounding happy. "My man! How's it going? I haven't seen you since you got out."

"There's a reason for that," Diego replied. A lengthy silence underscored this point.

"Oh. Umm… Anyway, we should hang out soon."

Diego snorted in response.

"I mean it!" Omar said. "We're good now, right? I helped you. You helped me. We're buds again!"

"Just because we're good, doesn't mean we're friends," Diego replied.

"Well you're *my* friend," Omar said, "whether you like it or not."

Diego rolled his eyes. "What do you want?"

"We're having a party tonight, and you're invited."

"Not interested."

"You will be," Omar continued unabashed. "It's for Ricky. To welcome him home."

Diego felt a stabbing pain in his heart. He clenched his jaw until the sensation went away. "No thanks."

"What?" Omar cried. "You *have* to be there! Ricky will be bummed if you're not."

"Not my problem."

"C'mon," Omar said, in the cloying tones a parent might use when trying to win over a stubborn child. "He's such a cute little guy. How can you resist?"

"He's not so little anymore," Diego replied.

"I guess not. At least think about it, all right? I'll give you the address. Ready?"

"Yup." Diego pretended to listen.

"Did you write it down?" Omar pressed.

"What do you think?"

"Read it back to me."

Diego sighed wearily.

"That's what I thought. Write it down, but for real this time."

Diego complied, if only to get him off the line. Once he'd proven he could repeat the address, Omar was finally satisfied.

"Lookin' forward to seeing you, man. For real."

"Yeah," Diego replied. "See ya."

He hung up the phone and leaned back while pinching the bridge of his nose. Ricky was getting to be a real problem. An easy one to solve. Diego only had to be mean to him. Like really cruel, so the kid would finally take the hint and fuck off. Except he couldn't bring himself to do it. For the same reason that he hadn't hounded Omar and Anthony after they ditched him. He could have made their lives hell. Diego hadn't been nice to them by any stretch of the imagination, but that was only when they happened to run into each other. Otherwise he left them alone, because he used to care, and that sort of thing mattered. To him anyway. Otherwise he would have cut the brake lines on Anthony's car by now and watched the idiots crash into the nearest tree.

The mental image brought a smile to his face, but it didn't last. People kept asking him for another chance. Omar wanted to be his friend. Ricky thought they could pick up where they'd left off. Too bad. Once burnt, twice shy. After trust had been broken, you couldn't glue it back together. You could try, but the cracks would still be there, and when trust inevitably broke again, the remaining shards were twice as sharp. He knew that from experience.

His eyes moved to the framed photo face-down on his desk. He raised it, ignoring his dead father and the impossibly happy kid who had stopped existing not long after the picture was taken. Instead he focused on his mother, the joy in her eyes something out of a mostly forgotten fairy tale. He couldn't remember the last time he'd seen that careless smile. They were different people now. Except…

"Gomez. You have a visitor."

Diego had been in the common room of the detention center when the guard called his name. He wasn't expecting anyone, but while being escorted to the visiting area, he figured Ricky had put one of his friends up to it. Huxley, most likely. Diego was prepared to greet a distant cousin he didn't actually have when he'd seen his mother standing there. Her expression had been every bit as uncertain as his own. They didn't do that sort of thing. Not anymore. If he got himself in trouble, Diego was on his own. He hadn't known what to think of her showing up like that. Conversation was stilted when they'd sat at a table together. Marti asked how they were treating him, and if there was anything she could do. He'd asked her to forward money from a future paycheck, so he could buy from the commissary, since they kept him hungry. That should have been the end of it, but she showed up the next week as well.

He opened a desk drawer and pulled out an old ledger his father used to keep, and that Diego had continued. Each line listed the make and model of a vehicle, the owner's name, and the work that had been done. He'd asked his mother to bring it with her a couple of visits in, wanting to keep it up to date even though he wasn't doing the work. His mom had sat there and recited from memory as many of the recent repairs as she could while he wrote them all down. The next time she came to visit, she brought the ledger, except it was already filled out in her handwriting. That was cool, because it gave them something to focus on. Diego had gone over each line with her. Sometimes they'd crack jokes about the owners and go off on other tangents, but they always had the ledger to fall back on if things got awkward. There wasn't much blank space left toward the back. Diego wasn't sure what he'd do when the pages ran out. He didn't want to buy a new one. He wanted his dad.

Diego swallowed, aware that his thoughts weren't making sense, but he also didn't care. Finishing the stupid thing wouldn't bring Lorenzo back to life. But it *was* proof that his legacy wasn't totally forgotten, and that Diego had kept it going for as long as he could. He sat there and documented the work he'd done today before shutting the ledger in the drawer again. Then he noticed the time and stood.

The repair shop was silent except for a rhythmic whisking sound. Diego followed this to the back of the garage, where a stooped old black man was sweeping up. Jasper was often the last to leave, besides himself.

"Time to go home," Diego said. "You can take the broom with you, since you're too damn stubborn to buy a cane."

Jasper stopped his work and leaned on it for support, his brown eyes twinkling. "I still outlast the youngsters who clock-in hours after I do."

"You're not kidding," Diego said. "You're worth twenty of them. Hey, speaking of which, I'm sweating bullets over the Volvo's timing chain. I could really use your help."

"I'll be your eyes if you'll be my hands," Jasper offered.

"Cool. See ya Monday."

"Take care of yourself, son," Jasper said before shuffling toward the lockers.

Diego walked around to shut everything down. By the time he got to the lockers, Jasper was gone. Diego stripped out of his coveralls while trying not to think about how Ricky would react. Disappointed, probably, since Diego was wearing a ratty old T-shirt and shorts beneath them. Then he went upstairs to the apartment he shared with his mom.

He expected to see Marti in her favorite recliner, watching some dumb game show or sitcom. That's how it always used to be. Instead he heard sizzling coming from the kitchen and smelled fried onions.

"Hey," he said, walking over to investigate.

His mother was almost as tall as him. She had a strong build for a woman. Diego never had to worry about her, since she'd blown through enough jerk-ass boyfriends to prove she could take care of herself. Not recently though. As far as Diego could tell, she hadn't dated anyone all summer.

"Are you done for the day?" Marti asked.

"Yeah."

She nodded before returning her attention to the stove. "I

thought I'd make macaroni and beef for dinner. You still like that, don't you?"

"I'm not picky," he assured her.

"Good. It'll be ready in about fifteen minutes."

He wordlessly went to his bedroom to change clothes. When he had come home at the start of the week, after his mom picked him up from the detention center, he'd discovered that his bedroom had been dusted and vacuumed. Even now, when he opened a dresser drawer, it revealed stacks of neatly folded shirts. That was unusual too. Diego normally did his own laundry, scooping clothes out of the drier and into a basket that he plucked from when needing something clean to wear. His bedroom floor was the hamper for his dirty clothes. He never bothered folding stuff and putting it away. Having it all so organized was weird. Nice, yeah, but it also made him nervous.

He grabbed a navy blue T-shirt and a pair of jeans so worn that the knees had split. Then he left his room and ducked into the bathroom for a quick shower. While under the steaming hot water, he thought of the way things had been in the weeks following his father's death. Back then he was just a dumb kid who kept waiting for his dad to return. He used to lay in bed each night listening for the front door to open, certain that his father's death was all some elaborate prank. Didn't matter that he'd been the one to find the body, or that he'd seen all the blood and gore up close. Horror movies were full of that stuff. If some guy in Hollywood could dye corn syrup red or whatever, then his father could too. The only thing Diego heard on those long sleepless nights was his mother weeping. Eventually the truth came home to roost and he started crying too. Diego remembered padding into her room and crawling into bed. Marti had pulled him close, wrapping her arms around him as they sobbed together. While clinging to her that night, he'd felt grateful only one of his parents had died. When his tears finally subsided, he'd slept better than he had in weeks. The next night…

Diego turned off the shower and grabbed a towel, burying his face so deep into it that everything past his eyelids was darkness as he forced himself to remember, because it was important.

When he'd shown up at his mother's bedroom the next night, the door was shut. And locked. He knocked of course, sniffling while choking out the same word over and over. *"Mama?"* Marti didn't answer. He could hear her in there crying, but she didn't open the door for him. As far as he knew, she still locked it each night. He'd given up trying long ago.

So this was nothing new. Over the years, the clouds would part on occasion, allowing his mother to see him clearly again. It never lasted. The specter of the man who had abandoned them would always return, but not to make everything okay. The sort of ghosts who live in your heart are only good for haunting.

Diego went to the refrigerator to take out a beer. He held it up and raised an eyebrow. Marti nodded, so he grabbed another for her, while she scooped mac and cheese tossed with ground beef into two bowls. She carried these to the living room area and turned on the TV. At least that hadn't changed. Diego would have fled in terror if she'd expected them to sit at the table together, like a normal family.

"What did you think of your first week of school?" she asked while flipping through channels.

"It was all right," he replied.

Marti eyed him and cracked open her beer. "How come you're not out with the cute redhead?"

"I dunno," he said, fighting off a smile. She'd found Mindy's photo in his room and assumed they were an item. And yeah, during one of the visits, he mentioned that she had volunteered. "I might see her later. There's a party but..." He shrugged.

"Go out and have fun," Marti said. "I'm all right."

He was too jaded to believe that, so he guzzled half his beer before grabbing the bowl of food. "It's good," he said after swallowing a bite.

"Thanks," his mother replied, raising the remote to turn up the volume.

They were back in familiar territory. Diego polished off his beer while eating and stood to get another. He thought of the address Omar had made him write down. The scrap of paper was still on the desk downstairs, in his father's old office. The same place where he'd danced for Ricky to make him laugh before those watery eyes had sought out his.

I love you. For real.

They were only words. Well-meaning but fickle and untrue. As always. How could you claim to love someone if you were planning on blowing your brains out? You didn't say it and then lock your bedroom door. And you sure as hell didn't ditch someone in their hour of need. Not if you really loved them. In recent years, nobody said those words to him at all. Ricky had though. And for whatever reason, Diego had said them back. So was he full of shit like the others? Or had he really meant it? Because if he did… maybe it was time to stop locking his door.

CHAPTER 8
SEPTEMBER 4ᵀᴴ, 1993

"So she just squished her boobs against his chest? And that's it?"

Anthony smirked. "While they made out, yeah."

Silvia pulled away from the powder brush that Mindy was dusting across her face, so she could look at him incredulously. "And he actually *liked* it?"

Anthony nodded. "You could say that, yeah."

He didn't share Omar's exact words, which were, *"I came so close to blowing a load, dude! Without having to touch myself or anything."*

Anthony cleared his throat. "So is that something straight people do?"

Mindy crinkled her nose. "Don't ask me!" She took hold of Silvia's chin, so she could turn it toward the light and resume her work.

"I think it sounds hot," Cameron said. He was stretched out on Mindy's bed while flipping through a magazine, which he lowered, so he could train bedroom eyes on Anthony. "Just imagine my bare chest pressed against yours while we make out."

"You do have a very nice chest," Anthony admitted before smiling demurely at him.

"Okay," Mindy said, pretending to fan herself with the powder brush. "Now I see what you mean. It *is* kind of sexy."

"You guys!" Silvia complained. "You're supposed to be helping me win him back!"

"For the record," Anthony said quickly, "they make an absolutely *terrible* couple. They're both so high-energy. Being in the same room with them is unbearable. Omar needs your chill to help balance him out."

"Thank you," Siliva said, seeming mollified.

"Eyeshadow?" Mindy asked, already bringing an applicator near.

"Do it!" Anthony said, moving closer. "Please!"

He'd been hovering near them the entire time, wanting to learn the techniques Mindy used.

"Do you really think this will work?" Silvia asked, her eyes darting over to him before they closed. "You know him better than anyone."

"Yes," Anthony said before second-guessing himself. "Maybe. Omar is really loyal."

"I don't want him to cheat on her," Silvia replied. "I only want him to remember that I'm an option."

"You're way more than just an option to him," Anthony assured her. "He simply—" Found someone who wasn't nearly as complicated. "—got distracted," he finished diplomatically, since he of all people shouldn't cast the first stone. "But I know he's still into you, because when I went over to his house the other day, he was watching *Record Store Girl*."

Omar had claimed he was considering using the new equipment at work to do a fresh edit, but he'd seemed too down afterwards for it to be that simple. "He still has feelings for you, I promise. But you might want to try some eyeliner, just in case."

Anthony added this last bit sheerly out of self-interest, and was thrilled when he got to watch up-close. He felt kind of foolish while doing so, because it was as easy as dragging a pencil of sorts along the edge of each eyelid. "Wait!" he said. "Why'd you go so far?"

"I'm adding a wing," Mindy said.

"A what?" Anthony and Silvia asked simultaneously.

"Oh my god," Mindy breathed. "Both of you be quiet. You'll see soon enough."

"I'm starting to think that Ricky had the right idea," Silvia murmured. "I could have dressed up in a costume, like he did. A clown maybe, since that would have involved less makeup."

"Hush," Mindy chastised.

"A clown wouldn't have worked," Anthony said. "You'd have to get into an Archie the Pizza Panda costume."

Silvia raised an eyebrow. "Do we still have time?"

"Tell her how beautiful she looks," Mindy said, leaning back.

"Wow!" Anthony didn't have to fake his enthusiasm. Silvia's eyeliner went beyond her eyelid slightly before curving upward. The effect was subtle but alluring.

"That does look nice," Siliva said, gazing into the nearby vanity mirror.

"Now let me do the other one," Mindy said, leaning forward

again. "I'm becoming quite the relationship counselor," she added. "I helped Ricky with his plan too. Does anyone know how it went?"

"No idea," he replied, "but Diego isn't big on second chances."

"So they probably won't get back together?" Mindy asked, an edge of desperation in her voice.

Anthony thought about it and shrugged. "I'm not sure. I never dreamed that Diego was into guys. When we were growing up, he only flirted with girls."

"Do you think it would have changed things if you'd known?" Silvia asked.

"What do you mean?"

She tried to shrug before Mindy placed a hand on her shoulder to hold her still. "Would you have fallen in love with Diego instead of Omar, knowing that it was possible to be with him?"

Anthony glanced toward the bed, where Cameron was peering over the magazine while awaiting his response. "Maybe," he lied. The truth was, he'd been in love with Omar his entire life. "Doesn't matter anyway. I can't imagine dating someone like him. I prefer nice guys."

The magazine raised again, but not before he saw Cameron's smiling eyes.

"Diego is nice," Mindy said. Somewhat wistfully, in fact.

"I guess I don't really know him anymore," Anthony replied.

Mindy finished her work.

Silvia applied her own lipstick while he watched enviously. "This is as good as it gets," she said after checking the mirror again.

"You look great," Anthony told her. "He'll definitely notice."

"Unless he's busy playing smoosh the boobies," Silvia said with an eyeroll.

Anthony laughed and checked the time. "We should probably get going."

"I need to use the lady's room first," Silvia said.

Mindy began touching up her own makeup while she was gone.

Anthony picked up the eyeliner pencil to examine it. "Don't you worry about blinding yourself?"

"Of course," she said. "You just have to be careful. Wanna try?"

"On you?"

"No, silly! On yourself. It'll look nice."

He would but… Anthony glanced at Cameron again, who had set down the magazine and was quietly watching him.

"I think boys look good in eyeliner," Mindy said.

"So do I," Cameron interjected.

Anthony felt his heart flutter. "Really?"

"Yeah!" Cameron swung his legs off the bed. "Whenever the guys in theater wore it, I thought it was hot. And a little gay."

Anthony was beyond flustered by this revelation. "I wouldn't know how."

"I'll do it for you!" Mindy said, clasping her hands together in excitement. "Please?"

"I mean, if it makes you guys happy," he said with a guffaw.

Soon he had a close-up view of Mindy's face, her tongue sticking out the corner of her mouth as she worked. "It really is as easy as drawing a line," she said. "You just have to make sure your eyes don't water. And if they do…" She deftly grabbed a tissue and dabbed at the tears that were forming. He nearly wept a few more when finally able to look in the mirror.

He looked cool. And yeah, maybe a bit more feminine. The breath caught in his throat when Cameron appeared behind his reflection.

"What do you think?" Mindy asked, voicing the question for him.

"You look stunning," Cameron said, draping an arm around Anthony's neck before nuzzling his ear.

"So cute!" Mindy stomped her petite little feet in excitement, like she couldn't take it anymore.

Cameron laughed. Anthony gulped down air to avoid crying. Out of relief mostly.

"How about some mascara?" Mindy asked. "You have beautiful eyelashes."

"No, that's all right," Anthony said, not wanting to press his luck. He considered putting on lip gloss, but if he did it would soon get worn off, because he planned on kissing Cameron a lot during the party. And maybe before. And definitely after.

Silvia returned to the room. They gathered up their things

and piled into Anthony's car. Cameron slid across the front seat to him, even though Mindy and Silvia climbed into the back. Once they were on the road, he placed his hand on Anthony's leg, occasionally sticking his fingers into the various tears in his jeans to tickle bare skin. Anthony had made sure not to wear too many layers tonight. He'd opted for a pair of T-shirts, but the outer one was full of holes like a family of moths had eaten their fill, revealing the pink long-sleeved shirt beneath. Cameron kept working his way up the jeans, higher and higher, which was driving him wild. Especially when Anthony checked the rearview mirror. He wasn't into himself, but he did feel a whole lot sexier with the makeup on. And his boyfriend was definitely getting him in the mood!

They didn't have far to go, which was probably for the best. Whitney's house stood out from the rest, the yard overflowing with flowering bushes and ornamental trees, like her family had wanted to live in the Garden of Eden. Cars already filled the driveway and lined the street.

"Just how many people does Ricky know?" Silvia asked.

"Not *that* many," Anthony replied, equally perplexed as he parked.

"Whitney is a social butterfly," Mindy explained. "Everybody likes her. Even though she's *terrible* for Omar," she added when noticing the betrayal on Silvia's face.

"Whitney came right up to me on my first day of school here," Cameron said. "Like we were old friends. That was cool."

"Yes yes, she's wonderful," Silvia said, before pretending to gag. "Now let's go wreck the place."

They walked to the front door and debated if they should knock or stroll right in. Cameron took the initiative and rang the bell. When the door swung open, Omar looked them over and grinned.

"Finally! I was wondering when my favorite people would show up."

"He means me," Anthony said. Then he casually tilted his head to the left, hoping that his best friend would notice how good Silvia looked.

"Oh wow," Omar said, "your makeup is different. Very cool!"

It was the right line, but he was looking at the wrong person. "Thanks," Anthony said, jerking his head to the left again.

Omar scrunched up his face. "Have you got water in your ear or something?"

Anthony blushed when everyone turned to him. "Just working out a kink."

"Hey, whatever gets you off," Omar replied. "Come on in!"

Beyond the entryway, a living room bled into the dining room. A handful of people were around, but none of them lingered. They all came and went from the stairs that Omar guided them to, the muted music growing louder. "Whitney has a karaoke machine," his best friend said. "The bad singing will make your ears bleed, but I've gotta admit, it's a lot of fun."

They descended the stairs to a finished basement. The large open space was normally used as a family room, judging from the big-screen TV and couches, but at the moment it was filled with two dozen teenagers. "Drinks are upstairs in the fridge," Omar said. "All non-alcoholic, but if you want them spiked, we have a few options. If you wanna sing, you've gotta write your name on the eraser board and wait your turn. Oh hey, there's the man of the hour!"

Ricky waved at them from the middle of a crowd. Anthony only recognized some of the people. David was there, as was Galen, who he hadn't seen since sophomore year.

"Hey everyone!" Ricky said, having managed to reach them. "What a party, huh? I can't believe it's for me! You guys are too nice. Who wants to sing with me?"

"Sign me up," Anthony said while giving him a hug. He was no stranger to karaoke and was eager to browse the options.

"Hey, you look *really* nice," Ricky said to Silvia, with more than enough emphasis to get everyone else to look.

All except for Omar, who seemed distracted. Whitney was jumping up and down while waving a microphone around.

"Looks like it's time for our big duet," Omar said. "Catch you guys later."

And with that, he began working his way through the crowd.

"You really do look nice," Ricky said to Silvia. "If it makes you feel any better, my plan didn't work either."

"The night isn't over yet," Cameron said, ruffling his hair affectionately.

"And besides," Silvia said. "We're here to welcome you home. Not to win back our exes."

"Right," Ricky said, glancing toward the stairs. "Speaking of which, have any of you guys seen—"

"No!" they all said, cutting him off.

Ricky laughed. "I'm just messing with you. Let's party!"

Cameron ran upstairs to get drinks while the rest of them talked. Which wasn't easy to do without shouting, because Omar and Whitney had hopped up on a coffee table that was being used as a stage and started singing Sonny & Cher's "I Got You Babe." They were really hamming it up too, making funny faces at each other and doing silly dances. They kept going even when the music stopped, seeming fixated on one part in particular as they took turns singing it to each other.

"You babe!"

"You babe!"

"You babe!"

"You babe!"

"I'm sorry," Anthony said, pinching the bridge of his nose, "but this simply isn't working for me."

"I agree," Ricky said, watching in horror. "Omar is usually so hot. And I really like Whitney."

"She's wonderful," Mindy said with a strained face, "but even I feel like throwing something at them. In fact, where's my drink?"

"Right here," Cameron said, reappearing through the crowd before passing out cans.

"You babe!"

"You babe!"

"Somebody stop them!" Anthony cried. He turned to his boyfriend. "What do *you* think?"

Cameron assessed the scene. "That table must be solid wood. Can we get a closer look at it?"

"That depends. Do you want to sing with me?"

"I do like the music we make together," Cameron replied with bedroom eyes.

They went to find out which songs were available. Omar hopped down to join them before they could. "Was that awesome or what?" he asked with a grin.

"Or what," Anthony deadpanned.

Omar didn't seem to take it personally. "Hey, it's not my fault. There aren't any metal bands to choose from." He leaned toward Anthony and in conspiring tones said, "Personally, I thought it would be more fun to play spin the bottle or seven minutes in heaven, you know what I mean? Get some action going."

"Sounds good to me," Cameron said, pushing his way between them and taking Anthony's hand.

"For real?" Omar arched an eyebrow and glanced around. "Let me see what I can do." He turned and disappeared into the crowd.

Anthony shook his head. "When you end up making out with half the girls at this party, you'll only have yourself to blame."

"I'm not interested in kissing anyone but you," Cameron replied before doing just that.

Anthony didn't know what had gotten into him, but he wasn't complaining.

"My dudes," Omar said, returning with a smirk. "Come with me. And then with each other."

Cameron looked to him for an explanation.

Anthony shrugged before they followed him upstairs, where it was easier to be heard. "We don't really want to play spin the bottle," he said.

"Yeah, I figured." Omar stopped in front of a closed door. "Nobody is allowed in here, but I asked Whitney, and she said it was cool." He used a paperclip that was hanging off his wallet chain to pop the lock. When he opened the door, a large bed was revealed.

"Her parents' room?" Anthony asked.

"Yup!" Omar replied. "Don't worry. They won't be back until midnight. Just lock the door after you and uh… try not to make a mess." He nudged Cameron. "Swallow, don't spit, all right?"

Cameron didn't seem as amused when cocking an eyebrow in response.

"We've got this," Anthony said, gently pushing his friend out of the room. "Thanks."

"Have fun, guys!" Omar said with a shit-eating grin.

Anthony laughed and closed the door, Omar peering into the narrowing crack until the very last second. When he turned around, Cameron seemed irritated. "What?"

"It's a bit much," his boyfriend said evenly. "Omar talks about our sex life like he's part of it."

"Oh stop," Anthony said. "We've known each other our entire lives. We don't have boundaries."

"I've noticed."

"And you and I don't either," Anthony said, walking over to kiss him.

"Is that a promise?" Cameron asked, pulling back.

Sex had continued to be one-sided lately.

"Yeah," Anthony said bravely, pressing their hips together. "It's a promise."

They kissed again and continued making out until Cameron tried to undress him.

"Wait," Anthony said, squirming out of his grasp. He saw the hurt on his boyfriend's face and smooched it away. "I just want to make sure the door is locked."

He went over to check, and while it was indeed locked, voices could be heard on the other side. Anthony held his breath until they went away. Then he turned around with a wince. "That lock is *really* easy to pick."

"I'm not too worried," Cameron said, openly adjusting himself.

Anthony stared and felt a little dizzy. Then he glanced around and saw another door. "How about in the bathroom? That way we'll be twice as safe."

"At this point," Cameron said in a husky voice, "I'll do it on the damn roof if you want!"

Anthony grinned, grabbed his hand, and led him to the bathroom door. Which turned out to be a walk-in closet.

"Oh the irony!" Cameron said, pushing him inside.

"No!" Anthony cried, rushing to the back wall as if to escape, but he was happy to turn around again so sweet pillowy lips could grace his with their caress.

They made out until Cameron began lifting both of Anthony's shirts at once. He swallowed against apprehension as they went over his head. Blue eyes filled with adoration looked him over before Cameron moved close again and began nibbling his neck. Anthony tried to focus on the pleasure, but he felt so exposed, and they were in a weird environment. One side of the closet was drab suits, pants, and button-up shirts. On the other side were blouses, dresses, and wide-hipped jeans. None of which he should be focusing on, because Cameron was slowly kissing his way south and would be disappointed if he didn't find a pole. Then again, a gorgeous black dress was hanging right next to Anthony, pink and white magnolias exploding across the surface to create an elegant pattern. The shimmering fabric looked soft to the touch. Anthony couldn't help it. He grabbed the sleeve of the dress, which was indeed silky, and nuzzled it against his cheek.

"Oh wow!" Cameron said. He was down on his knees now and very pleased with what he'd discovered there.

From the look of things, Anthony was happy too! He shifted to the left when stepping out of his underwear and jeans, bringing himself closer to the dress, which he pressed to his nose so he could breathe in deeply. A hint of perfume was trapped in the fabric. Anthony's eyelids fluttered shut in pleasure. With his free hand, he let his fingers sink into Cameron's brown hair, not minding at all when his boyfriend reached up to caress his stomach and play with a nipple. Anthony whimpered. Forget seven minutes in heaven. At this rate, it would be a miracle if he made it to five!

By the time Keisha showed up at the park, stars were beginning to twinkle in a sky that faded from indigo blue to tangerine orange. If she lived in a big exciting city, she might be on guard for muggers or worse, but all she saw was strolling couples, dogs on leashes, and the occasional jogger. So far, no sign of an athletic Chinese girl with an inviting smile. Keisha walked the length of the park twice over before stopping at a playground. She was sitting on the merry-go-round and beginning to despair when it started to spin. She glanced around in surprise and then laughed as she slowly rotated closer to her date.

"You nearly gave me a heart attack!" Keisha said, pressing a hand against her chest theatrically. "You sure are quiet."

"I'm really good at sneaking around," Hope said as they came face to face.

Keisha slid off the merry-go-round and stood. "Is that so?"

"Uh-huh."

Hope leaned forward and tilted her head, like she wanted a kiss. Was it really going to be that easy? Keisha didn't mind except… "My mother says you should always look before you leap. Mostly so you can enjoy the view. I wanna get to know you first."

Hope shrugged, and when withdrawing, briefly bit her bottom lip. "Okay."

"Let's walk," Keisha said, hoping to avoid temptation, because rushing in didn't seem like such a bad idea.

Especially since Hope was dressed in her usual: a simple T-shirt and nylon shorts, like she might break into a sprint at any moment. Keisha had agonized over the outfit she ended up choosing, wearing her brother's old letter jacket over a tight white tank top. And just to make sure she wouldn't get too heated while keeping things hot, she'd squeezed into a pair of denim shorts that gripped her butt and didn't go much lower.

Her head swam with all the questions she wanted to ask, so she started with the most pressing. "I get the impression you already know this song and dance."

Hope tucked a lock of hair behind her ear when glancing over at her. "Yeah. Do you know Abigail Cummings?"

Keisha stopped in her tracks. "The little blond cheerleader?"

Hope nodded rapidly. "Yup. Freshman year."

"Okay, I need you to hit me with an entire wall of exposition, because I am *starving* for details."

"You first," Hope said.

"Fine. My story is short and sweet. I figured out that I'm a lesbian in junior high."

"Same here," Hope interjected.

That came as welcome news. No need to gently hold her hand while she came to terms with herself and what other people would think. They could hit the ground running.

"I didn't see any good options in our school," Keisha continued. "Although from that tidbit you just dropped, maybe I wasn't looking hard enough. Anyway, I put a personal ad in the *Pitch Weekly* and had a few flings. Plus a short-lived relationship with a twenty-six-year-old woman who thought I was in college. I liked her but didn't want to build a relationship on a lie. So I quietly disappeared from her life and spent much of the next year chasing after a girl who is madly in love with a boy. That's my story. Now, for all that is holy, please tell me about Abigail Cummings. That last name is unfortunate, by the way."

"It was actually very appropriate," Hope said with a naughty smile.

"Mm!" Keisha said while fanning herself. "Do go on!"

Hope was quiet as they resumed walking, but only at first. "Abigail was in gymnastics with me and my sister. That's how I knew, because she kept staring at us. That's not so unusual when you're twins. People always do, but not like this. She wasn't comparing us while looking for differences. I could be on the other side of the gymnasium and I'd still catch her checking out Faith's butt while she stretched or whatever."

"Using your own sister as bait!" Keisha cried, as if scandalized. "I approve."

"It was very helpful," Hope said. "Especially when we invited her over. Me and Faith always wear the same thing on our birthday, and my hair was longer then, like hers is now, so it was hard to tell us apart. We hung out in our room with a bunch of our friends until it was time to go downstairs for cake. Abigail needed to use the restroom first, so I waited for her upstairs. Then I asked her if she could tell which sister I was."

Keisha made a face. "How come?"

"Because when she said she didn't know, I felt like I could get away with anything. So I kissed her."

"Oh, I see," Keisha said, tilting her head back toward the playground. "That's your opening move, is it?"

"Maybe," Hope said playfully. "It worked before. Abigail kissed me back. The messed-up thing is, by the time we went downstairs, I still hadn't revealed which twin I was. For the rest of the party, she had no idea. I told her at the end of it though. Mostly so she wouldn't try kissing Faith by accident."

Keisha laughed. "Having an identical twin must be fun."

"Sometimes," Hope said, her features creasing before she looked away.

"So how long were you helping Miss Cummings earn her name?" Keisha asked, wanting to keep it positive.

"Most of freshman year," Hope said. "Up until Faith found out."

"How did that go?"

Hope shrugged. "I wasn't ready. Abigail wanted to go public, but I didn't like the idea."

"Why's that?"

Hope skipped ahead and did a cartwheel on the grass, her flat stomach exposed in a pale blur. Then she came back smiling, like she wanted to try that kiss again.

"Don't leave a girl hangin'," Keisha said. "I need to hear the end of this story."

Hope's face became somber. "She made me choose."

"Who?"

"Faith. When she figured out that Abigail and I were… well, whatever it was. She made me choose between her and Abigail."

Keisha shook her head. "Why would she do that?"

Hope pressed her lips together before answering. "You don't know what it's like to be a twin. You're always part of a set. Our parents dressed us the same when we were little, and we *still* share a bedroom, even though there's a home office that my mom hardly ever uses. People like the idea of identical twins, so there's constant pressure to meet their expectations. They want you to do everything the same, because otherwise, twins are boring."

"I don't think so," Keisha assured her.

"I wish Faith felt the same way."

"But she doesn't?"

Hope shook her head. "We're really close. I'm not sure how to describe it to someone who doesn't have a twin. Your identities kind of get mixed up in each other. Not just who you are, but what you're going to do with your life. We always have to take the same classes and have the same goals."

"And date the same kind of people," Keisha ventured, "including their gender."

"Yeah," Hope said. "That's why she keeps pushing me to find a boyfriend. Faith thinks we're the same. Even though we're not. So she made me choose. And it felt like someone threatening to take away my appearance or my name or…" She shook her head. "I don't know. It's hard to explain."

"You've done a good job of it already," Keisha said in sympathy. "I bet she'll come around and accept you eventually. For now, I have a great group of friends who aren't quite so judgmental. They're having a party tonight, if you'd like to go."

Hope instantly shook her head. "This has to stay a secret."

For obvious reasons. Keisha had barely stuck her foot out of the closet before the news began to spread. She was more accustomed to keeping her personal life private.

"Do any of your friends know?" Hope pressed.

"About me? Yes. About us? Well, I suppose that's getting ahead of ourselves. But they don't know where I am right now, or who I'm with. I wasn't sure you'd want them to. I understand the importance of discretion."

"So you're okay with it?" Hope asked, already fighting down a smile.

"Sneaking around with you?" Keisha pretended to weigh her options. "Hmm. I don't know. Show me what you've got."

Hope did another happy skip. Then she grabbed the lapels of Keisha's jacket, walking backward as she led them toward the shadows. As soon as darkness enveloped them, lips found hers. They tasted sweet. And when that toned body pressed against her own, Keisha knew her answer.

Oh yes, she was very much okay with this!

Silvia hadn't been to many parties. Despite enjoying herself so far, she doubted that was going to change. She preferred to sing karaoke with Anthony while at work, when business was slow. And she would rather hang out in Mindy's bedroom, where it was quiet and easier to talk. In privacy. At the moment, a couple of white guys were flirting with them. They seemed okay but had these dumb grins on their faces, like talking to the opposite sex was a bigger thrill than anything she or Mindy actually had to say.

She glanced around for a lifeline. Anthony and Cameron had returned downstairs but were too wrapped up in each other to notice her. They were holding hands while flipping through the catalog of karaoke songs. Ricky had his eyes clenched shut while singing, although he opened them on occasion to search the room. Their eyes met and he smiled at her before looking around again. Omar stood in one corner, howling with laughter at a story told by a black guy with a contagious smile, but she couldn't remember his name. Gary? Galvin? Silvia wished they knew each other better, because catching up with him would be the perfect excuse to join her ex-boyfriend and get away from these two chumps, who were now talking about the Little League team they used to be in.

"Do either of you smoke?" she asked, cutting them off.

The guys shook their heads in unison.

"Too bad. I'm up to a carton a day. I really need to step outside to savor the flavor. What about you?"

The question was directed at Mindy, who glanced at the handsomer of the two boys. "I'm okay," she said.

Silvia excused herself, having to scoot diagonally to navigate past people when making her way through the basement. She breathed a sigh of relief when upstairs again and relaxed even more after reaching the sanctity of the backyard. Silvia moved to a shadowy corner of the house and took out a tin that used to contain mints. She brought a joint to her lips and was temporarily blinded by the flame when lighting it. She peered into the darkness while inhaling and exhaling until her vision adjusted. That's when she saw two pale figures poking around in the yard. Whitney's platinum blond hair and hyperactive movements made her easy to identify. At the moment, she was talking and pointing at the ground, squatting on occasion as if to inspect something up close. The guy standing next to her was vaguely familiar, although it wasn't Omar. Silvia was squinting in an attempt to see better when Whitney bounded over to her companion and touched his face while saying something. David! That's who it was. She could just make out the mustache under his—

The two hazy silhouettes kissed. Silvia stared in disbelief. The moon appeared from behind a cloud, casting enough light to banish any doubt. Whitney's laughter carried across the yard. Silvia's stomach sank. Why was she sneaking around behind Omar's back? With one of his friends, no less! She pulled on the joint while observing them. Whitney and David walked in a slow arc toward the patio. With the interior lights reflecting off their faces, she could see his dopey grin and her happy smile, like she didn't feel an ounce of guilt.

Whitney yanked on the sliding glass door. Then she sniffed. And kept sniffing until she looked in Silvia's direction, her eyes widening in recognition.

"I'll catch up with you later," Whitney said to David. "I need to talk to my friend."

Suddenly they were friends? She might play it like that, hoping that Silvia would keep her mouth shut, but it wouldn't work.

"Hey, girl!" Whitney said, sprinting to her side. "What's up? Are you enjoying the party?"

"I'm having more fun by the second," Silvia replied, holding up the joint.

"Sweet!" Whitney said, deftly taking it from her. "My parents smoke weed all the time. But I have *no* idea where they hide their stash. I've literally gone around the house smelling everything. It should be easy to find but—" She pulled on the joint with practiced skill and handed it back to her. "—no idea."

Silvia wasn't about to pretend that everything was okay. "What about Omar?" she demanded.

Whitney made a face. "Is he good at smelling things?"

"You know what I mean," Silvia said, pointing to the yard. "I saw you guys."

"Oh *that*," Whitney said. "David is really into Wicca, so I wanted him to see my mom's crystal garden. Do you want a tour?"

"That depends," Silvia said. "Do your tours always end with a kiss?"

"No way!" Whitney laughed and reached for the joint again. "Although I guess I *could* kiss a girl. Just for fun though."

Silvia stared in disbelief as Whitney took another hit. "What about Omar?" she repeated. "Don't you care about his feelings?"

"Of course!" Whitney said, as if there was no question. "He's so sweet. You know that though."

"I do. Which is why I regret hurting his feelings by kissing someone else while we were still together."

"Oh yeah, I heard about that." Whitney's expression was sympathetic. "That's why I prefer open relationships. I figure it's normal to get curious or whatever, you know? Like right now, the idea of kissing you is kind of exciting. Maybe it's the weed." She passed the joint back to her with a giggle.

"Wait," Silvia said, "are you and Omar in an open relationship?"

"Yeah!" Whitney replied. "He didn't tell you? Oh my gosh… You thought I was cheating on him!"

"Well, yeah. But you weren't?"

"Not at all! I would never do that to him."

Silvia studied her, but there was nothing duplicitous about Whitney, who wore her heart on her sleeve. But still… "An open relationship?" she repeated. "Really?"

"Yeah! You should try it." Whitney spread her arms and twirled. "It's so liberating!"

And it sounded very grown-up. Which made Silvia realize that Omar was more mature than she gave him credit for. Especially since he wasn't swaggering around, telling all the girls at their school that he was still available. Including her! What the hell?

"So the thought of him kissing other people doesn't bother you?" she pressed.

Whitney shrugged. "Nope!"

"What if he falls in love with someone else?"

"He's already in love with you," Whitney said, moving closer with wiggling fingers, as if wanting to tickle her. "He tries not to talk about you all the time."

Silvia gently pushed her hands away. "What do you mean?"

"He's always like—" Whitney made her voice deeper. "Oh, that's a really cool movie. I saw it with— Never mind. Hey, do you like fishing? Because— Never mind." She reverted to her normal voice. "It wasn't hard to figure out who 'Never Mind' is. I think it's nice."

"You do?"

"Yeah! He loves you so much, which is a good thing. That's the kind of guy I want to be with."

"Me too," Silvia said before she could stop herself.

Whitney didn't seem to notice. She gasped and pointed at a firefly. "So late in the year!"

"Just to be perfectly clear," Silvia said. "If I march into the house right now and kiss Omar, it wouldn't bother you?"

"I'd love to watch!" Whitney said, clapping in excitement. "It would be so romantic. Let's go!"

"That's all right," Silvia said, shaking her head with a chuckle. "I'm all bark and no bite."

"Wouldn't you love to be a dog?" Whitney said wistfully. "Or a cat." She pawed at the air experimentally.

Silvia reassessed her. Maybe she *was* perfect for Omar. They probably filmed funny sketches together all the time. "Do you love him?"

"Yes!" Whitney said instantly. "I love everyone at this party. Don't we go to a great school? I just wish we didn't have to go there *for* school, you know? Like if you got rid of all the homework and schedules and we got to decide what we wanted to learn each day or who we wanted to hang out with. That would be incredible!"

Silvia took another hit. Then she passed the joint back to Whitney. "You know what? I definitely want to see those crystals." When her hand was grabbed and she was yanked toward the yard, she added, "But *without* the kiss at the end."

Not that she would mind. Whitney was adorable and had an amazing personality. She simply worried that it would be too weird for Omar if his ex and his current girlfriend made out. Then again, maybe not. He'd changed more than she had realized.

Was that her fault? Did he prefer an open relationship now so he couldn't be hurt in the same way again? Silvia tasted guilt when she swallowed, but she took comfort in the knowledge that he'd ended up with someone with such a kind heart.

The party was winding down, Ricky's hope dwindling with each person who left, even though he was telling them they needed to go. Omar had asked him to help, and Ricky had readily agreed, imagining that the crowds would thin enough to reveal Diego sulking in a corner or something appropriately moody like that. All that became apparent, as Ricky went around declaring that his welcome home party was over, was that Diego hadn't bothered to show up. Which really bugged him, because after all they had been through, it wasn't much to ask. He didn't have to sweep Ricky up into his arms and promise to love him forever. That would've been nice, but he would have settled for a token appearance at the very least.

He approached a table where a group of guys clustered around open books. "Hey everyone," Ricky said. "You don't have to go home, but you can't stay here."

One of the guys looked up and grinned. "Ricky! Hey! Long time no see."

"Galen!" Ricky said in surprise. He almost hadn't recognized him. The last time they'd seen each other was in journalism class freshman year. Since then Galen had graduated from chubby to stocky, the poofy afro replaced by a short flattop. The easy-going smile was exactly the same though. "Hi! Wow! It really has been a while."

"Yeah." Galen stood up and brushed himself off while still grinning. "How was Seattle?"

"It was okay," Ricky said, peering at the table. "What are you guys doing?"

"Coming up with ideas for our next *D&D* campaign. Have you ever played?"

"No," Ricky said, moving closer. On the open pages of the nearest book, he could see gruesome drawings of monsters next to blocks of text. "I've always wanted to though."

"You should join us!" Galen seemed a little short of breath.

"That would be cool. Some other time. Whitney's parents will be home soon, and we still need to clean up."

"I can help," Galen offered.

"Okay. Would you mind spreading the word that it's time to go?"

"No problem." Galen nudged his friends, who began gathering up books and pads of paper.

Ricky left them to it. The house was really clearing out now, so he grabbed a trash bag and followed Omar around while tossing things into it. They mostly only had to worry about empty cans, plastic cups, and the occasional crushed potato chip. With everyone pitching in, the house was soon in good shape again.

"Anything I can do?" Galen asked when reappearing, this time without his friends.

"Sure," Omar said, kicking a cluster of bulging trash bags. "Take these to the curb. I gotta go kiss my girl goodnight."

There were only four trash bags, so they each took two.

"I'd love to hear about your trip," Galen said as they walked outside. "I've always wanted to visit Seattle. The home of grunge rock! Was it as cool as I'm imagining?"

"I was stuck with my grandparents the whole time," Ricky confessed.

"Oh." Galen's attention was on him as they walked, which is probably while he stumbled and nearly tripped. "You sure look different," he said, not seeming embarrassed.

"So do you," Ricky said, noticing the way the thin black hoodie clung to his round shoulders and protruding chest.

Brown eyes smiled in response. "I was really hoping we'd have a class together this year," Galen said, "but I didn't want to be on the newspaper or yearbook. I thought the creative writing elective would be more fun."

"I took the new computer sciences elective," Ricky said, the breath catching in his throat, because he'd just noticed a car parked across the street. A seventy-seven Trans Am with mismatched panels, to be exact.

"We should hang out sometime," Galen said as they reached the curb.

"Yeah," Ricky replied, having barely heard him. "I'll see you later, okay?"

He stumbled into the street, like he was in a waking dream, and prayed that the car wouldn't speed away before he got there. The driver-side window was facing him. Even before it rolled down, he saw the glint of eyes watching him.

"You came!" Ricky breathed.

"Yeah. I did my part." Diego reached for the ignition. "See ya."

"Wait!" Ricky cried, grabbing the side mirror with one hand and the door with the other while bracing to be dragged down the street. "Just give me a minute. Please!"

Diego sighed and leaned back. "Make it quick."

"I will, I promise."

Ricky moved around the front of the car, willing to be run over rather than let him get away. When he opened the passenger-side door, Diego was collecting beer cans from the footwell and tossing them in the back.

Ricky climbed inside, his feet causing an aluminum clamor. "Have you been drinking?"

"Yup," Diego said unapologetically.

"While driving?"

"Uh-huh."

Ricky stared at him in shock. "You can't do that!"

"Watch me." Diego reached for the ignition again.

"Not with me in the car," Ricky added hastily.

Diego hesitated. Then he dropped his hand. "What do you want?"

"Do you really need me to answer that?"

Diego studied him and shrugged. "I guess not."

Ricky shifted sideways in the passenger seat, one of his legs folded beneath him so his longing gaze could move across the furrowed brow and down the slope of a strong nose to downturned lips that he wanted nothing more than to kiss. "I'm really glad you're here."

The impressive chest rose and fell. "It's cool they threw you a party."

"I kept hoping you'd be there," Ricky told him.

"Here I am," Diego said, reaching into the back to hook a series of six plastic loops. Only a single can still hung from them. Judging from the mess on the floorboards, it probably wasn't his first six-pack.

"I'm worried about you," Ricky said. "What's going on?"

"Oh good, just what I needed," Diego growled. "Another heart-to-heart."

"I think you've had enough," Ricky said, the air between them sour with fumes.

"Oh yeah?" Diego cracked open the beer, locked eyes with him, and chugged the entire thing.

Ricky's attention darted down to the ignition, where the head of Frankenstein's monster dangled from a keyring. He grabbed it and yanked.

"Hey!" Diego tried to swipe the keys from him, but his hand was still filled with a can. "Give it back!"

"Nope!" Ricky rammed himself against the door and stumbled out onto the grass.

The driver-side door opened a second later, Diego's massive form a sinister shadow that swiftly grew taller. Ricky feinted to the right until Diego headed in the same direction. Then he dived back inside the car. Diego hustled around the hood and grabbed his foot as Ricky scrambled over the driver seat. He freed himself with a kick and slid out the other side. Then he made a break for Whitney's house. He saw Anthony and Cameron in the driveway—Omar standing just outside the front door— and imagined how much worse this would get if a drunk Diego confronted his former best friends.

"I'll find my own way home!" Ricky shouted at them before taking off down the sidewalk. Diego cut across the street at an angle, his massive arms pumping to reach him. Ricky kept running and glancing to his right until he saw a way through to the next street over. He darted into the shadows between houses and heard Diego coming after him like a T-Rex smashing through the forest.

He rounded a block and ran diagonally across the street to turn another corner unseen, even though losing Diego seemed unlikely. He must realize how close they were to Ricky's house. His destination was all too obvious, but where else could he go? His friends weren't home yet.

"I'm gonna kill you!" he heard Diego snarl.

He didn't sound too far away. Ricky's sides were hurting when he reached the end of another block. He checked over his shoulder and saw that Diego was still hot on his trail. Ricky turned down a familiar street, starting to stumble when his house came into view. He just needed a little more time. With the last of his energy, he sprinted to his yard and threw the bundle of keys beneath the front porch stairs. Then he hobbled back toward the street and plopped down in the grass before reaching it.

Diego slowed to a walk when noticing him sitting there. He was panting, the navy blue T-shirt he wore soaked with sweat. He stopped in front of Ricky and swayed.

"Gimmie," Diego huffed. "Keys." His massive form crumpled to the grass. Diego rolled over onto his back, staring up at the sky while his chest heaved.

Ricky scooted closer to him. "Hi."

Scowling eyes moved sidewise to focus on him. "I hate you."

Ricky swallowed. "Do you really?"

Diego didn't reply. He gulped down air before sitting up, groaning with the effort. "Give me the damn keys!"

"I don't have them anymore."

"What?" Diego started pawing at him to check his pockets.

"Or maybe I do," Ricky said before stretching out to make himself available.

Diego stopped frisking him a moment later. "Where'd you put them?"

"They're hidden. You can't have them again until you sober up."

"Are you kidding me? I'm fucking wasted! We'll be here all night!"

"That's okay," Ricky said. "You can stay with me."

"Hah!" Diego pushed himself up on his feet to consider the house. "No wait, that's a great idea! Let's wake your parents up and see how they feel about it."

"If you do, they'll drive you home," Ricky said softly. "That's okay too."

Diego rounded on him. "What are you doing? Huh? What sort of game are you trying to play?"

"I'm not," Ricky said. "This isn't one of my schemes. I just want you to be safe." He raised his hands when Diego's lip began to snarl in response. "Or whatever you want to call it. I want you to be okay, so stay with me. Just for tonight."

He watched Diego walk to the edge of the yard while shaking his head. Once he reached the corner, he buried his face in his big hands before slowly dragging them down. Then he turned around. "Fine."

Ricky silently stood and glanced at the house with apprehension. He wasn't supposed to be here tonight. He'd told his parents that he was staying with Omar, so he wouldn't have to worry about his curfew. They weren't expecting him. But what other choice did he have? "It's probably best if I sneak you in," he said.

Diego snorted. "I bet."

"Just try to be quiet, okay? Please."

Diego rolled his eyes. Ricky led the way inside, certain they would be caught, but that was preferable to someone dying in a car accident. They made it undetected to the entryway stairs and began climbing them when the light switched on.

"Ricky!"

The sound of his own name made him go rigid. He turned around to see Ken standing there with a perplexed expression that became a lot more concerned when he noticed Diego.

"Hey, Mr. Nishikawa," Diego said, his voice dripping with sarcasm. "Haven't seen you since you called the cops on me. Still got their number?"

"I'll meet you in my room," Ricky hissed, squeezing past him.

Diego tromped upstairs.

Ricky filled his lungs with air. "I ran into him at a party. He's too drunk to drive home, so I said he could stay here. I know I'm not allowed to see him, but I promise that he'll leave first thing in the morning. So please don't wake up Mom. She's going to be mad anyway, but at least this way, she'll get a full night's sleep."

Ken grimaced when glancing toward the master bedroom. Then he whispered, "I didn't see you. Okay? When I woke up to get a drink the house was very *very* quiet. Understand?"

Ricky nodded. "Thanks, Dad!"

Ken shook his head, like he'd lost his own mind, before turning off the entryway light.

Ricky hurried up the stairs, scarcely able to believe his luck. When he entered his bedroom, Diego was seated on the edge of the mattress with his head bowed. The lights remained off. Ricky shut the door behind him and locked it. In the limited gloom, he kicked off his shoes and sat on the carpet. He reached for one of the heavy black boots that Diego wore and tugged at the laces. Ricky carefully removed the first boot, then the other, cinnamon eyes watching him impassively the entire time. He stood and walked around the bed. Ricky was reaching for the lamp on his desk when an arm looped around his waist, lifting him off his feet. With a gut-wrenching tug, he was pulled into bed. Diego climbed on top of him, his arms rippling to either side of Ricky's head, his massive body eclipsing the last remaining light. Diego held himself there, his intent uncertain. Then he shifted to the left, the mattress bowing to one side of Ricky. One of those heavy arms curled around his torso, pulling Ricky close to a chest still hot from exertion. A leg pinned both of his down as a chin nestled against his shoulder, the breath warm against his ear.

"Don't say anything," Diego huffed. "I mean it. Not a fucking word. Understand?"

Ricky nodded, unsure what he was agreeing to. Diego didn't move much after that. Occasionally the arm around him clenched, as if there was still too much distance between them. Eventually his breathing slowed and his muscles finally went slack. The limbs draped across him were heavy. And reassuring. Diego was holding him again! Ricky had wanted this so badly. Endless questions sprang to mind, but he silenced them by focusing on how good it felt to be so close. The subtle smell of Diego's sweat, the radiating heat of his body, and the precious little places where their bare skin touched… Ricky tried to stay awake, wanting to savor every second while it lasted. But he must have fallen asleep, because the next thing he knew, he was lying on his side while blinking against daylight. When he rolled over, the mattress next to him was unoccupied. His stomach sank, the sensation remaining there.

Ricky got up, still dressed in yesterday's clothes. He opened his bedroom door and could hear his parents talking downstairs, but they didn't sound upset. He grabbed his shoes, noticing that Diego's boots were gone, and went to investigate.

"Ricky!" his father cried in artificial surprise as he padded into the kitchen. "I thought you were staying with a friend!"

"I had a bad dream and wanted to come home," he said, not caring how childish this made him sound. "Is everything okay?"

"We're fine," his mother insisted. "Come have breakfast."

"I will," Ricky said. "Umm… But I want to try going for a jog first. A guy at school does it, and he's ripped."

Ken and Ami shrugged at each other and resumed sipping their coffee. Ricky sat on the front porch before pulling on his shoes. There was no sign of Diego, but when he checked beneath the stairs and found the keys, Ricky knew he couldn't have gone far. He grabbed them and began the walk to Whitney's house. The Trans Am was still parked outside. He wasn't sure if it would be. Diego was a mechanic and could probably hotwire cars. Good thing he hadn't thought of that last night. Or maybe Diego had *wanted* to come home with Ricky, considering that he'd shown up at the party. That had to mean something.

He approached the car. The driver's seat was tilted all the way back. Diego's eyes were closed, a beam of sunlight warming his bronze skin. The window was still rolled down, so Ricky poked his head inside and considered those perpetually frowning lips. Would it be so wrong? Snow White hadn't seemed to mind, nor had Sleeping Beauty.

"Did you bring my keys?" Diego asked.

"Gah!" Ricky said, jerking upright and bumping his head. "You scared me!"

Diego opened his eyes. "What were you trying to do, kiss me?"

"Maybe," Ricky admitted. He walked around to the other side of the car and got in before handing over the keys.

"Finally," Diego said, eagerly taking them and starting the engine. "If you ever do that again, I'll break your damn fingers. Nobody comes between me and Frankenstein."

Ricky did his best imitation of the famous monster. "I love my dad."

Diego shook his head and shifted into gear. "He doesn't say lame shit like that. Even though it's true."

"Where are we going?"

"I'm taking you home."

Ricky watched as the houses began to blur. "Last night was nice. I missed you."

Diego clenched his jaw a few times but didn't say anything.

"We never officially broke up, you know," he added. "Not really. So we don't even have to start again, because it was never really over."

Diego looked at him. "Ricky?"

"Yeah?"

"I'm breaking up with you."

"Oh." Ricky swallowed, but the lump in his throat wouldn't go away. "Okay."

The car slowed again and pulled over in front of his house. Diego's fist clenched on the wheel. "Do you want a ride to school tomorrow?"

Ricky blinked in surprise. "Really? Yeah! That would be great."

"Cool."

Ricky studied him while chewing his bottom lip to distract himself from the pain he felt inside. At least they would be together again. In a way. "Does this mean we're friends?" he asked.

"No," Diego growled. "Of course not! People act like you can just go back to the way things used to be, but you can't, the stupid fucks. So no, you're not my friend. We have *way* too much history for that. You're my ex-boyfriend. It's a totally different thing."

"You're so right!" Ricky said. "People don't get back together with their friends. That doesn't even make sense. But sometimes they *do* start dating their ex again."

Diego made a face. "I guess."

"And sometimes people sleep with their ex. Right? That's a thing. I hear it's pretty common."

Diego laughed. "You wish."

"I really do," Ricky said. "I've heard breakup sex is great. I'm not sure if we'd have to do it right away, or if there's some sort of grace period. I guess we could experiment and find out."

Diego shook his head. "Don't make me change my mind."

"I won't," Ricky said, all levity leaving his voice. "I'll take what I can get, because I missed you. Really *really* bad."

"Yeah," Diego grunted, leaving it at that. He nodded through the windshield. "Now go home."

Ricky threw his arms around a thick neck. Diego didn't react, but that didn't faze him, because beneath the surface was the guy who had shown up at his party and held him throughout the night. That's who he would always love, no matter how damaged he might be.

"I'll see you tomorrow morning?" Ricky asked with his hand on the door.

Diego nodded. "See ya."

He felt conflicted when getting out and more than a little heartbroken as the Trans Am screeched and tore off down the street. But at least the long separation had finally come to an end. Diego was a part of his life again. And that meant there was still hope, no matter how small.

CHAPTER 10
SEPTEMBER 6TH, 1993

Cameron stood behind the garage door as it opened, the morning light bathing his shoes, legs, and then his upper body before he needed to shield his eyes from the sun. Another beautiful day! He yanked on the plastic over-sized trash container next to him and wheeled it toward the curb, tempted to whistle along the way. Cameron reached the street and ran a circle around the container while still holding on, like it was an unyielding dance partner, the wheels beneath grinding in protest. Then he let go with a bow, the trash container landing on its base with a thud. Glass clattered as the bags inside settled. Cameron froze, his happy expression shifting to one of concern before he shook it off. Yes, what he'd just heard had sounded like empty wine bottles knocking together, but it could have been anything, like a pickle jar hitting an old drinking glass. He had no reason to think it might have anything at all to do with booze.

Cameron swallowed while considering the trash container. He was being paranoid. Over the summer, his mother had gone with him to Alcoholics Anonymous, her consumption slowing and then stopping altogether. Brenda had continued going to meetings without him, assuring her son that she was back on steady ground. Which was obviously true, because she no longer passed out on the couch every night. She set her own alarm and went to work on time each day. His mom was up and taking a shower at this very moment. And here he was, biting his nails over a little clinking sound.

Cameron laughed and tilted the trash container up on its two wheels before letting it go again. He heard the exact same noise. Isn't that how trash always sounded? Glass was loudest by nature. But it *did* bother him that he couldn't remember finishing a jar of jelly or a bottle of ketchup recently. So what the hell was in there? He opened the lid to peer inside. All he saw were tied-shut trash bags. Cameron lifted the container and let it drop again, hearing the same sound. He was repeating this experiment when a car slowed and pulled into his driveway.

He turned and walked toward it, grateful for the distraction. Just moments ago, he'd still been buzzing from an amazing weekend. Hooking up with Anthony at the party had been incredibly hot, and reassured him that everything was good between them again. He'd been starting to think that Anthony didn't want to be touched by him at all. Jesus… He really was getting paranoid!

"Get out so he can see you!" he heard Omar say.

Cameron's eyes darted to the driver-side door just as Anthony stood. The first thing he noticed was the freshly dyed pink hair. He felt slightly disappointed by this, since he preferred Anthony as a blond, but his attention soon darted down to eyeliner so heavy and smudged that it made his boyfriend look like he hadn't slept in weeks. His lips were shiny and pink, his solid black clothes slashed to reveal pale skin beneath. As if he didn't stand out enough! Anthony was going to get his ass kicked! Anxiety surged through Cameron's system.

"What's wrong?" his boyfriend asked, having noticed his expression.

Omar stuck his head out a car window and shouted, "He's so punk rock! Don't you just want to bang him right here and now?"

Cameron clenched his jaw a few times.

"You don't like it," Anthony said.

His attention flicked back to him again. That's when Cameron noticed the vulnerable expression. "You look great," he said hurriedly. "I just…" Worry. About a lot of things, which come to think of it was the perfect excuse. "Come here."

Cameron kissed Anthony before taking his hand and leading him to the curb. He tilted the container and let it drop again. "Do you hear that?" He grabbed and shook the whole damn thing. "What does it sound like to you?"

"Glass?" Anthony said while looking uncertain.

"Yeah, but what kind?"

"Umm… Is this like your obsession with wood? Do you think there's an antique lamp in there or something?"

"Wine bottles," Cameron said. "That's what it sounds like to me."

Anthony's fine eyebrows shot up. "Oh."

"Yeah." He shook the container again. "What do you think?"

Anthony shrugged. "Let's find out." He lifted one of the trash bags and shook it. They heard some muted shuffling. "It's not that one," Anthony said, setting it aside before grabbing another.

"Forget about it," Cameron said, his face burning.

"I don't mind. We were digging through trash on our first date, remember? I knew what I was signing up for."

Cameron's embarrassment was replaced by gratitude. Especially when his boyfriend shook the second bag and they heard the unmistakable sound of glass.

"Wanna open it?" Anthony asked.

"Yeah, but I don't want my mom to see. Over here."

He took the trash bag and led the way to the side of the house. As soon as he set it down, Anthony began using his thin fingers to loosen the knot and dug right in once it was open, taking out item after item and setting each aside. Luckily there wasn't anything too filthy. An empty cereal box, some old coffee grinds, a plastic tub that used to contain ice cream… Anthony took a step back, like he'd seen a sharp-toothed rat. Cameron peered into the bag, his stomach sinking, because the narrow neck of a bottle was sticking out. He pulled it free to check the label, wanting to be absolutely sure. Cabernet Sauvignon. His mother's favorite.

"Here's another," Anthony said, still digging around. "Oh. Umm…"

"How many are in there?" Cameron asked.

"Just two more," Anthony said, trying to sound upbeat. "Maybe she found some old bottles and poured them out."

"Or maybe she had a party of her own on Saturday," Cameron said. "I knew she seemed tired on Sunday. She was hungover!"

"She didn't finish all of these in one night, did she?"

"Does it matter?" he croaked in response. "She's drinking again!"

"Sorry," Anthony said, his expression pure sympathy. "Let's check the other trash bags."

Cameron wasn't sure if he wanted to know. They were interrupted anyway.

"What are you guys doing?" Omar asked, appearing from around the corner. "Did you throw something away on accident?" He nudged Anthony. "Hey, remember when that happened to us? We'd stolen that nudie magazine from your brother, and I couldn't find it anywhere."

Anthony smiled at Cameron. "I'm afraid you're not the first boy I've gone dumpster diving with."

"I was freaking out," Omar continued, "even though it was only a *Playboy*. But hey, desperate times. Just thinking about that magazine used to give me a hard-on. What are you looking for? I'm not afraid to get dirty." He grabbed the trash bag.

Cameron yanked it out of his hands, sending garbage flying everywhere, which only upset him more. "Would you please fuck off?"

Omar recoiled. "Yeah. Sorry. I'll wait in the car."

Cameron scowled while watching him go.

"What was that about?" Anthony asked gently. "He was only trying to help,"

He didn't reply, choosing instead to collect the scattered garbage. "This stays between us," he said at last. "All right? I know you tell each other everything, but not this."

Anthony nodded. "Okay. Do you want to check the other trash bags?"

"No. I've seen enough."

The sun was shining and the sky was still blue, but Cameron's heart was heavy when they returned to the driveway. The trip to school was awkward. Omar sat sullenly in the back seat, the silence deafening. Cameron couldn't think of anything to say to his boyfriend. Not while they had an audience.

"You know what we need?" Anthony asked, reaching for the stereo system.

When he didn't get a reply, Boy George began singing about karma, but neither he nor Omar complained. At least it camouflaged the awkwardness. The music serenaded them all the way to the school parking lot. Omar didn't stick around after that.

"See ya," he said before skating away.

Anthony watched him go. Like always. He seemed to notice Cameron's irritation when finally turning toward him. "Is everything okay?"

"Yeah," he replied through gritted teeth, "but maybe it's time Omar found his own way to school. His family is rich. Can't they buy him a car?"

"They gave him a downpayment, but he's saving his money. *And* he pays for gas." Anthony shook his head, like it didn't matter. "I wasn't talking about him anyway."

Oh. Right. "I haven't had time to process any of it," Cameron said. "That's why it would have been nice to have some privacy for once."

"It's a five-minute drive," Anthony said, his tones playful. "We wouldn't have made much progress, even if he wasn't with us."

"Sorry." Guilt was added to the cocktail of emotions brewing in him. "I'll make sure to apologize."

"Don't worry about it," Anthony said. "I've said worse. And at least you were polite."

"I was?"

"Yeah. You asked him to *please* fuck off." Anthony laughed. "Which is just one of the many reasons I love you. Even when you're angry, you're still a nice person."

"Thanks," Cameron said glumly. "What a mess."

"We'll get through it," Anthony said, placing a palm on his chest. "Your mom is bound to have setbacks. That it took this long is probably a good sign. We'll figure it out together, and if we can't, there's always the next meeting."

Cameron pulled him into a hug. The day had just begun and he already wished he hadn't gotten out of bed. His boyfriend was right though. At least they had each other. This burden would be twice as difficult to bear on his own. That's how it used to be before they met. So when they turned and walked toward the school, he put an arm around Anthony and left it there, wanting everyone to see that his boyfriend was protected.

Anthony closed his locker and turned around. That's when he noticed someone watching him. A tall red-haired guy named Troy Mitchell, who had moved here recently. What few interactions they'd had were far from positive. He was one of Graham Fowler's friends, both of them bullies, albeit in different ways. Troy was more likely to stab you in the back than punch you in the face. Anthony averted his gaze and began walking to his next class. He counted under his breath before glancing over his shoulder.

Troy wasn't far behind. When they locked eyes, it only seemed to encourage him. Troy picked up the pace. Anthony forced himself to keep the same steady gait.

"Hey," he heard Troy say.

Anthony reached into his pocket for his earbuds.

"Hey," Troy repeated, appearing to Anthony's left while wearing an amused expression. "What are you supposed to be, some sort of drag queen?"

If he was, he'd probably have a witty response locked and loaded, but instead his mouth felt too dry to speak.

"You make an ugly girl," Troy said, still leering.

Anthony glanced at him. "That's better than having a repulsive personality."

The smile slid off Troy's face. "I don't know what you're aiming for, but there isn't enough makeup in the world."

"We'll see," Anthony replied. "I'm just getting started."

"Oh yeah?" Troy asked, in a way that felt threatening.

He just wasn't sure how exactly. Troy fell back. Anthony waited until he was about to turn the corner before checking the hall again. Troy was no longer there. Anthony shuddered and kept moving. He definitely preferred Graham Fowler. Which wasn't saying much.

"Hey!" This time the voice was in front of him and comfortingly familiar. Cameron was dodging people in the hall to reach him. "Sorry!" he said. "I ran into my shop teacher from last year and got held up."

"He robbed you at gunpoint?" Anthony feigned shock.

Cameron laughed. "Yeah. They really need to start paying teachers more." He put an arm around him as they continued walking in the same direction. "He was curious about the new antique shop. I told him to stop by after school, so he can get a preview before it opens."

Anthony thought of Charles and felt a longing like never before. "I might swing by too."

"Sure! I love having you there. Even though you haven't been around as much lately. You know the air conditioner got fixed, right?"

Anthony smiled. He was indeed aware of that fact. For much of the summer, Cameron had been working in blistering heat—necessitating the need to take off his shirt—while sanding and buffing his muscles to perfection. Oh sure, he was restoring furniture at the same time, but Anthony had barely noticed, his eyes only leaving that incredible body to visit the handsome face that resided just above it.

When they reached his next class, Cameron kissed him hurriedly and took off, so he wouldn't be late to his own. Anthony hardly thought of Troy after that, his boyfriend a much more welcome companion in his imagination. His fantasies carried him all the way to lunch.

"Thanks again for the party everyone!" Ricky said when sitting at their table. He nodded at Whitney. "You especially."

"I had *so* much fun," she replied.

"Yeah, me too," David said dreamily.

Whitney slapped her hand on the table. "We should have another party this weekend! Who else was gone over the summer?"

"Diego," Ricky said. "Sort of."

Whitney gasped. "That's right, he was in jail! Which sounds kind of fun." She turned to Omar. "Let's go rob a gas station after school!"

"I would," Omar replied easily, "but I've gotta work."

It wasn't clear if Whitney heard him, because she shot to her feet and waved. "Ms. Howard! I haven't seen you in ages. Oh my god!" And with that she went racing off.

Anthony smirked. "Always nice of her to drop by."

"I swear she never eats," Omar said, before shrugging and pulling her tray closer to get at her french fries.

"Speaking of Diego," Silvia said to Ricky, her eyes lingering on Omar's bulging cheeks with concern. "What's the latest between you two?"

"He broke up with me." Ricky's shoulders slumped, although he recovered quickly. "But we're actually talking again, so that's progress. In a way."

Anthony had spoken to him about it on the phone last night. "I'm sure it won't be long until you win him over," he said. "Not many people can turn a bully into a boyfriend."

"Thanks," Ricky said, managing a smile, "but I'm not sure he'll ever trust me again."

"You could always try an open relationship," David suggested. He looked at Omar. "How exactly do those work? Like are you allowed to have more than one girlfriend, or can you only mess around with other girls?"

Omar shook his head. "Huh?"

David's forehead creased. "Would it bug you if Whitney

started dating someone else? Or is it more like you're both swingers?"

Omar made a face. "My dude, I think you've been inhaling too much incense or whatever, because you're talking gibberish."

"He's asking how open relationships work," Silvia interjected.

Omar's brow furrowed up. "How the hell should I know?"

David's cheeks flushed.

Silvia looked to Anthony, as if for an explanation. He shrugged in response and tossed another Frito into his mouth. The show didn't make much sense to him, but there was nothing else to watch while he ate.

"It's a nice idea," Ricky said, "but I only want Diego. And I hope he only wants me."

"Give it time, my man," Omar said. "He'll come around."

They were discussing the most recent episode of *The X-Files* when someone approached their table. Principal Preckwinkle might be short and stout, but her mere presence was enough to snuff out conversation. And for whatever reason, she was looking squarely at him.

"Mr. Cullen," she said in clipped tones. "Would you please come with me?"

"What for?" Anthony asked.

She eyed the friends that surrounded him, her attention lingering on Ricky. "We can discuss it along the way."

He glanced down at his half-eaten food. "Should I bring my lunch with me?"

Preckwinkle nodded. "Hurry up. I'd like this taken care of before your next class."

That was ominous. His friends grimaced in sympathy. Anthony quickly packed up his lunch and followed her.

"Is everything okay?" he asked as they hustled down the hallway. All he could think of was that something had happened to his mom or dad.

Principal Preckwinkle sized him up with a judgmental air. "You are familiar, I hope, with the student handbook?"

Only in the general sense that such things existed, but Anthony knew that wouldn't make her happy, so he nodded.

"Good. Then you are equally aware of the school's dress code."

"Dress code?" he repeated before he could stop himself.

"Don't worry. You'll have the chance to refresh your memory. Vice Principal Freemont was hired to handle disciplinary matters. I suspect the two of you will be well-acquainted by the end of the school year."

"But I've always dressed like this," Anthony said in confusion.

Her eyes darted across his face. "The dress code applies to more than just your wardrobe, especially when it becomes enough of a distraction for other students to complain. This is a learning institution, not a Halloween party."

Anthony couldn't decide if that was a compliment or not. He loved Halloween! "Wait, are you saying that someone actually complained?"

"That's none of your concern," she replied. "If you turned that inquisitive mind to your studies, you wouldn't be in this situation now."

"My grades are pretty good actually," Anthony murmured.

She looked at him sharply, so he held his tongue as they went into the front office and down a side hall. Preckwinkle stopped in front of a door, knocked, and opened it without waiting for a response. "Vice Principal Fremont, this is the student I told you about." She gestured for him to enter.

A bull of a woman stood up, her expression hard, like she'd seen enough nonsense to last her a lifetime. The tight curls of her short no-fuss hairstyle fed into this impression. Anthony was taller than her by a foot, and yet it still felt like she was towering over him when she walked around her desk to look him up and down. She gestured to one of the empty chairs. "Have a seat."

"I trust you'll take things from here?" Principal Preckwinkle asked eagerly, like she was dangling a kitten over a crocodile's open mouth.

"Count on it," her new lackey responded.

The vice principal closed the door after Preckwinkle left and silently returned to her desk. She consulted an open folder before looking up. "My name is LaVern. I don't believe we've met. I was just reviewing your file, which is brief but interesting. You distributed an article in retaliation to a slur that was painted on your locker, and somehow this became a food fight that ended in a punching match?"

"Yes, ma'am," he replied, almost automatically, because something about this woman commanded respect. "Except that's not quite right. I distributed the article in response to censorship. The slur was only my inspiration for writing it in the first place." Ugh! Why couldn't he keep his big mouth shut?

She made a note in his file. Probably to deduct points, if there was such a thing. "Did Principal Preckwinkle explain why you're here?"

"She said something about the dress code."

LaVern nodded and slid a small booklet across the desk to him. "Does that look familiar? You were given a copy on your first day here as a freshman."

Anthony swallowed, not wanting to lie to her. If he'd been given such a book, it would have ended up in the trash or forgotten at the bottom of his locker. So instead of answering her, he stated the obvious after checking the title to be sure. "It's the student handbook."

"Open it to page thirteen," she instructed.

He did so. The title across the top of the page said "Dress Code Policy." He glanced up at her.

The vice principal appeared bored. "Start reading," she instructed.

Was this his punishment? Anthony cleared his throat. "Feet must be covered at all times. Slippers and flip flops are unacceptable but—"

"You have shoes on, correct?" she interrupted.

"Yes, ma'am."

LaVern nodded. "Skip to the next bullet point."

"Heads shall remain uncovered at all times. Hats will be confiscated if worn inside the building. Any headwear that doesn't provide protection from—"

"I can see your hair," La Vern said, sounding impatient. "That can't be the issue. Next."

"Clothing and accessories must not promote violence, risqué imagery, illicit substances, or display profanity of any nature." He looked up. She nodded for him to continue.

Anthony returned his attention to the handbook. He swallowed, not wanting to read the words aloud, because he knew what was coming. "Makeup and accessories must be of a modest nature that doesn't create a distraction for other students or faculty members."

"Hm," LaVern grunted. "Now that is interesting. Have you ever gotten distracted by someone else's makeup?"

"Only when it looked really good," he replied, trying a smile.

The vice principal eyed him coolly. "I don't like rules that leave room for subjective interpretation. I'm unsure what 'modest' was intended to mean in this context, but if a student is looking at the teacher or their assignment—like they should be—I can't imagine how someone else's makeup would break their concentration. Next."

Anthony stared, surprised that the subject was being brushed aside so easily. Then he blinked and hurried to read the next line. "Clothes worn by the student must provide complete cover from the mid-thigh to the upper chest so that no bare skin is showing."

"There you go," LaVern said, leaning back. "I don't see your underwear through the slashes in your jeans, so those are probably fine. The shirt, on the other hand, doesn't cover enough of your stomach or chest."

"I usually wear layers," Anthony said. He'd only gone without because he thought Cameron would like it but… "To be honest, I've been chilly all day, so I'm happy to comply."

"Good. I think we can skip the rest. I already reviewed it carefully before you came in. Feel free to keep that copy of the handbook so you can do the same."

"Okay," he said, wondering if he was allowed to go.

The vice-principal continued to eye him, taking in his hair, face, and no doubt the makeup that he wore. "Everyone's appearance comes with consequences," she said at last, "and rarely are they ever deserved. When I moved to this town, my new neighbor made sure to tell me how he felt about a black woman living next door. He was concerned about the devaluation of his property. I listened to his lecture and politely excused myself, because I do not make time for bigots. I do however treat all my neighbors with equal respect. So I continued to greet him when we happened to see each other, and I brought a package to him when the post office left it on my porch by accident. I suspect that none of the other neighbors treat him with such courtesy, because now when we see each other, he's often eager to chat. In other words, he seems to have overcome some of his reservations about my race. The experience wasn't pleasant for me—racism never is—but I do take solace that some good came of my response. People will always judge each other based on appearance. I've found a way of dealing with it that keeps my sanity in check. I advise you to do the same." Her shrewd eyes moved to a clock on the wall. "Back to class, Mr. Cullen."

Anthony stared in shock. Then he stood so fast he almost knocked over the chair. "Thank you!"

LaVern nodded and made a note in her file. He cleared the room, relieved that he didn't see Preckwinkle on the way out. The bell rang as he left the front office. The halls began filling with students. He was eager to return to his friends to tell them what had happened, but they wouldn't be in the cafeteria anymore. He scanned the throngs of people, hoping to catch them on their way to class. That's when he saw Troy, who smirked in satisfaction when approaching him, his eyes darting in the direction of the front office.

"Uh oh," Troy said, his voice dripping in sarcasm. "Did somebody get in trouble?"

"I don't know," Anthony replied. "Did a big baby tattle on me? Because it didn't work."

Troy's face scrunched up. "What do you mean?"

"Turns out there's nothing in the dress code against being so hot." Anthony smiled pleasantly, waving over his shoulder as he walked away. "Better luck next time!"

His new vice principal was kind of cool, but being civil to an asshole like Troy was too much to ask. Although what she had said did resonate with him. Leading by example was important. Anthony wasn't sure he'd have had the courage to wear makeup if not for Charles, or Robert Smith, or all the other guys who had done so before him. That was the reason he'd written his article in the first place, wanting other queer people in his school to realize that they weren't alone. He would keep on being loud and proud, no matter how often other people tried to extinguish his fire. Anthony wasn't a drag queen, but he did burn with pride, so if anything… he was a flaming queen!

CHAPTER 11
SEPTEMBER 6ᵀᴴ, 1993

Silvia locked the doors to Right Round Records ten minutes early. The store was empty and they rarely got customers this late. Most shops in town closed by eight on the weekdays for that reason, so she took the opportunity to get a head start while Archie's Pizza Pi remained open. She wasn't hungry (okay, maybe a little) but she *was* eager to see her ex-boyfriend again. Especially after the conversation she'd had with Anthony.

"Omar is definitely not in an open relationship," he had said. *"I would have heard about it, believe me."*

And she did. Except she also believed Whitney, who had apparently told David about the arrangement.

Silvia hopped on her ten-speed bike and pedaled to Archie's. When she went inside, the greeter looked surprised to see her.

"I'm sorry, but we're about to close."

"That's okay," Silvia said. "I'm here to pick up Omar."

"Oh! He usually stays after closing. I bet he's in the security office."

She followed the greeter's directions down a hall to a partially open door. The interior was filled with dim blue light radiating from a bank of monitors that displayed different areas of the restaurant. Next to this was a desk where Omar was sitting with his back to her, his wavy dark hair spilling halfway down his neck. She missed getting to touch it.

Silvia stood on the threshold and watched him a moment. Omar was normally so animated. She wasn't used to seeing him in a state of concentration. He barely moved at all except to alternate his attention between the two screens in front of him. Part of her wanted to walk inside, close the door behind her, and swivel that chair around before getting to her knees. She'd give him something else to focus on!

Instead she cleared her throat.

Omar turned, bleary eyes lighting up when he saw her. "Hey, babe!" He grimaced and shook his head. "Sorry. I'll never get used to that."

"It's fine," Silvia assured him. "Are you editing a birthday party?"

"Nah. I'm working on the video yearbook."

"Already?" she asked, walking closer to see. Girls in some sort of gymnastics formation were frozen on the screens.

"Yeah. Last year was super rushed. I really want this one to be perfect." He grinned at her suddenly. "It's so weird to see you in here. Usually it's just the security guy. He always smells like cabbage, for some reason."

She laughed. "I thought I'd come pick you up from work."

He perked up at this. "You've got your truck with you?"

"No. Just my bike. I thought we could hang out somewhere and talk. I can't remember the last time it was just the two of us."

"Yeah!" he said, glancing at the screens. "Let me shut all this down so we can go."

A few minutes later, they walked out into a warm night. The traffic on Main Street had died down. She saw other people locking up their businesses. Silvia got on her bike. Omar dropped his skateboard to the sidewalk. They went together to a nearby park, switching back to their feet so they could stroll across a green lawn to a gazebo surrounded by flowering bushes. She leaned her bike against the wooden stairs and turned to Omar, surprised to see that he'd stripped off his work Polo.

"I hate this thing," he said when stuffing it into his backpack.

"Aww!" she complained. "I like the colorful stripes."

"I don't," Omar said, the bare skin of his torso stretching over his muscles as he put on a Metallica T-shirt. "I keep trying to convince Mr. Dandy that customers will have an easier time finding an employee if we're dressed in all black. He's not buying it so far."

"That's your boss?"

"Yeah. He's cool. Should we just chill here?"

He nodded at the stairs. She sat there, wishing that Omar would move closer when he did the same.

"Hey!" he said suddenly. "Do you know what happened to Anthony? We haven't seen each other since Preckwinkle abducted him."

"Yes! He stopped by the record store." She filled him in on what had occurred.

"I'm glad he didn't get in trouble," Omar said. "Troy is a dick. He's in my English class, and the dude is a total kiss-ass with the teacher. Also, it's cool that you and Anthony hang out so much, but I can't believe he didn't come see me too. You are *not* allowed to replace me as his best friend."

Silvia smiled. "He'd already promised Cameron that he'd stop by the antique shop. But don't worry, you aren't forgotten. We talked about you too."

"Oh yeah?" Omar grinned at this. "How come?"

"We were trying to figure out open relationships."

He scrunched up his face. "Why does everyone keep mentioning about that?"

"Natural curiosity," Silvia ventured. "Is it something that you don't want people to know about?"

"You've lost me."

That was all the confirmation she needed. "When I talked to Whitney at the party, she mentioned that you guys are in an open relationship."

Omar scoffed. "We definitely aren't! She was probably joking."

"I don't think so." Silvia hesitated, not wanting to hurt him again, even by proxy, but he deserved to know the truth. "The only reason I asked Whitney about it is because I saw her kiss David."

"What?" Omar cried. "Are you for real?" His face became drawn when he saw her nod. "Aww man! What the hell?"

"Sorry," Silvia said, wincing in sympathy. "For whatever reason, she really seems to believe that's the arrangement between you two."

Omar looked skyward and groaned. "When we first started dating, I remember her saying something about how she wanted to stay open. I thought she meant open-*minded*. As in kinky sexual positions and stuff."

Silvia stifled her own amusement, which wasn't difficult, because he looked miserable.

"Why would she even want to kiss David?" Omar asked before touching his upper lip. "Is it the mustache? Should I grow one too?"

"Please don't."

"There has to be a reason this keeps happening to me." His eyes met hers and were filled with desperation. "Am I a bad kisser? Is that why? Be honest!"

"You're a great kisser," she assured him. "I was only curious about girls when I… You know. As for Whitney, it sounds like a misunderstanding."

"David though? Is he hotter than me? I wonder how many other guys she's kissed since we've been together." Omar's shoulders slumped. "I can't believe I'm in an open relationship."

"Is that such a bad thing?" she hinted.

He turned an incredulous expression on her. "What's good about it?"

"This." Silvia planted her lips firmly on his, his brown eyes widening in surprise. Then they became half-lidded as he got over the shock. She felt his fingers weave through her hair as he kissed her back. Which felt so good that she had to stifle a whimper. She'd missed this. No… She'd missed *him*.

Omar pulled away suddenly. "We shouldn't have done that."

Silvia tilted her head. "Why not? Whitney isn't going to be angry."

"She might be in an open relationship, but *I'm* not!"

"Too bad," Silvia murmured, feeling rejected.

Omar noticed. "I liked that," he said hurriedly. "Actually, I freaking loved it, because…" He shook his head and swallowed. "Because it's you," he finished with a sheepish smile. "Maybe I'm an old-fashioned kind of guy or something, I don't know. I just want to be with one person at a time. And they should actually want to be with me."

Silvia felt another pang of guilt. At the beginning of their relationship, she'd been uncertain about him. Had he picked up on that? Because she didn't feel that way now. If he wasn't with Whitney… "I guess you should talk to her about it all."

"Yeah," Omar said, shaking his head as if overwhelmed. "Sounds like I better before she goes around kissing everyone else. I mean… *David?* Are you sure it's not the mustache?"

"I can only speak for myself," Silvia told him. "I like you just the way you are."

"Thanks," he said. "God, I'm an idiot!"

"You aren't." Silvia took his hand and squeezed it. "Don't ever say that again, okay?" She let go of him to point in the direction of his work. "I wouldn't even know where to begin with that weird thing you were sitting in front of with all the buttons and sliders."

"You mean my editing board?" he asked with a toothy grin. "I could teach you how. It's simple."

"I doubt that. Just think what you managed to do without it. You're smart, Omar. And talented. That's why you don't need a mustache."

He laughed. "Oh man… I'm glad you were the one to tell me."

"Really? I was worried about that. Because of what happened when we were together."

"That's what makes it easier," he said. "We've got—I dunno—an intimate relationship. Even though we're not together anymore. We've been through some stuff."

"We have," Silvia said fondly. "I'm glad we can still talk like this."

"Me too."

Omar turned his head toward her and seemed to search her eyes. For permission to kiss her again? Or was he simply thinking about all the memories they'd made? Silvia wasn't sure, but she was more than happy to stare back.

"Hey!" Omar said, hopping to his feet. "I've been working on some new tricks. Wanna see?"

"Sure!"

Silvia leaned back, often laughing as he flopped around on his skateboard while trying to impress her. Whenever he messed up, he'd grin at her, like he didn't feel the slightest bit embarrassed. She was grateful for the easy comfort that remained between them. Even though, just beneath it, was a certain kind of tension, like tightly wound guitar strings that she longed to feel him pluck.

Mindy waited next to a ratty old sports car in the school parking lot and tried to look anywhere but at the awkward conversation happening just feet away.

"But I love the library!" Ricky was saying. "Why can't I come with you guys?"

She glanced over in time to see Diego's crossed arms tighten. "Because you always get this look on your face when I'm around Mindy, like she's a threat."

"What? I don't do that! Do I?"

The question was directed at her. "I really don't mind—" she began.

"I do," Diego grunted. "Get a ride with someone else or walk. I'll see you in the morning."

Ricky sighed before stomping off. As he passed her, a smile borne of politeness reluctantly tugged one of his cheeks before it disappeared. She smiled back, feeling nothing but sympathy for him.

"That was a little harsh," Mindy said when they were alone.

"It was the truth," Diego said. "Get in."

"Only because you asked nicely," she teased.

Diego held up an index finger, instructing her to wait. Then he walked around the car to open the door for her. "Is that nice enough?" he asked.

"Yes," she replied, fighting off a blush. "Thank you."

Mindy got into the car, thinking of the last time she'd been inside it. She had fled from Troy after their dreadful date and had been shaking from nerves and the cold when she'd run into Diego at a gas station. He'd been so sweet to her that night, in his own gruff way. Mindy could still remember how safe and warm she'd felt by the time he dropped her off.

"Ready?" Diego asked once behind the wheel.

"Yes," she said. "Just… take it easy. It's a short drive. There's no sense in speeding."

"If you say so," Diego replied with a smirk.

He was careful when leaving the parking lot. Mindy watched his big strong hand shift gears and wondered what his touch would feel like.

"Do you drive much?" Diego asked, having noticed her stare.

"No," she admitted. "I prefer to walk, so I can be alone with my thoughts. Even when it's cold outside. I like seeing the seasons change."

"What sort of stuff do you think about?"

"People and places." Mindy stared out the window as the world went racing by. "My favorite memories and my biggest dreams. The things that happened that day or what I read, so I can let it all sink in."

"I do that," Diego said to her surprise. "When I'm working at the garage and it's just me, I don't need music on. I like it quiet, so I can figure everything out."

"Like what?"

His hand clenched on the steering wheel, the knuckles turning white. "The past."

"You mean your dad?" she asked, feeling an ache in her heart.

"Yeah," he said hoarsely. "He was cool. I try to keep my memories of him fresh. Even dumb stuff like the sound of his voice, you know? That can be easy to forget when you go years without hearing it." He glanced over at her self-consciously. "You ever lose anyone?"

"Just a grandma," Mindy said, "which you expect to happen. Oh, and Miss Missy Kitty."

He cocked an eyebrow. "Who?"

"She was my cat when I was a little girl," Mindy explained. "I had her almost my entire life."

"Are you the one who named her?" Diego asked, sounding amused.

"Yes! Don't laugh, it's a great name. Very fun to say. Miss Missy Kitty. Try it."

"I don't want to."

"Please! Just once. It'll make you smile."

"Miss Missy Kitty," Diego grumbled without an ounce of joy.

Mindy laughed in delight. "Now say, 'I miss my messy Miss Missy Kitty.'"

"Never," Diego said, but his lips twitched a moment later, like he was tempted to try.

She probably could have goaded him into it if they hadn't arrived at their destination. After they had parked, Mindy skipped gleefully toward the entrance. There was no better place on the entire planet than the William S. Burroughs Public Library. She was always awed when going inside. Spiral staircases led up to the open second floor, tall windows filling the large space with natural light, like some sort of cathedral dedicated to reading. Hidden among the seemingly endless shelves of books were cozy nooks, art installations, and other little surprises that she enjoyed discovering. Mindy could barely contain her enthusiasm.

"Have you been here before?" she asked.

Diego shrugged. "Maybe when I was a little kid."

"Oh my gosh, so much has changed. Let me give you a tour!"

Diego humored her as Mindy led him here and there on impulse, unable to focus on any aspect for long before thinking of something else she wanted him to see.

"And out here is the meditation garden!" she said when they reached the back of the building.

Through the glass doors, cobblestones circled a fountain, a

number of paths diverging from this to wind between lush green foliage. Mindy knew that walking down them would lead past sculptures, bird feeders, a butterfly garden, and benches in leafy alcoves.

"I've never actually seen anyone meditating," she said, "although I guess it's hard to tell. I mostly go out there to read."

"Then we better find our next book," Diego said.

She turned to him. "What did you have in mind?"

"I liked *Lord of the Flies.*"

"Aren't you excited that it was chosen as our next production?"

"Yeah," Diego said. "When I play Jack Merridew, it's gonna give people nightmares."

"Or maybe you'll be Ralph." She could imagine him playing the charismatic leader.

"Not a chance in hell. Anyway, do you know of any other books about how bad the world sucks?"

Mindy thought for a moment. "Have you read *The Catcher in the Rye*?" She was pleased when he shook his head. Behind the main character's judgmental agonizing was a wounded sort of sensitivity. Maybe the story would be good for him.

Before long, they had a copy of the book and went outside to explore the garden, eventually settling down in a small circular offshoot that walled in a single bench. She sat at the very end, making room for him, but his arm still brushed against hers as they got settled.

"I've been looking forward to this," Diego said, a happy expression attempting to manifest before it faltered. "The sound of your voice is—" He turned his head away as if searching for the right word. Then he looked her right in the eye with an intensity that was electric. "—beautiful."

"I'm glad," she said, having to swallow just to get the words out. "I like reading to you too."

"Why?" He scrutinized her. "How come you showed up at that shithole this summer?"

The response inside of her was emotional rather than verbal, but she knew what she was supposed to say. "Ricky asked me to check in on you while he was gone."

"Like a pet sitter? I'm not his dog. Or even his Mister Man Kitty."

Mindy laughed, grateful that the tension was given an outlet. "He really loves you," she said, a sigh coming unbidden, because she adored the idea of two boys caring about each other so deeply. At least, that had been her impression. "Don't you love him?"

Diego averted his eyes. "Does it matter?"

"Yes! I'd give anything for someone to love me like that! Why throw it away just because he got cold feet about leaving town? That's a lot to ask of anyone."

"Is it?" he asked.

"On such short notice? Yes!"

Diego shrugged. "Love is overrated. You aren't missing anything."

She stared at him aghast. "How can you even say that?"

"Because," he said, taking her hand and curling the fingers until they formed a fist. "Love is like a dagger pressing against your heart." His hand wrapped around her wrist as he brought the butt of her fist to his chest with a thump. "And I mean *way* past all the muscle and bone. You have to imagine the tip of the blade piercing your heart. It fucking hurts, but the messed-up thing is that you don't even care. When you burn yourself, you jerk away without thinking about it, but no matter how bad love hurts, you don't want it to stop. And you can't get away from that pain, even when you want to let go."

Which is exactly what he did, releasing her wrist, but she didn't pull away as if burned. Mindy spread her hand over his chest. "Why does it have to be a dagger? Can't it be healing like, I don't know… a bandage or something nice?"

Diego laughed and shook his head. "This isn't one of your dumb romance novels."

"Hey!" she said, yanking her hand away. "Have you ever *read* a romance novel?"

"No," he admitted.

"Well just wait. You got to choose this book. I'll choose the next one."

"Oh great," he said, but with the hint of a smile. Diego searched her face. "So there wasn't another reason you volunteered?"

Mindy pressed her lips together. She hadn't volunteered at the detention center for Ricky's sake alone. She had cared about

Diego ever since they were kids, especially once he'd lost his father. But she worried he'd interpret that as pity, when really, it went so much deeper. "Who knows," she said at last. "I guess some people just have too much free time."

Diego grinned so wide that his dimples showed.

She was stunned by just how handsome he was when unbridled joy chased the clouds away. Mindy felt a flush spread over her body and up to her face, so she hurriedly opened the book and bowed her head, hoping to hide her red cheeks. "Are you ready?" she asked.

Diego leaned back, one of his arms ending up behind her as he gripped the bench. "Yeah. I'm ready."

Mindy cleared her throat. "Okay. Here we go!"

Anthony liked pep rallies. Mostly because it meant getting to skip a class, but this year was even better. He was on the bleachers in the school's gymnasium, surrounded by friends. Silvia and Mindy were sitting in the row in front of him. Next to them, Whitney and David were engaged in a thumb wrestling tournament. Cameron was on his left, his hand on Anthony's knee as a finger absentmindedly stroked his bare skin through a slash in his jeans. On his right, Ricky had finally given up searching the crowds for Diego and turned his attention to the spectacle. So far they had listened to Principal Preckwinkle give a speech and introduce the new vice principal. After they were both done talking, the cheerleaders rushed out to the center of the floor before launching into an energetic routine. Throughout all of it, a crinkle of concern had remained behind the frames of Ricky's glasses. He was hopelessly love-sick. Anthony talked to him about it on the phone almost every night, always wishing that he could give better advice, but Diego was a tough nut to crack.

"Oh my god," Ricky said, the tension finally leaving his face. "Is that Omar?"

Anthony returned his attention to the court. The cheerleaders had retreated to the sidelines, replaced by a small group of students dressed entirely in black. All of them were girls... except for Omar. His best friend was grinning with his hands on his hips, not seeming the slightest bit self-conscious about the tights he wore. A heavy beat began to play over the PA speakers, followed by a snarling synthetic riff. Culture Beat's "Mr. Vain" had been a pervasive hit all summer. The dance team played off the lyrics. Omar began moving his feet while eying the girls who circled him, his hips shaking like some sort of mating dance. He was the titular Mr. Vain, it would seem.

Sylvia turned around with a questioning expression. Anthony could only shrug. He knew that Omar was in the dance elective, of course, but he'd played this one close to his chest. They watched as he kept approaching different girls, who would each use a dance move to escape him. Keisha became his main target. She walked backward to avoid Omar while shaking her index finger left to right. Just when it seemed like he'd catch up to her, a pair of twins stepped in his way, the Song sisters locking arms and twirling to drive him back again. The other dancers spun in a circle that closed around him. When they dispersed, Omar's back was on the floor, his chest heaving from exertion. The other dancers turned away, each extending a flat palm in his direction, just as the music ended. Anthony was the first to start clapping.

"Wow!" Ricky breathed while doing the same. "And I thought Diego could dance!"

"Hands off," Anthony replied. "That one's mine."

Sylvia raised her eyebrows at this. "I'll fight you for him!"

They both looked at Whitney, who was shimmying her shoulders while murmuring the lyrics under her breath, unaware or unconcerned with the potential competition. Sylvia met his gaze again and laughed. Anthony's smile faltered when he glanced at Cameron and noticed the furrowed brow.

"I'm kidding," Anthony assured him while leaning close. "I've already got mine."

"Don't you forget it," Cameron murmured close to his lips before smooching him.

The football players took the floor next, tossing a ball to each other and doing other stunts he didn't pay attention to. Anthony was more interested in watching Omar and Keisha walk up the bleacher steps to join them. Keisha sat next to Mindy after they gave each other a high five. Omar shuffled past Silvia so he could reach Whitney, who clapped and hugged him. After releasing her, Omar looked at him with an upward nod. "How'd I do?"

"You were great!" Anthony enthused.

"Yeah?" Omar grinned. Then, while still standing, he turned sideways to show off his profile. "Hey, do you think these tights make my package look bigger or smaller?"

Anthony's eyes eagerly responded to the invitation, rushing straight down to the black fabric that gripped a considerable bulge.

"Why don't you ask your girlfriend?" Cameron grumbled.

"Anthony's been staring at it his whole life," Omar replied. "He's practically an expert."

"I think it looks smaller," Ricky interjected.

"How much bigger could it get?" Anthony asked incredulously.

"I'll tell you later," Ricky stage whispered.

Cameron rolled his eyes in exasperation. "I hate you both."

Anthony laughed. "Sit down, Omar. Please."

His best friend shrugged and plopped down. Then he began singing along with Whitney, but luckily, the noise generated by the football team mostly drowned them out. Anthony took his boyfriend's hand and leaned closed to murmur, "You need your own straight boy. They're fun, but no replacement for the real thing."

This seemed to appease Cameron, who squeezed his hand in return.

The football team finished their routine, getting much more applause, even though they'd mostly just tossed a ball around while music played. There was no accounting for taste.

Once the floor was clear again, the vice principal walked out holding a microphone. "You've seen some of what this school has to offer," LaVern said, "but the potential remains for so much more. The job of the school council is to steer you safely toward the brightest future. A president is elected each year to lead them. We only have two candidates this year, which is disappointing. I encourage you all to enroll in the student government elective I teach and take an active role in shaping the decisions that will directly affect you and your peers. For now, please give your full attention to the available candidates so you can cast an informed vote."

A small mousey girl took the mic and cleared her throat. "Hi everyone! My name is Jenny Keats, and I'd like to be your student council president. One of the first things I would do is to bring back the yearly science fair. Mr. Johnson used to run it before he passed away, which is why we didn't have one last year. I think it would be a nice tribute to his memory."

The crowd babbled, but not in response. People had already lost interest and were talking to each other instead of listening.

"I'd also meet with the school board regularly to be your voice," Jenny continued, "so that your needs are represented. Personally, I think we should focus on the lack of funding for science and art programs. I'll also work closely with the rest of the school council to make sure that—"

"Shut up!" someone shouted, resulting in a rumble of laughter from the crowd.

"—to make sure that we achieve our goals," Jenny continued, her face flushed now. "If you give me your vote, together we can make Pride High an even better place, not only for us, but for the next generation of students who will be here after we've graduated. Thank you."

A smattering of polite applause followed this speech as conversation continued unabated.

"You're in student government," Anthony said, leaning forward to address Silvia. "How come you're not running for president?"

"You just saw why!" she responded with a grimace.

"Tough crowd," Mindy said, nodding in agreement.

"All right everyone," a new voice said, sounding strong and confident. "Just chill out for a minute, because this is going to be good."

Anthony saw an expression of horror appear on Mindy's face, which probably mirrored his own, because he too recognized that voice. They both turned their attention to the center of the court, where a tall red-head was grinning at the audience.

"My name is Troy Mitchell, and I've got a serious question for you: How would you guys like an extra class each day? Don't be shy. Let's hear it!"

The crowd began to boo.

Troy's grin got wider. "I'm with you, but what if you could do whatever you wanted in that class? And it made all your other classes shorter? We learn stuff all day long, one period after another. When do we have time to actually take it all in, you know? So here's what I propose. Every class you have now gets ten minutes shorter." This already resulted in applause, Troy having to wave people into silence. "We're gonna take all that extra time and make a seventh period. You can use it to study or close your eyes to recharge. Whatever you need. Lunch break isn't enough, right? And it's really hard to concentrate afterwards, so why not have an extra period just to unwind? Do you like the sound of that?"

The crowd around them erupted in cheers.

"Awesome," Troy said when his audience calmed down again. "Just vote for me. I'll do that and way more. I'm going to protect you guys too. From what you ask? School uniforms. That's right, it's gonna happen. All because of how some people abuse the dress code."

Anthony's stomach sank. What the hell was he playing at? Cameron's hand tightened around his but he couldn't look away from Troy, who was now waving a copy of the student handbook above his head.

"Not only will you have to wear a uniform, but get this… Even makeup won't be allowed. Ladies, do you *like* wearing makeup? Make some noise if you do." He got the response he wanted, even more so when he added, "All my bros out there, do *you* like it when they wear makeup? Yeah, that's what I thought!"

Anthony couldn't believe this was allowed to go on! He could see LaVern having an animated discussion with Principal Preckwinkle, who shook her head briskly before taking a step away from the other woman.

"I've got you covered," Troy said. "It's an easy fix. We just need to make the dress code more specific. Girls will be allowed to wear what they want, as long as their skirts don't get too short. Sorry guys, but we've gotta compromise. And hey, you'll be able to wear whatever you want too… except for makeup and dresses. Are you okay with that?"

More cheering followed, deep and masculine, but Anthony barely heard it over the blood pounding in his ears. He shot to his feet, no longer able to take it. "What's wrong with wearing makeup?" he shouted.

"Oh great!" Troy oriented on him. "We have a question from the audience. The problem with a guy wearing makeup," he said, waving the handbook around again, "is that it's distracting. Speaking of which, take a look at that hair everyone. We better add that to the list because yikes! What an eyesore. Do you get yours done at the same place as the Joker?"

Laughter erupted, Anthony's face burning for a different reason now. He sat down, unable to bear the brunt of all those unkind stares. Cameron took his hand again, but it was hard to feel comforted when so many people were still looking at him with amusement.

"This is why we need a new dress code," Troy continued, "so *some* people don't ruin it for the rest of us. Now let's talk about those dances. Why can't homecoming be as big as prom? And why can't prom be even bigger? Like the biggest it's ever been!"

More cheers. Were people fooled so easily? Anthony was beginning to lose his faith in humanity.

Cameron shook off his hand and shot to his feet.

"Where are you going?" Anthony asked.

His boyfriend didn't seem to hear. Cameron hustled down the bleacher steps, their friends looking to Anthony for an explanation, but he could only shrug. Cameron cut across the gym floor, making a beeline for Principal Preckwinkle, probably to insist she end this farce. Anthony felt a surge of affection for him. The gesture was nice, even though it was too late to change anything. Troy had finished his speech. Most of the audience was cheering.

"We can't let him become president," Mindy said, turning to them. "He's horrible!"

"I don't think he has any real competition," Ricky grumbled.

"Don't be so sure," Keisha drawled, nodding toward the center of the gym. "Look."

The vice principal was standing there with Cameron at her side. LaVern raised the mic. "We have a last-minute entry," she said. "Nothing is more important in an election than having quality choices, so please, give him your attention."

The audience quieted down, mostly out of curiosity. Anthony held his breath in anticipation. And fear. He didn't want his boyfriend to be the subject of anyone's ridicule.

"Hey," Cameron said into the mic, reverb cutting him off. "I'm uh…" He cleared his throat and tried again. "I guess you can say I'm up here because…" His head slowly turned as he took in the rows of students, who were already beginning to lose patience. Cameron swallowed, seeming to panic. Then his eyes met Anthony's and regained their focus. "Think about the worst day of school you ever had," he said, his voice cutting through the chatter. "Doesn't matter what grade you were in. Think about the really bad times, because I bet they have one thing in common. Someone else made you feel that way. Maybe because of the way you dress, or how your voice sounds. Maybe it was your weight or acne or your teeth. Whatever the reason, it's not cool!" He pointed a trembling hand toward the bleachers. "Whoever told Jenny to shut up during her speech, that was wrong! So is making fun of someone's hair color or anything else about them. Instead of worrying about how we're allowed to dress, or how big the next dance is going to be, we should be thinking about who we are as people! Like the tradition of tripping freshmen on their way into the building on their first day of school. Did it happen to you? Or your little brother or sister? Because that can be even worse, when you see someone you love getting hurt." Cameron's eyes met his again as he placed a hand over his chest. "That's what I stand for. We need new rules that come down hard on bullying. And we clearly can't rely on the adults to take care of our problems for us. If they could stop any of it, I like to believe they would have already." He shot an accusing glare at Principal Preckwinkle. "So no, I'm not going to make a bunch of ridiculous promises that aren't going to come true. There won't be a new free period. There's already a study break elective. You can vote for the sort of people who want to dictate *their* version of how you should dress, but that's just another uniform. So if you've laid awake at night, dreading the next day of school, because you were scared of getting picked on... If you've worried about fitting in or being accepted… If you're tired of being judged and simply want to be who you really are, then vote for me, and I'll try. I can't promise results, but I swear I'll do everything in my power to make this school the sort of place where you feel safe and accepted."

Cameron dropped his arm to his side, the mic tightly gripped in his hand.

"What's your name?" Keisha shouted. "So we can vote for you!"

"Oh. Right."

Anthony watched his boyfriend raise the mic again, his heart nearly bursting at the seams.

"My name is Cameron Huxley. I want to be your president, but mostly—" Blue eyes sought him out again. "—I just want you to feel loved."

Anthony jumped up and started clapping, his friends right there with him. They weren't alone. Troy had gotten bigger cheers, but the people who were clapping now did so with a sort of determination that felt much more substantial.

"You're really *really* lucky," Ricky said to him.

Anthony swallowed against rising emotion. "Yeah, I really am." He was desperate to rejoin his boyfriend so he could reciprocate some of that love, but Cameron was on the sidelines talking to LaVern. As for Principal Preckwinkle…

"I hope the *unnecessary* delay didn't set us back too long," she said, checking her watch. "Please stand and join the choir in our school song."

Anthony stood, but only so he could continue to watch Cameron, who was deep in conversation with the vice principal. The pep rally concluded when the song ended.

"We need to have a campaign meeting," Silvia said.

"Yes!" Mindy clapped her hands in excitement. "Cameron can beat Troy, I know it!"

Anthony had nearly forgotten about his red-headed nemesis, his heart too filled with affection to harbor any anger or resentment.

"Your boyfriend is super cool," Omar said, offering him an elbow bump. "You know he's got my vote."

"Same here," Whitney said. "Although I *do* like Jenny. Science is hot!"

"Can I be his campaign manager?" Ricky asked.

"I'd be willing to raise some funds to support him," Keisha offered.

"Thanks everyone," Anthony said. "I'll um… Talk to him and get back to you."

He was already discovering the pressures of being a first lady! Or whatever.

His friends dispersed along with everybody else. Anthony sat on the bleachers and waited until his boyfriend was free. Then he stood and met him halfway.

"Good news, and bad news," Cameron said. "What do you want first?"

"You," Anthony replied before kissing him.

Cameron laughed and pulled away. "Careful! This could affect the whole election. I'll be under constant scrutiny from now on." His expression became somber. "I can't be in our creative writing elective anymore. LaVern wants me in her student government class. That way, even if I don't win, I'll be on the student council. That's the bad news. The good news is that I'm going to fight this, no matter what it takes. I won't let anyone get in the way of who you want to be. Okay?"

Anthony shook his head, but only in a failed attempt to stop his tears from breaking free. "I'm happy," he said when wiping them away. "I just love you so much."

"I love you too,' Cameron replied, taking his hand.

They walked together toward the exit, the intensity of Anthony's feelings for him stronger than ever, because his boyfriend was so much more than a presidential hopeful. Cameron was his prince.

Gomez Auto Repair was officially closed for the evening, most of the mechanics having left. Diego had already changed out of his coveralls. Normally he would go upstairs to the apartment he shared with his mother and crack open a beer, and he wanted to… but he worried that another home-cooked meal awaited him. Or maybe there wouldn't be any food at all. He honestly couldn't decide which would be worse, so he watched the sun sink lower on the horizon while smoking a joint.

The rear entrance to the garage squeaked open. Jasper walked out and noticed him standing there.

"It's Friday night," the old man said, hobbling over. "Don't you have plans?"

"You're looking at 'em," Diego replied, holding out the joint.

Jasper took it from him, pulling deeply before he breathed out. Then he handed it back. "Gotta be real with ya, son," he said. "Getting old has its perks, but I'd trade them all to be your age again and chasin' tail."

Diego grinned. "Yeah, well… You're not dead yet and I've got time to burn, so neither one of us is out of the game."

"Is there somebody?" Jasper pried.

Diego thought about Ricky. And Mindy. "I dunno. It's complicated."

"Good! That's how it should be at your age."

Diego took another hit. He offered the joint again while exhaling.

Jasper shook his head. "I've still gotta make it home. I won't be coming in tomorrow. We're nice and caught up anyway, especially with you back. The shop hasn't run this smooth in ages. I think your momma finally got a grip on the business end of things."

"Don't talk about my mom that way," Diego grumbled.

Jasper cracked a smile.

Diego did too, but it was short-lived, because he still didn't know what to think of her recent about-face. "Do you think people can change?" he asked.

Jasper turned toward the sun, as if seeking the answer there, his dark skin edged with orange light as he thought. "When I listen to Ella Fitzgerald here in the garage, the big space makes it sound like I'm seeing her perform at a jazz club. When I listen to her in the car, I feel like I'm in a black and white movie. And when I play her music at home, it's like she's there on the couch with me and in the mood for love."

"Hell yeah," Diego said.

"My point is," Jasper continued, "it's all the same song. Only the circumstances change."

Diego thought about it. "So you think people are like that? Because I'm *definitely* not who I used to be."

"Could've fooled me," Jasper said with a grin, his crooked teeth the color of aged ivory. "You were always a strong-headed boy with a nose for trouble. And smart as a whip."

"Me?" Diego said with a snort. "You're getting senile."

"Maybe so, but I knew you when you were still in diapers and watched you grow up. You aren't so different, no matter what you think. And there's more than one kind of smarts. Remember that the next time a doctor brings his Benz in and doesn't know the difference between a carburetor and a fuel injection system."

Diego nodded, his heart still troubled. "What about my dad?" he asked. "You knew him pretty well."

"Mostly through workin' here, although we did have a drink on occasion, and he'd always invite me to stay for dinner when he fired up the grill."

"Do you think he changed?" Diego asked, having to force the words out, because he didn't let himself talk about this very often. "He never seemed depressed or anything to me, but then all of the sudden, he blows his goddamn brains out."

Jasper's face tightened with remembered pain. "Could be that he had it in him somewhere. My sister was that way, happy as a lark most of the time, but every so often, she'd get down and nothin' anybody did would help. They'd probably give her pills these days, but back then..." He shrugged. "All I know is that your daddy didn't seem himself for a good week or so, like something had hit him hard. That can happen. I saw plenty of it during the second World War. And when my sons came back from Vietnam. They were still my boys, but they'd been put through the wringer. It can take a long time to recover from that sort of thing. Not all soldiers do, but given enough time…" He shrugged and peered at him. "Are you doin' all right?"

"Yeah," Diego said. "You?"

"I'll be a lot better when I get off my feet. I'll see you on Monday, son."

Diego swallowed. He liked it when Jasper called him that. "See ya."

He watched Jasper walk to his car and drive away. Diego took a few more hits, his stomach grumbling. Time to go inside for dinner. Except he didn't. Not yet. Diego continued to stand there, wondering if his mother would revert back to the woman she used to be. And if so… The circumstances were changing, sure, but he didn't know if he could ever be that carefree kid again. Or whoever he would have become, had circumstances been different. That unknowable other-self almost frightened him. Diego tried to imagine a happier life before he gave up and stubbed out the joint. He didn't have much patience for wistful fantasies. Diego was more interested in learning the truth, and only one person knew it. His mother. He doubted he'd get anything out of her tonight or anytime soon, but he'd settle for something to eat. With that in mind, he pushed away from the wall and went upstairs, already bracing himself for disappointment.

CHAPTER 13
SEPTEMBER 11ᵀᴴ, 1993

"I'm heading out!"

Cameron hovered in the living room entryway, watching his father's reaction. His dad barely glanced up from his newspaper. Even then he didn't say anything. That's how it had been all summer, chilly despite the heat. Cameron's mother was much more responsive.

"Are you going to your campaign meeting?" Brenda asked, setting aside her magazine.

"Yeah," he replied with a grin. "Don't be surprised if you see me on the evening news."

The newspaper ruffled before Trevor disappeared behind it completely. Cameron tried his best not to show how much that stung, since he knew his mother would rise to his defense, resulting in another argument. Instead he hid the pain behind a smile and said goodbye before heading for the front door.

"I love you!" Brenda called after him.

"I love you too!" he shouted.

His father's feelings remained a mystery, which was probably for the best. Their relationship had only gotten worse since Cameron came out. He didn't regret it though. Not one bit. Especially when he saw the old Dodge idling in the driveway. He ran toward the car, jumped in, and kissed the driver with such force that Anthony was practically shoved against the window.

"The feeling is mutual," his boyfriend said with a demure smile before kissing him back. "Ready to go?"

"Yeah," Cameron said. "Get me out of here."

He didn't mean anything by his choice of words, although they might have been percolating in his subconscious.

Anthony picked up on them regardless. "Is everything okay?"

Cameron took a deep breath before answering. "I don't know. Usually when my dad is in town, I'm not worried about my mom as much. At least, that's how it used to be." He'd searched the house recently and found more empty bottles. "Right now they barely say a thing to each other. Even at the dinner table. I was the only one making conversation last night."

"Sorry," Anthony said with a sympathetic wince.

"Thanks. I figure it's better than them arguing, but it's weird how quiet the house has been, even with him there."

"Maybe it's a good thing," Anthony suggested. "It sounds like they're getting along better at least."

"I guess so." He put the subject out of mind, exchanging one set of anxieties for another. "So what exactly is going to happen at this meeting?"

"Knowing our friends?" Anthony asked with a smirk. "We'll probably goof off for most of it."

"Don't be so sure," Cameron said. "Ricky is taking his role as campaign manager very seriously. He called me three different times last night, asking all sorts of personal questions."

Anthony snorted. "He's always had a thing for you."

"That was last year," Cameron said dismissively.

"If you say so." Anthony wore a playful smile, so it was hard to figure out if he was kidding or not.

They were pulling into the parking lot of Archie's Pizza Pi anyway. His pulse picked up and he felt the prickle of nervous sweat. What had he signed up for? Cameron didn't regret what he'd done. After asking Principal Preckwinkle to intervene during the pep rally, and witnessing her complete lack of empathy, he'd followed the impulses of his heart. But now there were so many expectations to contend with. Cameron didn't have a political bone in his body. And yet, here he was.

"Hi there!" the greeter said when they entered. "Are you here for lunch or just to play games?"

"There you are!" Ricky said, husting toward them. "Thanks, Shirley. I'll take things from here."

"No problem," the greeter responded, clearly perplexed by his behavior.

"Do you two know each other?" Cameron asked.

"Not really," Ricky said with a titter. "As your campaign manager, it's my job to know who everyone is. She could have been a voter. Turns out she graduated last year, but I *did* get her to agree to vote for you in theory."

"It's a start," Anthony murmured. "Where are the others?"

"Right this way," Ricky said, beckoning them to follow.

They were led through an area filled with dining tables and an indoor playground. Past this was a large space packed with video games, and beyond, the backroom where people their age usually convened.

"Everyone is here already," Ricky said over the sound of screeching children and video game explosions.

"Who exactly?" Cameron asked.

Ricky flashed him a bashful smile. "Your campaign team!"

A large table in the back corner was occupied with most of his friends. Mindy, Silvia, Keisha, and David all stood up and began clapping. Ricky and Anthony joined them. Cameron's face was already burning, but in a good way, because it was nice to have so much support.

"I asked Diego to join us," Ricky said, pulling out a chair for him. "He said there's nothing more fake than politics. But he *did* agree to vote for you."

"That's more than I would have expected," Anthony said, sitting down next to him as everyone else got settled too.

"I wonder if Diego would be my personal Secret Service agent," Cameron joked.

"That would be so hot!" Ricky breathed. "I'd love to see him in a suit."

"Hey, you're just in time!" a new voice said.

Cameron turned and saw Omar, dressed in a work uniform while carrying an extra-large pizza in both arms. "This is our ultimate party pie," he said with a toothy grin. "Gimme a hand, Anthony. This thing is so heavy you could crush a small child with it. Which would be really bad for business."

"I've got it!" Ricky said, leaping up to help.

Once the pizza had landed, Omar took out a pad of paper and a pen. "What do you want to drink, my man?"

Cameron eyed the huge pizza and all the drinks already on the table. Was he expected to pay for it all? "Um… A water is fine."

Omar made a face. "Don't be shy. It's on the house."

"Really? Thanks. Sprite would be nice."

"You got it." Omar winked at Anthony. "I know what you like. I'll be right back."

"Everyone dig in," Ricky said, still standing. "Some of you are here on your lunch break, so feel free to eat while we talk, but make sure to listen." He checked an open notepad on the table. "Here's the timeline we're dealing with: Each candidate has two weeks to campaign. Voting takes place on the twenty-seventh and twenty-eighth. We'll find out who the winner is on the thirtieth." Ricky looked at Cameron. "Don't worry about writing any of this down. I bought you a calendar."

That was one of the things he had asked on the phone last night, wanting to know if he had one already.

"Okay," Ricky said, addressing the group again. "We might have two weeks to campaign, but we need to come up with a plan right now so we can use all that time. Any ideas?"

Mindy raised her hand. "What if we do a smear campaign? We can tell people what a horrible person Troy is."

"Like starting a rumor?" David asked.

"Sort of," Mindy said, "except it would be the truth. He's a total sleazeball."

"Do you really want to explain to people how you know that?" Silvia asked.

Mindy made a face before her shoulders slumped. "Not really."

"That's okay," Cameron said. "I'd rather win because I deserve to, not because he doesn't."

Keisha gestured to him. "Which is exactly the sort of thing that gets my vote. Cameron has integrity. We just need to get him in front of the whole school, so everyone can hear him talk some more."

"I don't know about that," he said hurriedly.

"I could write an article about you for the paper," Anthony suggested.

"Can you make it an interview?" Keisha asked.

"Sure!"

"That's a great idea!" Ricky said. "When's the next issue out?"

Anthony grimaced. "At the end of the month."

"That's cutting it close," Ricky said, "but it's still a good idea. What else can we do?"

"I can try casting a spell," David suggested sheepishly.

"Yes!" Whitney said. "Do it!"

Ricky looked to Cameron. He shrugged.

"Okay," his campaign manager said. "So far we have an interview in the school paper and a magic spell. I feel like we need more."

"In the student government class," Silvia said, "the teacher talked about how most people have a key issue they vote on."

"Good point." Ricky made a note. "We should figure out what this campaign stands for."

"I'm against bullying," Cameron said. "And I agree with Jenny Keats about the funding issues. Ms. Deville, the theater teacher, has mentioned that before. She says the sports teams get plenty of financial support and that the art department receives almost nothing."

"It's true," Mindy said. "Most of the costumes are made from things that people bring from home or buy themselves."

"It's messed up," Cameron agreed. "But that's Jenny's campaign platform, not mine."

"She doesn't stand a chance," Keisha said. "If I was her and lost the election—which she will—I'd take comfort knowing that some of what I wanted was still possible because of you."

"How about censorship?" Anthony asked. "Like my coming-out article last year."

Preckwinkle had blocked it from being included in the school newspaper, so Anthony distributed it himself and had *still* gotten into trouble.

"I'm against it, of course," he answered. "We deserve to have a voice in our own school."

"You're a defender!" Ricky said, sounding excited. "That's your angle. You'll defend our right to be who we are and to say what we think."

Cameron blanched. "How am I supposed to do all that?"

"You won't be on your own," Silvia said. "The student council supports the president."

Anthony nodded in approval. "I like it."

"So do I," David agreed. "I'm tired of being made fun of, just because I worship the old gods."

He was so weird. Then again, they all were. That's what unified them. "Okay," Cameron said, nodding slowly. "I can get behind that message."

"But how do we get the message out?" Keisha asked. "Real-world campaigns blow most of their money on advertising."

They thought in silence until Whitney raised her hand, a half-eaten pizza slice in the other. "Why does free food taste so much better?"

David laughed. "It's true!"

"That's it!" Mindy said, snapping her fingers. "Do you guys remember Kandi Jackson?"

"Why does that name sound familiar?" Silvia asked.

"She was student council president during our freshman year," Mindy explained. "She passed out fun-sized candy bars to everyone with a note attached that said 'Vote for Kandi!' So I did, even though I had no idea who she was, because you know… free candy!"

"I remember that," Keisha said. "I voted for her because she was black and a woman, but the Snickers bar didn't hurt."

The others laughed. Ricky was beaming. "This is great!" he said. "We can include the campaign promises on the attached note. Maybe our slogan could be 'Vote for the sweetest guy in school.'"

Anthony shot Cameron a knowing look that he did his best to ignore.

"We'll have to work on that," he said tactfully.

"But with the interview in the newspaper and all of us dishing out sugar highs," Ricky said, "I think we have a real chance!"

They continued talking about it as they ate. Omar stopped by briefly to check on them. Whitney followed him when he went. Silvia and Dave had to get back to their own jobs. Keisha and Mindy had plans. Soon only Ricky and Anthony were sitting at the table with him.

"Oh yeah!" Ricky said, digging around in his backpack before handing him a wall calendar. "Here you go. I've already written the important dates inside."

"Cross-eyed kittens?" Cameron asked, reading the front cover.

"Have you ever tried to buy a calendar this late in the year?" Ricky retorted. "It was slim pickings. And it only cost two dollars."

"Thank you," Cameron said while staring at the photo of a visually challenged Siamese cat. "I kind of love it."

"I thought you would," Ricky said, his cheeks flushing happily.

"Is the meeting over?" Omar walked over to them with a crooked grin. "You know what they say, all work and no play makes Jack a dull boy. God I love that movie!" His cupped hands were filled with arcade tokens that he poured onto the table.

"Enjoy yourselves. I've got a birthday to film, so you probably won't see me again."

"What happened to Whitney?" Anthony asked.

"She joined the party. It's a family from India. Their English isn't great, but for whatever reason, they took to her right away. You're welcome to try cozying up to them for some free cake."

"That's okay," Anthony said. "Have fun."

"I always do."

Ricky scooped up some of the tokens. "Let's go play, you guys!"

"We'll catch up with you," Anthony promised.

Once they were finally alone, Cameron took a deep breath and exhaled. "That wasn't as bad as I was expecting."

Anthony pushed a slice of pizza toward him, as if wanting him to eat. "What were you worried about?"

"I don't know," Cameron said, struggling to articulate his feelings. "There's so much going on already. Charles wants to get the antique store ready to open before the holidays, and my mom is... Well, you know. And then there's this special guy that I like to spend lots and lots of time with."

Anthony smiled. "I don't mean to add to your burden," he said, "but I do have something you can write in your new calendar."

Cameron ventured a guess. "Your birthday?"

"No, it's much closer than that. Next month, in fact."

"Oh! You mean *my* birthday?"

Anthony bit his bottom lip and shook his head before dropping another hint. "Cast your mind back... an entire year."

Cameron was about to take a bite, but the slice of pizza stopped halfway to his mouth. "Oh my god... Is that how long we've been together?"

"Yeah," Anthony said. "Our first date was on October tenth. I kept a receipt."

"In case you wanted to return me?"

Anthony laughed. "I think it's a little late for that. And even if it wasn't, I wouldn't trade you for the world."

Cameron's heart did a little dance. "We have to celebrate! And come up with something amazing to do. I guess we could recreate that first date or... What about gifts? Are we giving each other something? You should have told me sooner!"

"Don't worry," Anthony assured him. "I only want to spend time with you. Although I *do* have something to give you. And that I want you to give me." He made sure his voice was laced with innuendo. "We've tried before but never succeeded."

"You mean…" Cameron's eyebrows shot up. "For real?"

"If you're ready."

"Oh yeah," Cameron said with a guffaw. "I'm definitely ready."

Anthony nodded at the still-hovering slice of pizza. "Then you better build up your strength."

Cameron took a bite and then another, chewing happily while his boyfriend watched and laughed.

Omar felt cool grass tickle his stomach where his shirt had ridden up, but he ignored it, intent on getting his shot. Through the camcorder viewfinder, a pair of guinea pigs were angled toward each other while eyeing him, their mouths working up and down as they chewed.

"Aren't they adorable?" Whitney cried, stretching out on the grass next to him.

She reached out to take one of them, rolling over on her back so she could cradle the guinea pig to her chest. Which ruined the shot, but that was nothing new. The whole reason Omar had started filming in the first place was to capture footage of Whitney fussing over her pets, since he thought it was adorable. He'd barely pointed the camera at her before she ran inside the house and returned with two miniature hats for the guinea pigs to wear—a sombrero and a beret. That had inspired him to film a sketch about two tourists who were trying to ask each other for directions, neither realizing that the other wasn't a native, but Whitney had other plans or had simply forgotten.

Omar gave up, setting aside the camcorder so he could mimic his girlfriend's behavior. Soon he was lying on his back next to her with a furry little critter on his chest.

"I love them so much," Whitney said with a sigh. "Don't you?"

"Yeah," Omar replied. "They're really cool. My sister is allergic to all kinds of stuff, so we never had any pets."

"I've had so many!" Whitney said. "Cats, dogs, gerbils, parakeets, rats… But I'd really like a raccoon."

"Is that a thing?"

"I don't know."

She was incredibly strange. Omar really liked her. Except…

He thought of that kiss again. The one Silvia had given him after work, which he still felt bad about. Mostly because of all the feelings that went with it.

"Hey," he said, lifting the guinea pig off his chest so he could sit up. "Can we talk about something?"

"Sure!"

Whitney sat up and placed her guinea pig in the grass between them, so he did the same.

"We're in an open relationship, right?" he asked.

Between work, school, and his own embarrassment, he hadn't brought up the subject until now.

"Yes!" Whitney said, gleefully baring her teeth. "Isn't it fun?"

He thought of Silvia again. "I mean… Kind of. I heard that you kissed David."

She nodded, her expression sympathetic. "He was so sad. I knew it would cheer him up."

Omar blinked. "Sad about what?"

"Because he lost his best friend."

Right. Dave had crossed over to the enemy. Omar couldn't remember the last time he'd hung out with either of them outside of school. So much had changed since junior high. He would try to include David in more things. "So that's the only reason you kissed him?"

Whitney shook her head. "I wanted to know what his mustache felt like."

"What did you think?"

She crinkled her nose. "Too scratchy!"

That was a relief. Omar was pretty sure he could grow one, but facial hair was more his dad's thing. And besides, Silvia had told him not to. Which didn't really matter except… "There's something I have to tell you," he said, licking dry lips. "Silvia kissed me the other day. And I kissed her back."

"Aww!" Whitney said. "That's so nice!"

"I'm not sure that it is. I mean, it felt good. Like, *really* good but…" He shook his head. "I didn't actually know that we're in an open relationship."

Whitney pulled back. "Really?"

"Yeah."

"That's hilarious! I went out with a guy for like… two weeks without knowing it. We were standing right next to the doors at school when he asked me out, and I thought he meant it literally, because it was raining and a really fun idea. And it's not like he made any moves after that. Drop some hints, you know?"

"Yeah," Omar said, feeling relieved. "But why do you want an open relationship anyway? What's wrong with just one person?"

Whitney shrugged. "I wanted to try something new. And also, what's wrong with more than one person? It's one of those rules that's a rule because it's a rule. But how come?"

"Because people don't like getting cheated on."

"But it *wouldn't* be cheating."

He thought about it. "I suppose that's true. So you've already been in a committed relationship and didn't like it?"

"I did," she said. "But you don't know if you like bubble gum ice cream until you try it." Whitney got to her feet and scooped up the guinea pigs. "We better go back inside. Too much sun is bad for them."

"Okay," he said.

He watched her smooch them repeatedly on their heads, alternating between each as they went into the house. Even if they weren't dating, he'd still want to be her friend. Which was different from how he felt about Silvia. They hadn't seen each other much over the summer. Maybe because when they were together, he felt all sorts of tension that was impossible to ignore. Slipping into their old roles was always tempting, because he really liked who he'd been while with her. Like he was better somehow. Part of a whole. That wasn't the case with Whitney. She was too much of a free spirit—a beautiful bird that you could admire while it was singing in your tree, but you knew it was only a matter of time before it flew away.

"Here's the thing," Omar said when they were in her bedroom. "I don't think I'm into open relationships. I've got nothing against them, but it's not for me. I'd rather just be committed to one person. If that doesn't work for you…" His pulse started beating rapidly. He hadn't planned on breaking up with her. "I'm not mad or anything. It's just what I need."

Whitney was quiet when putting the guinea pigs back in their cage. Then she stood and turned around. "I guess I've never been in an open relationship that became committed," she said, walking close. "That's new too."

"Yeah," he said, not sure what she was getting at.

Whitney smiled. "Great! Let's celebrate by getting naked!"

"Wait," he said, scrambling to keep up. His hormones tackled his brain, bringing it down. "Did you say naked?"

"Uh-huh."

Whitney was already stripping out of her clothes. Not slowly or seductively. She was throwing them off with reckless abandon so he hurried to do the same.

"You mean *everything*?" he asked, seconds before her panties hit the floor. "Holy shit! You weren't kidding!"

Whitney scowled and wagged a finger. "I'm a *very* serious person." Then she laughed and started doing a little dance.

Omar tugged on his boxers, which met resistance because he was already pointing at the ceiling. He managed to get them off and had absolutely no idea what to do with himself.

"Hooray!" Whitney said, staring at him openly.

"Have you um… seen many?" he asked.

"This is number three," she said. "And it's already my favorite."

He put his hands on his hips and grinned. "That's great! I uh… I really like what I'm seeing too."

Her skin was creamy white and she was blond all over, which was hot. Whitney's breasts were a lot smaller than Silvia's, but he didn't mind. All boobs were great! "So more kissing?" he asked, wanting to know what options were on the table.

"Yes!" Whitney said. "I'm going to kiss it!"

She sprang over to him and ended up on her knees, Omar forgetting to breathe until he got dizzy. He hadn't done anything like this since… No no no! He shouldn't be thinking about Silvia. Especially now that he was in a committed relationship. Which hadn't been his intent, but it was hard to argue with the results. Although he *could* be doing this with Silvia instead. If she was still interested.

Whitney leaned back and looked up at him. "I want you to rub it against me," she said before touching herself. "Down here. But you can't put it in no matter what!"

"I will literally do anything you say," Omar assured her.

Whitney scooted back, stretching herself out on the carpet, and soon became the only thing he was capable of thinking about.

— — —

Ricky didn't know what to think anymore. He'd ridden to school with Diego each morning for an entire week but struggled to understand where they stood. Or maybe he was just in denial. He could always count on Diego to be honest, although getting him to talk about his feelings took effort. And tact.

Ricky eased into it slowly today, already knowing where he wanted them to end up. He brought up a jail-break movie he'd watched over the weekend before asking, "What was your cell like? Was it as bad as you see on TV?"

"Basically, yeah," Diego said, his attention on the road. "Aside from bunk beds, there's a metal sink and toilet, and a couple of plastic storage bins that you can put your stuff in if you don't mind it getting searched or stolen."

"Sounds fun," Ricky said. "The bunk beds especially."

A smile tugged at Diego's cheek. "Oh yeah, it was a blast."

"Did you take the top or the bottom bunk?"

Diego shot him a glance, one of his thick eyebrows raised critically. "What do you think?"

Ricky grinned in response. "I don't have to. I know from experience."

"Damn straight," Diego said with a satisfied sniff.

"I guess it's safer up there at night too," Ricky said. "You said the guy in your cell was kind of crazy."

"Yeah. He'd always wake up in the middle of the night thrashing and kicking, like he'd just gotten jumped by a bunch of guys. The dude would fall right out of his bed and hit the floor. You'd think that would wake him up but..." Diego shrugged. "I don't know what did that to him and didn't want to find out, so we never talked much."

Ricky swallowed. He'd spent the summer in a sunny guest room that overlooked the Seattle skyline. "Weren't you scared?"

"Nah. Everyone in there is broken in some way. It's the guys who want to run the place that you have to watch out for. They learned not to mess with me."

Not before he'd gotten a black eye and a split lip. Ricky wished more than ever that he could turn back time. He'd have to settle for revisiting the past. His stomach clenched with anxiety as they parked outside the school. There was one question he hadn't allowed himself to ask, but he was going to now.

"Did you get any of my letters?"

"Yeah." Diego shut off the engine, his head remaining bowed. "I got them."

Ricky swallowed. "How come you never wrote me back?"

Diego took a deep breath. Then he exhaled. "I tried."

"What do you mean?"

Ricky stared at a clenching jaw and a furrowed brow, but he couldn't kiss away the anger like he used to. Not anymore. When it became obvious that he wasn't going to get an answer, he unbuckled his seatbelt and leaned to the side to pull out a folded piece of paper.

"I never sent this one," Ricky said. "But I can read it to you now. If you want."

Diego turned his head away, still unresponsive, but at least he didn't tell him not to.

Ricky unfolded the letter, his hands trembling as he began to read. "Diego. I know I messed up. Really bad. Maybe you're trying to punish me. I figure that's why I haven't heard from you. If so, that's okay, because I get it now. You've always told me the truth. When we were on the way to El Paso and I got scared, you said that we could last forever and—" His voice squeaked but he forced himself to go on, "—and that I had to make a choice. I did, but it was the wrong one. I see that now. So please… When you're free again and I'm back in Kansas, give me that choice one more time, and I swear that I won't let you down again. I'll miss my family and my friends because I love them—" His chin began to tremble. "—but I love you too, more than anyone I've ever loved before, and that will be enough. You're all I need. Give me one more chance and I swear…" Ricky set the letter in his lap and took Diego's hand so he could address him directly. "I swear I'll run away with you this time."

Diego shifted, his head lolling against the seatback. Those cinnamon eyes took in the tears coursing down Ricky's cheeks, but his expression remained impassive.

"Doesn't it hurt?" Ricky asked in disbelief. "I feel like my heart is breaking!"

Diego's beefy shoulders rose and fell. "Yeah. But I've felt like that for a long time now."

"Even when we were together?"

"You made it easy to forget. But the pain never really goes away. That's life."

"It doesn't have to be," Ricky croaked.

Diego's attention moved down to the letter resting in his lap. "How come you never sent it?"

"Because I wasn't sure if I could keep my promise."

"And now?"

Ricky took a deep shuddering breath and looked toward the school. All his friends were in there. He was excited about Cameron's campaign and wanted to support him. He loved talking with Anthony on the phone and getting to hang out in Omar's bedroom. Lately he even enjoyed stopping by the record store to say hello to Silvia. But there was one thing missing from his life that he needed back. No matter what it cost.

"Try me," he said defiantly.

Diego stared into his eyes, Ricky holding his gaze to show him that he wasn't kidding. The prospect of moving to Texas terrified him, but not nearly as much as losing the man he loved.

"I can't go to El Paso," Diego said at last.

"What?"

"Not anymore. Or at least… not yet."

Ricky shook his head in confusion. "How come?"

"There's some stuff here I need to figure out first."

"Like what?"

Diego pulled his hand away. "It's complicated."

"Okay, but what about us?"

Diego merely shook his head.

Ricky's chin trembled again as more tears broke loose. "Can't we start over? Please!"

Diego's gaze was sympathetic, his touch gentle when he used a thick thumb to wipe away one of Ricky's tears. "You'll get used to the pain," he said. "It becomes part of you."

"It's not pain," he cried. "It's love!"

Diego's brow furrowed. "There's no difference."

He was wrong! Diego couldn't see that now, but Ricky would find a way of showing him. They had gotten there before. He was certain they could find their way back. For now, he climbed over the center console so he could wrap his arms around Diego's neck, his head resting against a strong chest that shielded a wounded heart, and dotted the T-shirt with his tears.

CHAPTER 14
SEPTEMBER 14ᵀᴴ, 1993

Mindy bent over to touch her toes, rolling her eyes once she had, because beginning the day with PE was the *furthest* thing from ideal. Pretty soon they would start doing jumping jacks, which would make her sweat and defeat the purpose of the shower she'd taken this morning. Sometimes she wished she'd joined the swim team during her freshman year, but Mindy didn't enjoy competition. She just had to make it a little longer. Seniors didn't have to take PE so—

The PA system chimed to get their attention. Mindy welcomed the break. Although it was unusual for a Tuesday. Announcements were normally made on Monday mornings.

"Pardon the interruption," Principal Preckwinkle said with an accent that always reminded her of Rose from *The Golden Girls*. "The front office would like to remind students that the distribution of outside food and drink is strictly prohibited. Any food brought into the building must be for personal consumption only. Lunches from home are acceptable, as are a very *limited* number of snacks kept in your locker or backpack until needed. Anyone distributing food, including candy, will face disciplinary consequences. Thank you."

Puzzled murmurs filled the gymnasium. Mindy's mouth hung open. She'd stayed up late last night working on the candy hand-outs for the campaign. They'd settled on using Dum Dums—lollipops that came in a variety of flavors and were sure to be popular. Keisha had bought twenty bags and paid for the attached notes to be printed on quality paper. Now all that money would go to waste!

Mindy couldn't believe it. This was no coincidence. The day before they had planned to hand out candy, it just happened to get banned? She was relieved when reporting to the creative writing class she shared with Anthony and David, eager to get their opinion.

"Someone told Principal Preckwinkle," Anthony said. "Troy, probably. He tried the same thing when tattling on me for wearing makeup."

"How could he have known?" Mindy asked. "None of us would have told them our plans."

Anthony shook his head. David shrugged, his face red, like he too was angry. The class began soon after. Mindy didn't have a chance to discuss it again until lunch. She marched into the courtyard, her attention trained on Cameron.

"I know," he said when he saw her indignant expression. "We really put effort into it too. The tips of my fingers are still sore from tying so many knots, and that's coming from a carpenter."

"You've got nothing on a mechanic," Diego rumbled, holding out his hand. "You feel those calluses?"

"Yeah," Cameron said after poking one experimentally.

"Well I don't," Diego said. "It's like I'm wearing gloves year-round."

"This is serious, you guys," Mindy said. "What are we going to do?"

"Maybe find somewhere else to pass them out?" Cameron suggested. "Worse-case scenario, we give them away to trick-or-treaters next month. That way, in about ten years, I'll win the vote by a landslide." He looked to Keisha. "Sorry about the money you spent. I'll pay you back."

Keisha raised a palm and shook her head. "I'm all about a good cause. Besides, this is merely a bump in the road. Our wagon is still rollin' along. We simply need to adjust our strategy. How about an emergency campaign meeting?"

"Yes!" Mindy said. "I'll let everyone know."

"Or I could just beat the shit out of Troy," Diego suggested. "That would be way easier."

"Tempting," Mindy said, "but I'd rather see the whole school kick his butt by voting against him."

She'd been so convinced that was possible. Now she wasn't as certain. Mindy spent the rest of the day trying to organize a time and a place to meet. They settled on the parking lot, since many of her friends had after-school jobs to get to. She was so focused on arranging it all that she didn't have time to come up with an alternative plan. When the final bell rang at the end of the day, she went to the flagpole outside the school and counted heads until everyone had shown up.

"Don't panic," Ricky said, taking the lead. "This is just a small setback. Any ideas on how we can course correct?"

"I dunno," Omar said, "but whatever we come up with has to be something that Preckwinkle can't ban."

"That's a valid point," Anthony said. "Before we make a new plan, we should plug the leak."

"Yes!" Mindy said. "Think about anyone you might have told about our idea. We're not here to play the blame game, but loose lips sink ships."

"I told my mom," Whitney said helpfully. "Then we got the munchies and baked a cake together."

"Unless she's friends with Troy," Silvia said, "I think we can eliminate her as a suspect."

"I don't remember talking about it to anyone except you guys," Anthony said.

The others nodded. All except David. He was blushing again like before.

"What about you?" she prompted.

Everyone looked at him.

David squirmed. "I might have told Dave," he said at last.

"What?" Omar cried. "He's a traitor! Why would you do that?"

"Because he came over to my house on Sunday. He was acting like we were friends again and I..." David swallowed, his expression miserable. "I missed him."

"That's so messed up!" Mindy said, putting her hand on his shoulder.

"Yeah, it is," Anthony agreed. "Forget about him. You've got real friends."

"You're not mad at me?" David asked.

"Nah man," Omar said. "We're cool. And now we *know* he can't be trusted."

"That takes care of the leak," Cameron said. "So what's our new plan going to be?"

Mindy thought about it, different pieces rearranging themselves in her mind. "What if we do the same thing to them?"

"What do you mean?" Silvia asked.

"I might know somebody who can find out what they're planning. We'll go on the offensive!"

Omar grinned. "That would be rad!"

"Who do you know?" Anthony asked.

"I need to check with them first. Everyone has places they need to be, so leave it with me. Oh! Think about how we can spread the word about Cameron, because we'll still need to figure that out, no matter what."

Everyone dispersed, Mindy staying close to one person in particular until they were alone. She grabbed Keisha's hand.

"Hey!" she said.

"Hay is for horses," Keisha drawled. "When are you gonna visit the farm again and go riding with me?"

"Soon!" she said. "But you have work to do first."

Keisha averted her gaze. "What do you mean?"

"You know exactly what I mean! Do you really think you can hide what's going on from your best friend? Like on Saturday, when you were 'too busy' to hang out and couldn't explain why. I've seen the faces that you and Hope make at each other from across the cafeteria."

Keisha's eyes widened in concern. "Am I that obvious?"

"Only to me. So will you?"

Keisha swallowed. "You want me to find out what they're planning."

"Why not?"

"Because I don't use people like that."

"Then be honest about why you're asking her," Mindy said. "If she likes you, then she can't be all that bad."

"Are you saying that there's hope for Hope?"

"You're such a dork," Mindy said. "And yes. Even if she's not willing to tell you, maybe you'll pick up on something useful. Will you do it?"

Keisha sighed theatrically. "That means I'll have to see her again."

"Poor baby. Just be sure to leave an evening free for me, because you owe me some details."

"Do you really want to hear about the sort of things we get up to?"

"Have you seen the books I read?" Mindy asked. "I'm starved of romance, so yes, I want to know everything."

"Be careful what you wish for," Keisha replied playfully. Then she nodded. "I'll see what I can do."

"You're the best!"

Mindy had a spring in her step as they walked across the parking lot. Troy could pull all the dirty tricks he wanted, but she wasn't going to let him win. Not without one hell of a fight.

— — —

Anthony already had a smile on his face when he walked into his newspaper elective, but it got even bigger when he saw Mr. Finnegan sitting at his desk. His teacher often arrived mere seconds before the bell rang, so he took this as a sign that fate was in his favor.

"Hey," Anthony said breathlessly. "I know it's last-minute, but I have an idea that would be great for this month's issue of *The Lion's Pride Post*."

"Very well." Mr. Finnegan leaned back. "Let's hear your pitch."

"With the student council election coming up, I thought it would be a good idea to interview one of the candidates, so people can get to know him better."

"Hmm," Mr. Finnegan said. "Just one of them?"

Anthony hesitated. "Yeah. Cameron decided to run at the last minute, so he deserves a chance to tell people what he really stands for."

"He did a commendable job of that already," Mr. Finnegan said, "but you're right. This is exactly the sort of topic the school newspaper should cover. We'll have to push a couple of stories back until next month…" He frowned in thought before nodding. "I think we can manage, especially if I assign a reporter to interview each candidate. Let's talk about it again at the end of class."

Anthony didn't like that Troy would benefit from his idea, but Cameron would easily outshine him. He felt upbeat for the remainder of the period, jotting down a list of questions he planned to ask, including some heavy hitters. *How will your presidency affect the daily lives of every student? What policies will you institute that you're confident will be more than just another unfulfilled campaign promise?* He already knew that his boyfriend would have great answers, no matter what was thrown at him, because Mr. Finnegan was right: Cameron had nailed his pep rally speech without having prepared for it. This time he'd have the benefit of getting to choose and revise his words to perfection. They could work on it each day until the deadline, if need be.

With only a few minutes left in the class, Mr. Finnegan called him and two others to his desk. "Anthony. Steven. Tonya. A moment please."

He got there first, turning an eager smile on the other two, and patiently listened to Mr. Finnegan explain the assignment. Each of them would interview one of the candidates, asking the same five questions that they would need to agree on beforehand.

"Steven, I'd like you to interview Jenny Keats. Tonya, you'll interview Cameron Huxley. Anthony—"

His stomach sank as he opened his mouth, wanting to interrupt, because Mr. Finnegan had clearly misunderstood his intent.

"—you'll interview Troy Mitchell. I'd like each of you to come up with a list of potential questions tonight. We'll whittle them down to our chosen five tomorrow." The bell rang. "I'm looking forward to seeing what you come up with."

The others gathered their things and went. Anthony grabbed his backpack but didn't leave. He waited until they were alone before approaching Mr. Finnegan.

"I was hoping to interview Cameron," he said.

"I'm sure you were," his teacher responded, "and I can understand why you would want to, but I'm too concerned about bias."

"I'd be fair," Anthony promised. "I mean, yeah, I love him, but I can set that aside for the interview."

Mr. Finnegan stood and stretched. "When you approached me at the beginning of class, what were you really hoping for?"

Anthony shook his head in confusion. "Exactly what I said. I want Cameron to have a chance to express himself."

"And what did you want the end result to be?"

"For him to win the election," Anthony said with a shrug, "but like I said, I can leave my bias behind."

Mr. Finnegan nodded, as if in understanding. "I believe you can. Regardless, it's important to recognize that journalism isn't a tool to further your own agenda. Are you familiar with William Randolf Hearst?"

Anthony thought about it, remembering a test that he'd crammed for the previous semester. "He owned *The New York Times*."

"Close," Mr. Finnegan said. "His newspaper was *The New York Journal*. Hearst engaged in yellow journalism, which is a subject we haven't covered in this class yet, but we will. In the simplest terms, he relied on sensationalism, even though his causes would be viewed by many today as just. Some say that public support for the Spanish-American War was fueled in great part by the outrage his newspaper was so skilled in inciting. Some even called it The Journal's War. The topic is too nuanced to go into now, but I hope it demonstrates what a powerful influence journalism can have on American politics. So while I truly believe you can set aside your bias for Cameron enough to complete this assignment, as your editor, I feel your relationship to the candidate makes you an inappropriate choice to interview him."

Anthony considered his point. "I can respect that," he said, "but the truth is, I'm *way* more biased when it comes to Troy. There's a lot of bad blood there. To say the least. So I shouldn't interview him either."

"That's excellent critical thinking," Mr. Finnegan said. "You never fail to impress me, Anthony. That's why, as your teacher rather than your editor, I want you to interview Troy. The temptation to take down someone you dislike can be much harder to resist than wanting to help someone you love. I know you're up for the challenge. Use this opportunity to understand Troy better. Even if your feelings about him don't change, you'll walk away with the advantage." Mr. Finnegan nodded to the clock on the wall. "Better get to your next class."

Anthony took a deep breath. Part of him wanted to stomp his feet and refuse to interview anyone at all. But he also didn't want to let Mr. Finnegan down. Even if it meant having to spend time with someone he despised. "I'll do my best," he said.

Mr. Finnegan smiled. "Of that, I have no doubt."

Cameron pushed his way inside Sweet Tea Antiques, feeling a burst of relief as the door shut behind him. He smiled when considering the shop's interior, which had really come together. Three aisles separated rows of rustic tables, stately wardrobes, designer chairs, and so much more. He'd worked on many of the pieces himself and had repeatedly admired the rest. While here, he felt transported to the past, his problems reduced to a twinkling possibility on the far horizon of the future.

"There he is!" Charles said, approaching from the back of the shop. "The future president of the student council!"

Okay, so maybe his troubles were closer here than he cared to realize. At this rate, they wouldn't have to come up with a new plan, because everyone seemed to know about his campaign already.

"I only wish I'd been there to hear your speech," Charles continued. "Lover Boy did his best to paraphrase, and my heart was indeed moved, but I would have liked to have seen your boyfriend's face."

Lover Boy was his pet name for Mr. Finnegan. Cameron had only recently learned that his dearest friend was married to the journalism teacher at their school. The relationship was kept secret out of necessity, and no wonder, considering how hard it was to be an openly gay student. A teacher didn't stand a chance. The only downside is that Cameron's worlds weren't as separate as before, making it harder to escape.

"Anthony was pleased," Charles said, misinterpreting the reason for his silence. "Wasn't he?"

"Yeah," Cameron assured him. "We're in a really good place now. I'm just a little stressed about it all."

"I can imagine," Charles said with a sympathetic expression. "Being under public scrutiny is never easy."

"Sorry," he said hurriedly. For all appearances, Charles was a woman. He had long blond hair, expertly applied makeup, and currently wore a light blue sundress with frilly shoulders. "I guess you've gotten used to that sort of thing."

Charles cocked his head. "Oh, you mean the dead-eyed stares that small town yokels give me? Honey, I *live* for those! At the end of the day, I'm a passing distraction for most and an inspiration to the rest. No, I was referring to the pressures of the campaign trail. We compare ourselves to others enough as it is, but when the general public is invited to do the same…" He shuddered theatrically.

"It's not so bad," Cameron said, not wanting to come across like he felt sorry for himself, "but I wouldn't mind getting away from it all. Just for a little while."

"Then I have the perfect distraction. I've decided to rent some of this space to other dealers."

Cameron perked up. "Really?"

"Yes. Not everyone shares our passion for furniture. Customers will come looking for more, and we don't want to disappoint them. We'll be able to open much sooner this way, although it means moving some inventory to the back. Do you mind putting those muscles to work?"

"Not at all!" Cameron said eagerly.

Physical exercise always helped him iron out his thoughts.

For the next hour, he worked with Charles to rearrange the store, creating empty spaces for dealers to fill.

"It'll be interesting to see what people bring," he said when they had finished and returned to the front.

"I admit that was part of the appeal," Charles said. "I'll be able to shop and tend to the store at the same time. Best of all, we'll get first dibs on everything that comes through the doors."

"You're a genius!"

"I do try," Charles said, retreating behind the counter. He picked up a makeup compact and began patting his face with a powder puff. When he noticed Cameron watching, the compact snapped shut before he smiled. "Lover Boy promised to stop by," he explained.

Cameron continued to stare, his throat tight, maybe because of the question that had been stuck there for the past couple of weeks. "What were you like when you were my age?"

"Oh my goodness," Charles said, as if facing a very long voyage. "Let's see… How old are you again?"

"I'll be seventeen soon."

"Well, when I was your age, it was the sixties, which probably sounds more exciting than you're imagining. I didn't go to Woodstock or participate in any love-ins. I was a pimply-faced teenager who became obsessed with Star Trek because of the eyeshadow most of the cast wore, the men included. That planted a seed in my mind. And I had such a crush on William Shatner. What a dreamboat!" He must have noticed Cameron's puzzlement because he tried again. "I was still figuring out who I was meant to be. I saw tantalizing glimmers of it on television, or when watching movies like *Sunset Boulevard*—bless you Gloria Swanson—but the reality was much less glamorous. I would go to yard sales to buy women's clothing, claiming that I had a sister who became bedridden after a car accident. I borrowed that from *What Ever Happened to Baby Jane*. I wasn't very original, I'm afraid."

"But you already knew by then," Cameron pressed.

"To some degree," Charles said. "Yes."

He swallowed and finally asked the question that had been plaguing him. "Do you think Anthony might be the same as you?"

Charles didn't react as much as he'd expected. Like someone playing poker, the muscles of his face hardly moved at all. "Only he can answer that question. Is there a reason you're asking me instead of him?"

"I don't want to mess up and hurt his feelings," Cameron said.

"Oh." Charles seemed to relax. "Well, I *can* give you advice in that regard. If you do decide to broach the subject with Anthony, don't be surprised if he doesn't know the answer himself. Think how long it took you to come to terms with yourself and imagine how much more complicated it would have been, had your body and gender been a greater part of the equation. For me it was an ongoing discovery. Trying on women's clothing and learning to do my makeup was part of the process, but there was so much more to it than that. I weighed changing my name, for instance, before deciding that I like the sound of the one I have. And I had to make other decisions that, quite frankly, are nobody's business but my own. So had you asked me then or even ten years later, I might not have been sure how to answer. As much as we take comfort in labels that put everyone into easy-to-understand categories, they rarely communicate the complexity of who we actually are. You, for instance, are more than a carpenter or a teenager. At the moment, you're a high school student and Anthony's boyfriend. But all of those circumstances can change, and if they do, the labels would no longer apply. And yet, you would still be Cameron Huxley. Even that is merely a name. Who you truly are can't be defined by words. It can only be expressed by your actions." Charles shrugged. "That's my take anyway."

"You're amazing," Cameron breathed.

"Now *that's* a label I'm willing to wear," Charles said with a wink. "One last piece of advice: If you do ask Anthony about this subject, be prepared to answer the question he might not dare to ask."

"What's that?"

"If you would still feel the same way about him."

Cameron shifted to the other foot. "What if I'm not sure?"

"Then say as much. Respond to his truth with your own. What greater sign of respect can there be?" Charles looked toward the street and perked up. "Here he comes! How do I look?"

"Beautiful," Cameron said truthfully.

The bell above the door rang as Mr. Finnegan entered. He paused when noticing Cameron before nodding cordially.

"I better get going," Cameron said, not wanting to interfere with their private life. "Thanks for the pep talk."

"My pleasure, as always," Charles assured him.

"See you in school," Mr. Finnegan said warmly.

Cameron smiled and nodded. While slipping out the door, he glanced back just in time to see Mr. Finnegan leaning across the counter to kiss his wife. Cameron had a lot to figure out, but he knew love when he saw it, and nothing was more important to him.

CHAPTER 15
SEPTEMBER 17ᵀᴴ, 1993

Warm night air blew through the open window of Keisha's bedroom, sending goosebumps racing across her sweaty skin. She witnessed the same thing happen to Hope, her naked body on full display as they passed a joint back and forth. Inquisitive eyes were fixed seductively on her, the mysterious lights dancing within them rarely bound by words. Hope remained an enigma, despite two weeks of trysts. She didn't talk much. Keisha didn't mind that when she was in the mood to chase, but in moments like these, after they had sex, she found herself longing for a different type of intimacy.

Concerned that Hope's taciturn nature came from having a domineering sister, Keisha had decided to give her the chance to speak by holding her own tongue. So far it hadn't worked. Hope continued to study her with a probing gaze, her thoughts a mystery.

Keisha couldn't take it anymore. "How'd you learn to smoke?" she asked when passing back the joint.

"I dated a guy freshman year who couldn't stand cigarettes," Hope explained.

"Risking lung cancer to avoid kissing a boy?"

Hope shrugged. "Seemed like a good idea at the time. And it annoyed my sister. She was the one who pressured me into dating him. Besides, it's a useful skill." She held up the joint, examining it fondly. "Where do you get this stuff anyway?"

"I know a college student who sells it," she lied, for Diego's benefit as much as her own. They had taken a solemn vow not to tell anyone—without exception—about their secret arrangement. Keisha grew the cannabis on unused farmland that her parents had purchased and earmarked for future development. Before then, she really had bought it from a stoner who took classes at a local community college. She had intended to grow it only for her own use, but a green thumb ran in the family, and the crop had yielded much more than she could consume. These days, Diego helped her harvest and sell what she didn't need, netting them each a fair amount of cash.

"Can you hook me up with your dealer's number?" Hope asked.

"I can do better than that," Keisha said. "Be right back."

She ducked into her walk-in closet, unearthing a shoebox from beneath a pile. Inside, individual baggies were sealed in a glass jar to mute the scent. She took out an eighth. Keisha hesitated, normally cautious about such things. She had made Diego swear he would never sell to anyone at their school, since that was a recipe for disaster. Then again, if you couldn't trust someone who had just given you an earth-shattering orgasm, there was something very wrong with the world.

"Here you go," she said, tossing the eighth to Hope, who caught it deftly. "I bought too much last time. My guy was going on vacation, and I didn't want to run out."

"I can keep this?" Hope asked.

"Yeah," Keisha said, accepting the joint when it was passed back to her. "Just be careful. It creeps up on you. Speaking of which… Why don't you spend the night?"

Hope smiled at the suggestion. "Ready for another round?"

"I wouldn't mind," Keisha said, "but it's the time spent together that I'm more interested in. You never stick around for long."

Hope's gaze moved to the clock, her athletic body tensing. "My curfew is eleven."

"Which is why you should stay the night."

Hope shook her head. "Faith will want to know who I was with. Actually, I should probably get going. She won't be out with Troy much longer." She noticed the expression on Keisha's face. "It's nothing personal."

"Oh, I understand that," Keisha assured her. "It's the company your sister keeps that I find distasteful. What does she see in that wretched man?"

Hope shrugged. "I don't know. I think he's gross."

"I'm not too fond of him either," Keisha said, stubbing out the joint. "I assume he's the one who wrecked Cameron's campaign plans?"

Hope's eyes darted away, which was all the confirmation she needed.

"That was low of him," Keisha continued. "If he could win on his own merits, Troy wouldn't need to resort to dirty tricks."

"I bet he will, anyway," Hope said, sounding confident.

"Are you voting for him?"

"No way!"

"Then what makes you think he can win? Troy is new in school. He doesn't know many people."

Hope licked her lips before pressing them together.

"What?" Keisha pressed. "If he's got some sort of plan, I'd like to hear it."

"So you can tell your friends?" Hope asked.

Keisha nodded. "Yeah. That seems fair, considering what he did."

Hope turned to the window, even though it offered little more than murky darkness.

"Do you really want him to become president of the school council?"

Hope shook her head. "None of it really matters."

"So what's the harm in telling me?"

Hope finally met her gaze again. Then she shrugged. "You can't do anything about it anyway. Troy is throwing a big party at his house this weekend. All the popular kids are invited."

Keisha snorted. "That's it? He won't get enough votes. You're only talking about a dozen or so people."

"That's just the juniors," Hope replied, moving to the bed and sitting on the mattress. "He's inviting them from every grade. Freshmen, sophomores, seniors… All of them."

"Still won't be enough to turn the tide."

"Troy thinks it will be. He says most people are dumb sheep who believe what you say and do what they're told."

"A born politician," Keisha replied dryly. "So that's why he only invited the popular kids? He expects them to influence who the rest of us vote for?"

Hope nodded. "Do you think it'll work?"

Keisha thought about it and grudgingly concluded that it might. "Not if my friends come up with a better plan. Would it bother you if they did?"

Hope shook her head. "I don't like him." She reached for the pile of clothes on the floor, grabbing her shirt and sniffing it. Then she smiled. "I might start smoking pot in the nude from now on. No one will be able to smell it on me."

"Maybe not your clothes," Keisha said, "but it's on your skin.

Besides, you shouldn't drive so soon after getting high. Come take a shower with me."

Hope glanced at the clock and chewed her bottom lip. Keisha let her deliberate on her own, wanting to know where they stood. If she chose to rush home despite the risk, just to appease her sister…

Hope's eyes moved over Keisha's body. Then she tossed the shirt to the floor. "Think you can make me come again?" she asked.

Keisha offered her hand. "Only one way to find out."

The record store was full of teenagers. That wasn't so unusual for a Saturday, but Silvia worried her boss would discover that they were using his business as their campaign headquarters. Then again, Omar hadn't faced any consequences for offering the same service last week. Her attention returned to him, as it had repeatedly since her friends had filed in at the agreed-upon time. He was wearing the work-issued polo again with its muti-colored stripes, the fabric stretched across his pecs, which she swore had gotten bigger over the summer. His adam's apple bounced up and down at some joke that she didn't hear, but Silvia continued to watch him, liking how thick his neck was, and the way his dark hair curled flirtatiously around the back of it.

Omar finally noticed her stare, his grin shifting slightly, changing its meaning. His eyes sparkled before widening suddenly. Then he glanced self-consciously at Whitney, his gaze apologetic when it returned to her.

"Let's get down to business!" Ricky cried while clapping his hands.

Silvia checked the store and saw no customers. She went to the door to flip the sign indicating that she'd be back after her lunch break. By the time she returned to the group, Ricky had just finished reiterating what Keisha had told them both an hour earlier.

"So that's it," he said. "They're throwing a party for the cool kids. Pretty lame. I'm sure we can do better. Um… Anyone?"

Silence underscored just how few ideas they had until Anthony cleared his throat. "Let's do what they did to us and make sure their party gets canceled."

"No," Cameron said instantly. "I'm not stooping to the same lows. That would make us just as bad as them."

"Too much is on the line," Anthony shot back. "We can't let Troy become president."

"I agree," Cameron said patiently, "but I want to win this the right way. Ruining their plans won't win me any votes. I need to convince people that I'm the best choice."

"Does anyone know how to hack into the PA system?" Omar asked. "That would be a good way of getting your message out to everyone." He glanced at her, as if wanting to assess how impressed Silvia was with his idea, before he turned to Ricky. "Can you do it?"

"I'm not a hacker!" he spluttered.

"Neither am I," Cameron said. "I'm not sure how that system works, and it doesn't matter anyway. Preckwinkle would probably use it as an excuse to kick me out of the election. Like I said before, we have to keep everything on the level."

"Who cares what a bunch of snobs think anyway?" Mindy said. "Troy's plan is ridiculous."

"I don't know," David said. "If Angela Simmons came up to me and asked me to vote for someone, I probably would."

"Boys are so shallow," Mindy huffed.

Silvia arched an eyebrow. "What if it was Jacob Hammond who asked you instead?"

Mindy squirmed. "He *does* have the most adorable puppy-dog eyes."

Cameron sighed. "It's a good plan. The high school version of a celebrity endorsement."

"Whatever," Anthony said. "Troy and his friends can't possibly convince everyone."

"All they need is to win over more people than we do," Ricky said, his face drawn when he turned to Cameron. "As your campaign manager, I feel like I'm letting you down. Maybe I should resign."

Cameron fought down a smile. "Then I would too, because I can't think of anyone else I'd rather have." He looked at each of them in turn. "That goes for the rest of you too. Even if I lose, I'm really grateful to have your support. We're stronger together than we are apart."

"That's it!" Anthony said. "We outnumber the popular kids ten to one. Maybe even twenty to one."

"So we throw a party of our own!" Omar said, picking up on the idea. "And invite everyone who wasn't invited to *their* party."

He bumped elbows with Anthony, but their celebration seemed premature because, "That must be what—" Silvia said, "—five hundred people? Or a thousand?"

"Somewhere around that number," Mindy replied, sounding equally dubious.

"Even better," Omar said. "It'll be an absolutely *legendary* party of epic proportions!"

"Yes!" Whitney cried in excitement. "I love it!"

"But where?" Mindy pressed. "Your house isn't *that* big."

Omar began to wither before he rallied again. "Then we'll throw it at a park. Like we did for New Year's." His eyes darted over to meet hers again. She remembered standing with him on a hill, the Kansas City skyline twinkling in the distance, as he told Silvia for the first time that he loved her. She hadn't been ready then, but now…

"That many people will attract attention," Mindy said. "I'm pretty sure you'll need a permit."

"Unless it's on private property," Keisha said. "Like my farm."

"Would your parents be okay with that?" Cameron asked.

"They do love a shindig," Keisha said before looking doubtful. "Although we don't have much time left between now and the election."

"That's easy," Omar said with a lopsided grin. "My girl knows how to plan a party. You all were there for Ricky's. And that was like what… one day's notice or something?"

Whitney raised her palms and bowed her head, as if entering a state of deep concentration. They all held their breath until she straightened up suddenly. "You guys? I've totally got this!"

"We'll all pitch in," Omar said. "I'll invite the skaters. Anthony, you vibe with the goth kids more than the rest of us. Ask them. Mindy, you can take care of the nerds. I bet most of them have never even *been* to a party. Can you handle that?"

"Of course! Wait, why me?"

"Because you like to read."

"Ugh! You're such an—"

"That's a good start," Ricky quickly interjected, "but we need to figure out what we'll actually be *doing* at the party to further the campaign."

Silvia took out a sandwich, happy to let the deliberations

entertain her while she ate, since it really was her lunch break. Her input wasn't needed much as plans were finalized. Twenty minutes later, she unlocked the entrance and said goodbye to everyone as they left. All but Omar, who lingered behind.

"Do you have a second?" he asked when they were alone.

"Of course!" Silvia said, shutting the door and locking it again. She wasn't sure why exactly. Maybe it was all the looks they'd exchanged. The tension was thick in the air when she turned to face him.

"I've got some stuff I need to say," Omar began, his bronze skin flushed. "About us."

Silvia's pulse picked up. She nodded just as rapidly. "Okay."

"I kind of messed up this summer." He shook that dark mane of his. "No, I definitely did, because I only meant to take a break. I felt like I needed to heal or catch my breath or… I don't know. But I didn't mean to get distracted. Whitney just kind of happened, and it felt good, because we didn't have any baggage. But it turns out that I really like what me and you used to have together. Maybe not the problems, but wait, actually yeah, all that stuff too, because in a weird way, it made us even closer, you know?"

"Yes," Silvia said, wishing that she'd waited to eat that sandwich. What if she had mustard breath?

"So I talked to Whitney about the whole open relationship thing," Omar continued. "I told her that it's not for me."

He broke up with her! And had the decency to look sad about it, even though it cleared the way for them to be together again.

"She was really cool about everything," Omar said sheepishly. "So we're not in an open relationship anymore. We're committed. I just thought you should know in case you felt like kissing me again. Not that you'd want to! Right?"

Silvia pressed her lips together, only relenting when certain that she had control over the words that came out. Otherwise it would be all too easy to tell him the truth. She wanted to kiss him. Mustard breath be damned, she wanted to make the hell out with him! "I'm really happy for you," Silvia said carefully.

Omar pulled back, his expression wounded before he forced a smile. "Yeah," he said, sounding dejected. "Thanks. So um…" He swallowed and looked at the door. "I guess I should get back to work."

Silvia realized that she was standing in his way. She stepped aside.

Omar grabbed his skateboard from where he always leaned it against the wall. Although it wasn't there nearly as often these days.

"See you around," he said.

He had the door half-open before she pulled on his arm. "Wait!"

"What's up?" he said, turning toward her.

Silvia took the skateboard from him and set it aside. Then she wrapped her arms around his torso, squeezing him close. His hands slid around her back, one of them weaving into her hair. Omar held her while she breathed in his scent and remembered all the good times they'd had. The arguments and misunderstandings too, because he'd proven each time that he was a good person. Omar had never said anything unnecessarily cruel, even when she'd hurt him inadvertently. She only regretted all the time apart that could have been spent together. Of which there would be plenty more, now that he belonged to someone else. Sivia swallowed and forced herself to let go.

Omar's chest was heaving. He didn't give voice to whatever feelings overwhelmed him, but his smile was tinged with sorrow when he picked up his skateboard and left.

Anthony's stomach churned with nerves as he entered the school library. He scanned the room, his heart leaping when he saw Cameron speaking with Mr. Finnegan. Then he noticed a tall redhead talking to Jenny Keats—who had her arms crossed over her stomach—and felt just as vulnerable as she looked. He'd been dreading the interview with Troy. Enough that part of him was glad to finally get it over with.

Mr. Finnegan noticed their arrival and began directing everyone to their seats. Three different tables were dedicated to this task, one separating Anthony and his boyfriend, which was probably for the best. Otherwise he'd likely tune in to that conversation to escape the one he was about to engage in.

"You've gotta be kidding me," Troy said when Mr. Finnegan walked away.

"If it's a joke," Anthony replied as he got settled, "then it isn't very funny."

"So what's the plan here?" Troy asked. "You're going to trash me in the school newspaper so I lose the election?"

"Nope." Anthony opened his composition book and clicked his pen. "I'm going to ask you the same questions the other two candidates are getting and write down your answers. It's as simple as that."

Steely blue eyes studied him a moment before Troy shrugged. "All right. Do your worst."

Anthony checked the list of questions. "How would you sum up your campaign platform?"

Troy didn't need to think about his answer, which meant it was probably a canned response. "I want to advocate for the students. In most classes, we have to raise our hands to speak, and even then we have to stay on topic. When do we ever get to express our needs to the people in charge? I'm going to be the voice of the student body. Whatever they want, I'll make it happen."

Anthony wrote this down dutifully. Mr. Finnegan had told them that they were allowed to ask one follow-up question before moving on to the next. He wanted to press Troy on that promise, since he sure as hell wouldn't be representing Anthony's needs, but he tried to keep it neutral. "It's unlikely that everyone will agree on what should change," he said "What if the student body can't reach a consensus?"

"Easy," Troy said. "We'll go with what the majority wants. That's how elections work. So should politics."

Anthony documented this before moving on to the next question, which was one that he'd come up with. "How will your presidency affect the daily life of each student?"

"Everyone will be happier," Troy replied. "Everything is going to be really great. School can be cool. You'll see when I win the election."

Anthony took this down and glanced up, awaiting more. Troy stared back at him, seemingly finished.

"That's it?"

Troy sighed in annoyance. "People won't have to study as hard, because homework will be easier and there will be less of it. We'll get some real food in the cafeteria that doesn't taste like cardboard. Everything is gonna be *way* better than before. The best it's ever been!"

Compared to what? And according to whose standard? Troy wasn't actually saying anything of substance. Just a bunch of lofty promises that he couldn't possibly keep, because none of the issues were that simple. Anthony's hand sped across the paper so he could get to the next question, which was another of his choosing.

"What steps will you take to make your policies a reality?"

Troy leaned forward. "Listen, Jenny Keats wants to force everyone to participate in the science fair, even if they're not interested. What's next, a history fair? Or one for math? Science fair projects have to be worked on at home. As in homework. Then the rest of us have to go look at that boring stuff after school or on the weekends. So basically, if you want your free time taken away completely, then by all means, vote for her. Cameron is even worse, since he wants to tell you how to behave like some sort of nanny. He'll make even more rules to get you in trouble. If you're having a bad day and glare at someone, you better be ready to go to the principal's office, because that won't be allowed anymore. You can't force people to get along. That's not how the world works, but *he* wants to police your thoughts like a communist."

Anthony was pressing so hard as he wrote all of this down that the pen tore the paper.

"Am I going too fast for you?" Troy asked. "Cameron is a bully. That's what I'm trying to say. Write it down."

The blood was pounding in his ears as he tried to think of a follow-up question that wasn't laced with venom, because Troy was the one who told on people and policed their behavior. *He* was the bully! And now he had the nerve to accuse others of doing what he himself did?

Anthony glanced across the room to where his boyfriend sat. He was smiling patiently as his interviewer wrote down his response. Cameron didn't have a mean bone in his body. Not everyone knew that though, so they might read that he's a bully and actually believe it. Troy was such an asshole! Anthony's anger was beginning to blind him, so he checked the question again to find his place and was surprised that Troy hadn't answered it at all. "But what are *you* actually going to do?" he asked.

Troy rolled his eyes, like Anthony hadn't been listening. "I'm going to make everything better. School can be cool. Do you think the seniors who are graduating next year want to give up their weekends to look at a bunch of potato batteries? What about us? We're class of ninety-five, baby! I'm proud of that and you should be too. We can either go out with a bang or with tape over our mouths because we're not allowed to say anything that might upset a few weirdos who actually *like* negative attention. High school is hard enough. I'll make sure it feels more like a party."

He still hadn't really answered, but it was time to move on. Anthony checked the next question and forced himself to speak the words, even though much more important issues remained on the table. "School dances are the highlight of the year for many students. How will you make them memorable while ensuring a good time?"

Troy had plenty of opinions on the subject, all of them vague and dressed up with the same lofty promises. *Bigger! Better! More!* He finished with what was quickly becoming his catchphrase. "School can be cool. But that's only gonna happen if you vote for me."

The remaining questions brought similar answers. Troy used his responses to attack the other candidates, insisting that they were evil people who wanted to do bad things. He outright lied while doing so. Science fairs weren't mandatory and nobody planned on making them that way. Cameron sure as hell wasn't a bully. But if Troy repeated these things often enough, people might start to believe them. Just like all the empty promises he claimed would only come true if everyone voted for him, when in reality, none of it was going to happen because he clearly didn't have a plan.

"People are going to be talking about Pride High for a long time," Troy was saying. "They're either going to remember it as the worst school ever, because a bunch of bullies took away our weekends and freedom, or people are going to admire everyone who was lucky enough to go here, because it became one big party. Vote for me, and everything will be really cool, I swear."

Anthony had exhausted the list of questions and the allowed follow-ups. He checked the other tables and saw that the interviews hadn't finished yet, so they had time to burn. Anthony closed the notebook and set his pen on top of it. "I notice that you didn't mention the dress code."

Troy smirked. "I think the whole school got the message

during the pep rally. You know, where they could all take a good look at you."

Anthony didn't like being reminded of that moment, but he did his best to set it aside. "I want to ask you something. Off the record. Your answer won't be in the paper or used against you in any way."

Troy shrugged, as if he didn't care. "I've basically already won the election, so go ahead."

"Why do you have a problem with me wearing makeup? Is it a religious thing?"

Troy snorted. "Nope."

"Do you hate gay people?"

"I don't care what you and your butt buddy do together," Troy said, not even bothering to lower his voice. "I just don't want to look at you."

Anthony's mouth was dry but he managed to get one very important word out. "Why?"

"Because it's gross. I don't want to be with my girlfriend, see her makeup, and be reminded of people like you."

Anthony noticed Mr. Finnegan watching him with concern so he forced himself to take a deep breath. This was painful, but it was also an opportunity. He'd tried talking like this to Graham Fowler when they were in detention, but hadn't gotten a satisfactory response. Troy was a different animal. He wasn't a simpleton who didn't know how to express himself. Maybe he could be reasoned with.

"Do you find all women attractive?" Anthony asked.

Troy scoffed. "Of course not."

"Does it bother you when *those* women wear makeup? Do you think of them when you're with your girlfriend?"

"No," Troy said, "and don't get excited because I don't think of you either. But you ruin everything that I find attractive about them. I don't want girls to stop shaving their legs and armpits. And I don't want guys to wear lipstick and eyeshadow. That I even have to explain this to you is insane."

Anthony studied him. Troy was handsome, his gray-blue eyes filled with a sharp intelligence. He was a good-looking guy. Which probably made it harder for him to understand what it was like to be different. Although perhaps not. "What if people hated you because of your red hair? Enough that you dyed it and kept it a secret from everyone. Even your parents. But then one day, you decided you couldn't look at a fake version of yourself in the mirror anymore and you stopped dyeing it."

Troy was already shaking his head. "That's ridiculous. Babies are born with red hair. It's natural. They aren't born wearing eyeliner or whatever."

"But I *was* born this way," Anthony said, placing a hand over his heart. "Do you think I actually *like* being picked on?"

"No idea," Troy said without an ounce of sympathy. "I don't get what you're going for. Are you trying to turn yourself into a girl?"

Anthony felt the blood drain from his face. "No! I'm…"

"What?" Troy challenged.

He didn't have an answer. Not one that would remain still enough in his mind long enough for him to examine it. The truth kept darting away, which was annoying, because Anthony thought he'd already dealt with all of that when coming out.

"Even if you could turn yourself into a girl," Troy said, standing and stretching casually, "nobody would want you. We're done here. Right?"

Anthony nodded, his face burning so intensely that he felt feverish. Troy walked over to Mr. Finnegan. Anthony looked at Cameron, feeling self-conscious when noticing how handsome—and masculine—his boyfriend was. Bright blue eyes met his, Cameron's face falling when he realized something was wrong. He began to stand. Anthony shook his head. Then he opened his composition book and pretended to go over his notes, when in truth, he was staring at a blank page while searching inside himself for answers.

CHAPTER 16
SEPTEMBER 25ᵀᴴ, 1993

Diego had his Trans Am up on the rack so he could do an oil change. And inspect the suspension, because he thought there'd been a squeak the other day when going over a pothole. He hadn't heard it since, but he never needed much excuse to put Frankenstein on the hydraulic lift. Being underneath his car was kind of intimate, like seeing someone naked. Diego shook his head at the thought. Maybe he needed to get laid. Or he could whip it out and jack off while staring at the driveshaft like a total psychopath.

He heard the door to the garage open. Diego didn't need to cover himself. He wasn't turned on, but the amused grin remained on his face as he turned around. His mother walked toward him while surveying the repair bays.

"Has everyone gone home?" Marti asked.

"Yeah."

"I took care of payroll."

"I noticed."

His mother raised her chin to take in the Trans Am. "Did it finally break down?"

"Nah. Runs like a dream and always will, no matter what I have to do. Dad might be gone, but I still have a piece of him." He studied his mother's reaction. Mentioning his father came with risks. He never knew if she would flip out. Then again, if she really had changed…

Marti tore her attention away from the car. "I'm sure he'd like that."

She didn't look or sound upset. Diego stared at her, so fixated on deciphering her state of mind that he couldn't figure out his own.

"Are you sticking around?" she asked.

Diego shrugged. "I don't have any plans."

Marti nodded. "Dinner will be ready in an hour. I made lasagna."

"You what?"

She shrugged. "You always used to like it."

"I still do," he assured her. "Wait, you mean you made it from scratch?"

"It's not frozen, if that's what you're asking. I'll see you upstairs."

"Yeah," he said as she went. "See ya."

Diego felt a little dizzy as he tried to sort through his feelings. The hope that rose up was quickly squashed by bitter experience. He knew better. And yet, he couldn't ignore the need inside himself, no matter how many barriers he'd built around it. He'd never get his father back, but his mother… Maybe.

Or maybe not. Diego focused on his work, changing the oil before rotating and aligning the tires, out of affection rather than necessity. By the time he lowered the hydraulic lift, he had about fifteen minutes to spare. Diego stopped by his locker to get changed. Once he was in a maroon T-shirt and a comfortable pair of old jeans, he washed his hands and went upstairs.

His mom was pulling a bubbling baking pan out of the oven when he entered the apartment. His attention moved from this unusual sight to the small dining area table where he only had breakfast. He always ate dinner with his mom in front of the television, if at all. Now the small table had been set with napkins, cutlery, and a couple of glasses of ice water.

He joined Marti in the kitchen. "Can I get a beer?"

"Maybe after you eat," she said.

Why had he even asked? He'd never bothered before because his mother didn't care.

"Have a seat," she insisted.

"Need any help?"

"Nope."

Diego sat, unsure what to do with himself. Marti walked over and placed two bowls filled with leafy greens and freshly chopped vegetables on the table.

"What the hell is this?" he demanded

"It's called a salad," Marti replied.

"Yeah, I know, but what's it doing here?"

His mother rolled her eyes before returning to the kitchen. She came back with two small plates, each holding a square of the promised lasagna, which smelled amazing.

"Is this a special occasion or something?" he asked as Marti sat across from him.

"No. Just eat."

Diego did what he was told. The salad was fine. The lasagna was incredible. Better than anything he could buy out on his own. He'd forgotten how she would scatter fresh basil leaves over the top. Where had she gotten those? There used to be some growing in a little pot by the kitchen window. His mother had always reminded him to water it when he took care of the other houseplants. None of them had survived the years.

"Is it all right?" Marti asked.

Diego realized that he'd lowered his fork and had zoned out. "Yeah!" he said quickly. "It's fucking great!"

She smiled at this. "Eat the salad too."

"How come?"

"Because I want you to be healthy."

He made a face.

She nodded at the bowl in front of him. "I mean it!"

"All right, all right," he said, spearing a cherry tomato. "What's gotten into you?"

Marti took another bite and swallowed before responding. "I wanted to talk to you about that actually. I've been seeing a therapist."

"As in you're dating one?"

"No. I'm seeing him for the same reason everyone else does."

Diego bristled. He had nothing but disdain for the occupation. "Why bother? It sure as hell didn't do me any favors."

"Because you didn't need professional help," Marti replied. "You needed me. But I was…" She hesitated. This was uncomfortable territory for them both. "I was broken. That's the only way I can explain it. Otherwise I never would have let you down."

"I'm fine," Diego said with a dismissive shrug. "I can take care of myself."

"But you shouldn't have to," his mother continued. "It's been five years. Do you realize that? When I look back, so much of it is a blur. I thought I could work through the pain on my own, but all I really did was numb it with booze and bad boyfriends." She turned her head away, as if ashamed. "I'm sorry I wasn't there for you, but I will be from now on." Marti met his shocked stare, her eyes blazing with determination. "This year has been a wakeup call for me. When I saw you in your play…" Her chin trembled. Then she scowled before nodding at his plate. "Eat before it gets cold."

Diego shoved another bite in his mouth, panic pounding in his chest. Where was this going? And why did he feel like running away? Maybe because he was on the defensive this time. Since his dad had died, Diego was the only one who made attempts like these, wanting to reach through the maelstrom of torment that surrounded them both to grab his mother's hand, so they could stabilize each other. Which never worked. Why would it now? And yet he wanted it to. Really *really* bad.

"Do you remember when you were George Washington?" his mother asked.

Diego snorted. "I thought you were talking about the play I was in *this* year."

"I was. But seeing you up there reminded me of when you were in grade school. You were so excited, because you got to be the first president, and you thought—"

"Number one means you're the best," Diego said.

"I still remember how ridiculous you looked," Marti said, amusement twinkling in her eyes. "A little Mexican boy wearing a white wig… They should have had you play Lincoln instead. He looks more like one of us."

"I wanted to be the guy on the dollar bill."

"Your teacher had a soft spot for you." Marti swallowed. "When I saw you on stage for the most recent play, it was like a lifeline back to that day. And who I used to be. I felt like I'd gone into a coma and woken up to see you as a grown man. And when you got in trouble…"

"Sorry," Diego said.

"No," his mother began to slide her hand across the table before the fingers curled and she withdrew again. "I'm the one who let you down. I'm proud of how you've managed to take care of yourself all this time. You've always been a fighter. You get that from me. I just…" She shook her head, as if overwhelmed. "I should have been fighting *for* you, instead of fighting myself. That sounds crazy. Maybe it's good that I'm seeing a shrink, because I don't know what I'm doing."

Diego swallowed, despite not having taken a bite. "Is it helping?"

His mother gestured at the food. "I pulled it together enough to do this."

And to visit him over the summer when he was locked up. Diego felt the barriers inside him begin to crack, but he wouldn't let them come tumbling down. He'd learned not to.

"So anyway," Marti said, "that's that. Now tell me why you're home again on a Friday night when you could be out with the cute redhead."

"She's at a party."

"Without you? If you're interested, that's not a good move."

Diego cocked an eyebrow. "Now you're giving me relationship advice?"

"You didn't need it when you were twelve." His mother said, poking at her salad. "Now you do. So what's going on with her?"

"Nothing," Diego said. "We're friends."

"There's no chemistry?"

"There is," he admitted. "She uh…" A smile tugged at his cheek. "She reads to me. It's nice."

His mother had to fight down her own amusement before she could respond. "Is she at a party right now or a book club?"

"It's a real party," Diego said.

"And you don't mind that she'll be around a bunch of other guys all night?"

"Nope," Diego said. "We're not dating."

"Why not?"

"Because I was with someone else."

"Was?"

"Yeah. We broke up."

His mother leaned back with a knowing expression. "*Because of her?*"

"Not really."

"So if this other girl is officially out of the way—"

Diego shook his head. "It was a guy."

Marti peered at him. "You're fucking with me."

"Nope. I was dating a guy. Ricky."

"The little Asian kid that kept coming around?"

"He's not a kid," Diego said. "You make me sound like a sexual predator."

"Fine, fine, but you were really together? Did you have sex with him?"

"Yup."

"And you liked it?"

"Uh-huh."

Marti exhaled and set down her fork. "So you're gay."

Diego snorted. "Nah. I just do whatever the hell I want."

Marti studied him a moment longer before shrugging. "I made out with a girl when I was your age."

Diego was taking a drink when she said this, the water nearly spurting out his nose. "For real?"

"Yeah. She was interested… and I also do whatever the hell I want."

Diego grinned. "So what did you think?"

"Honestly? I didn't like that she was prettier than me."

They eyed each other before laughing.

"Tell me about Ricky," Marti said, picking up her fork again.

As they continued to eat, he tried to explain what they'd had together. His heart grew heavy as memories of their relationship came back to him, because it was the closest thing to carefree that he'd experienced in a very long time. Although the present moment was definitely a contender.

"So why'd you break up?" Marti asked as they carried their dishes to the kitchen.

"We come from two different worlds." Not wanting to linger on how much it all still hurt, Diego didn't expound further.

"Well if you're interested in the girl who reads to you," Marti said, "don't keep her waiting too long. You sure you don't want to go to that party?"

Diego thought of who would be there. That included his former best friends. "Yeah. I'm sure."

"Then you're stuck with me. What do you want to do?"

He shrugged. "I dunno."

His mother took his plate and set it in the sink. "Anything you want."

"For real?"

She nodded.

Diego wouldn't have guessed, when trudging up the stairs an hour ago, that he'd have a heart-to-heart with his mom about Ricky. And everything she'd gone through when his dad died. He felt close to her for the first time in years, even though he was still haunted by the past.

"Are you sure?" he asked.

Marti made a face. "Of course. Do you want to go to a movie or something?"

He shook his head, his throat tightening. "I want to see Dad's suicide letter."

He saw a flicker of madness in his mother's eyes before her expression went cold. "That's not funny."

"You know I'm not kidding." This wasn't the first time he'd

asked her to show him the note. Not by far. He was testing how much had really changed, driven by the same gnawing need that continued to eat him up inside, ever since that dreadful day.

"No." Marty turned toward the sink and began rinsing off dishes.

"Why not?"

"Because it wouldn't be good. For either of us."

"I'm not a little kid anymore," Diego said, trying to angle himself in front of her so she'd look him in the eye. "Like you said, I basically raised myself the past five years. I found his goddamn body! How much worse could it get?"

Marti's hands spasmed, cutlery clattering in the sink. "I'm still your mother. I know what's best for you, and I'm telling you no."

"What's best for me?" Diego spat, shaking his head in disbelief. "You think a stupid lasagna makes up for all the years of neglect? Only *I* know what I need! How come you won't show me the letter?"

Marti spun on him, her face contorting. "I already told you!" She raised a shaking hand to the bridge of her nose. "Don't ask me again."

"So I never get to find out why my dad killed himself." Diego scoffed. "That's great. Really fucking awesome." He spun away and marched toward the front door.

"Where are you going?" Marti called after him.

Diego was too pissed off to reply. And besides, he didn't know the answer. He only knew that he needed to get away.

Anthony's attention was locked on the amphitheater. That's how Keisha had described it earlier as she gave a quick tour of her farm. The word conjured up images of Roman architecture and major concert venues, when in reality, a half-moon of split tree trunks served as benches that faced a small wooden stage. Every seat was filled, as was the aisle where he stood, all attention on Cameron as he delivered a speech.

"My family moved to Pride when I was twelve," he was saying. "Going from grade school to junior high was scary enough. Imagine if you had to do so in a different town where you didn't know anybody. But really, it wasn't so bad. Most people here were really nice. They made me feel welcome. That wasn't luck. A good friend of mine went through the same thing."

Cameron sought out Ricky, who was sitting in the front row, and smiled at him. "Except he started *high school* in a new town. Can you imagine?"

Sympathetic murmurs traveled through the audience.

"He did all right too. Not everyone was nice to him, but more people cared about him than he probably realized at the time. That's Pride High for you. We have a good school full of good people. And I mean everyone, even the people I'm running against, because here's the thing: We all have reasons for acting the way we do. Life isn't perfect and cheerful like you see on TV. Each of us face some sort of challenge, whether it's our home life or self-doubt or whatever. Growing up is already tricky. Why make it worse for each other? All I want is for everyone to feel secure enough to be who they really are and to feel comfortable enough to ask for whatever help they need. I really mean it when I say everyone, because there's no such thing as a bad person. The guy that picks on you? The girl who makes fun of the way you look? I bet they're going through stuff of their own. In fact, I don't suppose Diego Gomez is here tonight?" Cameron shielded his eyes to see better. "Probably just as well, because he'd beat me up for saying something nice about him, but we used to be enemies. Not anymore. I've gotten to know him a little better since those early days, and he's a cool guy. I like him. I doubt there's anyone in our school I wouldn't like if given the chance to sit down and have a real conversation with them. So keep that in mind, no matter who wins this election, because you don't really need me to change anything. You've already got that power, simply by being nice. If someone seems lonely, invite them to join you and your friends. Or if you see someone getting picked on, stand up for them. If you get anything from my campaign, I want you to be proud of this town and its people. Be a friend to everyone and an enemy to nobody. If we all try our best to do that, the world will be a much better place. Thank you."

"Your boyfriend is so fucking awesome!" Omar said from next to him.

"Yeah." Anthony wiped at his eyes. "He really is. I love him so much!"

"How could you not? The dude is the complete package!" Omar nudged him. "And from what you've said, he's even *got* a nice package."

"He really does," Anthony said with a dreamy sigh.

Omar hooked an arm around his neck to pull him close. "I'm so happy for you, man!"

"Thanks. I'm happy for you too."

"Yeah." Omar released him. "Whitney is… really cool."

"You don't sound convinced."

Omar shrugged. "Nothing against her but… I'll put it this way. If it doesn't work out between you and Cameron, I feel sorry for the next guy, because he's got some great big shoes to fill."

Anthony peered at his best friend. "So you're saying that Whitney can't really compete with Silvia?"

"I dunno. That sounds kind of mean. But also… yeah."

Anthony thwapped him. "Then why aren't you dating Silvia?"

"I don't think she's into me anymore." Omar sounded just as distraught. "I was dropping all sorts of hints when I told her that I'm in a committed relationship now, but I swear she didn't care. Like at all!"

Anthony sighed. "Then you must have read her wrong."

Omar perked up. "How come? Did she say anything about me recently?"

"I mean, she asks how you are and stuff."

Omar's shoulder slumped. "That's it?"

"I'll dig a little deeper next time."

"For real?"

Anthony laughed. "Of course."

"You're the best." Omar offered him an elbow bump that was readily returned. "So are you going to congratulate your man? He totally nailed that speech."

A small crowd surrounded Cameron, Ricky at his side and trying to establish some sort of order.

"He's working," Anthony replied. "I'll tell him how great he is when we're alone."

"I bet you will," Omar said with another nudge. Then his eyes went wide. "Here she comes! Play it cool."

Anthony followed his gaze to where Silvia, Keisha, and Mindy were approaching them.

"I've gotta admit," Keisha said, "I didn't think we'd have near as much turnout. Not on such short notice."

Silvia nodded in agreement. "Whitney is amazing. She should make a career out of it somehow."

Omar glanced at Anthony meaningfully, as if his point was made. "Yeah," he said. "When my girlfriend gets an idea in her head, there's no stopping her."

"You aren't kidding," Mindy said. "This is a great party!" They had already passed out all the lollipops, dance music had begun blaring again now that the speech was over, and there was a literal buffet of food and drink available in a nearby building. "If everything we've done tonight doesn't win the election, nothing will."

Anthony's stomach lurched. Ever since the interview, he'd spent a lot of time imagining what the school would be like if Troy became president. Instead of the utopia Cameron described in his speech, anyone who didn't fit in would be mocked and shamed into submission, if not worse. Troy and his friends had proven through their behavior that they didn't value inclusivity. They were downright mean! That alone should be enough to cost Troy the election, but Anthony wasn't sure the world worked that way. Bad people often rose to the top.

He turned to Keisha. "Can I use your phone? I forgot to tell my parents where I was going to be tonight."

"No problem, hon," Keisha said. "Right this way."

Crap. Anthony had hoped she would simply point him in the right direction, because the request hadn't been spontaneous. His parents knew damn well where he was. He simply wanted to ensure that Troy wouldn't win. And so, against his better judgment, he'd lingered in the parking lot after school one day, sitting low in his seat while peering over the steering wheel, until he saw Troy get into his car. That's when Anthony had followed him home.

"I've known Cameron for years now," Keisha said while leading them toward a large two-story house, "but you and I have never talked much."

"Because I'm always worried I'll say something stupid," Anthony murmured, still distracted by his thoughts.

"Meaning?" Keisha asked. She looked him up and down, no doubt noticing his panic. "Oh. Because the color of my skin?"

"No!" he said instinctually. "Well, actually… Yeah. But not because I have anything against black people. It's the opposite really. I've always felt a huge amount of sympathy, even before I figured myself out. Not that it's the same thing," he hastened to add, "but it was relatable anyway. Especially now. I know

how it feels when people treat you different just because of who
you are."

Keisha's gaze was steady. "So you decided to do the same
thing to me?"

"No! I mean… I guess it might seem that way but—"

Keisha laughed. "Relax. If ignorance was a crime, we'd all
be locked up for one reason or another. And that doesn't make
you racist. Now if you dislike someone because of the color of
their skin or wish them ill, *then* you have some soul-searching to
do, because that's simply not right. For the record, I don't want
anyone to treat me differently, but if they happen to anyway, I
prefer when they err on the side of caution, like you were trying
to."

"I'll try harder," he promised. "Or I'll try to not try as much.
Um…"

Keisha smiled. "I can see why Cameron always uses the word
'adorable' to describe you."

"He does?"

"Mm-hm. And in many ways you're his inspiration. That was
some speech."

"Yeah," Anthony said, feeling a pang of guilt for the secret
mission he was on. "Do you think it'll be enough?"

"I sure hope so. I shudder to think what awaits us if Troy
wins. He's the sort of self-serving politician who doesn't care a
lick for the collateral damage he causes. All that matters to him
is what he wants and how he's gonna get it."

"You're absolutely right," Anthony said, his determination
returning. "Hey, do you think the black kids will vote for
Cameron?"

Keisha raised an eyebrow at this. "I'm beginning to see what
you were so worried about."

He shook his head. "Sorry! But isn't that… I don't know, a
demographic that can be polled?"

"Sure, but you're assuming I know all the other black kids at
school. Do you think all the gay boys will vote for him?"

"This one will," Anthony assured her, "but I get your point."

"Cameron wouldn't be the first white man to preach tolerance
in the hopes of winning over black voters," Keisha said, "but he
does seem much more sincere. Anyone who has reason to be
disillusioned with the system will be drawn to him. Whether or

not they are motivated enough to vote is another matter." She opened the front door to her house. "Come on in."

"Thanks for hosting the party," Anthony said. "All that food couldn't have been cheap. I'd offer to chip in, but I'm broke and your family is obviously rich. Was that a three-car garage outside?"

Keisha peered at him suspiciously. "Did Silvia tell you to say that?"

Yes, but Anthony wasn't ready to admit it yet. "She didn't have to. I know the smell of money. Omar's folks are loaded too."

"Oh stop," Keisha said. "We have a large property, that's all. You can't farm without a bunch of land."

"You have your own amphitheater," he countered. "You know what's in my backyard? An old swing set that's rusty and falling apart, but nobody will get close enough to tear it down, because wasps built nests in the tubes and my family is terrified of them. Doesn't matter if it's the dead of winter. We just assume the wasps are pretending to hibernate as a ploy to murder us."

Keisha laughed. "At least your life is rich in adventure."

They entered a large kitchen, Keisha directing him to a corded yellow phone on the wall. "There you go. I'm glad we had a chance to talk like this. In the future, don't worry so much about sticking your foot in your mouth. I know where you stand. You've been friends with Galen for a long time now."

"Oh, so you *do* know all the other black kids," he teased.

"Only most of them. Speaking of which, are you just as antsy around him?"

"No," Anthony admitted. "I guess because when you're an outcast, it supersedes everything else. Not belonging anywhere is our bond. You, on the other hand, are *way* too cool to be an outcast."

Keisha smiled at the compliment. "Just keep in mind that we're family now. The secret is out."

"That's right!" Anthony said. "Welcome to club gay."

"I prefer to think of it as planet lesbian," Keisha said with a wink, "but we share the same orbit. Come find me when you're done with your call. I'll introduce you to my older brother. He's handsome, the coolest, and even blacker than me. I can't wait to see you squirm."

"Sounds fun," he said with a smile that was returned.

The happy expression slowly faded when he was alone. Cameron's speech had moved him. Truly. But the world had been spinning for a very long time, and so far, humanity hadn't set aside their differences so they could be nice to each other. He wanted that to happen, but until it did… He took a scrap of paper out of his pocket. He'd written down Troy's address after following him home. Anthony swiped the phone off the receiver, glanced over his shoulder to make sure he was alone, and called a number on the flip side of the paper. Not one used for serious emergencies, but a line to the authorities regardless. His palms were sweaty as he pushed a series of numbered buttons.

"Pride Police Department," a gruff voice said. "How can I direct your call?"

"Hello there," Anthony said, trying to make his voice sound elderly. "Some teenagers are throwing a party next door and it's really getting out of hand. There's a weird smell too. I think it might be drugs."

"What's the address?" the voice asked.

Anthony raised the scrap of paper, which trembled slightly as he rattled off the information.

"Understood," said the voice on the line. "We'll send someone over."

"Thank you," he said. "Have a good evening now. Bye bye."

He hung up the phone. Hopefully the call had been too short to trace. Why would they anyway? The police would show up at Troy's house and find just what he'd described. A big party. And with any luck, it would get shut down, along with Troy's campaign. Anthony crumpled the scrap of paper and shoved it back in his pocket. Then he left the kitchen, intent on finding his boyfriend and their host, so they could celebrate.

CHAPTER 17
SEPTEMBER 25ᵀᴴ, 1993

Mindy bobbed her head to the music while enviously watching Omar and Whitney dance together. Not that she had any interest in either of them, although it *would* be exciting to develop a crush on a girl. She simply wished, for the millionth time, that she wasn't perpetually and hopelessly single. With so many people here, surely at least *one whole person* would catch her eye. Or notice her in return. She casually scanned the crowd while shimmying her shoulders. Silvia was on the amphitheater stage, playing DJ. Omar was dancing his heart out with Whitney. David was watching her while smoothing down his mustache, like he was working up the nerve to come talk to her. Uh oh!

Mindy started dancing for real, using the excuse to spin around and face in the opposite direction. David was nice enough, but she didn't feel any chemistry when around him. Like, at all. She knew that going on a date with the wrong person could be worse than being single and decided to simply enjoy herself. The night was beautiful. She always loved visiting Keisha's farm, no matter the occasion. And when did she get the chance to dance underneath the stars like this? It was incredibly romantic. For other people. She noticed a young pair nearby, holding on to each other's hands while stomping around and laughing. They had to be freshmen, but even they'd managed to pair up.

Mindy closed her eyes, wanting to lose herself in the music. As she danced, warm air caressed her skin like the breath from an invisible lover. Hey, that was a good turn of phrase! Maybe she should become a romance novelist. When people asked about her love life during interviews, she'd insist that she was married to her career, and that no living man could compete with the brooding boys in her books.

Mindy laughed at the idea and opened her eyes. Which got even wider when she realized that she wasn't alone. Someone was dancing with her!

"How's it going, princess?" Diego asked, his hips moving seductively.

"Oh my gosh!" Mindy placed both hands over her mouth, the blood rushing to her cheeks.

"Don't stop," Diego said, his feet stepping to the beat. "I've missed this."

"So have I," Mindy said, finding the rhythm again. "This is even better because we're not on stage."

"For now," Diego rumbled. "I'm gonna talk Ms. Deville into doing a dance version of *Lord of the Flies*."

"Could you imagine?" Mindy said with a titter. "All those filthy kids lurching around on stage?"

"While singing about how they got the runs from eating too much fruit."

Mindy laughed so hard that she missed a few steps. Diego's eyes were sparkling, putting the stars above them to shame. Although when his gaze darted to the right, his expression became annoyed.

"Looks like we have an audience after all," he said, just as the song came to an end.

Mindy glanced over her shoulder. Omar was moving in their direction, his girlfriend bounding ahead of him in her excitement.

"Hey guys!" Whitney cried. "The theater group is in the house!"

"He's not part of it," Diego said, nodding at Omar with a snarling lip.

"Aww!" Omar cried. "C'mon! I thought we buried the hatchet."

Diego crossed his arms over his chest. "What about the knife you stabbed me in the back with?"

"I think I've got it around here somewhere," Omar said while patting down his pockets. Then he grinned and opened his arms. "Come here, big boy. You can't say no to this."

"No," Diego growled before he turned and walked away.

"Hey!" Omar sounded genuinely upset. He watched him go before looking to Mindy for an explanation. "I'm not *that* annoying. Am I?"

"You're fine," she assured him. "I'm sure it's something else."

A new tune began to play, UB40's cover of '(I Can't Help) Falling in Love With You.' Whitney jumped up and down in excitement. "I love this song! Dance with me."

"Yeah, all right," Omar said, still staring after Diego with concern.

"I'll talk to him," Mindy said.

"Cool," Omar managed to say before being dragged away.

Mindy felt the pitter-patter of her heart before she gave chase. Diego hadn't made it far. He was heading toward the parking lot. She grabbed his arm to get his attention, her hand sliding off the round curve of his bicep as he turned around. A hint of relief betrayed itself when he saw it was her, along with something else that she interpreted as barely disguised pain.

"Where are you going?" she asked softly.

"This was a bad idea," Diego said, glancing in the direction of the party.

She shook her head. "No it wasn't. I'm really glad you're here."

Diego swallowed. "Yeah?"

"Yes."

"I'm not in the mood to be around a lot of people," he said. "Can we go somewhere else?"

"Sure!" She looked around to get her bearings. "It's a great big farm. Umm… I know something you'll like. This way!" She took his hand, but only briefly, so he'd begin to follow her. Although she wouldn't have minded if his hand had tightened around hers. Diego was always so unresponsive whenever she touched him. Mindy would try to respect his personal space from now on, even though it wouldn't be easy, because she wanted to be close to him. The urge came unbidden whenever they were together.

They wound between buildings until they came to an old pickup truck, rusting away behind a barn, thick tufts of weeds partially obscuring its flattened tires. The fields beyond stretched to the horizon, ending in a black wall of trees. Even though they could still hear the party they'd left behind, this place felt private and secluded.

"Nice," Diego said while inspecting the truck. "A classic Ford F-series. Probably from—" He walked around the front of it. "—fifty-seven to sixty. I wonder how long it's been out here."

"At least since I was a little kid," she said. "Keisha and I used to play here, and it was already rusty back then. My favorite game was when we'd be bank robbers. This was our getaway car. Or sometimes I'd pretend to be her mom and drop her off at school." Mindy laughed at the memories. "Keisha wanted us to camp out here one night. We put our sleeping bags in the back until I chickened out."

"Oh yeah? What spooked you?"

"Spiders!"

Diego snorted. "Next time you notice one, put your hand next to it."

Mindy recoiled at the suggestion. "Why would I do that?"

"So you can see how it runs away. Bugs are scared-er of you than you are of them.

"More scared," she corrected automatically.

Diego cocked an eyebrow. "I bet you liked playing school too."

"I did," she said, straightening up proudly. "And yes, I was *always* the teacher. Now please don't interrupt Ms. Beaumont again. Not without raising your hand first."

Diego grinned and went to the truck's open tailgate, which he began brushing off, seemingly unconcerned with how dirty and grimy it was. Then he gestured, as if inviting her to sit.

"Umm…" Mindy said, inching closer to inspect the spot before crinkling her nose. "My skirt will get dirty."

"Fine," Diego huffed before stripping off his shirt.

Mindy stared openly. What a chest! He could easily be on the cover of a romance novel.

Diego spread the T-shirt out on the tailgate. "There ya go."

Mindy hopped up, just as flattered as if he'd pulled out her chair at a fancy restaurant. This was even better, because dear lord, those shoulders! She couldn't stop staring!

Diego noticed and smirked when settling down next to her. His attention moved to the emptiness in front of them. She followed his gaze, tranquility spreading through her, because here everything felt distant. Her hometown was somewhere beyond the trees, reduced to a simple concept instead of the labyrinth of complex social situations and messy feelings.

The silence between them was comfortable, but she longed to hear Diego's deep voice again. Mindy turned toward him, surprised to see his jaw clenching.

"Are you okay?" she asked.

Diego thought about it. "Not really."

"What's wrong?"

He shook his head.

Mindy waited for him to say more. He didn't. "Well anyway, it's nice to get away from that party."

"Looked like you were having fun to me."

"I was! It's just…" She took a deep breath and sighed. "I don't think I like holding a grudge. Were you here during Cameron's speech?" He shook his head, so she did her best to explain. "It really hit home because I *despise* Troy. That's nothing new. But ever since the election started, I think about him all the time. I hate that he's in my head so much. I'd rather forget he existed. I only have myself to blame. It's not like he's trying to force his way into my life again." She nibbled her bottom lip and decided to switch streams. "That isn't always a bad thing, depending on the person. Omar only wants to be friends with you again. Troy was never my friend and never will be."

Diego remained perfectly still, only shifting slightly when he replied. "First of all, it isn't your fault. You have a damn good reason to hate Troy. That's why I like grudges. They keep the truth right there in front of you, so you don't forget. Otherwise you end up making the same mistake."

"Omar cares about you," Mindy countered. "So does Ricky. Don't you think they deserve a second chance?"

"Second chances," Diego said with a scoff. He scowled at the horizon while clenching his jaw again. Then he looked at her sharply, his gaze intense. "Do you trust your parents?"

She didn't understand the sudden change of subject, but it was obviously something he needed to talk about. "Of course!" she said.

"With everything?" he pressed, the fire in his eyes intensifying.

"Oh. I mean, within reason. When they were going through their divorce…" She thought back to how upsetting it had been. "I felt betrayed. They were supposed to keep me safe. And technically they did. I got to stay in the same house. Neither of my parents moved out. They sleep in different rooms now, but it's not so different really. Still…" She remembered how often she'd cried back then and shook her head. "I lost my sense of security. Your parents are everything when you're little. You think they're perfect and all-knowing. I didn't realize yet they're not and couldn't understand why they insisted on ruining everything. I get it now. I can see how much happier they are apart. They still love each other…" She shrugged. "They simply weren't meant to be together. I'm glad they had me, of course. My sister too. But I'm also glad they didn't feel the need to pretend like everything was fine, just to make us happy. I'd rather know the truth, no matter how bad it hurts."

"That's all I'm asking for," Diego grumbled.

"What do you mean?"

Diego eyed her a moment, his expression softening. "When my dad killed himself, he left a letter explaining why. My mom won't let me read it."

"Oh." Mindy had often tried to imagine what that loss must have been like for him, her heart breaking in sympathy each time. "Did she say why?"

"Only that it would be bad for me."

"What if she's right?"

Diego scowled. "You just said—"

She held up a palm. "I know! But maybe *that's* the truth. My parents hurt me by getting a divorce. I bet it would have been worse for everyone, even me, if they hadn't. So yes, our parents are flawed and don't always get it right. I just can't imagine your mom not letting you see that letter if it was harmless."

"How much worse could it get?" Diego snarled, the anger edged with enough pain to make his voice warble.

"I don't know," she said. "But do you really need another bad thing in your life? Maybe it's time to find something that makes you happy."

He searched her eyes, his chest heaving. Then he leaned forward.

Mindy met him halfway, wanting more than anything to take some of that pain away and replace it with what they both needed. His lips touched hers, thick and commanding. She breathed in through her nose to fend off the dizziness she felt, but it wasn't a lack of oxygen. It was him! When he started to pull away, she reached for his face, holding him near so she could kiss him again. And again. She finally relented and felt Diego smile against her mouth before he pulled away.

"What were we just talking about?" he asked.

"I don't know," Mindy said, pretending to adjust her hair. "Something about robbing a bank with a bunch of spiders?"

"Right," he said with a nod. "That must have been it."

They both laughed.

He was the first to grow serious. "I really liked that."

"So did I," Mindy said. "And I like you. I have for a really long time."

He lowered his eyes before they met hers again. "You know those Rice Krispies treats you gave me after my dad died?"

Mindy nodded, surprised that he still remembered. He'd never said anything about it, during or after.

"That meant a lot to me. So uh…" Diego searched her eyes again before shrugging those big shoulders of his. "Thanks."

Mindy felt drawn toward him, like her heart wanted desperately to snuggle up to his. "I wish I could have done something to help."

"You just did," he said, his gaze intense. "Really."

She leaned against him affectionately. Diego stiffened, but only momentarily. He shifted, put an arm around Mindy, and pulled her close. As they sat there listening to the insects hum along with distant music, Mindy felt like crying. Partly because of everything he'd gone though. But mostly because she was so incredibly happy.

Ricky's grin refused to quit. He was sitting on a picnic table near the amphitheater, Anthony and Cameron across from him. The evening had been a major success. After his speech, Cameron had been beset by people eager to talk with him. His speech really seemed to resonate with everyone. Victory felt closer than ever. Troy could be charming, but Cameron was something much better. Authentic! Ricky was certain that he would win. David and Galen had said the same thing when joining them at the table.

"If I do win," Cameron said, nuzzling Anthony's ear affectionately, "you're going to have to take on a lot of new responsibilities."

"As your first lady?" Anthony asked, seeming pleased by the idea.

"Uh-huh. You'll have to read to grade school children, decide how you want to decorate the cafeteria Christmas tree, and launch a war against drugs."

Anthony narrowed his eyes. "I'll get grade school kids to listen to The Cure, make sure there isn't a Christmas tree in school at all, and wage a war against stupidity. That's my final offer."

"Sold!" Cameron said, pretending to hammer the table with an auctioneer's gavel.

"I won't *really* have to do anything," Anthony said in concern. "Will I?"

"I'm not even sure what my duties will be," Cameron replied. "So probably not."

Anthony breathed out. "Good! I never wanted to be a public figure."

"I'm nervous too," Ricky said. "I'm auditioning for a role in the next school play. I've never been on stage before."

"You'll do fine," Galen said from next to him. "When you're in the moment, the pressure is great motivation."

"Have you been in a play?" Ricky asked, shifting to see him better.

Galen was zipped up in a purple hoodie that he filled out nicely. He opened his mouth to respond but David got there first.

"You haven't seen his act?" he asked in disbelief. "It's amazing!"

"Thanks," Galen said with smiling eyes.

Ricky shook his head, still confused. "What kind of act?"

"He can breathe fire!" David enthused.

Ricky scrunched up his face. "For real?"

Galen nodded. "Yeah. I guess you weren't at Omar's birthday party last year. That was my big debut. I've gotten a lot better since then."

Ricky looked at Anthony in excitement. "How much longer until Omar's next birthday?"

"I've gone exclusive since then," Galen said. "My dad and I put together a new act. We're really proud of it. You can only see it at the renaissance festival."

Ricky blinked. "The what?"

"Are you for real?" David said in disbelief. "It's the coolest thing ever! Like getting to travel back in time to the medieval days. Lots of people get dressed up and there's real jousting and actual swords you can buy. I got a magical talisman last year."

"Interesting," Cameron said. "We didn't have anything like that in Maine."

"Oh my god!" David cried. "You guys are killing me!"

"I think there's one in Colorado," Ricky said. "But I never went to it."

"I can get you a free pass," Galen said breathlessly. "If you'd like to come see my act. And everything."

"I'll take one!" David said.

"Me too," Anthony chimed in.

Galen's eyes widened. "I don't have *that* many passes!"

"I'll pay for ours," Cameron said, leaning against his boyfriend affectionately.

"The benefits of being married to a working man," Anthony said with a dreamy sigh.

Ricky laughed. "So we're all going?"

"How many free passes do you have?" David asked.

Galen glanced at Ricky. "Just one. You have a job bagging groceries, right?"

"Yeah," David conceded.

"I'm flat broke," Ricky said, raising his arms in victory. "That means I win!"

Galen laughed. "It's yours," he promised.

"Thanks." Ricky smiled at him. "I'm excited."

"About what?" a new voice asked.

Omar walked over to them, disheveled, sweaty, and grinning like a dog who had just played fetch to his heart's content.

"We're planning a trip to the renaissance festival," Anthony explained.

"Sweet! Count me in. I bet Whitney will want to go too. We might need a party bus. We'll load that sucker up!"

"I wonder if Diego would be interested," Ricky said while checking their surroundings, because hope sprang eternal.

"Not if I'm there," Omar said, plopping down next to Anthony. "You either, I bet," he said to his best friend. "I ran into him earlier and he stormed off."

"Classic Diego," Anthony murmured.

"Wait," Ricky said. "Do you mean at school?"

"Nuh-uh," Omar said, shaking his head. "He was on the dance floor. Or the dance field, I guess. Heh."

Ricky stood up. "When?"

Omar shrugged. "Not that long ago."

"Where'd he go?"

Omar jerked a thumb over his shoulder. "That way."

Ricky nearly tripped in his haste to get over the bench. "See you guys later!" he called while husting in the indicated direction.

He was already smiling, excited to be reunited with Diego once again. Hopefully he didn't show up drunk like last time. Ricky would take care of him no matter what. He kept walking until he reached the parking lot. He spotted Frankenstein and rushed over to check, but its owner wasn't inside. Ricky began backtracking to the party, remaining on high alert. This paid off when he saw Diego emerge from the shadows. Except he wasn't alone. Mindy was with him.

Instinct brought Ricky to a halt. He noticed the way they meandered together, as if in no rush to rejoin the party. Where had they been? And what had they gotten up to while there? He'd been jealous of Mindy before without reason. This was probably the same. Wasn't it? Ricky only needed to ask and his fears would be allayed.

Diego began turning toward him, as if sensing his need.

Mindy placed a hand on his arm and pointed toward the party. Diego looked in that direction before shaking his head. While standing intimately close, they exchanged words that Ricky couldn't hear. He ducked behind a tree to keep watching. Mindy began dancing. Diego grinned and did the same. Okay. No big deal. They were dancing together, but that didn't mean they were *together* together.

Ricky was about to join them when the song ended and a much slower one began to play. Diego offered his hand. Ricky felt like sprinting to where Silvia was DJing while shouting for her to stop the music, but it was already too late. Mindy placed her hand in Diego's. He took a step toward her, wrapping an arm around her waist. There was no mistaking the affection between them, or what was about to happen, especially when their faces neared.

Ricky rolled against the trunk of the tree until his back was against it and he couldn't see what they were doing anymore. Then he covered his mouth, whimpering against his hands as his heart began to break.

CHAPTER 18
SEPTEMBER 27ᵀᴴ, 1993

Something was wrong. Keisha had noticed it during the warm-up stretches of their dance elective. Hope would normally risk little peeks in her direction, Keisha making funny or flirtatious faces in response. Not today. Hope hardly looked at Keisha at all and when she did, there was no warmth there. She seemed angry. Keisha racked her brain to remember some unintentional transgression or broken promise. Did it have something to do with her sister? Faith had been shooting daggers in her direction, although that wasn't so unusual.

"I need you to run interference," Keisha said as the class was coming to an end.

"For real?" Omar asked with a grimace. "Faith keeps giving me the evil eye."

"Please," Keisha said. As soon as he nodded, she rushed to the hallway that led to the locker rooms. She waited there until Hope showed up. Alone, thank goodness. "Hey! How are things?"

Hope stopped in her tracks and glared at her. "How do you think?"

"I really don't know. Did I do something wrong?"

"Why?" Hope asked, narrowing her eyes. "Do you have a guilty conscience?"

Keisha shook her head. "I'm at a loss."

"You're a backstabber!" Hope hissed before pushing past her.

"Wait!" Keisha said. "We've gotta hash this out!"

"After what you did?" Hope only slowed enough to scowl at her. "No way!"

"But I didn't do anything! Tell me what's going on."

"Nice talking to you!" Omar bellowed.

That had to be for her benefit. She leaned back to check the gym and saw Faith marching toward the door.

Keisha sprinted to catch up with Hope. "Meet me in the library at the beginning of lunch," she said. "Please! I don't know what you think I did, but you're mistaken, I swear."

Hope glowered at her before doubt softened her features. "Really?"

"Yes." Keisha reached for her before remembering that they were in public. "I'll see you then?"

Hope chewed her bottom lip. Then her eyes moved farther down the hall. She spun around and walked away, Keisha's stomach sinking until she saw her nod from behind. Even then she wasn't certain if it was only her imagination.

During her next class, Keisha repeatedly audited her past behavior, clearing herself each time. What did Hope think that she had done? When lunch finally arrived, Keisha paced near the entrance of the school library. Five minutes went by. Then ten. She was just about to give up when Hope finally showed.

"Thank god," Keisha said, leading her through the stacks until two rows of books hid them. "What's going on?"

"You set me up!" Hope snapped.

"Set you up?" Keisha repeated in confusion. "I literally have no idea what you're talking about."

"Troy's party," Hope said, peering at her in suspicion.

Keisha splayed her hands and shook her head. "What about it?"

"You didn't call the police?"

"No! Of course not." Keisha could tell that Hope still didn't believe her. "I promise, if I were the sort of person to make a move against you and your friends, I'd have the balls to admit it. Now tell me everything."

Hope exhaled. "The police busted Troy's party. They were looking for drugs. I got searched."

Keisha felt the blood drain from her face. "Did you have weed on you?"

"Yeah." Suspicion returned to Hope's features. "Funny how they knew to look for it."

"I sure as hell didn't tell anyone!" Keisha hissed. "That would get me in a whole heap of trouble, considering that I'm the one who gave it to you. Why would I do that to myself? Or to you?"

Hope bowed her head in thought. When she raised her chin again, the accusation had finally left her eyes. "Really?"

"Yes, really. Did you get in trouble?"

Hope shook her head. "I had enough time to hide the weed, but it was scary, because I didn't know if they had drug dogs with them. The whole house smelled because we'd been smoking up. And drinking. The police sent everyone home, but Troy got in trouble."

"Oh shit," Keisha said with a wince. "Was it bad?"

Hope shrugged. "They didn't arrest him or anything."

Keisha rolled her eyes. "Of course not. He's white."

Hope glowered at her again. "It's not funny. His parents were really angry. He's grounded."

"That sucks," Keisha said. "I'm glad you're okay though. So… Are we good now?"

Hope crossed her arms over her chest with a frown. "I don't know. I better go before Faith gets suspicious."

"Wait," Keisha said. "This whole situation is a mess, but it doesn't involve us. No matter how your friends feel about mine, or vice versa, what we've got is entirely separate. I have no interest in pissing off either side. I just want us to keep going. And I think you want that too."

Hope chewed her bottom lip again before nodding.

Keisha took a step closer, relieved when their lips met and her kiss was returned. Although she saw a hint of doubt when they broke it off.

"So who called the police?" Hope asked.

"A neighbor? That's usually how it goes."

"Well my friends are convinced it was you guys so…"

Keisha didn't like the sinister undertones. "Should I be worried?"

Hope shrugged. "I have to go."

"When do I get to see you again?"

"I don't know. It'll be harder now that Troy is grounded. See ya."

Keisha sighed while watching her leave. This wasn't good. But it also wasn't the end of the world. Surely it would blow over. She let Hope get a head start before heading for the cafeteria. Along the way, she reassessed the situation, which seemed more and more ludicrous. It was quite the assumption that she or any of the others had called the police. Especially since they'd been busy with their own party. When would anyone have had the chance?

"Could I use your phone?"

She slowed to a halt. Anthony! He had every reason to do

such a thing. Especially after all the bullying he'd gone through sophomore year. Keisha hadn't stuck around to listen to the phone call he'd made, so she couldn't be sure. Maybe she was wrong, but if not... the boy was seriously misguided. And messing with her love life, not that he could have known. About the weed especially. Damn it! She shouldn't have broken her own rule. This was exactly why she and Diego had agreed not to sell to anyone at school. And technically she hadn't... but this was the next worst thing.

Keisha sighed. The election would be over this week. With any luck, things would soon go back to normal, because at the moment, her relationship with Hope mattered more to her than politics.

Mindy placed her hand on her chest, her heart fluttering as it had all through the weekend. Was this the beginning of love? Or did she have a medical condition? Either way, she could die happy, because Saturday had been a dream come true. She brought the tips of her fingers to her lips, where Diego had kissed her, and remembered how good it had felt to be held in his big arms as they danced beneath the night sky. Neither one of them had felt like socializing afterwards, too wrapped up in each other, so he'd given her a ride home. They ended up parking outside her house and talking until the very last minute of her curfew. She didn't know where they stood now. Was this a relationship? Were they merely dating? Or had his need been driven by circumstance and already satiated? Mindy wasn't sure. She'd had plans with her family the next day, although Diego had been a constant companion in her mind. Once home again, she had remained close to the phone while trying to read, even though she'd been too distracted to take much in. Her vigilance paid off when Diego called as she'd been getting ready for bed.

"I just wanted to say goodnight," his deep voice had rumbled over the phone.

"What did you do today?" she'd asked, unwilling to let him go.

"Worked mostly. What about you?"

"We drove out to Missouri to visit some relatives."

The call hadn't lasted long after that. Nothing important or revealing was spoken. Hearing from him was enough. Mindy had leapt into bed, giggling with glee while imagining all sorts of romantic scenarios.

Lunch at school the next day felt like any other, although their gazes often met, Diego smirking playfully each time. Mindy was glad they shared a class this year. Even better, they were holding auditions for *Lord of the Flies*, which meant staying after school, extending their time together. So far, Whitney had been the best contender for the leading role of Ralph. Mindy watched as another hopeful thanked them and left the stage. They grouped the auditions by character and that meant—

"Diego Gomez," Ms. Deville called.

The man in question sauntered out of the wings. Mindy's pulse became a telegram that spelled out "I'm over here! I'm over here! I'm over here!" until Diego finally looked at her. He gave an upward nod and shaded his eyes so he could find their teacher.

"I'm gonna play Jack Merridew," he said. "Do you really need me to audition?"

"That's how these things normally work," Ms. Deville replied.

"Do I have to stick to the script?"

"That would be preferable, yes."

Diego tossed the script aside. "Too bad! From now on, we're doing things *my* way. No more keeping the stupid fire going or worrying about the damn beast. If it messes with us, we'll kill it like the pigs we hunt. Anyone who has a problem with that will end up as a head on a stake. Understand?"

He said the final word with such force that Mindy could swear she heard it echo through the resulting silence.

"He's got my vote," Keisha murmured.

"Mine too!" Mindy chimed in.

"I'd still like to hear an actual line from the play," Ms. Deville pressed.

"You mean this?" Diego asked, sweeping up his script. "Call a meeting if you want. Doesn't matter anymore. *This* is what I think of your dumb conch!" He dropkicked the script into the audience. Then he grinned broadly. "Not bad, huh?"

Mindy clapped. She couldn't help herself.

"You certainly know how to make an impression," Ms. Deville said. "Now then… Scott Mooney, you're up."

A pale guy took the stage, Diego feinting to make him flinch as they passed each other. The poor guy stammered as he introduced himself, glancing over his shoulder as if afraid that Diego would sneak up on him. Mindy covered her mouth to hide her smile. She had no doubt as to who would get the role. None of the auditions that followed managed to capture Jack Merridew's menace.

The role of Piggy was up next and—not surprisingly considering the character's name—only two people chose to audition. The first was a chubby senior who was even taller than Diego. His voice was whisper-quiet, forcing them all to lean forward in their seats, just to hear what he said. Still, with a little coaching, he might get the job done. Even though he looked big enough to tangle with anyone else on the island, Diego included.

"Riku Nishikawa!" Ms. Deville called out. "You're up!"

Ricky walked on stage, blinked against the light, and adjusted his glasses. "Uh… Hi everyone! I'm auditioning for the role of Piggy. Umm…" He began flipping through his script to find the right page.

Mindy felt a pang of guilt. He was such a sweet guy, and even though he had only officially joined this semester, Ricky already felt like a part of their theater troupe. He'd been there during the previous two productions, always following Diego around with a happy smile. Was she getting in the way of that now?

"Okay," Ricky said, having finally found his place. "Um…" He squinted against the light again. Mindy couldn't be sure, but she thought he was looking at her. "This isn't how things are supposed to be!" Ricky cried, his voice suddenly full of emotion. "We should be tucked in our beds at night, where we feel safe. Only our parents know how to go about the business of making and mending, but until they're back, someone has to take their place." His voice warbled. "And it should be someone who's good and nice and trustworthy. And that's why I vote Jack as leader—" Ricky shook his head. "Sorry, I meant to say Ralph. Um… Oh! I've been practicing this recently." He took off his glasses and put them in his pocket. Then he began casting around. "Give em' back! It isn't fair. I can't see a thing without my spectacles. You've gotta give 'em back! It's cruel, I tell you!" He put a hand over his chest and began hyperventilating, simulating the character's chronic asthma. The effect was so believable that Mindy found herself rising from her seat with concern.

"So there's that," Ricky said, instantly returning to normal.

He put his glasses back on and squinted at them. "Um… Thanks."

"He's perfect," Keisha breathed from farther down the row.

"No he isn't," said a guy sitting between them. "He'd need to put on about two hundred pounds between now and the premiere."

"So we'll call him Twiggy instead," Mindy suggested. "We always make changes to the source material anyway."

"Twiggy works for me," Keisha said with a nod of support.

"I have no objections," Ms. Deville said. "Let's move on for now."

The rest of the auditions went fine, aside from the roles of Sam and Eric, since no actual twins had auditioned. Keisha cleared her throat, as if to suggest a pair, until Mindy glared her into submission. She did *not* want Hope and Faith spoiling another production! Although she cared less and less about them lately. Mindy hadn't been focusing on her disdain for Troy and his friends as much. Not since the weekend. She was eager to get backstage where the others would be hanging out so she could see Diego. Mindy wanted to talk to him about everything. Did he want to kiss her again? What month should the wedding take place? Was it too soon to name their future children? Except when she finally got backstage, someone else was clearly waiting for her.

"Hey!" Ricky said. "Do you have a minute?"

"Sure!" she said, casually checking their surroundings.

Diego was talking to a few of the others while watching her, one of his eyebrows raised quizzically. She shrugged her uncertainty before focusing on Ricky, who was glancing around as if wanting to find somewhere private they could speak.

"Do you want to go outside?" Mindy asked. "It's always so cold in here. I'm eager to warm up."

"Yeah," Ricky said. "That'll work."

As they walked toward the nearest exit, Mindy said, "Your audition was great! I feel like you really captured the essence of the character."

"Thanks," he replied. "It felt good to have somewhere to put everything that I'm feeling."

Mindy had wondered if that was the case. His "give 'em back!" had been much too heartfelt to refer to a pair of glasses. Ricky turned when they reached the door, leaning his weight against the push bar while considering her sullenly. The last of the day's heat hit them as he led the way outside. They only made it a few paces from the door before Ricky stopped and placed a hand against the school's brick wall, as if needing support. Mindy was about to ask if he was okay when Ricky spun around to face her.

"I saw you guys at the party," he said in a strained voice. "You and Diego, I mean."

Mindy's stomach sank. "Oh. I'm really sorry."

"Don't be," he said. "It's not like I don't get it. He's everything to me. Even now." He swallowed and forced a halfhearted smile. "I'm glad he found someone nice and not some girl who just wants to use him or whatever. I know you'll actually be there for Diego. That's what I wanted to talk to you about. I have a few tips."

"But we're not—" Mindy started to say. She shook her head. "I'm not really sure what's going on with us."

Ricky's smile was tight. "I remember what that was like. Enjoy it while you can. Not that I think it'll be over soon. I can help you avoid the mistakes I made. If you ever need to ask me anything, I'm okay with that. I just want him to be happy."

"I want you *both* to be happy," Mindy said.

Ricky shook his head, as if that was no longer possible. "This won't take long. There are just a few things you need to know. Diego doesn't always have the best judgment. When that happens, you need to call him on it and stick to your guns. He'll listen. You just have to be stubborn. Don't let him drive when he's drunk or anything like that, okay?"

Mindy nodded and felt herself begin to panic, like someone who had stopped to pet someone else's dog and was now being told what she'd need to feed it and how often to take it for walks.

"Diego isn't great at expressing his feelings," Ricky continued. "He definitely can, but it doesn't come naturally to him. It helps to keep things physical. Sometimes just—" His chin began to tremble. "—just touching his hand works better than telling him how you feel. He doesn't trust words. When you use them, you've gotta be completely honest, because he only respects the truth."

Mindy felt torn between wanting to assure him that nothing had really happened and wanting to take notes because it most definitely had. "Ricky—" she began to say.

He held up his hand and shook his head wearily, as if unsure if he'd be able to continue. "Last thing, and it's the most important of all. You have to be there for him. No matter what it costs. Diego has been abandoned by everyone who ever loved him so—" His voice squeaked to a halt. Ricky turned his head away to hide his tears, even though she could still hear him sniffle.

Mindy felt terrible. Like a homewrecker. Yes, she really *really* liked Diego, but Ricky's feelings went much further. What right did she have to interfere with that? "Listen," she said, placing a hand on his shoulder. "Yes, Diego and I danced together at the party. And we kissed. But that's all. He'd had a bad argument with his mom and needed someone to talk to. We aren't dating. I know how much you love him, so I'll back off. Okay?"

Ricky wiped his nose on the back of his hand and shook his head. "Diego doesn't want me anymore. And I don't want him to be alone again. That would hurt even worse, so it has to be you. Please! You really care about him. Don't you?"

"Yes," Mindy admitted. And it was painfully clear that Ricky cared for him too. Even more than she did, because if Diego refused to ever see her again, she would be sad, but not enough to cry. "No matter what happens," she said, "even if Diego and I end up as friends and nothing more, we'll both continue to look out for him. Okay? That's all I was trying to do during the summer, and it's what you're trying to do now. Diego won't be alone. He's got us. And we're on the same side, right?"

Ricky's chin trembled again. "Yeah," he said.

"Good. Now let's take a moment to collect ourselves. Then we'll go back in and have some fun."

Ricky leaned against the wall and took deep shuddering breaths that slowly became steadier.

Mindy joined him and thought about how nice the weekend had been. Not just the dancing and kissing, but all the dreams that had filled her heart since then. She'd caught a glimpse of something truly special. That would have to be enough to sustain her, because it was clear that Ricky needed Diego more than she did. Now all Mindy had to do was figure out how to make that happen.

Cameron was overwhelmed with jitters while awaiting the election results. At the beginning of their student government class, Vice-Principal LaVern had escorted him to the front office along with Jenny Keats and Troy Mitchell. That's where they were now, each squirming nervously as Preckwinkle lectured them on how this would play out.

"After the winner is announced," she was saying, "the new president will be allowed to make a *brief* statement on the PA system. So decide now what you'd like to say." She turned to LaVern. "Are you ready?"

The vice principal nodded and sat at the receptionist's desk. She picked up the telephone and dialed a code. In the distance, Cameron heard the chime that was designed to get everyone's attention. "Students and faculty of Pride High," LaVern said in a commanding tone. "This is your vice principal speaking. It is my pleasure to announce the results of the student council election." She opened an envelope, like they were at the Oscars.

"Good luck everyone," Cameron whispered to the other candidates.

"You too!" Jenny said with a smile.

Troy merely rolled his eyes.

"With three percent of the vote," LaVern said, her attention darting over to them, "Jenny Keats made a compelling case for restoring the annual science fair."

Jenny sighed but didn't look surprised. Cameron patted her on the back. "You deserved way more than that!" he said.

"With forty-seven percent of the vote," LaVern said, "your runner-up wanted to give you a break from hectic learning schedules. Troy Mitchell deserves a round of applause for running such a memorable campaign."

Cameron began to clap until LaVern covered the receiver and shook her head. Then she gestured for him to come closer.

"That means, with fifty percent of the vote, Cameron Huxley is your new student council president. I'll let him remind you of the promises he made in his first student body address."

Cameron's mouth went dry as he walked around the desk, his palm slick with nervous sweat when he took the receiver. He glanced around. Jenny was smiling at him encouragingly. Troy was glaring openly. The two adults were difficult to read.

"Hey," he said into the receiver, foolishly awaiting a response. He was on the PA system, not a phone call. "Um... Hi, everyone. This is Cameron Huxley. Instead of your president, I'd rather you think of me as your friend. I'm gonna get to work on my promises right away. I look forward to making this school an even more inclusive and safe place that you can truly be proud of. Thank you for your faith in me!"

He handed the phone back to LaVern, his hand shaking with adrenaline. This was exciting!

"There are many more positions available in the student council," LaVern said, addressing the entire school again. "If you want to take a more active role, I encourage you to consider my student government elective next semester. For now, I'd like to thank everyone who participated in this election, most especially the candidates themselves, all three of whom demonstrated the power of their convictions when taking the podium. That makes each of them a winner. Enjoy the rest of your day."

"Congratulations!" Jenny said, clapping for him.

"Thanks," Cameron said sheepishly. "I guess this is where the hard work starts. I'll need your help."

Jenny nodded. Troy clenched his jaw and looked away.

Preckwinkle cleared her throat. "Better tend to your class, LaVern. We don't want to leave them unsupervised."

"Of course," LaVern said. "There's much to discuss."

She was ushering them out the door when Preckwinkle cleared her throat again.

"I'd like a word with you, Mr. Huxley. We'll be working together, from time to time."

"Yeah, of course!" he said. "That would be great!"

LaVern met his eye but didn't say anything as she left with the others. Preckwinkle gestured for him to enter her office.

"Have a seat," she said, shutting the door behind them. "I have good news for you."

"Oh yeah?"

Preckwinkle nodded before settling into her chair. "You'll no doubt be busy in your new role. I've taken the liberty of relieving some of that burden by meeting with the school board." She slid a copy of the student handbook across the desk. "We've made some revisions. Take a look at the dress code in particular."

Cameron studied her in confusion before complying. Why would she make changes before he had a chance to get involved? He flipped to the page that contained the dress code and tried to read what it said before he was interrupted.

"You'll notice that we clarified the rules that were causing confusion," Preckwinkle said. "Second paragraph, third line down. Go ahead and read it aloud."

Cameron tried to scan the text in silence.

"Go on," Preckwinkle prompted.

Apparently that was the only way he'd get to the bottom of this. "Makeup and accessories must be suitable to a healthy learning environment," Cameron read aloud, glancing up at her with unease. "To avoid creating a distraction for other students or faculty members, only naturally occurring colors of makeup will be allowed. For instance, hair cannot be dyed green. Blue or purple eyeshadow is unacceptable. Likewise, makeup and accessories shall only be worn by the appropriate gender. For instance, boys are not allowed to wear dresses, and girls are not allowed to wear bowties." He lowered the handbook and shook his head. "But these are some of the issues that I promised to deal with."

"Now you won't have to," Preckwinkle said. "You can focus on more urgent issues, such as planning the homecoming dance."

"I'll make sure that gets done," Cameron said. "but I'd appreciate the chance to work on a revised dress code."

"There's no need," Preckwinkle said, her face impassive. "The school board voted unanimously to ratify the new rules."

"Could I meet with them?" Cameron asked. "I'm supposed to represent the needs of the student body. The school board could vote on whether or not they'd be willing to accept further changes."

"That sounds like a waste of everyone's time," Preckwinkle said. "The issue has already been dealt with. I'm sure you'll find plenty to occupy yourself with. Now please report to class."

Cameron didn't move. He stared at the student handbook, his brow crinkled in concern.

"You can take that with you," Preckwinkle said. "Copies will be distributed to everyone on the first of the month. The new rules go into effect the following Monday. Congratulations on running a successful campaign."

"Thanks," Cameron said.

He took the revised handbook and left the office, his despair increasing with each step, because the only reason he'd run for president was to fix an unfair rule. And now it had been made even worse! He could already imagine Anthony's face when

Cameron broke the news to him, how his boyfriend's mouth would form a hard line, the anger failing to disguise how hurt and rejected he felt inside. What was the point in having won the election if he couldn't use his new position to protect the person he loved?

Cameron glanced up in startled surprise when reaching his class and everyone started clapping. Most of them anyway. Troy still looked pissed.

"All right, everyone," LaVern said. "This is where the real work begins. In the United States government, a newly elected president is in charge of selecting their cabinet. Cameron will submit a list of his picks to me that we'll go over together before making a final decision. Now then, let's quickly remind ourselves of those positions before volunteering for what interests you most."

He did his best to pay attention to the proceedings, even though it all felt so pointless. Part of him was tempted to offer the presidency to Jenny, so he could go rejoin the creative writing elective and be closer to Anthony. Then again, if he stepped down, Troy had the most legitimate claim to the presidency, and he couldn't imagine that helping the situation.

Cameron's thoughts were still troubled when the bell rang. As he stood to collect his things, Jenny walked over to him.

"I look forward to working with you," she said, "in any capacity that you feel I'd be the most effective."

He gathered what little enthusiasm remained. "Yeah! I look forward to working with you too. You were right about the science fair. I'm also interested in bringing it back." Maybe this wouldn't be a total loss. He could still do some good. He noticed Troy walking past them with a glower. "In fact, I hope we can *all* work together," Cameron said, looking directly at him.

"No way in hell." Troy slowed to a stop. "You stole the election!"

Cameron shook his head in confusion. "What?"

"When you had the cops bust my party," Troy hissed. "Don't play dumb! And don't think you've won either, because I'm still going to be here, getting in the way of anything you dweebs want to do. You'll be sorry!"

"I already am," Cameron murmured while watching him go.

"I'm so glad he didn't win," Jenny whispered.

"Me too. Will you be my vice president?"

She perked up at this, her smile giving him renewed hope. "Absolutely! Thank you!"

"My pleasure," Cameron said. "I would have been just as happy to see you win."

Jenny had a spring in her step as she walked away.

Silvia was the next to approach him. "Congratulations," she said. "I can't wait to see Anthony's face. He's going to be so thrilled."

"I don't know about that," Cameron replied, but he didn't get a chance to explain, because LaVern walked over.

"I'd like a moment of your time," she said.

He looked at Silvia apologetically. They said goodbye. The last stragglers left the classroom.

"I assume you've heard the news," LaVern said, nodding at the student handbook on his desk.

"Did you know about this?" he asked.

"Yes," she admitted.

"Then why didn't you say anything? Now it's too late, and the whole election was for nothing!" He winced at his own outburst. "Sorry."

"I understand your frustration," LaVern said. "You're welcome to vent it here. How did you react when Preckwinkle told you?"

Cameron shrugged. "I tried to reason with her. Not that it helped."

"I'm glad you kept a cool head. That bodes well for the future."

"But what can I do? She won't let me change the dress code or talk to the school board about it. I already asked."

"You won't get her to budge on the dress code," LaVern said with a frown, "but do you know what's missing from the student handbook?"

He shook his head.

"An anti-discrimination policy." LaVern's powerful gaze bored into him. "Are you familiar with those?"

"Yeah," he said. "It's so people can't be discriminated against based on their color or creed."

"And a good many other things," LaVern said. "That's where you should make your move."

Cameron blinked in surprise. "You agree with me?"

"I'm here to guide your education," LaVern said. "And in this class—given your position—that means supporting your political ambitions. Which I do have some sympathy for, yes."

Cameron licked his lips, always nervous about having to come out, but it wasn't exactly a secret anymore. "I wanted to become president to protect my boyfriend."

LaVern didn't blink an eye at this confession. "An anti-discrimination policy could provide him and countless others with that protection."

"But the new rules are going to make it so he can't be himself!"

LaVern raised an eyebrow. "When I was in grade school, I grew my hair out until it was a big beautiful afro, just like my grandma had. My homeroom teacher sent me home with a note that I needed to have my hair cut or straightened. My mother and father tried talking to the principal, who wasn't sympathetic. I didn't want my hair straightened. So I cut it all off."

Her hair was still much shorter than most women wore it. Almost militant.

"My homeroom teacher didn't care that it was part of my cultural heritage," LaVern continued. "Of course, the school didn't have an anti-discrimination policy back then, or I might have had more of a voice."

"Do you think that would work for my boyfriend too?" he asked.

"If not, would you still find it a worthwhile pursuit?"

Cameron didn't need to dig deep for the answer. Preckwinkle had stolen his thunder, but LaVern had given him a lightning bolt. He was going to keep his promise and make the school a safer place.

For everyone.

CHAPTER 19
OCTOBER 2ND, 1993

Ricky sat on the couch in his living room, alternating between yawning and sighing while watching old reruns of *The Beverly Hillbillies*. Those usually made him laugh—Granny's antics especially—but not today. He hadn't so much as smiled. After swiping the remote control, he turned off the TV, the resulting silence resonating with him. Ricky felt empty inside. He'd been aching for Diego since they'd been forced apart four months earlier. Only hope had sustained him through the long grueling separation. Not anymore. Diego had moved on. It really was over.

Ricky stared at his murky reflection in the glassy-gray screen of the television and tried to imagine another world, one where he'd conquered his fear and gone to El Paso. By now he would be enrolled in a new school. Once class was out for the day, he'd walk to where Diego worked and tell him about the new friends he'd made, or what they'd gotten up to. After the work day was over, they would return to their little apartment so Ricky could cook dinner. Something easy, like a box of macaroni and cheese. Diego would eat most of it while Ricky watched and laughed, never needing much himself. His appetite would be satisfied later, when Diego would finally unzip his coveralls, stepping out of them while asking in that deliciously deep voice of his, "So… Whaddya wanna do now?" Afterwards, when they were both worn out and exhausted, they would stretch out on the couch to watch TV, Ricky falling asleep in Diego's big arms. He'd wake up in them again the next morning, except in bed, where he'd lovingly been carried to during the night.

Ricky took off his glasses and wiped at his eyes. He could have had it all. Although he doubted his El Paso friends would've been as cool as the ones he had here. That included Mindy, because Ricky couldn't bring himself to hate her. Not after she'd been there for Diego during the summer and ever since. This way only one of them ended up alone. Diego deserved to have someone. Especially after all the terrible things he'd been through. Ricky's life was a walk in the park by comparison.

He glanced around, his face crumpling with the realization that he'd trade everything happy in his life for one more day together.

"Honey?" he heard his mother say.

Ricky quickly put his glasses back on. "Hey!" he said, trying to sound upbeat.

Ami sat on the couch next to him, her features already concerned. "What are you up to?"

"Just thinking," he replied.

"About what?"

Ricky shrugged, not trusting himself to speak.

Ami smoothed down his hair, even though he preferred it swept to the side. "Do you have any plans today?"

He shook his head.

"Oh really? You aren't hanging out with any of your friends?"

Ricky shook his head again.

"Oh. Why don't you have one of them over for a sleepover? Omar is such a sweet boy. What's he up to?"

Ricky shrugged. "I'm not really in the mood to hang out with anyone."

His mother studied him, always seeing more than he wanted her to. "Are you okay?"

Part of him resented her for prying. Then again, none of this was her fault. Not really. Although her rules and punishments sure hadn't helped the situation. Then again, Diego's mom let him get away with murder, and while a loose leash might sound good on paper, the reality wasn't so great. Maybe it was good that his mom cared a little too much. Especially during moments like these, when he felt vulnerable.

Ricky's chin trembled. "No," he admitted. "I'm not okay."

"Oh honey!" Ami said, patting his hand. "What's wrong?"

"Diego," Ricky squeaked, unable to get out any other words.

His mother took a deep breath. "You're allowed to see him again."

Ricky blinked. "What?"

"Your father told me," she said. "Eventually. He waited until it was a good time, but I know that Diego was over here the other night. If you promise to always be home before your curfew, and to keep your pager on so we can get ahold of you, then we'll take it from there."

Oh the irony! Ricky gulped down air so he could respond. "It's too late. He has a girlfriend now."

Ami's mouth became an "O" of sympathy. "So you aren't..."

He shook his head.

She squeezed his hand. "I'm so sorry!"

"It's fine," he lied. "Just don't tell me that I'll meet someone new, because I—" He swallowed and forced the words out. "I only want Diego."

Ami put her arm around him and pulled him close. "The mother in me wants to say whatever it takes to comfort you. The truth is, you just have to live with the pain. It really will get better with time, but I suppose that's not much help now, is it?"

He shook his head, leaning against her for support before making himself sit upright. "I'll be okay," he said.

She searched his face. "Are you sure you don't want to hang out with your friends? It'll help get your mind off of him for a little while."

He shook his head. "I'm too depressed."

The lines on her face deepened. "Have you had any suicidal thoughts?"

"No!" he answered immediately. "I'll never try that again, believe me."

Ami studied him a moment longer. "Would you like to see Dr. Sharma?"

Ricky sat upright. "For real?"

His mother nodded. "If you think it would help."

Of course it would! She was the wisest woman he'd ever met. Dr. Sharma would know what to do. "I'd really like that," he said. "The sooner the better."

"Okay. I'll make an appointment. For now..." She patted his leg and stood. "Come help me in the kitchen."

"With what?" he asked. "It's too early to start dinner."

"I'm in the mood to bake. I just can't decide what. Cookies? Brownies?"

"I haven't had your lemon bars in a long time," Ricky said, mustering some enthusiasm.

"That's it then," Ami said with shining eyes. "Like the old saying, when life gives you lemons, make lemon bars."

He made a face, but when her back was turned, Ricky was surprised to find a smile playing about his lips. He knew it wouldn't last. Tonight, when he was alone in his room, the sorrow would return to weigh him down again. But for now, a break from it all would be nice. Especially one that was so citrusy sweet!

Anthony stood naked in front of the bathroom mirror and frowned at himself. He had bags under his eyes from insomnia that had plagued him the entire weekend. Ever since his boyfriend had sat him down and explained, with an apologetic expression, what the new dress code entailed. Cameron had even said he was sorry, as if it was somehow his fault. Anthony knew who was to blame. Troy. Preckwinkle. An entire culture that insisted on rigid gender lines. Why? He wasn't hurting anyone. *They* were the ones hurting *him*, because lately, Anthony felt rejected and persecuted by the world he lived in. All because he'd found something that made him happy. And now?

The face in the mirror sagged with misery. Yesterday's eyeliner was smeared and fading. God it looked good! His downturned lips were bare and begging for some extra shine. He had taken out his earrings and rubbed off the intentionally distressed nail polish with a solvent. As for his pink hair... It wasn't too late. He could show up at school this morning, looking like he did now, and face the consequences. Where would that end? His parents being called in? Suspension? Expulsion? Preckwinkle would love any excuse to throw the book at him. She would delight in getting to punish him for being so queer. Anthony clenched his jaw. Then he reached for the electric clippers and turned them on.

He stared at the jagged blade as it vibrated back and forth. No guard was attached. Those razor-sharp teeth would greedily consume his hair, right down to the blond roots. He met his green eyes in the mirror. Then he leaned over the bathroom counter, brought the clippers to his scalp, and mowed a strip right down the middle, resulting in an inverse mohawk. There was no turning back. Even his mother couldn't salvage his hair at this point. Anthony kept running the clippers over his head until the sink appeared to be full of cotton candy.

Once sure that he'd gotten it all, he grimaced at his own reflection before stepping into the shower. Anthony scrubbed his face under the steaming water before continuing with his usual routine, although there wasn't really anything left to shampoo and condition. After stepping out of the tub, he was glad the mirror was too fogged up to see himself. Anthony went to his room and put on the outfit he'd carefully shopped for over the weekend. The shirt and slacks were both beige. He'd tried to get as close to his skin tone as possible when picking them out.

He returned to the bathroom and wiped the mirror with a towel. A stranger stared back at him. His features were gaunt and unhealthy, the clothes he wore tight fitting, making him appear naked. Almost like one of those horrible photos of Holocaust victims piled up in mass graves. Some of those people were just like him, but they had been sentenced to hard labor and ultimately death for being queer. High school was nothing by comparison. He could handle this.

Anthony switched off the light. He grabbed a pair of cheap beige sandals that he'd bought to go with the rest of his outfit. Then he went downstairs, already braced for his parents' reaction.

His father was the first to see him. Joe dropped the fork he was holding, his mouth hanging open. "Who the hell are you and what did ya do with my son?"

"Just following the rules," Anthony said bitterly.

He'd already told them about the new dress code.

"Oh honey," Dawn said, eyeing him sympathetically. "I wish you had let me dye your hair instead. Even if you didn't want to be blond, you could have gone back to black."

Anthony had considered that, but it felt too much like giving Preckwinkle what she wanted. This was much more of a statement. His parents tried to put a positive spin on his appearance as he ate. "At least I made a beautifully-shaped head," his mother said at one point. He appreciated their support. Not so long ago, he would have worried about what they'd think, but ever since he'd come out, his parents had proven their love to him through acceptance. Here, at least, he felt safe.

Anthony was much more nervous when leaving for school. As always, he stopped by Omar's house first.

His best friend started scowling the second they saw each other.

"Preckwinkle is a fucking psychopath," Omar grumbled when meeting him in the driveway. "Maybe I should cut my hair too. You know, in solidarity or whatever."

"Please don't," Anthony said, adoring those dark locks too much.

"Well no matter what," Omar said while tossing his skateboard in the back seat, "you look badass. Like some sort of Joan of Arc. Even though I prefer it when you're pretty."

"Thanks," Anthony replied from around a lump in his throat. It was exactly what he'd needed to hear.

He was nervous on the way to Cameron's house. Anthony had already warned him of his intentions. The only people he wanted to shock with his appearance were the detractors at school. Regardless, this would've been a much easier plan to execute if he didn't have to worry about someone finding him attractive. He parked in his boyfriend's driveway and got out, so they'd have privacy. Anthony met him at the front door.

"Wow!" Cameron said, clearly taken aback. "That's a big difference, but you look great!"

"What?" Anthony asked in disbelief.

"You look nice," Cameron said with a smile before leaning forward for a kiss.

Anthony pulled back instinctually. "*Nice?* I hate how I look!"

Cameron's face contorted with confusion. "I don't. You're still my boyfriend. Your eyes haven't changed. Neither have your lips." He leaned forward again.

Anthony kissed him, feeling wounded without knowing why.

"Are you okay?" Cameron asked on the way back to the car.

"Yes," he said, forcing a reassuring smile.

Today was going to be tough enough emotionally. The last person he wanted to alienate was the guy who loved him. Anthony considered lifting his spirits by playing Culture Club, but he was pretty sure it would only upset him more. Although he did turn on the radio hoping to hear "The Crying Game" because if anyone could understand what he was going through, it was Boy George.

The fates weren't on his side, although they did hear Nirvana, which was a welcome reminder that he had something to look forward to.

"Seventeen more days until the concert!" Cameron said.

Anthony grinned. Especially when Omar groaned from the back seat.

"I'm so frickin' jealous!" his best friend moaned.

Cameron craned his neck to look at him. "I thought you were more into heavy metal?"

"And punk," Omar said, "but anyone with ears likes Nirvana. How could you not?"

They talked about their favorite songs the rest of the way. After they'd all gotten out, Anthony surveyed the parking lot. He spotted Troy and his friends hanging out around a sports car.

"Hey," he said. "Get your camcorder ready."

"How come?" Omar asked, already taking it out of his backpack.

Anthony nodded in Troy's direction. "I want you to get their reaction when they see me like this."

"You mean right now?"

"Yup." Anthony began marching toward them.

"Why waste your time?" Cameron asked while keeping pace.

"I need to do this," Anthony replied. "For me."

Graham had Dave in a headlock and was giving him a noogie. Troy laughed while keeping an arm looped possessively around Faith's waist. Hope stood nearby with her arms crossed. They were going to have a field day with Anthony. He felt shaky while approaching them until a surge of anger set his blood aboil. Then he picked up the pace.

"Ready?" Anthony murmured.

"I'm on it," Omar replied.

Graham was the first to notice him. He let go of Dave and nodded in his direction. "Check it out."

"What the fuck?" Troy said, looking him up and down before laughing. His amusement quickly turned to disgust. "Jesus Christ! Even without makeup, you still look hideous."

"Hey!" Cameron snarled.

"It's fine," Anthony said. "I just wanted to make sure that nothing had changed. Troy is still upset, even though he got his way. What are you going to do now? Run off to Preckwinkle again, like you did before?"

Faith made a face. "What's he talking about?"

"Nothing," Troy said. "He's crazy."

"You didn't tell her?" Anthony pressed before addressing Faith directly. "He worries about imagining me when he's with you."

"That's *not* what I said," Troy growled.

Anthony smirked. "So you *did* tattle on me."

"You mean the dress code?" Faith spat. "I already knew about that. And I agree with him."

"What about you?" Anthony said, looking at Dave now. Not the goofy guy with a mustache, but his former best friend, the one who had betrayed them all.

Dave averted his eyes. "This is why we don't hang out anymore," he mumbled, steeling himself before adding. "You're a freak!"

"Yeah, well it's better than being a fascist."

Graham took a step forward, his attention on Omar. "Stop pointing that thing at me," he said, his massive hands balling up into fists.

"It's for the video yearbook," Omar said. "Your parents are going to love this."

Graham took another step forward and reached for the camcorder. "I said stop!"

"Make me!" Omar dropped his board to the ground and skated an arc around them while still filming.

"Let's go inside," Hope murmured.

Troy didn't budge. He was looking at Cameron with a cruel expression. "I get that you're gay," he said, "but now that you're president, surely you can do better." His glare moved to Anthony. "You look like an old rawhide that my dog barfed up."

Cameron took Anthony's hand. "You don't know what love is," he said before walking away to a chorus of laughter.

Anthony glanced over his shoulder long enough to make sure they weren't being followed. "That was fun," he murmured.

Cameron looked at him like he was crazy, but the grinding of skateboard wheels cut off any response.

"What a bunch of dicks!" Omar said as he came to a halt.

"Did you get everything?" Anthony asked.

"Yeah. Nice and up close. So what's the plan? Are you gonna show Preckwinkle the footage?"

Anthony shook his head. "It's for me. If I ever feel like I'm crazy, or wonder if they're right, I'm going to watch that tape to remind myself who they really are, and who I never want to be."

Omar grinned. "You're so cool, dude!"

"Thanks."

When they heard the distant imitation of a screeching eagle, Omar glanced around until he located Whitney.

"That's my cue," he said. "See you guys later."

They watched him skate away, Cameron's grip tightening on Anthony's hand.

"I wish you wouldn't provoke people," he said.

Anthony recoiled in shock. "Are you kidding me?"

"No," Cameron said, his expression pained. "You're going to get hurt."

"I'll be fine."

"You don't know that. And frankly, you're only making things worse. I need Troy to be on my side."

Anthony rolled his eyes. "Because of the student council?"

"Yes! I'm trying to help you."

"You do things your way," he said, giving Cameron a quick peck on the lips. "I'll do them mine."

"Why can't we all work together and figure out a compromise?"

"Oh I don't know, maybe because this is the real world? I appreciate what you're trying to do. Really! The anti-discrimination policy is a great idea, but we don't know if it'll ever happen. Until it does…" Anthony exhaled and shook his head helplessly. "I still have to figure out a way to be myself."

"Okay, but maybe you should give them the same benefit."

Anthony scrunched up his face. "You agree with them?"

"Of course not!" Cameron said with a flush, "but you can't expect people to let you do whatever you want while telling them what they *aren't* allowed to do. Even if they are assholes. Like you said, this is the real world. It's never going to be a fairy tale where everyone holds hands and sings Kumbaya. People are always going to disagree. The only thing left to figure out is how we can get along despite not seeing eye to eye."

Anthony considered these words. Then he nodded. "You're right. I'll stop poking the hornet's nest."

"Thank you," Cameron said with transparent relief.

"After today," Anthony added.

His boyfriend groaned. They walked into the school hand-in-hand, Anthony grateful for Cameron's support, because they were attracting even more stares than usual. Which is what he'd wanted, but it was still a lot of scrutiny to bear. He was on his own when the first class began and as the rest of his day progressed. Lunch was especially trying.

Principal Preckwinkle stopped by their table as they were

eating and sized him up. He stared back defiantly as she did so, even standing up so she could get a better look.

Preckwinkle nodded. "Much better," she said in approval before walking away.

Anthony swallowed, feeling small and foolish, even with his friends there.

"Do you think Troy was trying to get you in trouble again?" Omar asked.

Anthony shook his head. "I knew she'd come check on me."

He had hoped, like Troy, that she would express frustration that he'd found a way of standing out despite staying within the lines. Instead she actually *preferred* him this way! He shouldn't be surprised.

All the stares and comments began to take a toll on him during the second half of the day. He wouldn't dress like this tomorrow. Not because he was giving into pressure or wanted to conform. This simply wasn't who he was. He still hadn't figured out how to be that person without breaking the rules.

As soon as he was free for the day, Anthony got into his car, wishing that everyone wasn't so busy. Cameron was expected to stay after school for the student council. Omar and Silvia had to work. Ricky and Mindy were rehearsing the next play. He went home and dressed in clothes that felt more comfortable to him. Then he put on his makeup before searching the house for a hat. Ballcaps always made him look like a little boy, he was reminded when trying a few on, so he settled for a black bandana that he found in his brother's old room. After covering his head with it and tying it around the back, he walked to Main Street, needing to see his boyfriend again. Anthony opened the door to Sweet Tea Antiques, a bell chiming above his head as he entered, and while he didn't see Cameron inside, a friendly face awaited him regardless.

"Oh thank goodness!" Charles said, already rushing around the counter to meet him. "I've been absolutely *dying* to talk to you!"

Anthony smiled. "You have my phone number."

"And you have mine, but all this business with 'Mr. Finnegan' makes it so much more complicated. I can't wait until you graduate from high school."

"Me neither," Anthony grumbled.

"Well there's nothing I can do about someone walking into my store from the street. Come! Let's share some tea while spilling it."

Anthony followed him back to the counter. Next to it was an antique serving cart with a glass jug of sun tea and vintage plastic cups. "Wow," he said, "it's not just the name of the store."

"I never do anything by halves," Charles said. "Remind me, do you take sugar?"

"Yes, please. You even have ice? That's doing things by three halves instead of two."

Charles chuckled when placing a cup in front of him. "Now then, how have you been? I was absolutely mortified when Lover Boy informed me of the interview he asked you to conduct."

"You mean the one with Troy?"

"Is that his name?" Charles said with a shudder. "I told my husband that it was a terrible idea. He insisted it would be good for your personal growth. I informed him that people like us face enough challenges as it is. We certainly don't need to go seeking them out!"

"People like us?" Anthony said, a smile coming unbidden.

"Queer people in general," Charles amended with a twinkle in his eye. "Was the experience as dreadful as I imagined?"

"Yeah, but it was just more of the same. The new dress code is worse."

Charles's attention darted to the bandana Anthony wore, and not for the first time. "Is that what inspired the new look? They're making you cover up your darling hair?"

"I wish," Anthony said. "I don't think I'd be allowed to wear this at school. I actually did something really stupid." He pulled off the bandana.

Charles gasped.

"I know," Anthony said miserably. "It made sense at the time. Now I wish I hadn't done it. I feel like I'm going crazy."

"The world will do that to you," Charles said, tilting his head while clearly trying to find something positive to say. "I suppose the new look has a touch of Sinéad O'Connor."

"I hate it," Anthony said, his voice cracking.

"I'm so sorry." Charles reached across the counter to pat his hand. Then he perked up. "I have an idea! Follow me."

He circled the counter and led the way down one of the aisles.

The place had really taken shape since Anthony's previous visit. In addition to all the furniture, there were squared off booths that featured a variety of smaller antiques. Charles ducked into one of these and emerged again while shaking what appeared to be a blond pom-pom.

"Tah-dah!"

Anthony stopped and stared. "Is that a wig?"

"Either that or someone lost their pet. I thought you might want to try it on. Just for fun."

"Are you kidding?" Anthony said louder than he intended.

"So you want to?" Charles asked.

"Yes!"

"Right this way." The older man led him to the restroom, stopping outside the door. "We don't have many clothing items at the moment, but I should probably set up a changing booth anyway. For now…" He held out the wig.

Anthony started to reach for it. Then he glanced around. "Cameron isn't here?"

"Not yet, but he did say he intended to stop by. How come?"

"Doesn't matter," Anthony said, taking the wig. "So I guess I just…"

"I'm sure you'll figure it out," Charles said warmly. "Go right ahead. I'll give you some privacy."

Anthony entered the restroom, distracted by how much it had changed. The last time he'd seen it, there hadn't been anything but a grungy toilet and sink. Now the porcelain was polished, the walls decorated with vintage art and a shelf full of knickknacks, all of which were for sale. Very clever!

Anthony noticed his reflection in the mirror. He really did look like Sinéad O'Connor, who was beautiful in her own right, but he felt a disconnect, like he was seeing someone else. Anthony turned the wig over, noticing the netting inside. His pulse picked up in excitement as he put it on, crooked at first, until he made adjustments and brushed the long locks out of his eyes. When he looked in the mirror again…

He saw a woman.

That's when everything clicked. He brought a hand to his mouth, overcome by a strange mixture of laughter and tears. Anthony wasn't sad. Not in the slightest. His heart was bursting with joy! He took a step back, turning his head from side to side while his eyes remained locked on his own reflection. The wig's hair was golden and straight, reaching down to his shoulders. He wasn't sure if the style suited him, but it was leagues better than his buzzed scalp. And much closer to who he really was. He smiled, his twin sister matching his gleeful expression.

"Hello beautiful," he said. "Where have you been hiding?"

Just beneath the surface, waiting to be let out. Anthony spun around, wanting to share his new discovery with Charles, but nobody was standing in the doorway. He hurried out of the restroom and saw someone else instead.

"There you are!" Cameron said, his expression puzzled before he laughed. "What are you doing?"

"Nothing." Anthony ripped the wig from his head. "Umm…"

"Charles said you were busy, but I couldn't wait. How did the rest of the day go? Are you okay?"

"Yeah!" Anthony said. "I'm fine."

Cameron nodded at the wig in his hands. "Do you want to see what that looks like on me? It'll be funny."

"No," Anthony said. "Your big head will stretch it out."

"My head isn't big!" His brow creased in concern. "Is it?"

Anthony managed a smile. "Just a little. But I like it."

Cameron put his hands on either side of his head, as if trying to squish it into shape. "Is that why most hats don't fit me?"

"Doesn't matter," Anthony said before smooching him. "You're perfect."

"So are you. What do you think of the store? Hey! You should see the chair I'm restoring right now. It has all sorts of weird things carved into it. Come look. It's in my workshop."

He was referring to a room at the back of the store. Charles had designated the space for the carpentry Cameron did, so he'd always have a place to further his projects.

"I'll meet you there," Anthony said, jiggling the wig. "Let me give this back and grab my drink."

He went to the front counter, where Charles was ringing up a purchase. "My apologies," he said once they were alone. "A customer came in and I wasn't sure how much longer you'd be in there."

"I thought it was just a few seconds," Anthony said in surprise.

"Closer to ten minutes." Charles nodded at the wig. "What did you think?"

"I love it," Anthony admitted. Everything else he felt was too monumental to put into words just yet.

"Then why aren't you still wearing it? If you don't like the style, you can have it cut, just like normal hair. Your mother is a beautician, isn't she?"

"Yeah." Anthony stroked the wig fondly and noticed the price tag dangling from it. Fifty dollars? Yikes! "Thanks for letting me try it on," he said, setting the wig on the counter.

"You don't want to take it home with you?"

"I can't afford it. Besides, they won't let me wear it at school. Even if I get it cut to look more masculine."

"I've seen the new dress code, and it doesn't say *anything* about how long a boy's hair can be. Grow it out, honey. For now…" Charles pushed the wig toward him. "You've got this to tide you over. On the house."

Anthony looked up in surprise. "Are you sure?"

"If you don't take it, it'll probably still be here a year from now. You deserve a treat. Especially after everything you've been through lately. Go spend some time with your boyfriend. I have the original box around here somewhere. By the time you're ready to leave, it'll be all packed up and waiting for you."

Anthony went to find Cameron. But not before walking around the counter to give Charles a great big hug.

CHAPTER 20
OCTOBER 6ᵀᴴ, 1993

Mindy was curled up on the couch in her living room while reading aloud from *The Catcher in the Rye*. Each time she looked up from the book, she'd find Diego's eyes smoldering as they watched her. She had invited him over under the pretense of helping him learn his lines for the upcoming play, but they were nearing the end of the novel and eager to finish. She had just reached the titular scene, where the protagonist thinks about how he'd like to be the catcher in the rye, so he could stop people from getting hurt, revealing how wounded he is beneath all the anger and rebellion.

"Would you read this part to me?" Mindy asked, holding the book out to Diego.

"How come?" he asked.

"My eyes are tired," she lied.

In truth, she thought the perpetual edge of rawness in Diego's voice was perfectly suited to Holden Caulfield. And she liked getting to study his strong features when he was distracted. As he continued to read, she stretched out and rested her head in his lap, Diego not missing a beat as he shifted to accommodate her. She closed her eyes to take in the rumble of his words, only opening them again when he reached the end of the chapter. Diego had set aside the book and was staring down at her.

"Sit up," he said.

"Sorry," she said while complying. "Is my head too heavy?"

"No," Diego replied with half-lidded eyes. "You're perfect. I just wanted to do this."

He leaned toward her, his intent unmistakable. And irresistible. Mindy kissed him back, placing a hand on his cheek before she moved it down to his chest, so she could gently push him away.

"Wait," she said.

Diego pulled back, affection dancing in his gaze. "What's up?"

Mindy gathered all her strength, but even then, it almost wasn't enough. "We shouldn't be doing this."

His face scrunched up. "Why not?"

Mindy rocked backwards until she tumbled into the far corner of the couch. "Because of Ricky."

Diego glowered at this. "I already told you—"

"I know," she interrupted. "But he's really upset. The other day, in theater, Ricky pulled me aside to give me his blessing."

"You never needed it," Diego huffed.

"You don't understand. He was trying to tell me everything I would need to do for you, to keep you happy."

Diego's lip snarled as he struggled to articulate a response. "Like I'm some sort of emotionally challenged kid who needs a babysitter?"

"No! It was really sweet. That's why I think he deserves another chance. He obviously loves you."

Diego considered her. "And you don't?"

Mindy took a deep breath. "I think I could. I already care about you. Deeply. But it's not the same as being in love. Or do you not feel the same way about him?"

Diego averted his eyes. "It doesn't matter how I feel."

She shook her head in confusion. "Then what does?"

"Him being happy."

"That settles it then," Mindy said, her heart breaking a little. "Ricky was sad before you came along. You just need to be with him again."

"It's not that simple." Diego pushed himself off the couch, seemingly without a destination in mind, because he began to pace. "You think Ricky was sad before he met me? That's bullshit! Who do you think pushed him toward the brink of suicide? And yeah, I wanted to make sure that wouldn't happen again, and he kept asking to be with me, so I figured why the hell not. What happened then, huh? I fucked up his life! He was in trouble the entire time we were together, and if he'd been dumb enough to listen to me, Ricky would be in some other state by now. I'm the *last* thing he needs." Diego rounded on her with a scowl. "Same goes for you! Remember when I wanted us to toilet paper Faith's house? If we had, *you* would've been the one getting hounded by the police. I'm not the sort of person you should associate with. Jesus fucking Christ! What am I even doing here?"

He reached for the script on the coffee table, like he intended to leave. Mindy placed her hand over his. Diego didn't pull away.

He hesitated, so she stood, walked around the table, and gave him a hug.

Diego didn't hug her back. "You don't get it," he grumbled. "I always fuck everything up."

"You're way too hard on yourself." she replied, still clinging to him. "Most people don't get it right on their first try. Or even their second or third. That's just how it is." She released him and took a step back. "Do you still have feelings for Ricky?"

Diego swallowed. "Yeah," he said hoarsely.

Mindy nibbled her bottom lip, torn between what she wanted and what she thought was right. "I really like you, Diego… but Ricky *needs* you." She straightened up and put on a brave face. "I'm a big girl. I do just fine on my own."

Diego shook his head while scowling at a nearby wall.

"I can't tell you what to do," Mindy said. "I only know what feels right to me. I couldn't live with myself, knowing that us being together would hurt Ricky, so I think it's for the best that we stay friends and nothing more."

Diego exhaled, the tension draining from him with the released air. "Smart thinking," he said. "You probably just dodged a bullet."

Mindy didn't think so. In fact, it felt as if that bullet had struck her right in the heart. But when she thought of the way Ricky's chin had quivered and everything he'd gone through since moving here, she felt the strength of her convictions.

"He's the lucky one," she said. "Now let's start practicing your lines. I'll get us something to drink. Okay?"

Diego nodded.

Mindy waited until she had left the room before she stopped, pressed her hand to her chest, and sighed. She'd finally met a knight in shining armor. But she couldn't be his damsel in distress.

Ricky felt dizzy from talking so much, having to gasp between sentences on occasion, because there was so much he needed Dr. Sharma to know. From the comforting confines of her office, he told his therapist everything that had transpired since they'd last seen each other: the arson that sent Diego into hiding, the magical first time with him in Candle Cave, the drive to El Paso that came to a premature end, and the long summer of separation which followed.

Ricky glanced at his Casio calculator watch and felt a jolt of panic. They were already nearing the end of the session! He hurriedly described what he'd been through since returning to Pride—how Diego had remained distant before moving on completely.

"Mindy is really nice," he said, "so maybe it's for the best, but I feel so guilty for hurting him, and if I'm honest, I wish we were still together. So what do you think?"

"That you should take a deep breath," Dr. Sharma said with a hint of amusement, "both figuratively and literally. You're only fifteen years old, and you've already had a more adventurous love life than many of the adults I know."

"I just want to be with one guy," Ricky said. "Diego is all I need. So is it too late? Have I already ruined my chances?"

He watched Dr. Sharma quietly consider his question, the only sounds in her office a ticking clock and the pen she tapped gently on her notepad. "What I think," she said at last, "is that it's unrealistic to expect a relationship to last when trust has been broken so early."

Ricky's shoulders slumped. "I figured. I really messed up, huh?"

"I don't mean you," Dr. Sharma said. "Diego is the one who broke *your* trust."

Ricky scrunched up his face before shaking his head. "He didn't do anything wrong."

"Perhaps not on purpose," Dr. Sharma replied, "but good intentions don't allow you to dictate what the other person does under penalty of separation. Think of it this way: Let's say you had a bad dream that Diego died in a car accident, which you found so upsetting that you asked him to never drive again. He would probably refuse this request, considering how important cars are to him on both a professional and a personal level. Would it then be fair of you to threaten to leave him if he didn't comply with your wish?"

"Like an ultimatum?"

"Precisely," Dr. Sharma said. "I'm proud of you, Ricky. You found yourself in a very difficult situation, and even though it was painful, you made the right choice. Your family and friends are important to you. So is a sense of security. You've always impressed me with your insight and maturity, but even then, I don't believe you're ready to live on your own in a different state.

Especially cut off from your family and friends. No matter his intentions, it was unfair of Diego to expect you to choose between his love and everything else. That isn't how a healthy relationship is supposed to work."

"But he came back," Ricky croaked, "even though he knew it would get him in trouble. Diego spent his entire summer locked up for me."

"A noble sacrifice, and a much healthier manifestation of his feelings for you. I'm not asking you to blame him. Diego is a product of his upbringing, and it sounds to me like he's doing the best he can with what he's been given. What I'd like you to take away from this session is the alleviation of your own guilt. Forgive yourself, Ricky. You made a hard decision in the most trying of circumstances. You didn't intend to hurt Diego. You've already apologized for doing so. Had you sacrificed your own needs and gone with him, the relationship would have ended sooner rather than later, but not before more damage had been done. You did the best you could. Diego probably did as well. It's time to move on."

"Completely?" Ricky asked in disbelief.

"Can you truly accept being his friend? Will that be a constant detriment to your own happiness and well-being? Only you can answer that. Think about it. Carefully."

Ricky did so. He imagined climbing into the back seat of Diego's car each morning, Mindy already in the front, having been picked up first. He envisioned them going to prom and having sex, neither of which he was likely to see in person, but it would still sting when he found out. Even then, Ricky hated the idea of being cut off from him completely. Not knowing how Diego was doing, and what he got up to, would be torture. He'd already had a taste of that during the summer. In a way, Ricky was being asked to choose between two different kinds of pain.

"I'm not sure," he answered at last.

"That's the best answer you could have given," Dr. Sharma said with a nod of approval. "Continue to weigh the question as you go forward. If being around Diego hurts too much, then you'll know it's time to prioritize your own happiness. But for now…"

"No more guilt," he said.

Dr. Sharma smiled. "That brings us to the end of our session."

Ricky thanked her, already feeling lighter when he stood and made his way outside. A black Dodge idled in the parking lot, the boom boom boom of bass audible behind the rolled-up windows. Anthony sat behind the wheel. A pink bandana covered his scalp, which combined with the eyeliner and lip gloss, was feminine and unmistakably gay. Ricky thought it was awesome. He waved to get Anthony's attention before running over and climbing in.

"What are you listening to?" he asked as the music was turned down. "It sounds like something my dad would play."

"The Doobie Brothers," Anthony replied sheepishly. "They're *way* better than I care to admit, so pretend it was something cooler than that."

Ricky laughed. "Your secret is safe with me."

Anthony shifted the car into reverse and began pulling out. "How did it go?"

"Amazing!" Ricky said. "If you ever need help, you should talk to her. Dr. Sharma is even wiser than Yoda."

"Hopefully she has a better handle on grammar," Anthony said, "or confused I will likely be. And uh… Speaking of wisdom, I need your help."

"With what?" Ricky asked.

"Don't make a big deal out of this, or tell anyone else, but my one-year anniversary with Cameron is tomorrow and um… I want to give him something special."

"So let's go shopping," Ricky said with a shrug. "Wait! Do you mean…" When he saw his friend blush, he clasped his hands together in excitement. "You're going to go *all the way* with him?"

Anthony bit his bottom lip and nodded. "I want to. But I don't know how. We tried before and it really hurt."

Ricky waved away his concerns. "I've got this. Drive us to the nearest pharmacy. Actually, choose one that you never ever go to, because it's about to get embarrassing. But I promise that it's worth it!"

Anthony grimaced in concern before accelerating. Ten minutes later, they were standing in an aisle dominated by feminine hygiene products. Ricky grabbed a box off the shelf and smiled.

"This is your new best friend," he said.

"An enema?" Anthony said, peering at the label before glancing around to make sure they were alone. "You're kidding, right?"

"You really just need the bottle, so you can spray water up

your butt. I tried using the laxative it came with once and it was a *very* bad idea. Not romantic at all. Hey look, this one is more like a hot water bottle. I guess that works too."

Anthony's face was burning. "What if I don't eat anything from now until our anniversary? That works too, right?"

"Trust me," Ricky said, "after the first time, you'll want to do it again. And what if it's spontaneous instead of a special occasion?"

"So I what… Do a seductive dance for Cameron before pulling out that bottle?"

Ricky laughed. "Tell him you need to get ready and lock yourself in the bathroom. It's easy. We can try it today if you want to practice."

"No!" Anthony said hurriedly. "I'm not sure I want to do this at all!"

"You'll love it," Ricky said, feeling a pang of sorrow as he remembered how gentle Diego had been. "You'll feel so close to him. I know giving yourself an enema is the opposite of hot, but you'll want to be as clean as humanly possible, so you don't have to worry. Once you are…" He sucked in air before exhaling again. "It can be really beautiful, I swear. Oh! You'll need lube too. This way." Ricky led him down the aisle. "My mom says the water-based kind is best, since it's more natural."

"You've talked to your mom about this stuff?" Anthony asked in disbelief.

Ricky nodded happily. "She's a gynecologist. You should hear the sort of topics that come up at the dinner table."

Anthony laughed. "Water-based lube it is," he said, choosing a small bottle.

"What about condoms?" Ricky asked. "Oh wait, you've only ever been with each other, right?"

Anthony nodded.

"That's lucky," Ricky said. "Otherwise, you should always wear one. Or I guess *he* should. Unless you plan on mixing things up on occasion."

Anthony blushed again and shook his head. "I can only speak for myself, but when I fantasize about being with him, Cameron is always on top."

"Same here," Ricky said before catching himself. "I mean, in general," he added hurriedly. "I'm always the bottom, no matter who I'm thinking about. Not that I fantasize about your boyfriend."

Anthony peered at him before laughing. "I'd be disappointed if you *didn't* think of Cameron on occasion."

"In that case," Ricky said with a grin, "he's in my top ten list. Easily. Who's in yours?"

"Lately?" Anthony said. "Mostly just my boyfriend."

"Wow, you *are* in love!" Ricky said. "I envy you. But I also like that I get to help. This is even more fun than being a campaign manager!"

Anthony laughed before looking self-conscious. Probably because a mother and daughter were coming down the aisle. "Have we got it all?" he asked.

"Yes," Ricky replied. "Let's go." Wanting to prove there was nothing to be embarrassed about, he proudly marched toward the cash registers at the front of the store.

"This is mortifying," Anthony murmured as they were waiting in line. He was still clutching the lube and enema bulb, even though they could be placed on the conveyor belt in front of them.

"I've got this," Ricky said, taking the things from him. "What a beautiful day!" he said to the cashier when it was their turn. He set the items on the counter. "Too bad we have to stay inside and work on a science project. At least we found the things we'll need."

The cashier rang up the items, raising one of her eyebrows at the enema bulb, so Ricky waggled his in response. Once they had paid and were handed the bag, they stumbled out of the store laughing.

"She totally thinks we're about to do it!" Ricky cackled.

"For our science project," Anthony said, before clearing his throat and standing up straight, as if giving a presentation. "For the school's consideration, we'd like to demonstrate the most efficient way to have anal sex."

"Yes!" Ricky said. "We'll win first prize, I know it!"

Once in the privacy of the car, Anthony turned an overwhelmed expression on him. "I'm so nervous. What if I can't do this?"

"Then tell him that," Ricky suggested. "You shouldn't force yourself. Do you *want* to do it?"

Anthony nodded instantly. "Yeah. I'm just scared I'll mess up somehow."

"Don't worry," Ricky said. "Dr. Nishikawa will teach you everything you need to know."

"Um… Do we *have* to get your mom involved?"

"No silly, I was pretending to be a doctor, although I'm sure she'd be happy to help."

Anthony shook his head. "Let's keep this between us. Like… forever."

Ricky nodded his agreement, his heart still heavy with sorrow, but there was plenty of room inside for other emotions. Like the love he felt for his honorary big brother, and how fulfilling it was to help him chase after his own happiness.

Cameron's cheeks were sore from smiling so much. He'd been with Anthony for an entire year now! He could scarcely believe his luck. After wanting so long to find someone, he'd ended up with the perfect guy on his first try. And now they were celebrating their anniversary together. The night had been a major success so far. They'd decided to recreate their first date, beginning at Turing's Arcade, where they played a bunch of games. Mostly the kind that awarded tickets, so that Cameron could finally win Anthony the plush pig that he'd wanted.

"I think I'll name him Troy," Anthony had joked while snuggling it.

It wasn't until afterwards, when they went to a vegetarian restaurant called The Garden of Eatin', that the pig was properly christened.

"Tempeh is a cute name," Anthony had said while perusing the menu. "I don't like eating it, but that works, because I don't like eating pigs."

"And when he's bad," Cameron had responded, "you can tell him not to have a tempeh tantrum."

Anthony had laughed, like he always did when Cameron made a dumb joke. Okay, maybe not *always*, but often enough that he felt his goofy sense of humor was appreciated. After they'd finished dinner, they decided not to go to a movie, as they'd done on their first date. Mostly because Anthony's parents were on a date of their own, which meant they would have the house to themselves. That's where they were now, the anticipation thick in the air as Cameron waited in Anthony's bedroom. Their personal mixtape was playing on the stereo. They'd already slow danced together. And made out. When things had gotten heated and Cameron tried to undress him, Anthony had excused himself.

"I have to get ready," his boyfriend had said enigmatically before rushing from the room.

Cameron was reminded of all the movies and TV shows he'd seen where a woman would lock herself in the bathroom on her wedding night, the man waiting impatiently in the bedroom like he was now. Although he didn't expect Anthony to return dressed in gauzy lingerie. Then again…

His attention moved to the featureless Styrofoam bust that sported a blond wig. Charles had given it to Anthony. Cameron wasn't sure what to make of that. Besides the obvious. Anthony hadn't mentioned the wig or worn it again, as far as he knew. Maybe he'd only accepted the gift out of politeness. If so, it sure was displayed prominently. Anthony was literally sleeping next to the wig, since the bust was on the nightstand Cameron had restored after they'd found it together on their first date. Had they not driven home tonight, maybe they would have lucked out and walked past another trash pile to dig through. That would have been *really* romantic!

He was laughing at this train of thought when Anthony finally returned to the room wearing nothing but a red bathrobe and a pink bandana.

"Hey," his boyfriend said sheepishly. "I could have gotten dressed again but it seemed kind of pointless since…" He shrugged. "You know."

"Makin' it easy on me?" Cameron asked with a grin as he walked over. He playfully tugged on the robe's belt while leaning forward for a smooch. Anthony smelled great! "Wait," he said when pulling back. "Did you take a shower?"

Anthony shrugged. "I want everything to be perfect."

"Should *I* take a shower?"

Anthony laughed. "You're already perfect. Except for this." He grabbed the hem of his shirt and lifted.

Cameron took over and pulled it over his own head. "What about these?" he asked, placing his hands on the waist of his jeans.

"Those have to go too," Anthony said. "Let me help."

He got down on his knees. Cameron started gasping soon after. He would have been happy to remain there if it wasn't such a special occasion. "Get back up here," he said, stepping out of his underwear and jeans as Anthony stood.

He slid his hands inside the folds of the robe, his palms caressing the soft skin there before he pulled his boyfriend close. They resumed kissing, his hands never idle. He pushed the robe over Anthony's shoulders until it fell to the floor. Cameron kissed his neck before working his way down, Anthony squirming. With impatience, as it turned out.

"I don't want to rush anything," he said. "But I also don't want to wait any longer."

Cameron grinned. Then he grabbed Anthony around the waist as he stood, draping him over one shoulder, and carried him over to the bed, where he put his boyfriend down again on his back. Cameron climbed on top of him.

"Okay," he said. "We're moving into the fast lane."

Anthony looked slightly panicked. "Maybe not *too* fast."

"Vroom vroom!" Cameron said when grinding against him.

Anthony laughed and relaxed again.

To prove that he was only kidding, Cameron kissed him with careful intent. When he pulled back, joy was dancing in those emerald eyes. He pressed his lips to Anthony's forehead affectionately, just beneath the bandana he still wore. Wanting to see the frizzy hair beneath it, Cameron reached up and started to pull it off.

Anthony's hand came down on top of the bandana. "Don't!"

"I wanna see you naked," Cameron said. "All of you."

Anthony's cheeks grew red. "I hate my hair."

"Why?" Cameron asked. "It's cute. And I like how it feels."

He pulled on the bandana again. This time Anthony didn't resist. Fine blond hairs covered his scalp, like bristles made of the softest silk. Cameron ran a hand over the curve of his scalp and laughed happily at the tickling sensation. Anthony only looked more miserable.

"I hate it," he repeated.

"You look cute!"

Anthony glowered at him before he seemed to find some cause for optimism. "I have an idea," he said. "Sit up."

Cameron complied.

"Close your eyes," Anthony said.

He did so, unable to resist a smile. And another joke. "I'm not ready for whips and paddles," he said, "but my safe word is 'soy bacon.'"

"That's more than one word," Anthony replied. "Okay, you can open them again."

Cameron did so, his smile faltering when he saw that Anthony was wearing the wig. His boyfriend's eyes were wide open, like he was seeking reassurance instead of amusement.

"You always wanted to see me as a blond," Anthony said, brushing at the bangs.

"That's a little longer than I was imagining," Cameron replied diplomatically.

"I'm going to have my mom cut it. I just need to decide on a style."

Anthony flopped back on the pillow again, like they were going to continue with him still wearing the wig. Cameron stared, unsure what to do or say, because all that hair was really throwing him for a loop.

"Oh wait!" Anthony sat up again.

Cameron felt relief. But only momentarily.

"Let's switch positions," Anthony said.

"Why?" Cameron asked, not hiding his unease.

"So I can fuck you up the butt," Anthony deadpanned. "Ricky said it'll be easier to start if I'm on top. Not as *the* top, but... You'll see."

Cameron made a face. "What does Ricky have to do with any of this?"

"He gave me some pointers. Now get off me, so we can get off together."

Cameron rolled to the side. Anthony climbed on top, straddling his hips and pushing him back down into a horizontal position.

"I see," Cameron said with bedroom eyes. "You want to go for a ride."

"Yeah," Anthony said before looking doubtful. "I think so. Um..."

"Maybe we should page Ricky and ask him to come over. Sounds like we might need a personal trainer."

Anthony laughed. "I'm sure he'd love that."

He fell forward and they resumed kissing. Which felt great, except the wig kept tickling him. Cameron's mouth continued to work as his eyes darted around, his view reduced to a blond curtain that walled in their faces. Which was different. And kind of weird.

Anthony sat up, his gaze filled with affection. Then he leaned back and reached behind him, his expression becoming concerned when he took hold of Cameron. Probably because he wasn't hard anymore.

"What's wrong?" Anthony asked.

"Nothing," Cameron said. "I just got distracted."

He looped a hand behind Anthony's neck to pull him back in for another kiss. Time to get his head in the game! He didn't want to let his boyfriend down. Or their personal trainer. He imagined Ricky in a chair angled toward the bed, so he could coach them. But of course he wouldn't just sit there. Cameron imagined his dark eyes glittering mischievously before Ricky reached for his zipper, so he could enjoy himself too. What a hot scenario! The next time Anthony reached for him, he got a firm handshake. His boyfriend began pressing his weight against him before he leaned in for another kiss. When a strand of hair tickled his nostril, Cameron brushed it away before doubling down on his concentration. In his mind, Ricky was still sitting nearby, stroking himself while whispering words of encouragement.

"Grab his ass cheeks and spread them wide. Make room for that great big—"

"Are you okay?" Anthony asked.

Cameron nodded with his eyes closed. He'd been acting out his fantasy, Anthony's tight little butt gripped in each of his hands. "Yeah. Keep going."

Anthony began pressing against him again. Ricky resumed stroking himself in his imagination.

"Hey," Anthony said.

"What's up?" Cameron asked.

"I really love you."

Cameron's eyelids fluttered open. He quickly shut them again. "I love you too."

Anthony remained perfectly still.

"Is it silly that I want you to look at me?"

Cameron opened his eyes again. "Of course not!"

Anthony smiled down at him, all that hair impossible to ignore. Especially when he kissed him on the nose, the wig pooling into curls on either side of Cameron's face. His boyfriend reached for the nightstand, opened the drawer, and pulled out a small bottle of lube. He squeezed some into his hand and reached behind him, which was bad timing because Cameron had gotten distracted again and—

Anthony looked at him sharply. "What's wrong?"

"Nothing!" he insisted.

Anthony swallowed. "Do you actually want to do this? It's okay if you don't."

"I do," Cameron said. "For real. It's just..." He pressed his lips together, unwilling to say anything that might hurt the person he loved. But he had to tell him *something* because Anthony was looking increasingly wounded. "I'm a little off my game tonight, that's all."

Anthony didn't seem reassured or relieved. He continued to study Cameron. "Well there must be a reason," he said. "You usually stay hard even after we've both finished. Is it me?"

"It's not you," Cameron said, tasting guilt. "It's the wig."

Anthony reached up and started to pull it off before he seemed to reconsider. "I was planning on growing out my hair, so if you don't like the idea, you should tell me now."

"How long?" Cameron asked.

Anthony shrugged. "Does it matter?" Then he glanced over his shoulder again and finally let go, since the rhythmic squeezing wasn't helping. "Apparently it does."

"Come on now," he said with injured pride. "I've never had trouble performing before."

"So what's the issue?" Anthony pressed.

"I'm gay!" Cameron snapped. "Which means I'm attracted to guys!"

He regretted the words, but they'd already been set free to wreak havoc on his world.

"Fine," Anthony said, tearing the wig from his head and tossing it aside. He attempted to rub off his eyeliner with the butts of his hands before giving up. "Go ahead and tell me how I should look and dress, just like everyone else does."

"That isn't fair!" Cameron growled. "You think I *want* to be student council president? I did all of that for you!"

"I know," Anthony said, "but I need you to actually be attracted to me even though— " His face fell before he sighed and shook his head. "Even though I'm a big fucking mess."

He rolled off Cameron and swung his legs over the bed.

"Wait!" he spluttered. "I messed up! You just caught me off-guard. I hadn't seen you in a wig before, not for that long at least, and it... You know I'm cool with this! I wouldn't be friends with Charles if I wasn't."

"But you don't find him attractive."

"Well no, but he's three times my age."

"And he looks like a woman." Anthony sounded defeated rather than angry.

What was he supposed to say? He couldn't pretend that if Charles was their age it would change anything. So yeah, when being completely honest with himself, he was much more attracted to Anthony before all this began. Cameron didn't like the makeup. And he sure as hell didn't like the wig. But did that really matter when love was involved? Wasn't it supposed to fix everything? If so, he could really use a miracle right about now.

"I don't blame you," Anthony said suddenly. "I've been worried about this." He looked over his shoulder, expression sympathetic as he chewed his bottom lip. "I wouldn't want to see you in a dress. For fun, sure... But not when we're about to sleep together, because what you said is the truth. We're gay. And that means we're attracted to men."

"Mr. Finnegan is gay too," Cameron said before second-guessing himself. "I think. Anyway, he obviously doesn't have a problem with it or he wouldn't have married Charles."

"True. But you aren't him."

"And you aren't Charles," Cameron replied. "But um... are you *like* him?"

Anthony broke eye contact, facing forward again. "Maybe."

"That's okay," Cameron said, scooting across the mattress to embrace him from behind. "Really."

"Is it though?" Anthony challenged, his voice raw. "I don't want to lose you."

"I'm not going anywhere," Cameron said, tightening his arms around him. "You just sprang this on me at a *really* inconvenient moment." He tried to inject some humor in his voice, relieved when he heard some of it back.

"You're right," Anthony said. "I should have waited until you were inside me."

Cameron laughed, mostly because the tension needed an outlet. "We could always try again."

"Okay. Let me put the wig back on."

Cameron tensed until he saw a smile. Which was good, because it meant his boyfriend wasn't devastated, Even though his feelings must be hurt. "Can we talk about it?" he asked. "I want to understand you better."

"So do I," Anthony said. "I'm still trying to figure everything out. All I can say is that it makes me feel…" He was quiet for almost an entire minute before finding the right word. "Aligned."

"I don't get it," Cameron said, scooting back while pulling on his boyfriend's arm, so he'd turn around. "What do you mean? Explain it to me."

Anthony shifted to face him. "You know when you're trying to tune in to a radio station, and you keep turning the knob left and right? That's what it's like. I can hear music, but it keeps cutting out, or sometimes there's too much static. So I keep making adjustments, because it's a really good song. The kind that makes you happy inside."

Cameron nodded. "That's how I felt when I figured out that I'm gay. Like I had finally tuned in to the right frequency."

Anthony nodded. "Same here. I thought I was done but… maybe not."

Cameron licked dry lips, almost scared to ask, but he had to know. "Do you wish you were a woman?"

Anthony swallowed. "I wish I could try being one. So that I'd know for sure. But maybe it's not that simple either. Charles is…" He shook his head as if overwhelmed. "He's so awesome. For him, it wasn't a choice between one or the other. So I don't know if it'll be that for me either. Maybe I fall somewhere in the middle. But um…" Vulnerable green eyes tacitly promised forgiveness. "I get if this is a dealbreaker for you. Really. I mean it."

"I'm not sure," Cameron admitted. "I guess you'll have to figure out who you are before I can react to it. But I do know that I want you to be happy."

"Even if it means we can't be together?" Anthony asked, his voice warbling.

Cameron shook his head, the thought unbearable. "I'm not

leaving you," he said. "No matter what. We can make this work. We just have to figure out how. Okay?"

Anthony nodded, a couple of tears breaking free before he wiped at them. "Sorry," he said. "I really screwed up our anniversary."

Cameron reached for him. "No you didn't. Getting to know you better is the best gift you could've given me."

He pulled Anthony into his arms. They stretched out on the bed, Cameron holding him from behind, their voices murmuring to each other long after the mixtape had clicked and fallen silent. While it wasn't the evening that either of them had imagined, they had learned an important lesson: There was more than one way to make love.

Omar's fingers drummed impatiently on the armrest of Anthony's car as he listened to his friend talk. The morning was crisp and beautiful, which made it unbearable that he would be locked up in school. He already yearned for the carefree days of summer, despite having spent many of them working. Omar loved his job, but the leaves had changed color. He longed to lie beneath the trees so he could stare at canopies made of gold, orange, and crimson. The light today would be *perfect* for filming.

"Wait," he said, catching up with the conversation. "So you guys didn't do it? Like at all?"

"No. As soon as he saw me in the wig, he couldn't get it up anymore."

Omar made a face. "For real? Even with a naked guy in his bed? And the promise of butt sex?"

Anthony pulled over. Probably because they were only a couple of blocks from Cameron's house. "Don't tease him about it," he said. "You can't breathe a word of this to anyone."

"Of course!" Omar assured him. Anthony could drive him to where he'd buried a body and his lips would remain sealed. "So are you pissed at him or what?"

"Not at all! I'm the one who was using the wrong bait. I want points for the fishing reference, by the way."

Omar laughed. "I guess it would be like if Silvia and I were about to get it on, and she came back from the bathroom with a mustache and beard. That would freak me out too."

Anthony was looking at him funny. "Don't you mean Whitney?"

"Oh right!" Omar said quickly. "I guess that makes more sense."

Anthony shook his head. "Just ask her out again."

"Silvia? No way! I'm not a clueless freshman anymore. I actually have experience with women now. I get the way they think, and trust me, she's not interested. Anyway, I'm sorry your anniversary sucked."

"It didn't," Anthony said, his cheeks turning pink. "We actually talked about a lot of things I've been scared to say out loud. Cameron was so wonderful about it all. I love him even more now. And feel closer to him, which is what I wanted in the first place."

"That's really cool," Omar said with a grin. "I hope you guys get married someday. If it's ever allowed."

"Thanks," Anthony said with a bashful smile. "Me too."

"That having been said," Omar added as they resumed their trip. "He still should have stayed up half the night banging you. I would have."

"You're a hopeless romantic. My parents came home, or who knows, maybe he would have."

"That makes me feel a little better."

Anthony was awesome. He deserved to have someone who appreciated him, and Cameron sure seemed to be that guy. When they reached his house, Omar climbed into the back seat and watched them greet each other in the driveway, mouthing words he couldn't hear. They were obviously into each other. They didn't let go after hugging, like they needed to hold each other for a while.

Omar longed for that kind of closeness. Which was ridiculous because he was about to see his girlfriend. But that was more like hanging out with a friend who let him touch her boobs. What he'd had with Silvia had been on an entirely different level. True love maybe.

When they got to school, he was reminded just how much he liked Whitney. She was still rockin' his sister's old skateboard and was really getting good at it. He helped her practice kick turns until the first bell rang. Omar was tempted to suggest they cut class together, since he still had so much pent-up energy. He found an outlet for it in his dance elective, which he was really getting into.

"I need your help," Keisha said to him during their warm-up routine.

He nodded at the twins. "Need me to run interference again?"

"No. My aunt wants a copy of the birthday you filmed for us."

"You mean Little Bee? How's she doing?"

Keisha smiled. "I'm surprised you remember her name."

"Hey, that was my first paid gig! It was a big deal. And yeah, I can help with that. You'd have to bring me the tape, since we don't keep backups, but it won't take long. I got my boss to invest in a unit that does high-speed dubbing, and it's really great because it has time base correctors, which means—"

Keisha raised a palm to silence him. "So I just need to stop by your work?"

"Yup."

"I'll do that. Thank you."

Omar felt calmer after dancing his heart out. His next class passed in a haze of slowly fading endorphins. His pulse picked up again during lunch, because Silvia was wearing an open-neck sweater that revealed a lot of skin. She caught him staring but didn't seem offended. Instead she nodded at his tray.

"Going heavy on the carbs again, I see," she said playfully.

He glanced down, a pile of french fries untouched in one corner. He'd bought an extra portion for Whitney, but once again, she'd run off to socialize. "I was thinking of bulking up," Omar said casually. "Maybe put on some extra muscle. You're welcome to them though."

Silvia perked up. "Really?"

"Yeah, but they've gotta be cold by now."

"I don't mind," Silvia said while taking one. "I kind of like that actually. Have you ever found an old french fry in your car and eaten it?"

"That's so gross!" Omar said with a guffaw. "And yeah, I totally have. They taste—I dunno—extra starchy."

"Exactly," Silvia said. "Would you mind dumping the rest of these on the floorboard of my truck? They need to sit for a few days."

Omar laughed again. She was so damn cool!

He noticed Anthony giving him a knowing look. As if he knew the first thing about women! Then again, she *had* kissed him not long ago. If he hadn't gotten freaked out about the whole open relationship thing, maybe she would have again. Omar could be drowning in babes right now! Which sounded like a hot fantasy, but if he was honest with himself, he'd rather be out on the lake with someone special.

Whitney returned then with fresh news. "Mr. Spencer's toupee fell off during third period!" she said. "It landed right on Marcy Nichol's desk while he was helping her with a math problem." She gasped suddenly. "Are those french fries for me? I'm starving!"

He shot Silvia an apologetic expression as the tray was pulled out of her reach. She didn't seem to mind. At all. Which was disappointing but obviously for the best. He just couldn't think of a single reason why. Omar wouldn't have minded a *little* jealousy, or even a subtle eyeroll.

Silvia returned to his thoughts at the end of the day while on his way to work. Omar was skating down the sidewalk across the street from Right Round Records. He slowed and stopped before leaning against a tree. From there he watched the storefront, so much nostalgia welling up that it almost made him want to be a sophomore again, so he didn't have as many responsibilities to worry about. He'd go inside, leave his board by the door, and spend the next couple of hours filming her or listening to her talk or getting a little romantic. He couldn't actually see Silvia through the heavy reflections on the window, but if she happened to look outside, maybe she'd see him standing there and miss some of what they used to have.

Duty called, so he got back on his board and skated to work. He rarely needed to film birthday parties on a Monday, but there was always plenty of footage leftover from the weekend to edit. He was in the dark room that he shared with the security guard when, toward the end of his shift, someone knocked on the door.

"Omar offered to help me with this," a familiar voice drawled.

He turned around to see Keisha holding up a VHS tape.

"I've got this, Steve," he said to the guard.

"I'm done for the night anyway," Steve said, grabbing his coat and leaving them on their own.

Keisha eyed the monitors and editing decks. "This is quite the setup."

"Yeah," Omar said, taking the tape from her. "I'm really lucky. Whenever we need something, I just tell my boss and he makes it happen. Hey, your aunt doesn't live overseas or anything crazy, does she?"

"No, she's down in Alabama, which is almost as foreign to me."

"Then where'd you get the accent?"

"My parents. They brought it with them."

Omar deftly pushed some buttons that sent spools whirring. "One copy in NTSC format, coming right up," he said. "It'll be about fifteen minutes."

He grinned at her. She smiled back politely. They never spent much time together outside of school, so this was new territory.

"How are things going with Hope?" he asked.

"Could be better," Keisha said. "We haven't seen much of each other since her sister's boyfriend got grounded."

He scrunched up his face. "Huh?"

"It's complicated." Keisha nodded at one of the monitors. "Is that for the school yearbook?"

He swiveled in his chair and saw a freeze frame of Mindy and Cameron sitting on a picnic table together while eating ice cream. "Nah, I'm making a tape for Diego. Watch this."

He pushed play, the still frame coming to life.

Cameron offered his ice cream to Mindy. "It's really good," he said. "Try it."

"Only if you try mine," she said, offering hers. "At the same time. One, two, three!"

They thrust the ice cream at each other. Cameron's fell off the cone. Mindy jerked to avoid it and ended up slamming hers into his cheek. Then they both looked at the camera, clearly mortified.

Omar cackled. "Anthony ended up licking it off his face. Wish I'd gotten footage of that. Hey, speaking of which!"

The scene cut to Anthony sitting on a pink skateboard while clinging to the sides. He was positioned on the precipice of what looked like an empty swimming pool at the skate park.

"I don't think this is a good idea!" Anthony said, turning fearful eyes on the camera.

"Sure it is," Omar's voice replied before his foot appeared on screen to nudge him.

That sent Anthony spilling over the edge. After a blood-curdling scream and some shaky footage, his fate was revealed at the bottom of the bowl. Anthony was flat on his back, his arms and legs spread wide.

"It was the final straw for him," Omar said to Keisha while grinning. "He didn't skate anymore after that."

She cocked her head. "And this is all for Diego? As in, Diego Gomez?"

Omar nodded. "Yeah. I felt bad that he had to miss the whole summer, so I recorded a bunch of it for him to see. What do you think?"

Keisha raised an eyebrow. "If it's all footage of you and your friends suffering, then he'll love it. If you're trying to show him what he missed out on while locked up…" She shrugged. "That might be a bitter pill to swallow."

Omar grimaced. "You're probably right." He glanced at the monitor. A ladybug was crawling across Whitney's hand. When it reached the tip of her finger, he paused the tape just as the little critter spread its wings to take flight. Diego wouldn't care about that! No matter how beautiful it was. His shoulders slumped. "I've gotta do *something* for him."

"Why's that?" Keisha asked.

"Because he still hates my guts for ditching him after his dad died. Even though I keep trying to get him to see that we could be buds again."

Keisha plopped down in the chair vacated by the security guard. "Have you told him that you're sorry?"

"Yeah. He doesn't like apologies."

"Sounds about right," Keisha murmured.

"You know him?" Omar asked in surprise.

She went still before answering. "He's in my theater group."

"Oh. Right. Hey! Maybe I should make a tape of the school plays he's been in. I have a bunch of rehearsal footage. I could make a demo reel of Diego's greatest hits."

"Maybe," Keisha said. "Some actors *love* seeing themselves. Others not so much. I'm guessing Diego falls into the second camp. Do you have any footage of back when you guys were friends? Maybe that would remind him of how things used to be."

Omar shook his head. "He came over to my house with Ricky and watched a bunch of old home movies with us. He didn't like those either." The only interest Diego had shown was during one of the prank videos, because he'd thought his dad would be in it. Omar blinked. Then he grinned. "You're a fucking genius!"

"I'm merely gifted," Keisha said, batting her eyelashes. "What exactly did I do to earn this acclaim?"

"You just reminded me of what Diego really wants," Omar said. The dubbing equipment clicked and went silent, a green light turning on. "There's your tape!" he said, ejecting them both. "You're good to go."

"What do I owe you?" Keisha asked.

"Nothing."

"Your boss doesn't charge for duplicates?"

"He does," Omar said, handing the tapes to her, "but this one is on the house, because you might've just done the impossible. If you see me getting a piggyback ride from Diego soon, you'll know why. For now, let's keep this between us."

"I don't have a clue what you're talking about," Keisha said, "so your secret is safe with me."

He grabbed his things, shrugged on his jacket, and walked her out since Archie's Pizza Pi was closing for the night. Keisha offered him a ride home but he declined, wanting to catch the tail-end of the day, even though the sun had already set. He skated down Main Street, stopping by the same tree as before. This time when he looked at Right Round Records, the lights were on, making it possible to see inside. He watched as Silvia walked around, shutting everything down. Then she wheeled her bike outside. Silvia leaned it against the building before locking up. When she turned around, their eyes met.

He smiled at her and gave an upward nod.

She tucked a lock of hair behind her ear before raising her hand.

"See you at lunch tomorrow?" he called.

"Yes! See you then!"

"Have a good night!"

"You too, Omar."

He reluctantly got back on his board and kicked, his heart thumping as he raced off. He glanced back to see Silvia heading in the opposite direction. Then he breathed in the evening air before letting it out again in a sigh. All in all, not a bad day.

Cameron rubbed his eyes and wished he could take a quick nap. If he was alone, maybe he would have crawled onto the desk and done just that.

"Time to make some decisions," LaVern said. "So we can both go home."

He dropped his hands, light and color returning to the world. He had pulled up a chair to the front of the room, where the teacher's desk was covered in index cards and a spread of forms. He was supposed to use them to choose who would get each role on the student council.

"Let's start with the vice president," LaVern said. "Only two people requested the position."

"Jenny," he said instantly.

LaVern considered him. "Troy asked for it as well."

Cameron shook his head. "I don't trust him."

The vice president would make decisions in his absence. He couldn't imagine letting Troy take the reins, even for a day.

"Very well," LaVern said, pairing Jenny's form with the appropriate index card. "That brings us to the secretary. Four people volunteered."

He knew two of them, one more personally than the other. He tapped on the form that Silvia had filled out. "Her."

"Any reason why?" LaVern asked.

"Because of the reason she wants it."

Each form included the person's name, the positions they were vying for, and a section to justify why they should be chosen. Silvia had written, *I'm here to learn how the political system works. This would give me a front-row seat to everything that happens.*

"She's motivated to pay attention. Which is important when taking the minutes of meetings. And I know that she's responsible."

"Works for me," LaVern said. "How about the treasurer?"

Cameron gave the role to a guy who claimed to have gotten straight A's in math since grade school, and whose mother was a tax accountant.

"Aside from the various committee chairs," LaVern said, "that just leaves the student representative. This is a popular one, since it's basically equivalent to the Speaker of the House. This person will liaison with the representative of each grade, who are similar to the members of Congress. These are your choices."

Troy had thrown his hat in the ring for this position as well. Cameron moved his form aside, whittling it down to five. All of them seemed like good candidates, but none truly stood out. "I'm not sure," he said at last.

"If I may make a suggestion…" LaVern said, moving Troy's form front and center.

Cameron shook his head. "I don't think he represents the voice of the student body."

"His campaign speech seemed to resonate with a good many people. And it was a close race."

"Yeah, but he already told me after I won that he'd do everything to get in my way." Cameron's face grew hot. "And to be frank, I really don't like him."

LaVern leaned back. "Ursula Franklin once said, 'Peace is not the absence of war—peace is the absence of fear.' Think about that a moment."

He was happy to because it resonated with what he wanted most for Anthony and himself—to live without the threat of persecution. "I like that," he said.

"Good. Now let's invert it. If war is not the absence of peace, then what is it the absence of?"

He thought about it and shook his head.

"War is the absence of diplomacy," LaVern said. "A last resort when all other avenues of negotiation have been exhausted or abandoned. Where reason fails, destruction will follow."

He took a deep breath. "Okay, but with all due respect, that's the real world. This is only high school."

"A student council is a far cry from the United Nations," LaVern said with a nod. "That's certainly true, but you'll find that high school is a microcosm of the so-called real world. You don't have to look far in American politics—or any other country—to find adults squabbling like children while failing to get anything done. That's why I want you to learn these lessons now, in an environment that might indeed have lower stakes, despite how affecting they can be for some of us."

"Speaking of which," Cameron said, "when are we going to start working on the anti-discrimination policy?"

"In due time," LaVern responded. "You've already seen that Principal Preckwinkle likes to take an active role in such things. I intend to have fully formed legislation that can be brought before the school board before she has a chance to… exert her influence, shall we say. For now, we need to establish your cabinet. I feel it would be worthwhile for you to try working with Troy, even though he expressed his unwillingness."

He frowned at the choices in front of him. "How about we put him on the events committee instead?"

"That would be better than nothing. What reason did he give for wanting to be the student representative?"

Cameron checked the form and read aloud. "'It would allow me to fulfill my campaign promises.'" He wasn't sure how much to buy into that. Troy was probably worried about his reputation more than his ideals.

"A government should represent the people," LaVern said, "and the people rarely agree on anything. We need a variety of perspectives. Even those that aren't in harmony with our own."

That sounded reasonable. He wasn't eager to interact with Troy again, but he did prefer the idea of working with him to fighting against him. "All right," he said with a sigh. "He can be the student representative. Faith wants to head the events committee anyway. She's his girlfriend, so that should make him twice as happy. Which is more than I can say about *my* significant other."

"There's an art to balancing your professional life and your personal life," LaVern said with a hint of amusement. "Unfortunately, such things aren't taught in school. But you might learn about it anyway, during your political career."

He imagined how Anthony would react when learning that Troy was on his cabinet, and judging from the sinking sensation in his stomach, Cameron did indeed expect there to be some tough lessons ahead.

The Trans Am slowed at a stop sign, Diego glancing over at Ricky. This was noticed, of course, a friendly smile the standard response. Ricky no longer seemed tortured that they couldn't be together. Instead he was content to talk about TV shows that Diego had never seen. He didn't know who Mulder and Scully were, but they sounded like a couple of idiots. If there *were* such things as aliens advanced enough to travel to other planets, they sure as hell wouldn't choose to visit this one. Diego tightened his hand on the wheel and returned his attention to the road, just as the light turned green.

For the past week, ever since Mindy drew a line in the sand, everything had played out the same. He'd pick up Ricky in the morning, they'd talk a little on the way to school, and then they'd go to their separate classes, not seeing each other again until the end of the day. Theater didn't provide much opportunity to spark things up again. Not with both of them starring in the play. Diego never had much time afterwards, wanting to make sure his dad's business was running smoothly. That felt especially important as of late. Probably because the time of year, but he didn't want to think about that. Even dancing around the thought caused sorrow to gnaw at his insides, leaving him emptier than before. He needed to fill himself up again.

He shot another glance at Ricky. The weekend was almost here. They could hang. But as he pulled into the school parking lot, Diego decided he wouldn't be able to wait that long. His hunger was too great. Mindy had enough sense to realize that she didn't want to be with him. His mom was still acting weird, fussing over him in superficial little ways when all he wanted from her was the truth. Diego felt like he was trying to find his footing at the top of a sand dune, everything sliding out from underneath him. He needed something solid that he could rely on.

"So…" he said when shutting off the engine. "I've been thinking. About everything that happened."

Ricky looked surprised before shifting to face him, his expression open and eager.

Diego swallowed. He wasn't good at this sort of thing. Nothing made him feel more foolish than doubling back on his own convictions. Like a kid who threw a temper tantrum at the dinner table before stomping off, only to return later when he wanted dessert, sullenly wiping his snotty little nose while mumbling apologies.

"Do you mean the trip to El Paso?" Ricky prompted. "I've been thinking about it too."

"Oh yeah?" Diego said, relieved that he was taking the lead.

He'd never had to seduce Ricky before. Oh sure, when it came to sex, he'd flex his muscles or lean back to show off his package. Diego had a great big fucking dick, which he could only assume was a consolation prize from God for all the hell he'd been put through. In the bedroom, Diego knew exactly what he was doing. The emotional stuff was a lot trickier. So he'd been waiting for Ricky to make another move, to say they should try again—that they belonged together—and once he did… Diego would smirk, nod, and give in to love. He needed that. Really bad.

"I've been meaning to talk to you about everything," Ricky said, his voice gentle. "But um… Do you want to go first?"

Diego shook his head. "Please," he said hoarsely, hoping that it didn't sound like he was begging, even though he was on the verge.

Ricky nibbled his bottom lip. "I can't go to El Paso."

Diego scrunched up his face. "I'm not asking you to."

"I know. But the last time we talked about it, I said that I would. If you wanted me to. Which you don't right now or anymore so um… I guess what I'm really saying is that I made the right decision. Even though it wasn't easy. For you especially. I hate that they put you in that terrible place. I still wish I could change that part—" Ricky looked him square in the eye and jutted out his chin. "—but not the rest. At least I was brave enough to tell you that I was scared."

Diego studied him, the respect he felt eclipsing his disappointment. "I was scared too," he admitted.

Ricky blinked. "Of moving to El Paso?"

"Nah." Diego peered out the window at a gloomy autumn sky, the bad memories way too close for comfort. "I was scared of being on my own again."

"You're not though," Ricky said, his voice laced with emotion. "I'll always be your friend. No matter what. I promise."

Diego was impressed again by his maturity. He'd done a lot of growing up since they'd met.

"Is there anything else you wanted to say to me?" Ricky asked.

That I love you. And I'm sorry for fucking everything up, like I always do. These words remained unspoken. Ricky had finally moved on. Dragging him back into the mess that was his life would be an act of selfishness. He seemed distracted anyway. Ricky's face lit up before he reached for the door. "It's Cameron!" he said, grabbing the sleeve of Diego's jacket and tugging. "Come on! We have to tell him how terrible the new set designer is."

"Yeah yeah," Diego said, wanting to grab that hand and press it to his lips. It slid off of him before he could. He got out of the car and talked to Cameron on the way inside the school. It sucked that he was no longer with the theater group, but at least they saw each other during lunch. He supposed he could invite Cameron to hang out on the weekend or something. Diego wasn't sure how that sort of thing worked anymore.

In the old days, Omar would always have some scheme that he was excited about, dragging Diego and Anthony along with him. Everything had been so easy. Not anymore. Diego had been on his own for so long that the prospect of having a friend was intimidating. Although apparently he had a couple of them now, Ricky and Mindy, even though he wanted more from both of them. God he needed a beer!

Diego managed to get through the day despite the temptation to get high in his car during lunch break. Doing so would mean being alone with his thoughts. Which he really didn't want to do when leaves would be skittering across the parking lot, reminding him of the past. He used to think it was weird that Ricky was frightened of trees, but maybe the kid was on to something. Besides, chilling with Mindy, Cameron, and Keisha for an hour helped keep the demons at bay.

He was eager to get to his theater class for the same reason. They were rehearsing, running through the entire play to figure out what needed to change and how it would all work. That meant he got to be a different person. Diego didn't have to figure out the right words to say. They were all written down for him.

"I've got the conch now and you're all going to listen to me!" Ricky cried from on stage. He was holding a seashell above his head that looked like it was bought from a tourist trap. "Why can't you be sensible?" he cried. "Why must you ruin everything?"

"Okay," Keisha said, pointing to a guy who was standing on scaffolding while clutching a giant inflated ball. The kind sold in toy stores. "That's when you, Roger, push the boulder over the edge. Get ready, Twiggy."

"Okay," Ricky said.

Keisha held up a finger. Then she pointed at Whitney, whose face became a mask of terror.

"Look out!" she cried.

The ball was tossed toward Ricky, who spread his arms so it would hit him in the chest. He collapsed onto the stage with a groan, the ball bouncing away.

Diego continued to watch its trajectory until Keisha hissed, "Jack!"

He blinked before twisting up his face and rushing toward Whitney, his anger eager for release. "That's what you get!" he snarled. "You aren't a part of the tribe anymore. There's no more conch!" He pointed in Ricky's direction. "See? That's what's gonna happen to you!"

"Not bad," Ms. Deville said, walking to the front of the stage with the ball, which she rolled toward them. "But we need a moment of silence first, so the audience can process the shock of Twiggy's death."

They ran through it again, Diego having to catch the ball when it bounced off Ricky. He started to dribble it while everyone else crowded around his fallen form.

"Mr. Gomez?" Ms. Deville said pointedly. "Jack feels just as much shock. This is the first death the children have witnessed with their own eyes."

"This is dumb," he said, holding up the ball. "Boulders don't bounce."

"I'm going to cover it in papier-mâché," the new set designer said. "Which come to think of it, might get damaged if we aren't careful. Maybe if Ricky kind of catches the ball while falling over?"

"Worth a shot," Keisha said. "Let's try that."

Diego wasn't gentle when tossing the ball back to the set designer. It didn't do any damage. The ball was big enough to knock down a toddler, but that was about it.

"Places, everyone!" Ms. Deville called.

Diego growled his frustration. In the novel, Piggy gets knocked off a cliff by the boulder, hits the rocks below, and gets swept away by a wave. Nice and convenient. Not at all like what happens with a real body, which just lays there covered in flies that he'd tried to... Diego had known that it didn't matter anymore but it felt wrong to just sit around while they crawled on his dad and—

"Give it your all this time," Ms. Deville said, looking at him in particular. "Treat these events as if they are real, and the audience will too."

Diego clenched his jaw and retreated to his mark. Keisha gave the signal. Ricky raised the conch above his head while pleading with everyone to be reasonable. A stupid magenta ball hit him square in the chest, knocking him down. Everyone rushed over to see. Diego took his time and swore he could hear the leaves crunching beneath his feet. He looked up at the rafters, his attention remaining there.

"I don't understand," Ms. Deville called. "Is this character work? You think that Jack wouldn't allow himself to look? Because I suspect he wouldn't be able to tear his eyes away."

That hit a little too close to home.

"Nobody can see what I'm looking at anyway!" Diego snapped.

"He's right," the set designer said. "Maybe I should make a raised platform for Ricky to fall on, so the audience can see him too."

"*Something* must be done," Ms. Deville said before waving a hand dismissively. "Continue with the scene."

Finally! Diego launched into his lines with such force that spittle went flying from his lips. Then he picked up a spear with a rubber tip and chucked it at Whitney, who reacted with appropriate terror. They moved on to the next scene after that, thank fucking god! There wasn't much left in the play that involved him. He just had to bark orders at some of his hunters and show up for the ending.

Everyone was dispersing on stage when Ms. Deville walked to the front again, gesturing for him to come over. "Is everything all right?" she asked.

"Yeah," he replied. "It's just been a weird day."

"We all have those," she said. "You have exceptional talent, *when* you focus. I understand that the unfinished sets can make it difficult to lose yourself in the role. I recommend you find something you have in common with Jack's character that lets you fully embody him, no matter your surroundings."

Diego stared at her evenly. "I'll dig a little deeper."

This seemed to appease Ms. Deville. When he turned around, Ricky was standing there, which was odd, because he didn't have any scenes after dying. Piggy's ghost never showed up to rattle his chains and say "Remember the conch! Remeeembeeer!"

Diego snorted at the thought.

Ricky swallowed, his eyes watery, which brought back some memories. "Are you okay?" he asked.

"Yeah," Diego replied. "Why does everyone keep asking me that?"

"I don't know. You just seemed..."

"Haunted?" he suggested. As if that was news. His dad had died a long time ago. It still sucked. So what?

"Yeah, I guess," Ricky said. "If you need to talk or whatever..."

Diego was definitely interested in that whatever. Even if they just sat on Ricky's bed together, watching shows he didn't really care about. "What are you doing this weekend?" he asked.

Ricky perked up. "I'm going to the renaissance festival with Galen!"

"Who?"

Ricky pointed. Diego followed his finger to the auditorium seats, where a pudgy black guy sat. He was grinning like an idiot, as if starstruck. Or maybe he was in love.

"Hi, Galen!" Ricky called to him. "You can come up here, if you want."

Diego turned his back to the seats. "What's he doing here?"

"I told him about the play. He wanted to watch me rehearse."

"And he's taking you out this weekend?"

Ricky nodded happily. "He gave me a free ticket. Do you wanna go with us?"

"Fuck no," Diego said before walking away.

Now he knew why—and how—Ricky had moved on.

He went backstage and made a beeline toward Mindy, out of habit mostly. She noticed him, her body language becoming more demure. She opened her mouth to say something as he neared. If she asked if he was okay, Diego was going to lose his mind.

"Guess what?" she said.

He cocked an eyebrow in response.

"I figured out what book we're reading next."

"Oh yeah?"

She nodded happily. "It's called *Outlander*."

"That sounds cool," he said before peering at her in suspicion. "Wait, I thought you were going to make us read a romance novel."

"It's more of an adventure," Mindy said, squirming under his gaze until she cracked. "Okay, fine, it's also *super* romantic! But there really is more to it than that."

"I don't mind," he said. "Maybe I'll learn something useful."

"About love?" she asked before glancing toward the stage. "How is that going anyway?"

"It's not," he said.

He eyed her for a moment, feeling vulnerable, but then again, he was used to bearing pain. "Do you wanna hang out this weekend?" he asked. "We could start the new book."

Mindy perked up, but thankfully, not because she had exciting plans with someone else. "Sure! That would be great."

Diego felt like salve had been spread over the open wounds of his heart, soothing it. Although when he glanced back toward the stage one last time, he still felt an ache.

Ricky was walking toward city gates from an era long since passed. Banners fluttered from the towers that flanked either side, a number of costumed people in the crowds around them. They had piled into Anthony's car and driven east to reach the Kansas City Renaissance Festival, Ricky grinning in anticipation the whole time. Despite his excitement, he couldn't help noticing that he was the odd man out. Anthony and Cameron were walking ahead of him, their hands often bumping, as if they couldn't stop touching each other. He watched their fingers intertwine briefly and felt envious. Especially when he looked to his right.

Omar had his arm draped around Whitney's shoulders. His girlfriend was wearing layers of gossamer fabric and a pair of forest green tights, her blond hair braided delicately. She resembled some sort of elven creature. All she needed was pointed ears. Omar was dressed in black as always, the waves of his dark hair almost reaching his shoulders. He was incredibly handsome. Ricky found himself longing for the earliest days of their friendship, when everything had seemed so easy. Getting to blow him had been fun. There hadn't been any complicated feelings afterwards. Or resentment when Omar started dating Silvia soon after. Ricky had been horny—as always—and found someone to mess around with. Nice and simple.

Maybe that's what he needed now. He noticed a chisel-chinned knight wearing chainmail, his attention lingering on the manly scruff. All manner of potential partners could await him here. A dashing thief. Or a cleric with healing hands. He began scanning the crowds, an extra bounce in his step.

Omar caught his eye and grinned. "This is going to be so fun, dude!"

"Yeah!" Ricky said. "I can't wait!"

He felt a jolt when noticing a muscular guy dressed in nothing but a leather chest harness and a pair of furry underwear. For a split second, he thought it might be Diego, who would look *incredibly* hot in such a getup... But the long hair and carefree smile didn't match. Ricky tore his gaze away. Which did nothing to banish the barbarian in his imagination, who glowered at him with cinnamon eyes while gripping the thick hilt of his impressive sword.

"How come Galen didn't give us free passes too?" Omar asked as they neared the gates. "We've known him way longer than you have."

Ricky shrugged. "I guess I just have one of those faces."

He didn't get it either. They hadn't interacted much in journalism class last year. Galen seemed nice, but they weren't friends by any stretch of the imagination. Whatever the reason may be, as the others bought their tickets and they all passed through the gates to the festival beyond, he was even more thrilled by the invitation. Tents and primitive buildings lined dirt paths that snaked off in various directions, merchants hawking a variety of wares—mostly clothes, weapons, and accessories appropriate to the era. Many of the visitors around them were snacking on massive drumsticks or drinking from tankards. They passed a group of minstrels, Omar and Whitney falling behind briefly so they could dance together. Ricky found it easy to suspend his disbelief and pretend he'd been spirited away to the past, or better yet, to some fantastical version of history where magic was real.

They had stopped to watch a knight parade by with his retinue when an arm wrapped around Ricky from behind, restraining him. He felt cold steel touch his throat and a portly belly press against his back. From above his head, a voice hissed. "Don't move or you'll be smiling from your throat from now on."

He didn't recognize the voice, but it sounded older, like an adult.

"Um, you guys?" Ricky squeaked helplessly.

The others had already turned toward him, the surprise not leaving their faces.

"What do you want?" Whitney demanded.

"Your gold!" the voice growled. "How much is your friend worth to you?"

Anthony shrugged. "I've got ten bucks."

"You can keep your filthy animals," the man responded. "I want gold!"

"Do you accept checks?" Cameron tried.

"From the strange way you speak," the man shot back, "I can tell you're from foreign parts, so I'll make it easy on you. I'll take *all* of your worldly possessions! Now empty your pockets or your friend is going to start losing weight the easy way. Let's begin with that shiny bauble on your wrist. If you're lucky, I'll let you keep your clothes."

Cameron immediately began undoing the strap of his watch.

"Unhand him!" a new voice cried.

A wizard leapt into Ricky's field of view, waving a magic wand that was shooting sparks. It was Galen! He was dressed in shimmering purple robes and a floppy pointed hat.

"I'll take *your* money too, wizard!" the man behind Ricky growled.

"You'll do no such thing." Galen began tracing an arcane shape in the air. "I'm going to turn you into a toad, but if you let my friend go now, I might not step on you afterwards. *Or* you can try outrunning my magic."

The blade finally left his throat.

"Curse you!" the man shouted before releasing him.

Ricky spun around in time to see an older man dressed like a highway robber flee into the crowd. People around them clapped, as if they were part of the show.

"Sorry about that," Galen said, returning the wand to the inside of his robes. "My dad can be a real *rogue* sometimes."

Ricky stared. Then he started laughing.

"My hero," he managed while wiping at his eyes.

"I would have saved you," Cameron said with a sniff.

"Before or after you gave away all our stuff?" Anthony teased.

"I was willing to let him gut you," Omar said. "This is my favorite jacket." He nodded at the shimmering purple robes. "Although your threads are cool too."

"You really think so?" Galen asked.

"Yeah!" Ricky answered for him. "You look great!"

Galen grinned at this. "When did you guys arrive?"

"I was *born* here!" Whitney said while twirling around.

"About an hour ago," Omar translated.

"Then you haven't seen it all yet," Galen said to Ricky. "Would you like a tour?"

"Yes please!"

They resumed walking as a group, the others pairing up again.

"Is that a magical amulet?" Ricky asked, his eyes lingering on Galen's beefy chest.

"Sure is. A clan of wood elves gave it to me after I saved their grove from orcs. If ever I find myself in mortal peril, I only need to push this gem here and I'll be teleported back to their— Oops!" Galen trembled and shook, as if magic forces were about to whisk him away, before he stopped and peered at the amulet. "False alarm. That gem must control the massage feature."

Ricky laughed again. "You're really into all this stuff, aren't you?"

"To say the least," Galen replied shamelessly.

"It's really cool that your dad is so supportive."

"Oh, you mean because of the little show we put on back there?" Galen shook his head. "You don't understand. I'm here *because* of my dad. In more than one way. This is where he met my mom. They're both huge fantasy geeks. And apparently that's hereditary, because I am too."

"I'm also a proud nerd," Ricky assured him.

"Do you like to read?"

"Yeah! I prefer sci-fi over fantasy, but I've read some of the obvious choices—C.S. Lewis, Tolkien, that sort of thing. What about you?"

"Oh let's see," Galen said, counting down on his fingers. "I like Piers Anthony, Robert Aspirin, Terry Brooks, Jack L. Chalker—"

"Wait," Ricky said, "are you going in alphabetical order?"

"Of course!" Galen said without blinking an eye. "That's how they're organized on my shelves at home. I'm not a savage!"

This made Ricky laugh, especially when Galen continued to name authors. He stopped at Alan Dean Foster but assured him that he could keep going. The group lingered at a tent that was selling exotic masks. As neat as they were, the cute guy with a contagious smile interested him more.

"Did you buy that outfit here?" Ricky asked.

Galen nodded. "It's what I wanted for my sixteenth birthday. I've gotten a lot of mileage out of it so far. RenFest is only open six weeks a year, but I also wear it when playing *D&D*."

"As in *Dungeons and Dragons*?" Ricky asked, not hiding his awe.

"Yeah! We like to get dressed up as our characters. My dad included. He's our Dungeon Master."

"All my dad is good for is watching *Star Trek*," Ricky grumbled in mock frustration. "Although he does know even more about computers than I do. Are you into those at all?"

Galen shook his head.

"I'll make you a deal," Ricky said. "I have a lot of great fantasy games for the PC. You can come over to my house to play them, *if* you let me come play *D&D* with you guys."

"Sounds nice," Galen said. "We're already too deep into our current campaign for a new player, but I'm thinking of running my own soon."

"Sign me up," Ricky said. "Please! I've been wanting to play since forever."

There was something about Galen's cherub face that he found endearing. Ricky liked his thick features, and how passionate he was about his interests. They continued to talk as the others browsed, Galen often pointing out different details so Ricky wouldn't miss them. Such as a couple of women dressed as mermaids who sunbathed on the rocks that surrounded a small pool.

"Listen," Galen said after pulling out a pocket watch from his robes. "There's somewhere I need to be, but later today, the king is going to give his final address of the year. Will you be there? It's important to me."

"Of course!" Ricky said.

He made sure the others were listening as Galen described the details, so he wouldn't get lost along the way. Then he was left alone with two infatuated couples again, although he didn't feel as down about it as before. Instead he kept thinking of Galen's happy face. Ricky could very easily imagine kissing those full lips of his. The thought helped entertain him while the others were busy flirting and holding hands.

They stopped to get some food, and afterwards, watched a truly impressive joust. "Huzzah!" Ricky shouted gleefully as the riders left the field. What a cool place! He didn't understand why it wasn't open year round. He'd like the option to escape into a fantasy world, no matter the season.

"Time to get going," Cameron said. "We have a date with the king."

"And a wizard," Anthony said, nudging Ricky playfully. "You two seem to have hit it off."

"Not like *that*," Ricky spluttered. Then he reconsidered. "You've known Galen a long time, right?"

Anthony nodded. "Since grade school."

"And he's into girls, right?"

"Probably. I don't remember him ever talking about them, but then, that's not the sort of subject I would broach. Hey, Omar!"

"What's up?"

"Did you ever talk to Galen about girls?"

"Uh… Yeah! He had a crush on Courtney Applegate in junior high."

"He offered me a brownie once," Whitney added. "During lunch."

"What happened?" Omar asked.

"I ate it."

Anthony peered at her before returning his attention to Ricky. "Are you interested in him?"

"I'm not sure," Ricky admitted, "but it would be nice to know if we're compatible in that way."

"You seem to manage regardless," Anthony said pointedly.

Ricky grinned. "I'm tenacious!"

"You're adorable," Cameron said. "If it's not Galen, it'll be some other lucky guy."

"Who isn't taken yet," Anthony added, clinging to Cameron's arm possessively, but he winked to show he was only kidding.

They wound their way through the wooded festival grounds, working their way back toward the gates, where a crowd had gathered. Ricky might have grown over the summer, but he was still slender enough to step sideways between people until he reached the front. A bearded man was already giving a speech. Judging from the crown on his head, and the courtiers surrounding him, he was the king.

"From the most skilled artisans and craftsmen to the hardworking souls who tend the fields, my loyal subjects have made these lands a richer place for their efforts." He gestured to a plinth, glittering gems resting on the pillow that topped it. "In a show of gratitude, I thought you would all appreciate a rare viewing of the crown jewels. As you gaze upon them, I hope that you'll be reminded of what unites us. I am your king, yes, but also your humble servant. Now then—"

"—how about you stop wagging your jaw and hand over

your riches!" A masked man swung from a rope, landing in front of the king before swiftly drawing his sword. Ricky recognized Galen's father, but was so caught up in the action that he didn't feel any relief. The man was too villainous. "Do as I say or you'll no longer have a head to place that crown upon!"

Figures in dark robes burst forth from the shadows, wielding daggers, but they weren't coming to the rescue. They looked more like assassins!

"There's no need to panic!" the king shouted to the audience. "My royal guard is never far behind!"

A man wearing nothing but boxer shorts covered in hearts hopped toward the king, his wrists and ankles bound with rope. "I have some bad news, your majesty," he said. "The ale was much stronger than usual when my men and I partook of our midday meal."

"Because I spiked it with a drop of sleep draught!" the chief thief said, opening a large bag. "And now it's time for me to earn *my* dinner." He plucked the crown off the king's head and tossed it into the bag, along with the jewels. Then he turned toward the crowd menacingly. "While you're all gathered here so conveniently," he said, "why don't you make a donation to a good cause: my retirement!"

The crowd laughed nervously. Ricky didn't. He was too caught up in the drama. He gasped with excitement as multi-colored smoke bombs were tossed into the center of the court, causing enough of a diversion for five heroes to rush forward from the audience. Ricky noticed a fighter wielding dual swords and an elven archer, but his attention soon locked on the wizard, who was of course Galen. Sparks flew from his wand as a synchronized battle played out. The assassins recoiled from the unexpected attack before rallying, the situation looking desperate for the heroes as one after another fell in battle. Front and center to all of this, the chief thief and wizard continued to square off.

"You think your little wand scares me?" the thief cried before slashing his blade through the air, forcing the wizard to leap back. "A spell is no match for a sword!"

"Then perhaps this calls for a potion," Galen said before guzzling from a red glass bottle. He held his wand before him and spit the potion out again, the liquid igniting to create a plume of flame. The thief was forced to drop the bag of loot in order to shield himself with his cloak. The crowd erupted in cheers. Galen took another sip from the potion, advancing on the thief and driving him back with more fire. Elsewhere on the field, sensing that the tables had turned, the assassins fled the scene.

"Retreat!" the chief thief shouted, only then seeming to realize that his cronies had already abandoned him. "Those cowards!" he snarled before rounding on the audience. "You haven't seen the last of me. I hope you all remembered to lock your strange metal carriages!" And with that, he fled through the gates, out into the parking lot.

The band of heroes helped each other up and gathered in front of the king, returning his crown to him. There was another speech and plenty of cheers from the audience. All of it was great fun, Ricky grinning nonstop, his attention rarely leaving Galen. The performance was the grand finale. The king thanked everyone for coming and urged them to check on their carriages—a playful way of asking them to leave.

Ricky's friends found him as the crowd dispersed.

Galen joined them shortly after. "If you want to stick around," he said, "everyone's going to be hanging out, since it's the last day."

"Yes!" Ricky said instantly.

"I'm kind of tired," Anthony said before nudging Cameron meaningfully.

"Oh right, me too!" his boyfriend said dutifully. "Could you give Ricky a ride home?"

"Sure!" Galen said with a wide grin.

Omar and Whitney were talking to the elven archer, who was letting them practice with the bow. Judging from the wink that Anthony gave Ricky, they'd be going home too.

He felt a little nervous when left alone with Galen. Excited too. Especially when they walked through the fairground together, which was unpopulated now except for employees. That meant it felt even more like a fantasy world, since he didn't see as many people dressed in sweatshirts and ballcaps.

"Next year I'm going to wear a costume," Ricky said.

"What class would you play?" Galen asked, referring to the game mechanics of *Dungeons & Dragons*.

"I'm not sure. It's a big decision, but after seeing you in action, you make me want to be a wizard. That was amazing!"

Galen grinned. "Speaking of which, I need a drink. Magic potions always leave a bad taste in my mouth. Have you ever tried mead?"

"No!" Ricky said. "Isn't it alcoholic?"

"Yeah, but I know a guy who works at one of the booths."

Before long, they were seated on a bench in a cozy outdoor alcove, each holding a ceramic mug. They clinked brims before taking shy sips, the sweet taste of honey lingering on Ricky's lips.

"Wow, this is delicious!"

"Just go easy," Galen warned. "I know it tastes like candy, but it'll get you buzzed."

"Good to know." Ricky already felt intoxicated anyway. After another sip, he set aside the mug. "How do you do all that fire-breathing stuff?" he asked.

"Trade secret," Galen said with a wink. "Don't try it at home. I've been training for a very long time. With a professional."

Ricky made a face. "I didn't realize fire-breathing was a career path."

Galen laughed. "I doubt it is for many people. The guy who taught me is a stage magician. I'm really into sleight-of-hand."

"For real? You can do other tricks?"

"Sure!" Galen reached behind Ricky's ear, where he plucked something out of the air—a small folded piece of paper that was handed to him.

"I thought it was going to be a quarter," Ricky said while unfolding it.

Inside was written, *Only grandpas pull quarters from people's ears.*

He looked up in surprise. "How'd you know what I was going to say?"

"I didn't," Galen chuckled. "It usually gets a laugh either way."

"Oh. How do you make your wand shoot sparks? You have to show me at least one trick. Otherwise I won't be able to sleep tonight."

"You'll be disappointed," Galen said, pulling the wand from his robe and handing it to him. "It's just a wooden stick that I tape sparklers to. The same kind you can get from anywhere that sells fireworks."

"I used to love spelling out my name," Ricky said, waving it through the air. "Hey! Instead of tape, you could have a special wand with holes on the side to slide the sparklers into. I bet my friend Cameron can make one for you."

"That would be cool!" Galen said, their fingers touching briefly when the wand was handed back.

Ricky was pretty sure he felt sparks of a different kind. "Can I ask you something?"

Galen shook his head. "I can't reveal any more magic secrets or I'll end up sawed in half. That's what happens to people who break the magician's code."

Ricky smiled. "It's not that. I've had a wonderful day. I'm really glad you invited me out here." He steeled himself for disappointment. "But is there a reason why? Aside from you wanting me to see your amazing performance."

"Yeah, actually, there is." Galen seemed self-conscious, swiftly pulling off his floppy hat, revealing a short flattop. "Umm... I had a dream about you."

"A dream?" Ricky repeated in confusion.

"Yeah. During the summer."

"Oh! Do you mean like a wet dream?"

A rosy hue spread across Galen's milk chocolate cheeks. He took a gulp of mead before nodding rapidly. "Yeah," he rasped. "That sort of thing."

"How flattering!" Ricky said, wanting to assure him that it was okay.

"*And* I think you're cool," Galen said hurriedly. "I didn't invite you out here expecting you to um..."

"Make your dreams come true?" Ricky suggested.

They both laughed.

"I thought it would be fun to get to know each other better," Galen explained. "And yeah, I'm curious about all the other stuff too."

"Have you always been attracted to guys?" Ricky asked.

Galen shook his head. "This is new for me. I never have much luck with girls. I wish being around them was as easy as hanging out with my guy friends. You know what I mean? It would be the best of both worlds. The comfort of hanging out with a friend, but with sex involved."

Ricky certainly found the idea appealing! Except… "What about feelings?" he pried. "Do you think you could fall in love with another guy?"

"I'm not sure," Galen admitted. "I've never fallen in love with *anyone* before. Not really. Maybe we could find out together. If you are um… into me too."

Ricky was tempted to lean over and kiss him. If that went well, they could take things further. Worst case scenario, Galen was a curious straight guy. Just like when Ricky had messed around with Omar, it would be fun and probably stop when the right girl came along. Or maybe they'd discover that they were truly compatible and fall in love. The mere thought put a lump in Ricky's throat. He felt a desperate longing, but not for the person sitting next to him.

"I'm really sorry," he croaked. "You're definitely my type. I want to explore this with you but—" He struggled to get the next word out. "Diego."

Galen looked confused. "I thought you guys broke up?"

"We did," Ricky said, "but I'm still in love with him. My heart isn't ready to try again. My body…" He looked Galen over, not hiding his interest. "My body is *more* than ready! But I think that would be a mistake right now. I've learned the hard way that I need to slow down sometimes and take care of myself."

"Oh," Galen said, seeming crestfallen. "Can we be friends anyway? I wasn't only trying to hook up with you. I really do think you're cool."

"Yes! I would love that. And for the record, I think you're cool too."

Galen smiled and raised his mug. "Then here's to new friendships."

"I'll drink to that!"

Sorrow lingered in Ricky's heart, mingling with newly discovered joy. He only hoped, no matter where Diego was today, that he found himself in equally good company.

Anthony spread the blanket out beneath the willow tree, his boyfriend hurrying to grab two corners so he could help. Cameron smiled at him from over the slowly sinking fabric. Anthony returned the gesture, feeling pure adoration.

"Sit down," he instructed. "It's your special day. I'll take care of everything."

"Is that a promise?" Cameron asked flirtatiously.

"Yes," Anthony replied. No sense in keeping him in suspense. The sexual tension between them was almost tangible. It really would be later, when they had enough privacy, because Anthony couldn't wait to touch that beautiful body. For now, he set a picnic basket on the blanket between them and got down on his knees to unpack it. He'd wanted Cameron's seventeenth birthday to be memorable, and so far, it had been.

They'd begun the morning by having brunch with Cameron's parents at the same café where they had come out to his mother. His father's presence there—meeting him properly for the first time—had made the occasion especially interesting. Trevor had been cordial but otherwise detached, his attention often elsewhere, as if he couldn't stand to see his son with another man. Or maybe he was troubled by Anthony's appearance, because Trevor's features had tightened whenever forced to look directly at him.

Anthony was still wearing the pink bandana, but as a headband now, which made him feel like a throwback from the eighties. This left the top of his head exposed, his hair having grown out enough that he resembled Annie Lennox more than Sinéad O'Connor. Which was a big improvement, both in terms of appearance and his musical preferences, but he still wished it was longer. Cameron seemed to appreciate the new style anyway, since he kept making excuses to touch Anthony's hair whenever they were close.

After brunch, they'd gone to Sweet Tea Antiques to visit Charles, who told Cameron that he could choose any one thing in the store as his gift. Anthony had watched with amusement as his boyfriend went around, agonizing over the options. In the end, he selected a small lamp with a stained-glass shade.

"You know there's an actual Tiffany lamp in the window," Charles had said when seeing his choice.

"I couldn't," Cameron had replied. "They're too expensive."

Anthony was grateful that his boyfriend was so humble, because he didn't have money to spend on a birthday present. So he'd made something instead: the meal they were about to enjoy.

"Tuna salad," he said, setting a Tupperware container on the blanket.

"My favorite!" Cameron replied. Then he blinked. "Wait, you don't eat meat."

"I'll make an exception. We also have English muffins, which seems weird, but okay."

"They go together so well! You'll see."

Anthony took another container out of the basket. "And here we have a variety of three different melons, balled not cubed."

Cameron laughed. "Perfect!"

"Last but not least…" He was most careful with the final container. "Your birthday cake. Only a slice of it. The rest is at my house because it was too big to bring with me, but we do have candles."

Cameron was grinning from ear to ear as the picnic was set up in front of him. "I love the blue frosting," he commented.

"As requested," Anthony replied with a little bow.

"And you really made the cake all by yourself?"

He nodded. "From scratch. I read the instructions on the back of the box *very* carefully."

Cameron laughed.

Anthony stuck candles in the cake before lighting them, singing all the while. He didn't have much of a voice, but traditions were important. "Okay. Make a wish."

Cameron shook his head and leaned forward on his knuckles, bringing his face near. "I've already got everything I want."

Anthony was all too happy to kiss him. Once they broke apart, he nodded at the cake. "You might as well," he said. "Since we have to blow them out anyway."

"More of this," Cameron said. "That's my wish."

He blew out the candles and kissed Anthony again.

"Maybe we should work up an appetite," Cameron murmured against his lips.

"Or we could eat the tuna salad before it goes bad in this heat," Anthony teased.

In truth the weather was mild, the afternoon sun shining through the yellowing leaves of the willow tree. He was very interested in giving Cameron what he wanted. Anthony simply hoped to make it extra special, and that meant waiting. They settled down after a few more kisses and began snacking.

"How do you think it went with Ricky and Galen yesterday?" Cameron asked.

"It didn't," Anthony informed him. "Ricky called last night and said that he's not ready to date anyone new."

"You sound disappointed."

Anthony shrugged. He'd been elated when Galen had approached him to inquire about Ricky's relationship status. "I want him to find someone who is… I don't know. Softer, I guess."

"He's more than a little crazy about Diego," Cameron replied.

"Yes, and Diego is more than a little crazy." He shook his head. "I just thought they'd make a better match. They're both the same age and share similar interests."

"Just like us," Cameron said playfully. "Remind me again, my sixteen-year-old boyfriend, what your favorite period of antique furniture is."

Anthony laughed. "Who's your favorite music producer, you old fart? I see your point. It all comes down to chemistry."

"Exactly. Do you think Galen is gay?"

"No idea. I didn't think Diego was interested in guys, and I deluded myself into thinking that Omar might be, so obviously I have terrible gaydar. I just want Ricky to be happy."

"He'll find his way," Cameron assured him, holding up an English muffin topped with tuna salad. "This is really good."

"Thanks, but my mom helped me with it. If home-cooked meals are important to you, you should marry a different girl."

This jest was followed by what Anthony was beginning to think of as the supportive smile. A slight upturning of the lips and a friendly gaze that said *I don't get it but I'm here for you.* Which was nice, even though the supportive smile was never accompanied by questions. Cameron was probably too scared to ask. Anthony felt just as intimated, unwilling to talk about what little he understood before figuring out one important detail: How could he become the person he was meant to be without losing the man he loved?

Tonight might be the ultimate test.

For now, such concerns grew distant as they stretched out on the blanket, idly chatting and using each other as pillows while the sun slowly sank toward the horizon. Anthony read aloud a poem that he'd written for the occasion, which was equal parts sappy and silly, all of it sincere. Cameron was always making nice things for people. Anthony admired that. Along with everything else about him. He'd never been in love before. Okay, he supposed Omar counted, but that was unrequited. Cameron was right there with him, in tandem. Anthony was astounded at just how deep his affection could go while continuing to grow. So when the light faded and they began to feel a chill, they packed up the picnic, the desire inside of him increasing in intensity.

"Do you think we'll have any privacy at your place?" Anthony asked.

"Why's that?" Cameron replied, even though the goofy grin on his face suggested that he already knew the answer.

"I figure your mom might be excited to see you again, since it's your birthday. You know how mothers can be."

"I do," Cameron said. "What about your folks?"

They would probably be home, but with his brothers having both moved out, and some music set at just the right volume, it might work. "Let's go there," Anthony said. "You need to pick up the rest of your cake anyway."

"You're the best gift I've ever gotten," Cameron said as they walked to the car. "I mean it," he said when seeing his smirk. "We started dating a week before my birthday. How perfect is that?"

"*Almost* perfect," Anthony teased. "I should have held out for another seven days."

"I wish we would have met even sooner," Cameron said, still dead serious. "Like my first day after moving here. We could have fallen in love in junior high. Wouldn't that have been nice?"

"Yeah," Anthony said, trying to imagine that life.

Instead of his love for Omar, Cameron would have been the catalyst that made him accept himself. What about the rest? Would he have started wearing makeup sooner? Had coming out unleashed what Anthony was struggling with now?

When they got to his house, Dawn greeted them in the living room and hugged Cameron as if he was her own. Eventually, after enough social pleasantries, they went up to Anthony's room where he began setting the scene. First by taking off the aviator jacket that Cameron wore, their lips meeting repeatedly during this process. Anthony hung it up for him, which wasn't easy with Cameron at his heels, attempting to undress him as well.

He continued to duck and dodge so he could put on music—Depeche Mode's *Black Celebration* album—and light the candles on his window sill. Anthony turned on a table lamp and switched off the overhead light. Cameron correctly interpreted these signals, flopping back on the bed with a grin, like he was about to get the best blowjob of his life. Although he looked puzzled after Anthony opened the bedroom door.

"I'll be right back," he promised before remembering everything he needed to do. "Maybe not right away, but pretty soon, I promise. Um… Do you need to use the restroom first?"

Cameron shook his head. "There's only one thing I need."

Anthony's attention darted down to the bulge between his boyfriend's legs and decided to hurry. Once in the bathroom, he rushed through the routine Ricky had taught him. Then he shook off his clothes and stepped into the tub. Once he was underneath the steaming hot shower spray, Anthony scrubbed all the makeup off his face, like he did every weekday morning. If he could go to such great lengths to appease a draconian dress code policy, then doing the same for someone he loved was a small sacrifice. He wanted Cameron to be as turned on as possible, especially after last week's debacle.

That just left how he felt about himself. After drying off, Anthony considered himself in the mirror. His hair was short, his body lanky. There wasn't much in the way of curves or rosy hues. He didn't hate what he saw but felt a disconnect, like he had borrowed the body from someone else. He got dressed again, wanting to give Cameron something to unwrap since Anthony didn't have any real gifts to offer. He paused at the bathroom door and closed his eyes. He wouldn't see his own reflection again after leaving this room. So why not pretend?

He stood up straight and brought the tip of his finger to his lips, tracing red lipstick there. He did the same with his eyeliner, carefully using a fingernail to simulate the sensation. Anthony patted his cheeks and forehead to apply powder and base. A moment of concentration made his hair grow out long enough to frame his face and tickle the base of his neck. He considered himself in an imaginary mirror, seeing his twin sister again, and felt pretty as fuck.

And ready to *get* fucked!

Anthony swept gracefully into the hallway, feeling himself transformed. When he reentered the room, Cameron sat up slowly with transparent awe.

"You look—" He blinked and shook his head before smiling. "—really nice," he finished at last.

"Thank you," Anthony said, his voice soft.

He moved toward the bed with a purpose, placing his knees to either side of Cameron's lap and sitting there while kissing him. He only relented to pull off his boyfriend's shirt, revealing a raised chest and flat stomach. Cameron did the same, but for once, Anthony didn't shy away. He felt a moment of disconnect when his nipples were touched, like they were in the wrong place, but his imagination kicked in again and all was right with the world. They rolled and tumbled in bed, their clothes tossed to the floor one item at a time until Cameron was finally on top of him. There was no doubting how turned on he was, since Anthony kept getting poked. While still kissing his man, he groped around for the nightstand until his hand landed on the knob of the drawer.

Cameron caught on and helped, fishing out the bottle of lube. "Same position as last time?" he asked.

Anthony shook his head. Warnings be damned, he wanted to do it just like this, with Cameron above him.

"Just be really *really* careful," he said.

Cameron nodded solemnly. That made Anthony want him even more. Who else could he trust with something like this?

They took their time, doing things much more familiar to them, until Anthony wrapped his legs around Cameron's waist meaningfully. Then came the moment of truth. They were staring into each other's eyes, both of them tense. The second Anthony winced, Cameron began to retreat.

"You finally got it in," Anthony hissed. "Don't take it out again!"

"Yeah, but that's just the tip," Cameron replied. "Are you sure about this?"

"You don't seem to have any doubts," he breathed in response.

Cameron was *definitely* not having the same problem.

"Just tell me what to do," his boyfriend said.

"Go slow," Anthony suggested.

"Like this?"

He nodded despite the pain, which was a mistake because it only ended up hurting worse.

"Actually, can you get more lube on it? *Without* pulling out!"

Cameron complied as best he could. And it helped! His motions were gentle and shallow enough that it actually started to feel good.

"Do you like that?" Cameron asked.

Anthony nodded, this time with more conviction. "Yeah! Do you?"

Cameron smiled tenderly and bent over for a kiss, sliding deeper inside, but it was okay this time.

"That's all of it," he said, pushing himself up on toned arms. "Think it'll be enough?"

"I'm glad it's not any bigger!" Anthony spluttered. "There's such a thing as too much!"

His boyfriend grinned at him, his hips beginning to move in a gentle rhythm, sending waves of pleasure through Anthony's body. His eyelids fluttered shut. He could still see himself, in his mind's eye, looking exactly the way he wanted. His thoughts soon became fleeting as the physical asserted itself. Cameron's body was writhing against his now, their mouths interlocking as they huffed through their noses.

"Does that feel good?" Anthony pulled away to ask him.

"Yeah," Cameron said. "Really good! I'm having trouble holding back."

"Don't," Anthony said. "We can always do it again."

"Are you sure?"

"Oh yeah!"

He was already addicted. The physical sensations were one thing, but the emotional side of it, giving himself to Cameron in this way and being so impossibly close…

"I love you," Cameron grunted.

"I love you too," Anthony panted.

Their mouths met again, mostly to muffle their moans, because the big finale was anything but anticlimactic.

Cameron collapsed on to him, wrapping his arms around

Anthony before rolling over, as if wanting to use him as a blanket. He smiled, his eyes darting around Anthony's face, as if pleased with everything he saw there. Then he laughed joyously.

"That was beautiful," Cameron said. "*You're* beautiful."

"You really think so?" Anthony asked, feeling vulnerable.

"Yeah. No one could ever compare. You're my soulmate."

Anthony felt it too. More than ever. He kissed Cameron before settling down to rest a cheek on his chest. "Happy birthday," he murmured.

"Thanks," Cameron said. "I'm already looking forward to that wish."

"You mean the more part?" Anthony asked.

"Yeah." Arms wrapped around him possessively. "I don't think I'll ever get enough."

Diego cracked open another beer, guzzling it down nonstop until it was empty. Then he crushed the can and tossed it out the passenger-side window, where it clattered noisily on the school parking lot. He belched, taking no joy in the act, because today sucked. Just like it always did.

Five fucking years! He couldn't believe it had been that long. Time was supposed to heal all wounds. At this rate he'd need a century, because Diego didn't feel any better. Not a goddamn bit! All he'd learned was how to carry the pain, but he still felt like someone had blown a hole right through his chest, just like the one his dad had—

Diego's stomach lurched as the beer landed. He probably should have eaten something today. But when he'd woken up this morning, he hadn't felt like living at all. So he had lain there in bed, listening to an annoying clock tick in the kitchen as the sun slowly moved across his room. When he'd finally gotten up to take a piss, he saw that it was eleven in the morning. After getting ready, Diego drove to school, but only because he wanted to see Mindy again. He showed up at lunch like he'd been there all day but didn't talk much. Keisha kept looking at him funny, which was no surprise. She was the type of person who saw everything, even if you didn't want her to. That seemed to include him not wanting to talk about his problems, which he appreciated.

Being around other people had—to his surprise—made him feel a little better. Enough that, after driving around aimlessly, he'd picked up a six-pack and circled back around to the school. There he had sat, occasionally checking the clock while drinking. He did so again and saw that fifth period was about to begin.

Diego got out of the car, his head woozy as he went inside the building, and wished someone would cross this stupid day off the calendar. Permanently! He wanted it erased from history, including everything that had happened. Some girl in the hall excitedly screeched news to her friends, making him wince. With his eyes closed, he could see golden light filing an overgrown field. Diego swiftly opened them again, his heart thudding, and barged through a group of guys who were in his way. They complained and made tough guy faces, but when they recognized who they were dealing with, they lost interest in him real quick.

He finally reached the auditorium, the backstage area seeming to sway left and right like a ship at sea. His stomach lurched again, but not because of the booze. Mindy was organizing a rack of costumes. She noticed him on his way over, her smile chasing away the shadows.

"Wass goin' on?" he asked, trying to lean against the rack, but it was on wheels and slid away. Diego stumbled, caught himself, and tried again. "S'up, princess?"

Mindy's face crinkled with concern. "Are you okay?"

He pulled himself together before answering. "Yeah, of course. Did you miss me?"

She didn't seem reassured, her nostrils flaring. "Have you been drinking?"

He tried a smile. "Either that or I hit my head on something."

Mindy glanced around worriedly. "You better not let Ms. Deville find out! You'll get in trouble."

"She can't do anything to me," Diego retorted. "All of this stuff around us, rules and things, it's just…" He gestured aimlessly, trying to find the right words. "It's the conch, right? Some dumb kid decided it had power, but that's all bullshit. We can do whatever we want." He laughed. "I'm Jack fucking Merridew! Juss try and stop me!"

"Shh!" Mindy said, placing a dainty hand on his forearm. "Maybe you should sit down. Please."

He plopped into the makeup chair, where he'd often talked to her while slowly falling in… well, whatever. It didn't matter how he felt because she wasn't having it. "You're too damn smart," he said. "Way too smart for the likes of me. Thass good. Don't date some stupid loser, okay? Don't let some idiot drag you down with him. Or get you knocked up."

"I wasn't planning on it!" Mindy said, recoiling from the suggestion. She began looking around. "Um… Wait here. I'll be right back."

She wasn't though. Diego felt like he sat there for hours as crushing despair slowly seeped in from around the edges, eager to consume him. That empty field, the sound of crunching leaves beneath his feet…

"Hey!"

The voice was so familiar that it made his heart ache. Diego lifted his head. Ricky was with Mindy when she returned, worry already lining his face.

"Places, everyone!" Ms. Deville called from elsewhere.

"Cover for us," Ricky hissed after peering at him. "We'll be there soon."

"Okay," Mindy said before rushing away.

She probably welcomed the excuse.

"Too damn smart," Diego muttered.

"What's going on?" Ricky asked, gingerly moving in front of him.

Diego felt a different sort of pain rise up as he stared into two dark eyes wet with concern. "Come on man," he croaked, feeling crippled by his need. "Don't make this hard on me."

Ricky shook his head in confusion. "Did something happen?"

Diego laughed humorlessly. Then he forced himself to stand. "The show must go on," he spat. "Still gotta wake up. Still gotta eat. Still gotta go to school." He began marching, like some sort of wound-up robot. Isn't that how he'd felt since his dad died? If only. Part of him ran on autopilot. The rest wallowed in agony.

"Where are you going?" Ricky asked, grabbing his arm.

Diego shook him off. He didn't need to be pestered by stupid questions. He was glad they had broken up!

"There you are!" Ms. Deville said when he stomped on stage. "Oh good. Ricky, this involves you as well."

Diego trudged over to where everyone was gathered on stage. He watched as a bunch of padded gym mats were dragged together to form a pile. A sheet painted to resemble stone was draped over it.

"I figure if Ricky falls onto this…" The set designer said without confidence. "I guess he'd have to sort of turn toward the audience, so they can see him. Um."

Diego got a running start and belly flopped onto the pile, which flattened beneath him. He rolled over onto his back, feeling rather comfortable.

"Always the jokester!" Mindy said in the awkward silence that followed. She took his hand and pulled on his arm. Ricky came over to do the same for the other. He shook them both off and stood.

"Very amusing," Ms. Deville said in a clipped tone. "Now put things back the way they were."

Diego helped. Hell, he did a better job of making it look like the sort of rock that would be jutting out of the water. That's what they wanted, a sacrificial altar for Ricky to die on, so the audience could say they actually felt something, no matter how briefly.

"Come on," Ricky said, trying to guide him away.

"I'm fine!" Diego snapped. "Don't touch me."

"Sorry," Ricky replied glumly.

Diego crossed his arms over his chest and glared as the others went to work. Ricky kept practice-falling on the fake rock. The big bouncing ball was brought back out, Diego eager to kick it.

"Let's try the scene again," Ms. Deville called. "Actors, take your places. Everyone else, give them room."

He watched the set designer climb the scaffolding. Whitney handed the ball up to the guy before going to her mark.

"This is an important scene," Ms. Deville said. "The entire final act hinges on this moment. Let's give it everything we've got. Understood?"

Diego nodded, having to fight down a maddened grin. She didn't know what she was asking. Or what he kept inside. None of them did.

The stage lights were shining on him. Diego squinted against their brightness. He remembered how the sun had been in his eyes as he walked home. He'd just been kicked out of the house where he was supposed to be spending the night. Omar's family used to have an aquarium in their living room, which had looked a little low on water, so he'd suggested they refill it using the garden hose just beyond the patio door. The hose didn't quite reach when they dragged it inside, so Omar had done that thing where you partially cover the opening with your thumb to make it spray in a certain direction. Diego went outside to turn on the faucet, and when he came inside again, Omar was freaking out, because water was getting everywhere.

"Just plug the hole!" Diego had said, trying to wrest the hose from him. Which only made it worse. And more amusing. They got a little carried away, to say the least. Omar's parents returned before they had a chance to clean up. That's when they sent Diego home, which had been a bummer, but he'd also been aware that Omar was in way more trouble than he was. The mess hadn't been bad enough for them to call his parents. Even if they had, his dad would've probably thought it was funny. By the time Diego had reached the field behind his family's home, he'd been eager to tell his dad the story.

"I've got the conch now and you're all going to listen to me!" Ricky shouted from on stage. "Why can't you be sensible! Why must you ruin everything?"

Because of that day.

His twelve-year-old self began to cross the field. The leaves were crunching beneath Diego's feet as he shielded his eyes against the intense orange glow on the horizon. He noticed something dark on the ground, lying there like so much roadkill. At first he thought it was a dog, since there was a black labrador in the neighborhood who liked to chase Diego whenever he passed by. Propelled on by morbid curiosity, he moved closer to see. That's when the wind picked up, fluttering the brim of the old cowboy hat his dad always wore. His favorite hat that he'd never leave in a field used for parking cars in need of repair.

Dread settled over him when he realized that it wasn't a dog lying there but a person. The wind blew again, leaves skittering around his feet as Diego crept forward until he was close enough to see the same flannel shirt and old jeans that his father had been wearing that morning. Then he ran to him while laughing, certain that his dad had stretched out in the sun and fallen asleep. He reached the hat first, noticing that it was splattered with red paint.

"Daddy?"

His father's legs were bent at an uncomfortable angle, like they'd collapsed beneath him.

"Dad?"

Diego reached the body and fell to his knees, an unpleasant smell reaching his nose, like the summer sun beating down on a hot metal trash can full of meat. That's when he saw the dark hole in his father's temple, his face resting in a pool of congealed blood. A Halloween prank! What else could it be?

"Look out!"

Back in the present, he was barely aware of the large ball that was sailing through the air in front of him. Although he noticed when Ricky caught it with a grunt, his legs bending as he twisted and fell, as if wanting to demonstrate what had happened.

"Daddy? You're scaring me! It's not funny anymore!"

He shook the body, panic overtaking him when there was no response.

"Help! Someone call an ambulance. Help!"

Diego swatted at the flies, brushed off the dried leaves stuck to his father's face, and pressed his hand over the wound, wanting to stop the bleeding, but it was all coming out the other side, or had already, and he didn't know if CPR would still work or —

"Somebody help!"

Diego pushed his way through the circle of onlookers, except it wasn't his father lying there, but Ricky. The sweet kid he'd picked on and harassed, just because he reeked of innocence and happiness and all the things that Diego had lost long ago. And it worked, because as the school year went on, the joy had begun to fade from his eyes. Even that hadn't been enough. Diego kept chipping away at him until finally…

Ricky had tried to kill himself.

Diego stared in horror at the pale body, crumpled up on a cheap spray-painted sheet. Ricky's pupils would no longer dilate when looking at him. His lips wouldn't shape ceaseless irritating questions. He'd never feel that small hand take his again. Ricky was dead.

Diego fell to his knees, just as he had five years ago, but he wasn't a helpless kid anymore. He was strong. Diego scooped the body into his arms, cradling his father to him protectively. No wait, it couldn't be. That spark had been snuffed out long ago.

Ricky's eyes fluttered open in confusion. "Diego?"

Hearing that voice was such a relief that sobs wracked his body. He clung to Ricky, unwilling to let him go.

"Clear the stage!" Ms. Deville shouted in commanding tones. "All of you, backstage, *now!*"

He didn't think these words were directed at him, nor did

he care either way. Diego pulled Ricky closer. "Don't ever leave me," he croaked. "I can't—" His voice faltered until he managed to force the rest out. "I can't lose you, so just don't. Okay?"

"I won't!" Ricky said.

"I won't leave him!" Diego had cried when someone finally came to see what all the commotion was about.

Jasper, who was more spry back then, had bounded across the field. After uttering some unanswered prayer to God, he'd picked up the fallen cowboy hat and placed it over his father's face.

"You've got to help him!" Diego pleaded. *"Please!"*

"He's in safe hands now," Jasper told him. *"Ain't nothin' can hurt him where he's gone. Come on, son. Let's go home."*

"I won't leave him!"

"Your daddy wouldn't want you to see this. Come on now."

Arms wrapped around him before Jasper stood and carried him away from the grisly scene.

"I need you," Diego said, standing up with Ricky still cradled in his arms. "Please."

They were alone now, except for Ms. Deville, who kept a respectful distance.

"Of course," Ricky said, his chin trembling. "I'll always be there. Whenever you need me."

"Do you swear?" Diego asked, his face twisting up. "I can't lose someone else. Not ever. I mean it!"

Ricky's eyes wavered as tears broke free. Then he nodded. "I swear."

"Good." Diego kissed him, needing to ensure that his intent couldn't be mistaken, but just in case… "Because I love you."

Ricky stared in disbelief. Then he looped his arms around Diego's neck, and after a sob, he gave his answer.

"I love you too."

CHAPTER 24
OCTOBER 21ST, 1993

"This isn't a date," Silvia said as her truck pulled up to Omar's house. No one disagreed with her. Probably because she was alone. "And he's not your boyfriend anymore," she added.

There. That should do the trick. Silvia had reminded herself of the basic facts, which should make it easy to resist everything her heart—and her body—wanted. Right?

She parked and went to the front porch to ring the bell. The door swung open a minute later, a grin already plastered on Omar's face.

"Hey," he said with an upward nod.

"Hey," she replied.

"Careful, or we'll look *and* sound like twins."

He was dressed in a black T-shirt and matching jeans. She was too, with the addition of a suede jacket that she hadn't worn much since junior high. The fringe tassels that went halfway down the arms and around her back felt a little too out-of-date. When she used to wear it, she'd imagined herself as a modern-day Sacagawea and would wander the woods near the trailer park, secretly hoping to find a stray horse that would whisk her away to adventure. But now it was almost November, and she'd wanted something in black that would keep her warm.

"I better put a jacket on too," Omar said while eyeing her. "Come inside real quick."

Silvia hadn't been here since they broke up. Hanging out in his bedroom would create way too much temptation. Omar disappeared up the stairs, but she didn't follow. Silvia was still looking up them, kept company by memories, when a squeak attracted her attention. An older woman wearing a burgundy hijab rolled her wheelchair into the entryway.

"Silvia!" Mamani said, her voice just as leathery and ancient as her skin. "Thank goodness. I thought it might be the blond one."

"You mean Anthony?" she asked.

"No no, the girl who is always zipping around while talking nonstop. My neck is still sore from trying to keep up with her."

"Oh, you mean Whitney," Silvia said with a laugh. "Has she um… been over here a lot lately?"

"I'm not sure I should answer that," Mamani replied shrewdly.

"It's fine. Omar and I are only friends now."

"Then why have I seen so little of you?" Mamani's eyes were twinkling. "Summer is full of carefree days. Could you not spare one of them to visit a friend?"

Silvia got the impression that she was being toyed with. "To be fair, I *was* working full-time."

"Ah! That is exactly the sort of 'friend' my grandson needs. You were always a good influence on him. Unlike that flighty girl who thought it would be funny to push me around. In my chair," Mamani added when seeing her concern. "We were out for a walk. I think she was trying to be helpful, but I almost went over a curb. She seemed to get the point when I smacked her hands away."

Silvia laughed.

Omar groaned as he came back down the stairs. "Grandma! You're not trash-talking my girlfriend again, are you?"

"Blame the wrestlers on those silly TV shows that you like me to watch with you. Although the drama *is* often better than my soap operas."

"Right?" Omar said. "Not that I ever watch soap operas," he added hurriedly. He patted the pockets of the leather jacket he was now wearing. "I'm ready to go. Are you?"

"Yes," Silvia said, smiling at Mamani. "I'll try to visit again soon."

"Very soon, I hope," the older woman said, taking her hand and patting it affectionately.

"I've missed her," Silvia said once they were outside.

"She's always asking about you," Omar replied.

"I thought she only used her wheelchair in the winter. Is everything okay?"

Omar stopped next to the truck, looking worried. "I hope so. She *has* been using it a lot more lately. I was kinda hoping that she's just been feeling lazy."

Of all the words that could describe Omar's grandmother, lazy wasn't one of them, but she didn't want to upset him unnecessarily. The body got older, but Mamani's mind was still razor-sharp.

"Is it wrong that I feel super lucky?" Omar said as they drove away from the house. "I mean, my best friend is barfing his guts out right now, but me and you… We're going to see freaking Nirvana!"

"I was conflicted too," Silvia admitted. Anthony had called her this morning, sounding on the verge of vomiting, when he explained that both he and Cameron had gotten food poisoning from expired milk. "I don't know if I'll ever be able to eat cereal again," Anthony had said. "Or if I want to go on living, because it's my favorite night-time snack. Ugh… Give me a minute." She had listened to him choke down air before he got his stomach under control, her own turning out of sympathy. "I don't want the concert tickets to go to waste," Anthony said when able to speak again. It was *who* he chose to give the tickets to that baffled her. "Don't you think it would make more sense for you and Whitney to go together?"

Omar shook his head. "Doesn't matter. Anthony got the tickets as a birthday present, and that means he gets to decide what happens to them. We're his two closest friends, so it makes sense."

She supposed it did. Silvia turned on the radio as they left Pride and headed toward Kansas City. They were both thrilled when "Heart-Shaped Box," the first single off Nirvana's newly released third album, began to play.

"That's gotta be a sign!" Omar crowed before turning it up. He was still grinning when the song ended and commercials compelled him to turn the radio down again. "I love this time of year," he said. "Tonight is going to be amazing, Halloween is just around the corner, and then it's my birthday. So awesome!"

"Are you doing anything special this year?" she asked.

"Nope. I don't have any plans yet. What about you?"

"I already celebrated mine."

"Yeah, I know," he said. "July sixteenth. You didn't invite me to the party."

"Because I didn't have one!"

"But you did something fun, right?" he asked, as if genuinely concerned.

"Yes, I had a nice day with my family. And then I had a girls' night out."

"Cool. I actually meant Halloween. Do you have any plans then?"

"Oh. Keisha's family always has one of their big community events. She has to help each year, so I volunteered. Mindy did too. Mostly because we think it's a sad way for Keisha to spend Halloween. So this year, we're bringing the party to her."

"What are we talking here?" Omar asked. "Bobbing for apples? That sort of thing?"

Silvia shrugged. "All I know is that there's a corn maze."

Omar perked up. "Really?"

"Yeah. Why? Do you like those?"

"No idea. I've never been to one, but it *does* sound like the sort of thing Whitney would like."

"Bring her with you," Silvia said, keeping her tone neutral.

"You wouldn't mind?" Omar pried.

"Why would I?" she asked evenly.

The last thing she wanted to do was make him feel conflicted. Conversation was easy on the rest of the drive. They had time enough to grab a burger after parking the car. Then they went to Memorial Hall, a rectangular building with towering columns out front that made it look like a beige version of the White House. The interior was packed. And noisy! One of the opening bands was already playing. She grabbed hold of Omar's jacket sleeve so she wouldn't lose him as they slowly got their bearings. They began working their way through the crowd as the first band left the stage and another took its place. Silvia didn't know much about either, only that the vibe here was electrifying. From the way that Omar was grinning, he thought so too, but it was much too loud to discuss anything. Between acts, when people who were old enough left to get more beer, they managed to squeeze their way to the very front. Right up against the metal barriers put there to keep people from rushing the stage. Nirvana came out soon after, launching immediately into a grinding track called "Radio Friendly Unit Shifter" from the new album.

Silvia had listened to music her entire life, but this was something new. She could literally feel it! There wasn't any choice. The massive speakers shook everything around them, the crowd going wild. Dave Grohl was bludgeoning the drums like he had a personal grudge against them. Pat Smear finished smoking a cigarette and flicked the butt over the heads of the audience, not missing a single strum on his guitar. Krist Novoselic bounced up and down—like much of the audience—

while plucking his bass. Front and center was Kurt Cobain, his blond hair windblown and covering half his face. He was dressed in a T-shirt and an open cardigan, his eyes squinted shut as he crooned into the microphone. Silvia decided right then and there that he could have her virginity and anything else he wanted, should he decide to pull her on stage and carry her back to the tour bus.

She felt like she'd smoked a bowl, despite being stone-cold sober, as the tracks kept coming: "Drain You," "Breed," "Serve the Servants," "About a Girl." Omar was banging his head, often with one fist raised in the air. Silvia was whipping her head left and right. "Heart-Shaped Box" began to play. Omar put an arm around her as they jumped up and down in unison. The crowd got wilder and wilder as the show went on. Mosh pits surged into existence before dying out again. Silvia was repeatedly jostled to and fro, almost losing her footing a few times.

They were deep into the set when the band started playing "School," which had a fast beat and thrashing guitars. The crowd around them went ballistic! Someone slammed into Omar from the side. Silvia turned in surprise and saw him being sucked into the crowd, like he was caught in an undertow. They reached for each other, his eyes filled with panic before he disappeared. Silvia was knocked backward, then to the left. She continued to get battered around, often by people who had themselves been shoved. The music was soon forgotten as remaining upright became her sole focus.

Silvia shrieked in surprise when she felt a hand wrap around her ankle. She looked down, ready to kick the offender, until she saw Omar's wide eyes staring back up at her.

"What are you doing down there?" she yelled.

"Rescuing you!" Omar shouted back. "Help!"

She grabbed his hands, and together, they managed to get him to his feet.

"My hero!" Silvia shouted.

He opened his mouth to respond before both of them were knocked to the side again. This was getting out of control! Silvia tried to shove her way to somewhere calmer and ended up against one of the metal barriers. She turned, relieved to see that Omar had managed to follow. He put his arms to either side of her, grabbed the metal barrier, and used his body as a shield.

He smiled, his eyes on her rather than the show. She continued facing him instead of the stage, too worried about his welfare.

A couple of frat boys plowed into Omar from behind, his expression contorting in a wince, but he managed to hold his ground, the reassuring smile appearing again soon after. This happened a second time, pushing Omar closer to her. And again, their bodies colliding, but he managed to brace himself and take the brunt of the collision. His face was close to hers now. She could feel the heat radiating off his body. His eyes kept darting down to her lips, maybe because hers were doing the same thing. She almost wished someone would shove him from behind once more, which was silly, because she only had to lean forward, like she was doing now, and tilt her head slightly...

Omar's eyes became half-lidded. Hers fluttered shut, but she didn't feel anything touch her lips. Instead, a sweaty forehead gently came to rest against her own. She opened her eyes again to find that Omar's were filled with desire... and an apology. The song came to an end.

He moved his mouth close to her ear. "I can't," he said. "I want to... But I can't."

Because he didn't want to hurt the girl he was already with. This only magnified Silvia's desire. She pulled him close as an acoustic version of "Polly" began to play. Omar's arms wrapped around her and squeezed. He didn't let go. She didn't either. No matter what Mamani might think, *he* was actually a good influence on *her*. Silvia never would have allowed herself to live so freely before meeting him. And she'd once again been willing to break someone's heart to get what she wanted, but he hadn't let it happen. Omar was too good of a man. No longer hers... but loved just the same.

The minivan pulled into the small parking lot of Gomez Auto Repair. Not for service, although Ricky liked the idea of his parents taking their vehicles there. In fact, he would suggest that they do so from now on! His enthusiasm might be a little premature, because Ricky still wasn't sure where they stood exactly. That's what he was here to find out.

"Does he work every weekend?" his mother asked, leaning over to see past him.

"Pretty much, yeah. Most weeknights too."

Ami leaned back again, her expression sympathetic. "That can't be easy to balance with school. Can't his family hire someone else?"

Ricky shrugged. "They did earlier in the year. And it helped, but Diego still works a lot. I think because he wants to keep his dad's legacy alive."

"The poor child!" his mother replied.

He wasn't sure why, but her attitude toward Diego had changed. Maybe because Ricky wasn't trying to hide anything from her. He refused to sneak around behind her back. What sort of message would that send? He'd asked his mom to drive him here instead of begging one of his friends, hoping to trade transparency for trust, but they weren't out of the woods yet.

"Are you two together again or just friends?" Ami asked with an edge of concern.

"I'm not sure," Ricky replied. "I want to be with him but… we're taking it slow this time."

She gave him a smile unique to mothers that was a mixture of pride and barely contained tears. "Remember your curfew. If you need a ride home or anything else…"

"I'll call you," he promised before hugging her.

He grabbed his backpack and climbed out. Ricky walked across the parking lot, pausing to wave at his mother as she drove away. He avoided the front desk and went directly to one of the open bays. An elderly black man noticed him first. He said something to the car nearest him, or so it appeared before Diego rolled out from underneath it dressed in blue coveralls.

"You're early,' he said after an upward nod.

"I know," Ricky replied. "I just wanted to be close to you."

The man who had first noticed him suddenly became distracted and hobbled away.

Diego's reaction was tougher to read. "I still have some work to do."

"That's okay," Ricky said. "I won't get in the way, I promise."

Diego eyed him again. "Wanna wait in my office?"

Ricky shook his head. He noticed a large metal barrel against one wall. "Just pretend I'm not here," he said. "Really."

Diego watched him walk over to the barrel and use it as a seat. There was a hint of a smirk before he rolled beneath the car again. Ricky could hardly wait for him to reappear. While he waited, he thought about the past week, having mixed feelings about Diego's breakdown during rehearsals. Part of him had been thrilled to be kissed and told that he was loved, but the circumstances... Diego had been drunk. And grieving the death of his father. So it hadn't seemed right for Ricky to celebrate their reunion, or to take advantage of the vulnerable state Diego had been in.

The next morning proved the wisdom of his caution. Diego hadn't been cold when picking him up, but some of the distance had returned. Ricky didn't feel like he was being held at bay, more like Diego was protecting himself out of necessity. Trust wouldn't magically spring back into existence. Not for either of them. Ricky hadn't broached any complicated subjects with him during the week, or tried talking about what they felt for each other. All he'd done was place his hand in Diego's on occasion, always reassured when it was accepted and squeezed. All that having been said, Ricky was only human, so when Diego had asked if he wanted to hang out on Saturday, he couldn't help but feel a thrill.

The auto shop slowly emptied as cars were pulled out for customers to collect. The daylight grew dim and the mechanics went home, one by one, until only Diego was left. Ricky hopped off his barrel and walked with him as he closed the garage doors and locked up.

"I'm all yours," Diego said at last. He scratched at his chest. "Guess I should take a shower real quick."

"Please don't!" Ricky said.

Diego eyed him before smirking. "You haven't changed one bit."

"And you probably need help *getting* changed," Ricky said, taking his hand and leading him toward the lockers.

As soon as they reached them, Diego pressed him up against the cold metal for a kiss. Ricky was very into that, especially as it went on. Diego's love language was physical. Sexual. So he took this as a sign that things were good... except he was a part of this relationship too—if it could even be called that. Dr. Sharma wouldn't want him to sacrifice his own needs. Ricky's love language was verbal.

"Wait," he said.

Diego backed off. "What's up?" He grabbed himself through the coveralls. "Besides this."

Ricky glanced down, his brain needing to reboot before he could remember how to speak. "Are we back together again? I mean like… all the way."

"I was hoping to go all the way," Diego said with bedroom eyes.

Ricky did his best to resist them. "Are you my boyfriend again?"

Diego cocked an eyebrow. "Why buy the cow when you get the milk for free? Is that the sort of thing you're worried about?"

Ricky thought about it. Then he shook his head. "I'll milk you no matter what. But I want to know if this is just a casual fling, or if it's a new start for us."

"First of all," Diego said. "You can't milk a bull. Although you're welcome to try. Secondly, what we had together never really ended. Not when they locked me up or sent you away. Hell, you could walk out right now and it wouldn't be over, because I still feel it. And I know you do too. So let's make it official."

He tugged on the zipper of his coveralls before letting go and spreading his hands wide, like the choice was his. Ricky didn't even hesitate. He pulled the zipper down, revealing beefy muscle. The great thing about coveralls is that the zipper went *all* the way, past even the waist. Ricky got down on his knees and took Diego into his mouth. Or as much as he could fit anyway. He kept looking up as he worked, at first because Diego had shrugged off the coveralls, revealing his round shoulders and that incredible chest. But mostly he wanted to see the different expressions play out across his handsome face. Diego had a tendency to curl his lip, especially the closer he got, his stare filled with a carnal intensity. With a hint of love. Ricky was sure of it when Diego stopped grunting and finally groaned with relief, his gaze softening.

"Goddamn, I missed that!" Diego said, pulling him to his feet.

"Me too," Ricky said, wiping his mouth on the back of his arm.

Diego breathed in and exhaled again before looking him over. "All right. Take off your clothes. Let's see if anything else has grown while you were away."

"It has," Ricky said, undoing his jeans. "By almost half an inch."

Diego made a face. "How would you know?"

"I measure," Ricky said. "Doesn't everyone?"

"I don't need a ruler to know that I'm big."

"I guess that makes sense. Can *I* measure it though?"

"Some other time," Diego said. "It's your turn."

His turn? Ricky wasn't sure what to make of that, used to finishing himself off. Was he expected to put on a show? At the moment, he was so horny that anything sounded like a good idea. If Diego wanted him to fuck an exhaust pipe, he only needed to point Ricky in the direction of a willing car. Although he'd still prefer a date first. They could go to a drive-thru for dinner and then a drive-in movie. This made him laugh.

"I'm not joking," Diego grumbled as he stepped out of his coveralls and tugged on Ricky's shirt. "I wanna see you naked."

"Um… Are you sure that nobody will come in here?"

"I already did," Diego said. "You've got nothing to worry about. My mom is out with her best friend. And also, I'm the goddamn boss. I'll do whatever the hell I want."

Eager to discover what exactly that was, Ricky quickly complied.

"I guess it does look bigger," Diego said appraisingly.

"Thanks," Ricky said, reaching for himself before his hand was smacked away.

"I'll take care of that," Diego said, a big paw wrapping around Ricky to pull him close.

He stumbled into those massive arms, one of them continuing to pump. This was new territory! Diego had never shown much interest in that part of him before. Ricky whimpered against his lips, loving how the strong calloused hands felt.

"I don't get on my knees for anyone," Diego said when pulling back. "So let's try it this way." He reached under Ricky's arms and lifted him up. "Swing your legs over my shoulders," he instructed.

"Are you kidding?" Ricky asked.

He didn't wait for an answer. He scrambled up the muscled torso as quickly and carefully as he could. Soon he was riding on those meaty shoulders, Diego's face buried in his crotch. Ricky's back hit the lockers, but he barely registered any discomfort. He was too overwhelmed by the intense pleasure. All he could do was hold on for dear life while gasping. He didn't last very long.

Diego looked smug when helping him down again. "That was some Olympic-level sex," he said.

"It was incredible!" Ricky said, his voice warbling slightly.

"Come tastes weird." Diego didn't sound too off-put as he put on the boxer briefs that had been the only thing beneath his coveralls. "Let's go to my office. I need a drink."

Ricky hastily pulled on his underwear and T-shirt before gathering up the rest of his clothes and following. Once in the office, Diego took out two bottles of Orange Crush from the mini-fridge, opened them, and handed one to him.

"Thanks," Ricky said after taking a sip. "So it's official now?"

Diego shrugged, although a hint of amusement made his lips twitch. "That depends. Did you sleep with that pudgy guy?"

"You mean Galen?" Ricky asked. "First of all, he's not pudgy. He's stocky."

Diego snorted.

"I like his body!" Ricky said. "And I would have slept with him… if I wasn't so in love with you."

"So nothing happened?" Diego asked, sounding more serious this time.

"Nothing at all. Not even a kiss. Can you say the same?"

"I kissed Mindy," Diego said, his gaze not wavering. "A bunch."

"Because you like her?" Ricky asked, feeling vulnerable.

"Yeah," Diego admitted. "I do."

Ricky swallowed. "Then how come she's not here instead of me?"

"Because I don't love her," Diego said, setting his soda on the desk and walking toward him. "And because you love me. So yeah, it's official now."

"You're my boyfriend?" he asked.

"You're *my* boyfriend," Diego said possessively. "And it's my turn."

"Again?" Ricky asked. Even though experience had taught him, on numerous occasions, that Diego wasn't kidding.

He felt worn out in the best way possible at the end of the night. They did more than mess around. Diego invited him upstairs to the apartment for the first time. Getting to see his room, and cuddle with him on the bed, felt like another act of trust. His mom came home around the time they were leaving. She was a tall woman with a strong build. Ricky wasn't sure what to make of her yet. Marti seemed equally uncertain of him, but it was only a short introduction. He hoped they would meet again, and that he'd continue to be invited into Diego's life. Ricky was very aware, on the drive home, that some areas were more sensitive than others.

"I have something for you," he said after they had pulled up to his house. "It's not from me, but I want you to treat it like it is."

"What's that supposed to mean?" Diego asked while watching him dig around in his backpack.

"Omar wants you to have this," Ricky said, pulling out a VHS tape.

"He didn't have the guts to give it to me himself?"

Ricky rolled his eyes. "He was worried that you'd smash it or something, tough guy."

"I probably would have," Diego said, snatching the tape from him. "And I might still. What's on it?"

"All the footage he could find of your father."

Diego's mouth fell open. It closed again when he swallowed. His brow furrowed as he considered the tape anew. "For real?"

"Yes."

Diego carefully set it in the back seat. "Okay."

Ricky wanted to know what he was feeling, and when he'd watch it, or if he would at all… but the night had already been emotional enough. And besides, there would be plenty of time for that later, now that they had truly reunited. Just the thought filled his heart with joy.

"I love you," Ricky said.

"Yeah yeah," Diego replied, leaning over to kiss him. "Better get inside before your folks call the cops on me again."

"Okay." Ricky bit his bottom lip to stop himself from saying more. But he would. One glorious day at a time.

CHAPTER 25
OCTOBER 31ˢᵀ, 1993

Anthony couldn't remember the last time he felt so at peace with himself. He'd always enjoyed Halloween. Although it was much more fun back when they were kids. Who could resist the opportunity to become someone new? This year felt different. Like he'd been given the chance to be his true self. So even though none of his friends were wearing costumes, Anthony had gotten dressed up. After listening carefully to his needs, his mother had trimmed the wig, and it turned out just like he'd imagined. The hair now spilled across his forehead and over his ears, framing his face. He rolled his neck to feel it tickle the skin there, goosebumps prickling in response and making him laugh.

Cameron noticed, glancing over at him from behind the wheel of Anthony's car. He hadn't wanted to drive, too drunk on everything he felt inside.

"You know," his boyfriend said, briefly checking the road. "As much as I like blonds, I have to admit that it's good to see you in pink again."

Anthony smiled demurely. His mother had dyed the wig for him, and best of all, the color wouldn't fade as quickly as his own hair. Not if he was careful to keep the wig clean, so it wouldn't need to be washed too often. "Thanks," he replied. "I like seeing you in brown. Although if you *were* going to dye your hair, what color would you choose?"

"Purple," Cameron said without needing to think.

"Purple?" Anthony repeated in surprise. "How come?"

"Because it would look nice next to yours. I'd really go for it though. I wouldn't hold back."

Anthony arched an eyebrow at this. "Meaning?"

Cameron nodded at his own crotch. "Upstairs *and* downstairs."

"Purple pubes?" Anthony laughed. "I'm not sure if the world is ready for that, but I am. I'll make an appointment for you with my mom."

Cameron didn't respond right away, his attention on the road. "Is this the right way?"

"Yeah, keep going."

They were driving on the outskirts of town, heading toward Keisha's farm.

"Do you think Ricky will be there?" Cameron asked.

"I doubt it, now that he's back together with Diego."

"Are you disappointed?"

Anthony shrugged. "As weird as it might sound, I'm happier for Diego than I am Ricky."

Cameron glanced at him. "Why's that?"

"Diego has been on his own for way too long. I know he's dated a few girls, but that's not the same as having a friend. Ricky will be there for him, even if they don't last. I guess that helps alleviate some of my own guilt, because knowing what I do now..." Anthony sighed. "Well anyway. I'm happy for Diego."

"But not Ricky."

"I *am*," he said tentatively, "but I'd worry less if he'd ended up with someone better suited to him."

"They could always rent matching tuxedos."

Anthony needed a second to get the joke. Then he groaned.

Cameron seemed pleased with himself. "So what sort of guy should he be with then?"

Anthony thought about it. "Someone sweet who will never do anything to hurt him, intentionally or otherwise." He felt a rush of warmth for his boyfriend. "Someone like you."

"Even I can't make that promise," Cameron said. "I've hurt you without meaning to."

"When?" Anthony said, all previous transgressions intentionally forgotten. "I don't remember anything like that."

"Then I won't remind you," Cameron said with a chuckle. "Hey, there's the sign!"

An iron gate with the words *Hartland Farms* worked into the design stretched over the small road they turned onto. A short drive took them to an area set aside for parking. Anthony flipped down the visor to check himself in the mirror. His eyeliner was smeared to perfection, his pink lip gloss still popping, but most of all... that wig! It sat upon his head like a totem of power, lending him confidence and grace.

"Do you want to be alone with that thing?" Cameron teased.

"Would you mind?" Anthony asked with a straight face.

After a moment of shocked silence, his boyfriend laughed. "I do *not* need more competition than I already have."

He got out of the car without explaining.

Anthony hurried after him to ask what he meant.

"Doesn't matter," Cameron said. "It was a dumb joke."

Anthony could only think of one person he might view in those terms. Omar. But there wasn't really any competition there. Anthony would work harder to prove that to him. For now, it was probably for the best that Whitney had insisted on going trick-or-treating instead of coming here. They'd have the entire evening to themselves, more or less, with the others busy volunteering. They passed Silvia's truck on the way in.

The night air was crisp, just chilly enough for Anthony to wear his favorite long coat that reached his shins. With so much of his body concealed beneath the black fabric, he wouldn't be surprised if someone mistook him for a woman. Was it weird that he hoped for that to happen? Maybe. But the thought also made him smile.

He turned his attention to Michael Jackson's "Thriller," which was playing over outdoor speakers. They followed the sound to the heart of the festivities and began exploring. They saw little kids in costumes run from station to station to collect candy. A horse-drawn cart forced them to stop when crossing their path, happy families sitting on the haystacks it hauled. Most of the activities were aimed at younger audiences, but that didn't discourage either of them. Cameron practically dragged him to the Halloween petting zoo, where they met the first of their friends.

"Excuse me ma'am," Anthony said to Silvia in formal tones, as if they didn't know each other. "I'm afraid I must express my disappointment. None of these animals are wearing costumes."

"Don't be fooled," she said, nodding at a pony. "That's actually a pig." She leaned closer to whisper, "And between you and me, most of the goats were summoned from Hell."

He sniffed snootily before nodding in concession. "I stand corrected."

"I love the wig," Silvia said, dropping the act. "You look gorgeous!"

"Thanks," Anthony said. "Your makeup is even better than usual. I think you've found your new style."

She was wearing brown and white face paint that made her resemble a deer, down to a little black nose and two tiny antlers drawn on her forehead. "Thank you," Silvia said. "Mindy helped me with it. I've already decided to never wash my face again."

"Good call," Anthony said. "You won't be single for much longer."

She glanced around, as if searching for potential partners. "Who all is with you?"

"Just the guy over there with the big cock."

In one corner of the pen, Cameron was cradling a rooster while looking thrilled.

"That bird is so sweet," Silvia said. "So is your man. Oh! You have to meet Bacon Junior!"

She gave Anthony a tour, introducing him to livestock as if they were real people. He forgot sometimes that she was so into animals. It made sense that she would volunteer for this station. They hung out together until a family needed Silvia's help with an especially nervous child. Anthony collected his boyfriend so they could continue exploring.

They were passing the amphitheater when Cameron grabbed his arm. "Hey, there's Mindy! Let's go say hi to her."

They had to navigate past a small crowd of costumed characters who were milling about for some reason. Cameron took the lead. He'd gotten a lot closer to Mindy over the past year, which benefited Anthony as well. They'd known each other since they were kids but rarely ever hung out. Not until recently, which was great, because she was undeniably cool. Mindy hugged Cameron before noticing him.

"Oh my gosh!" she said. "You look stunning!"

"Why thank you," Anthony replied, fluttering his lashes to draw attention to his eyeliner. "I've learned from the best."

"I don't know the first thing about cutting hair." Mindy reached up to gently touch the wig. "Is this your mom's work?"

"Yeah," he said with a grin. "I'm very lucky to be surrounded by talented women who are infinitely patient with me."

"Only because we love you," Mindy said before taking stock of him again. "You look so happy!"

"I really am." Blissfully so! He had an understanding boyfriend, an accepting family, and the best group of friends anyone could wish for.

"Can we do a makeover sometime?" Mindy asked. "Not that you need it. I just think it would be fun. We can have a sleepover!"

"I would love that." Anthony noticed an unusual number of people looking in their direction. Probably because they were standing on the small stage. "Are they expecting us to put on a show?"

"Just me," Mindy replied. "I'm hosting the costume contest."

"The girl with stage fright?" Cameron asked with a wry grin.

"I've conquered my fears," she said casually, as if having just arm-wrestled a grizzly bear without breaking a sweat. Her face became distressed. "But you know what's horrible? Being one of the judges. We already had the little ones up here. You just know they all have their hearts set on winning. It was terrible!"

"Why don't you give them each a prize?" Cameron asked.

"We do, but there can only be one first place winner. Keisha says that losing helps build character. And that I'm too much of a softy."

"Don't you ever change," Cameron said affectionately. He scanned the crowd. "So who's on your short list?"

"The kid dressed as Sonic the Hedgehog because that is a *lot* of blue paint. If he's willing to risk a full-body rash, then he deserves to win. When it comes to the adult category, my vote goes to the guy dressed as Homer Simpson."

Anthony made a face. "He's just a bald guy wearing a white Polo and jeans."

"That was my first thought too," Mindy said, "but he actually shaved himself bald. For real! He usually has a full head of hair. Talk about dedication. And he can do the voice."

Anthony narrowed his eyes critically while studying the other contestants. "Is that a white guy dressed as Michael Jackson?"

Mindy shook her head. "I thought so too, but he's supposed to be Corey Feldman."

"Huh," Cameron said. "I thought he was trying to be Prince."

"The artist formerly known as," Anthony murmured.

One of the judges joined them just long enough to give Mindy a couple of index cards.

"This is it!" she told them. "The winners of the next round!"

"Let me see," Cameron said, trying to peek.

"No way!" Mindy shielded the cards. "You have to wait like everyone else. Actually—" she checked her watch. "It's time!"

They cleared the stage and joined the audience, watching as the winners were declared one by one. Sonic was victorious. The guy even did his best to zip around the stage after collecting his prize. They both felt too restless to stay for the next round, which hadn't been decided yet.

"Let's check out the haunted corn maze," Cameron suggested.

Anthony nodded. Of all the attractions, that one held the most appeal. He could already imagine how fun—and romantic—it would be to get lost with his boyfriend. The corn maze was on the far side of the farm, the entrance tended by another friend of theirs.

"Here comes trouble," Keisha said as they approached. "Do I need to lecture you boys about public indecency? We all know how much gay men love doing it in the bushes."

Anthony laughed. "Don't worry, we'll keep *most* of our clothes on while doing it. We aren't depraved."

"I rest assured," Keisha said with a smile. "So nice of y'all to come out here tonight."

"It's really cool that your family puts this on each year," Cameron responded. "We didn't have to pay for admission. Is that right?"

Keisha nodded. "We do it for the community. Although it isn't all free. Make sure to stop by the gift shop on your way out."

"We will," Cameron assured her. "Is there some other way I can contribute? I don't mind helping."

"Yes, actually," Keisha said. "I didn't have a chance to get a drink when I took my break. Too many little fires to put out. Would you mind grabbing me a Dr Pepper from the food hall? Just tell them it's for me and you won't get charged."

"I'm happy to pay for it," Cameron said. "Be right back."

He took off, leaving them alone.

"So just how haunted is this corn maze?" Anthony asked.

"We've had reports of zombies, a poltergeist or two, and I saw a werewolf digging around in there earlier, like he was looking for somewhere to bury a bone. I hope that doesn't give you any ideas."

Anthony snorted. They both toned it down when a group of kids approached. Keisha counted them in using a little clicking device. She did the same thing when a pair of adults left not long after.

"This is my first year as a bouncer," she explained. "I'm usually in there scaring people but that torch has been passed. All I have to do now is make sure it doesn't get too crowded, and that everyone finds their way out again."

"This whole thing is amazing," Anthony said in awe. "The closest thing my family ever did is the year we left the garage door open and the lights off, so Omar and I could leap out and scare the trick-or-treaters."

As if on cue, they heard screams from inside the corn maze.

"You're both welcome to put those skills to work here next year, if you'd like." Her features crinkled in confusion before widening with surprise. "What are you doing here?"

Anthony followed her gaze and saw one of the Song sisters emerge from the maze.

"Hey," Hope said sheepishly. "Um..."

"You must have gone in while I was on break. How long have you been here?"

"Not very," Hope said, her eyes darting to him and away again. "There's something you should know."

More screams. This time they went on for quite a while.

"What's up?" Keisha asked.

"I'm here with my friends," Hope said.

Keisha shrugged. "That's fine. Everybody is welcome."

"You don't understand." Hope eyed Anthony with unease. Then she pressed her lips together.

"You can trust him," Keisha said. "We're all part of the same family."

Considering the contrasting skin tones on display, Anthony was pretty sure she meant they were all queer. The rumors he'd heard about them were true then.

Hope hesitated a moment longer before angry shouting from the corn maze seemed to spur her on. "Troy wants to get revenge. For you guys ruining his party."

Keisha's eyes flicked to Anthony briefly. Did she know what he'd done? If so, she didn't betray him.

"But this *isn't* a party," Keisha stressed.

Hope shrugged. "That's what I tried to tell him."

Keisha sighed. "What's his big plan?"

Hope chewed her bottom lip before answering. "They came here to raise hell. Whatever that means. I got separated from the others on purpose so I could tell you."

They heard another scream from the corn maze, except this time it was high-pitched and drawn out, like a whistling tea kettle.

"That's my little sister!" Keisha said in shock. "I'd recognize those pipes anywhere!" She rushed toward the entrance.

Anthony was right behind her.

"I'll never forgive them if they do something to Little Bee," Keisha said, sounding panicked.

After another shrill scream, they both broke into a run, turning one corner and then another, their world reduced to corridor after corridor lined by corn. The frequently diverging path was strewn with hay. Keisha seemed to know where she was going until they stopped at a four-way junction.

"They're either that way," she said pointing in one direction, "or that way," she said when pointing in another.

"Let's split up," Antony suggested.

Keisha nodded. "If you find her first, just have Little Bee keep screaming. That'll be my homing signal."

"You've got it." Anthony took off running, only slowing when the path split in two. He chose randomly and kept going. When he heard the high-pitched scream again, it sounded farther away instead of closer. Anthony took another turn that he hoped was the right direction but ended up in a dead end. He turned around, intent on backtracking, but didn't get far before his path was blocked by a group of people wearing gruesome masks.

"Holy shit," one of them said, nudging his friends while laughing. "Look who it is!"

Troy, his worst enemy. Anthony would have recognized the voice, even if Hope hadn't tipped them off. The hulking giant next to him must be Graham, the bully who had decked him sophomore year. He was flanked by some other guy nearly his size. Faith Song appeared from behind them, a black hood drawn over her head, but not enough to fully conceal her face. She seemed distracted as if searching for her sister. Rounding out their group was someone he knew a lot better, even despite the demonic face paint, because they used to be friends. Dave seemed nervous.

"How's it going, Troy?" Anthony asked, wanting them to know that he had their number.

"I'm having a blast," Troy said, pulling off the mask. "Just one question." His expression was amused as he looked Anthony over. "Is that a costume? Or do you always look like a prostitute when you're not in school?"

"You'd know if it wasn't for the dress code," Anthony shot

back. "Just think how many opportunities to make fun of me you're missing out on now. You really shot yourself in the foot."

"Maybe we'll shoot *you* in the face!" Graham grunted from behind his mask.

"Easy, boy," Troy said, waving him into submission. "That would be overkill, don't you think? Like running over a dandelion with a bulldozer."

"Are you saying I should just use my fists?" Graham asked, balling them up.

"Maybe," Troy replied, as if the idea intrigued him.

"Let's get out of here," Faith suggested with an irritated sigh. "This whole thing is stupid."

"Go find your sister," Troy snapped. "Leave this to us."

Faith shrugged before wandering away, abandoning him to four other guys. Anthony tried to ignore his rising sense of dread. Some animal instinct inside was telling him to run. He did his best to ignore it.

"Why are you doing this?" Anthony asked, choosing to reason with them instead.

"Because you tried to burn down my house!" Graham growled, taking a step forward.

"That wasn't me!" Anthony shot back.

"Yeah, but it was your friends!"

If only that were true. Ricky was his friend, but Diego sure wasn't. His presence would be welcome right now regardless. "I had nothing to do with that," Anthony said, remembering his own guilt. He addressed Troy instead. "You can stop trying to ruin things here, because it's not Keisha's fault that the cops busted your party. None of my friends had anything to do with it. I'm the one who called the police."

Troy's leering smile faded. "Are you serious?"

"Yes," Anthony said, hurriedly adding, "but to be fair, you made it so we couldn't distribute our suckers. Right?"

"That was just politics," Troy snarled, thumping his chest. "*I* got in trouble with my parents. They're making me take a fucking drug test every week!"

"That wasn't my intention," Anthony said with a swallow. "I shouldn't have done what I did. I'm sorry. But again, you threw the first punch."

"Yeah, but not the last one," Troy said. "Start running."

"What?"

Drops of rain began to pitter patter around them.

"You heard me," Troy grumbled. "Start running."

There was nowhere to go. The path behind him was a dead end. Anthony looked to Dave, silently pleading with his old friend to defend him or argue on his behalf, but all he saw in that gaze was trembling fear.

"Fuck it," Graham said, cracking his knuckles. "I'll beat the shit out of you right here."

"No you won't!" Anthony turned and ran, faster than he'd ever run in his whole life, his brain working overtime.

Yes, he was running toward a dead end, but this was a corn maze. The walls weren't solid. The corn was planted close together, but he could still make it through. Drops struck his cheeks as he fled. They weren't tears. He was too freaked out to cry, but it did give him hope. If it started raining hard enough, maybe they'd abandon the chase and seek shelter. Please let it rain!

He saw the dead end ahead of him. The others must have too, because there were howls of laughter. They sounded much too close for comfort. He pumped his arms, not daring to look back in case it cost him the lead. He burst through the wall of corn, slipping into one of the narrow spaces between rows while praying for a miracle: Omar showing up unexpectedly. Dave tripping his new friends on "accident" to give him the chance to escape. Or maybe Anthony would burst through to another path with some adults on it. He saw no sign of the maze around him, just rows and rows of dark shadowy corn that he sprinted between.

He had just decided to turn at a right angle and try a different direction when a hand grabbed the back of his coat.

"Got ya!" he heard Troy say.

Anthony wiggled out of the coat in an attempt to escape. He made it a few more steps before something struck him from behind. Graham's shoulder, if he had to guess, in a classic football tackle. He hit the ground and tried to roll away, exposing his stomach just in time for a booted foot to kick him there. The air left his lungs, his eyes wide in fear as he saw four towering shadows gather around him. A hand reached out to rip the wig from his head. A shoe struck him across the chin, lights blinding him. He sucked in air and managed to roll over, clawing the ground to get away. A heavy weight landed on his back, making it impossible to move and difficult to breathe.

"Come on, you guys," he heard Dave say weakly.

"Help him get that makeup off," Troy spat.

A big hand wrapped around the back of his head before his face was shoved in the mud. It hurt like hell, but all Anthony could think about was suffocating to death, because he was still struggling to breathe.

"Let me take a look at him."

Anthony's head was pulled back. He used the chance to suck in air, the sound haggard. All he heard in response was laughter and a rumble of thunder.

"Nope. Still ugly as sin. Try again."

His face was shoved in the mud again. This time they really rubbed it into the ground, hard enough that Anthony worried they'd break his nose. Which was a laughable concern, considering that he'd soon be dead. He was on the verge of losing consciousness. At least he wouldn't feel the moment when it came.

The weight lifted off him suddenly. He was kicked in the side again and rolled over in agony. That's when the rain finally broke and became a heavy downpour.

"Fuck!" one of the guys yelled.

"Let's get out here," Dave shouted. "Come on!"

Anthony shielded his head with his arms before curling up into a ball, fearing parting shots or that they'd finish him off entirely. He wasn't sure how long he remained there before he gathered enough courage to look around. He was alone in the dark, which he found oddly comforting, since they probably couldn't find him again. He managed to sit up, a trembling hand checking his face, which hurt all over.

The rest of him wasn't any better. Anthony unsteadily got to his feet, his entire body aching. He was too scared to return the same way. How ironic would it be if the bastards couldn't escape the maze? He didn't want to run into them. Lights cut through the field briefly before disappearing. He walked in that direction, stumbling and falling along the way, until he finally broke through the rows of corn. In front of him was the road that they'd driven down to get here. The idea of being safe and dry in the car's interior—to be close again to Cameron's reassuring presence—seemed like a distant dream. Anthony wanted to return to that far-away place. He managed a hobbling sort of run, loping his way to the end of the corn field.

Cars were leaving in droves, but he didn't see many people. Everyone who had decided to stay must have sought shelter. All except for a solitary figure hovering near the entrance of the corn maze. When it turned and rushed toward him, he reacted with fear and squeezed his eyes shut, too shaken to escape. That's when he heard a heart-achingly familiar voice.

"Anthony?"

He opened his eyes again. Cameron!

Anthony tried to respond, but only a sob came out. Cameron was soaked to the bone, his hair plastered to his head. He took off his jacket anyway, using it to shield him from the rain. Anthony wrapped himself around Cameron's torso with desperate need, clutching him like his life depended on it.

"Are you okay?" Cameron asked, still trying to use his jacket as an umbrella.

Anthony wanted to tell him what had happened, but as it all flashed through his mind like a horrific nightmare, all he could do was cry.

Cameron woke an hour before his alarm clock was set to go off. He lay there wearily, anger and sorrow having battered him for most of the night, making it difficult to find sleep. He'd been too haunted by the memory of Anthony's face, scratched and swollen from the violence he'd suffered. His boyfriend had whimpered in pain as they made their way back to the food hall, where most people had taken shelter. Once there… Cameron had done his best to comfort him. As had the rest of their friends. Anthony only wanted to be somewhere private, out of public view, and had insisted that the police not be called, despite the wishes of Keisha's parents. Only when they were completely alone did he tell Cameron in a shaking voice what had befallen him.

Troy. Graham. Dave.

Cameron thought about hurting each of them in different ways, the twisted fantasies alien to his normal way of thinking. In the end, the dark desires did little to alleviate the ache in his heart, because what stung the most, was that Anthony had been the victim. Cameron would have gladly taken his place, a hundred times over if need be, rather than to see him suffer. That would have been so much easier to bear.

His alarm finally went off, a cheerful song playing over the radio. He silenced it with the butt of his fist. Cameron got out of bed and forced himself, despite his exhaustion, to run through his usual routine of push-ups, sit-ups, and pull-ups, since he'd likely need the strength to defend his boyfriend. Then he stepped into the shower, finally allowing himself to weep beneath the steaming water. Once it was out of his system, he got dressed and went downstairs.

He ate a bowl of instant oatmeal while listening to his mother move around upstairs. She was still doing good… in that regard, at least. He was getting ready to leave and decided to take the kitchen trash to the curb. The bag clinked as he pulled it free from the plastic tub. Cameron felt the bottles from the outside, their long necks confirming an uncomfortable truth: His mother was still drinking.

She was downstairs and pouring herself a cup of coffee when he re-entered the house.

"Good morning!" Brenda said, unaware of what had transpired last night.

Cameron glowered at her, his patience thin.

"Is everything all right, hon?" she asked when he was at the sink.

"No," he said, spinning around to face her. "I'm going to be late to school, if they call you. I have to go to Anthony's house first. He got beat up last night."

"No!" His mother's face creased with concern. "What happened?"

"He was gay-bashed," Cameron said, having to steel himself before he could continue. "He's not going to school today. His parents don't want him to. But I really need to see him, so I'm going to skip first period. Maybe more."

"I'll call the office and let them know. Do you want to take the whole day off?"

"No," he said, his voice warbling, "because we have the first student council meeting today, and I really can't miss it. Especially now. I also have work after school. Charles is out of town and nobody will be there to take over from the woman he hired." His hands were beginning to shake.

His mother noticed. "Everything will be fine," Brenda said, moving toward him.

"Nothing is fine!" he shouted. "I know you've been drinking again!"

She paused. "I slipped up, it's true. Don't worry about that. I'm still going to my meetings."

"What's the point if you keep getting drunk?" he demanded, before the anger drained from him, despair taking its place. "I'm sorry I haven't been there for you. I've just been so busy and... Everything is so crazy right now. I don't know what to do."

He dodged when she tried to hug him.

Brenda dropped her arms to her sides. "I'm going to be okay," she said. "I stopped once. I can do it again. The last thing you need to worry about is me. Focus on Anthony. He should be your top priority right now. The rest can wait. Okay?"

His chin trembled as he nodded. When she tried to hug him again, he didn't resist. Cameron needed it too much. Once he'd calmed down somewhat, he drove over to Anthony's house, waiting impatiently for him to answer the door. When he did… Anthony was wearing makeup. And the stupid pink bandana. The panic Cameron felt must have shown, because Anthony gently rolled his eyes and said, "I won't let them change who I am."

"They're going to kill you," he barely managed to croak in response.

Anthony shook his head. "If I become who they want me to be, I'll die on the inside, and that will be much worse."

"For you maybe," Cameron said miserably.

Anthony's expression softened. "Get in here."

Cameron hugged him in the entryway, pulling back to check his face, which did look better. A little swollen in places and scratched up. His demeanor surprised him more. Anthony didn't seem nearly as distraught as he felt inside.

"Let's call the police," Cameron suggested once they were in the living room. "You can file a report with them. Just look at how much trouble Diego got into. They deserve to be locked up. All of them!"

Anthony shook his head. "I already called the police. *Before* the election. I'm the reason Troy and his friends were out there last night."

"What?" Cameron asked, the pieces falling into place.

"Please don't be angry," Anthony said, wincing as he settled down on the couch. "I've already received my punishment."

"I don't care what you did!" Cameron said. "You didn't deserve *that!*"

"Oh, I don't know," Anthony responded in lofty tones. "I can be a self-righteous asshole." The amusement left his face. "But yeah, that was—" He swallowed while searching for the right word. "—harrowing."

"I won't let it happen again," Cameron said. "I swear. I've already talked to everyone. You'll never be alone at school. Not between classes. One of us will always be there with you."

"That isn't necessary," Anthony said, starting to shake his head.

"We did it for Mindy," Cameron said firmly. "We're doing it for you."

Anthony considered him. Then he nodded. "Thanks. That helps."

"And I'll fight for you," Cameron continued. "Through the

student council, on my own in front of the school board, in the ring with Principal Preckwinkle… whatever it takes."

Anthony seemed genuinely moved before he forced a smile. "I'm so glad I have you," he said. "Not everyone is so lucky."

"I know," Cameron said, barely staving off tears. "I'll also be fighting for them."

"Speaking of which, won't you be late to school?"

"I have time," Cameron said.

The relief on Anthony's face was heartbreaking. "Will you hold me?"

"Yeah," Cameron said. "I need that too."

He felt a little better once his boyfriend was wrapped in his arms. Cameron wished they could remain that way, even though Anthony was handling the situation with surprising resilience. He was stronger than most people realized, and would likely need all his strength going forward, but he wouldn't face that challenge alone. Cameron would be there with him every step of the way, protecting him from the hardships of the world with his love.

"Hello?"

Diego stood perfectly still in the living room of the apartment he shared with his mom. He didn't hear a response, so he checked her room, needing to be certain that he had complete privacy. For an entire week, he'd been working up the courage to watch the tape that Omar had made for him. He wasn't sure why the prospect made him so nervous. Maybe because he didn't want to be disappointed. His dad had become a giant in his mind, as seen through the eyes of a twelve-year-old boy. What if the truth didn't live up to the legend? Time to find out. That last thing Diego wanted was to delude himself. Nothing sacred. Even this.

He went to his bedroom to fetch the tape, returning to the living room to feed it into the VCR. Then he sat on the couch, chastising himself for feeling so nervous. Diego couldn't remember recording any videos with his dad, so at most, he'd probably only see him for a few fleeting seconds here and there in the background. He hit the play button on the remote and frowned in irritation when Omar's big dumb head filled the screen.

"Hey, man! I thought an intro was called for to manage

expectations. There's only about ten minutes of footage on this tape, so not a lot, but it's everything I could find. Sorry for being such a dick after your dad died. I was a clueless kid. I wish I could go back in time and smack some sense into myself. Uh… That's not an invitation for you to do it for me. I know it's too late to change things, but I'm still your bud for life. Whether you like it or not. Okay. Enjoy the show."

Diego tried to cling to his irritation, but it was hopeless. The footage jerked before stabilizing again, revealing his father on a riding lawnmower. Lorenzo noticed that he was being filmed and raised his cowboy hat in greeting. Then he began driving around like he was drunk, the straight lines of mowed grass transitioning to loops as he did donuts.

"Don't quit your day job, Mr. Gomez!" Omar called from behind the lens.

"Too late!" Lorenzo called back, waving his hat in the air like he was riding a bull at a rodeo.

Diego's throat was already painfully tight from the effort it took to hold back tears. He wasn't sure if they were the sad or happy kind. Maybe both, because seeing him again… Lorenzo wasn't a big man. He was short and thin, with a lopsided mustache. Diego hadn't thought of that in ages. One side was always slightly higher than the other. Hearing his voice was surreal. His father had a heavy accent from growing up so close to the border that he'd never managed to shake, despite being fluent in English. Diego wasn't sure if he'd been able to speak Spanish.

The scene changed to the repair shop, a Trans Am raised on the hydraulic lift… and not just any. It was *the* Trans Am! His father's old car that Diego had later dubbed Frankenstein. Some of the panels hadn't been replaced yet. He'd nearly forgotten how dinged up they'd been. The firebird symbol on the hood was crisper, since the vehicle hadn't spent years baking in the sun after being abandoned. Anthony was sitting in the passenger seat, scrawny as ever and impossibly young.

"Put your seatbelt on Tony," Lorenzo said. He'd always called Anthony that jokingly. The camera panned to where he stood. "I don't want your parents suing me if that thing goes flying off."

"It won't though, right?" he heard Anthony ask nervously. His voice was especially girlish, since it hadn't broken yet.

"Let's find out," Lorenzo said gleefully before hitting the up and down buttons in quick succession.

The camera returned to Anthony, who was clinging to the steering wheel for dear life as the car bounced like a carnival ride. Omar was giggling from behind the camera. Digo could hear himself laughing too, the sound anything but familiar.

"How come you make me wear a seatbelt?" Diego asked when it was his turn. "I'm not going to sue you."

"Yeah, but when your mom is mad at me, she's scarier than a lawyer. So buckle up!"

The hair stood up on the back of Diego's neck. Hearing his father talk to him, even from so long ago, was powerful. He wanted more of that, no matter how unlikely. The scene continued, eventually replaced by another and another, his father making brief cameos in all of them. Footage panned across a birthday party—one of Omar's probably, since it was his backyard—the adults chatting and drinking. Seeing their folks together like that was interesting, but not very satisfying. Diego kept checking the display on the VCR, the seconds ticking by much too fast. He didn't want this to end. He felt a jolt of panic when reaching the nine-minute mark. Was the intro Omar recorded part of the ten minutes? If so, the tape was as good as over.

The screen cut to a new scene. His father's office. Lorenzo looked up from his desk, his demeanor more subdued this time.

"Where's your friend?"

"Upstairs pooping," Diego heard himself say.

Lorenzo made a face. "Why's he have to stink up our place? He could have used the restrooms down here."

"He says he's poop shy," Diego replied before snickering.

Lorenzo grabbed the phone off his desk and dialed a number, a glimmer of mischief in his eye.

"Who are you calling?" Diego asked.

"I'm making the phone upstairs ring. Hopefully he'll clench and won't be able to finish his business until he gets home."

Diego had laughed, the lens panning across the office. Even before his dad died, it had seemed like a mystical place. The epicenter of his father's power, who back then had seemed like a god.

"I'm glad you like it in here," Lorenzo said, the camera

swinging back around to him. "You know whose name is on the building?"

"Yours," Diego answered, admiration lacing his young voice.

Lorenzo shook his head. "It's *your* name. I'm doing all of this for you. When you're old enough, the business will be yours."

"This office too?" Diego asked.

His father nodded in confirmation. "That's right. But not this chair." Lorenzo kicked, the chair rolling backward.

"Where will you work then?" Diego asked. "Here?"

"Nope," his father replied. "That's the best part. You're going to do all the work and take care of me instead. Sucker!" Lorenzo cackled while rolling around the office.

The footage shook as Diego chased after him. It slowed again when Omar entered the room.

"Did you manage to go?" Diego asked.

"No," Omar said, looking miserable. "I got interrupted."

Diego's laughter joined that of his father.

"You guys suck," Omar complained. "Give me back my camcorder."

The footage swung around, and for one glorious moment, a young boy could be seen standing next to his father, the grins on their faces identical. White static filled the screen.

Diego hit stop and rewind, intending to watch the tape again. The door to the apartment swung open while he was waiting. Diego leapt to his feet, like he'd been caught watching porn.

Marti paused in the doorway. She was holding a grocery bag, something leafy and green sticking out the top. Fresh produce was practically alien to him. Diego had grown accustomed to nuking frozen food or opening a can.

"Hey," Marti said, kicking the door shut behind her. "You aren't working today?"

"I might later," he said. "I was watching something."

"Oh yeah?" his mother asked. "Anything good?"

He followed her into the kitchen. "Old home movies of dad."

She paused again. "We don't have any."

He explained what Omar had done while helping her put away the groceries. "It's a real trip," he said. "Do you want to see?"

She thought about it in silence. Considering that he'd needed a week to decide, he didn't judge her for it.

"Okay. Why not?"

They sat on the couch together. He wanted to fast-forward through Omar's intro, but she made him play it. "He's gotten so handsome!" she raved.

Diego rolled his eyes. "He's still a dork. Here comes the good stuff."

Her reaction was similar to his. He could tell how overwhelming it was to see her husband move and talk again, when they'd gotten by on stationary photos for so long. Once the shock wore off, she laughed at all the same parts he did. By the end of it, their eyes were wetter than either of them preferred.

"I need to know," Diego said, taking advantage of the moment. "It drives me crazy, Mom. Please." He didn't have to explain what he meant. Diego wanted to read the suicide letter his father had left behind. "Or at least tell me the reason why."

Marti shook her head. "I wish I could have protected you back then. You shouldn't have been the one to find his body. He never wanted that. You weren't supposed to be home that night! The letter was for me, so I'd know where to find him."

"Does it say why he killed himself?"

Pain flashed across her face before she managed to hide it. "Yes. And you don't need to know. You've been through so much already, all of it horrible. I'm not sure how you managed to survive. Especially when I failed to be there for you when you needed me most. If I thought that letter would help you heal, or accept what happened, I would show you. I wouldn't hesitate, but this is the last chance I have to protect you. Even if it means you can't forgive me or love me or—" She had to press her hand over her chest before she could continue. "Let me be your mother this one final time. Please."

Diego studied her, recognizing that they had both been through a horrendous loss. Like his father, she was flawed and human. He knew that now. Marti had done her best. And was still trying to.

"Okay," he said hoarsely. "I'll let it go."

The words must have been of great relief to her because she started crying. Diego pulled her close, fearful of the unknown, and grateful that he wouldn't have to face it just yet. Maybe someday, when enough years or decades had gone by, but not now.

324

Marti took a step back, seemingly embarrassed. "I better start dinner," she said. "Are you gonna stick around this time?"

"Yeah," he said. Not only had he found a missing piece of his father. He'd gotten to reconnect with his mother as well. Diego didn't know which mattered to him more, but for the first time in a very long while, he felt like he was home.

Omar hammered the buttons of the controller mercilessly, trying to purge the violence from his system. They were playing one of those shoot 'em ups where wave after wave of bad guys needed to be slaughtered. And yet, he didn't feel any better because the *real* enemy was out there, probably having a grand ol' time, while his best friend was—

Stoically playing a video game, Omar saw after checking on him. Anthony had insisted on doing something fun, unwilling to talk much about what had gone down. Omar squeezed plenty of details out of him anyway, because today had been absolute torture. He'd only found out last night when Cameron called him and seriously undersold just how bad it had been.

"Troy and his friends gave Anthony a hard time tonight. We really need to look out for him, between classes especially. Before and after school too, I guess."

Anthony was just as casual when calling him this morning to say that he was staying home and couldn't give him a ride. Only when Omar went to his dance class did Keisha clue him in. He heard more details from Silvia during lunch. He had been tempted to skip the rest of the day, and regretted not doing so when finally seeing Anthony after school. He looked a little beat up, which was bad enough, but he could tell the damage went way deeper than that.

They'd hurt him, the fuckers! His best friend! The guy he'd shared every single adventure with since they were kids.

Omar tossed aside his controller in frustration. "I'm going to kill them," he growled.

Anthony paused the game. "You can't," he said.

"Just try and stop me!" Omar snarled.

Anthony smirked. "And if I do, you'll what? Beat me up for not giving you permission to beat them up after they beat me up?"

"I'd never hurt you," Omar replied, his voice raw.

"I know," Anthony said softly. He looked toward the window of his bedroom. "Do you want to go for a walk?"

"Okay," Omar said, "but it won't change anything. They're fucking dead!"

Anthony pressed his lips together and stood. Omar followed him outside, noticing that his friend put on an old denim jacket that he hadn't worn since junior high. His long black coat had been lost. Presumably it was—along with the wig—still in the muddy cornfield where those pieces of shit had ganged up on him like cowards.

Omar clenched his jaw as they began their walk. He felt like punching a goddamn tree!

Anthony must have noticed, because he said, "This has to stop."

"Oh, I plan on finishing it!" Omar assured him.

"For real," Anthony said. "No more feuds. Not with Graham or Troy. Not with Diego either. LaVern is right. We need to start building bridges."

"How can you say that?" Omar demanded. "Especially after what those assholes did to you!"

"Only after what I did to them, because of what they did to us. I don't know how far back it goes anymore. I'd have to write it all down. I bet they're the same way. After a while, you forget the reasons and just start hating each other out of habit."

"Fine with me," Omar said, crossing his arms over his chest.

"It's not okay with me. What if it's Cameron next time?" Anthony's voice was strained. "Or you? I don't want that."

Omar stewed in silence as they walked toward a public park. "So what's the deal?" he said at last. "We're all going to be buddy-buddy somehow?"

"I doubt that," Anthony replied. "But we've got to find a way of getting along with them, even if we don't agree on much. Otherwise it will only get worse."

"How do you plan on doing that?"

"No idea," Anthony admitted. "I think I'd like to try making amends with Diego first."

"I haven't had any luck," Omar said with a sigh.

"Did he ever watch the tape you gave him?"

"I dunno. He's probably using it as a paperweight."

"Maybe if we both try," Anthony said. "We need him. And he needs us."

"Don't worry about Graham or any of the others," Omar said. "I'll be your bodyguard."

Anthony stopped and turned toward him. "No more fighting. Promise me."

"Only if you promise me something in return."

"What?"

"Quit acting like everything is okay! You might be able to fool the others, but not me."

Anthony's face started to crumple before he caught himself. Then he nodded solemnly and resumed walking.

"I hate that I wasn't there," Omar said as they cut across the park. "I should have been, even if we both ended up getting our asses kicked. Were you scared?"

Anthony's chin trembled. "Yeah. I thought I was going to die."

"That would have killed me too," Omar said, grabbing his arm to stop him. "It'll never happen again. I'll always be there for you, no matter what. I love you, man!"

The mask finally slipped and fell away. Anthony began to cry. Omar took his best friend into his arms, holding him and not letting go as the autumn leaves broke free to spiral through the air around them.

Anthony pressed his back to the bedroom door and exhaled, relieved to finally escape everyone's well-meaning concern. He appreciated that they cared so much about him, but the pain in their eyes made it hard to forget his own. He needed to stay strong. That was crucial, because inside himself he was standing on the brink of a life-changing decision. Part of him wanted to give in, to fall back in line to avoid getting attacked again. He'd pretend to be like any other boy, and while the bullies wouldn't let him forget who he really was, they'd probably get bored and find a more interesting target. A sacrificial lamb to spare Anthony from further harm.

He stood there in the darkness of his room, the temptation overwhelming as flashes of the violence he'd suffered played through his mind. Unable to take it anymore, he switched on the light. He felt safe here. Although he couldn't shake the feeling that the poster of Robert Smith was staring at him, an unasked question on his red painted lips.

How long until you start hating yourself?

Because that's what it would take. If the bullies sensed any pride remaining in him, they'd do everything they could to snuff it out, grinding it beneath their heels. Similar to what they'd done to his face. Anthony reached up to touch his cheeks and nose, wincing at how tender parts still felt. The rest of him was even worse. His body twinged painfully with every movement, making it impossible to forget. Even here.

He sighed and put on *Disintegration*, his favorite album from The Cure. Anthony stretched out on his bed and tried to lose himself in the maudlin melodies, and while they were comforting, something inside him remained restless. He needed to make a decision. He would have to go back to school eventually, and when that happened, he wouldn't have the benefit of makeup to give him artificial confidence. Anthony could no longer be himself while there. Troy had made that impossible. Or maybe Preckwinkle was to blame, he didn't know, but what was the point in trying anymore when he'd already lost?

And yet, if that was true, how come he'd gotten up this morning and carefully applied powder and base to his swollen face? Eyeliner and lip gloss too. He remembered standing taller after doing so, feeling that he'd magically erased the damage they'd inflicted. If only. Maybe it was time to take off the makeup and face reality. He got up to do just that, passing by Robert Smith's judgmental stare on the way out.

Last year had been tough but doable. He'd gotten shit for coming out, but nobody had attacked him for it. Aside from the time Graham decked him, but that had involved some provocation on Anthony's part. He could tone down the public affection so people wouldn't be reminded. No more holding Cameron's hand in the hallway or kissing him in the parking lot. Anthony wouldn't be giving up exactly. He would simply be more cautious. Discreet.

He closed the bathroom door behind him and avoided his own reflection. He wet a washcloth in the sink and brought it to his face. He hesitated when forced to look in the mirror. Anthony still liked the person he saw there. No… He loved her. Even though she was clearly shaken by what had happened. And what he was about to do to himself. The least he could do was give her a parting gift.

Anthony tossed the washcloth aside and opened a drawer

to take out the lipstick he'd bought but never worked up the courage to actually try. He took off the lid and twisted the tube, revealing a bright red slope. Then he leaned forward over the sink and tickled his bottom lip with waxy pigment. His upper lip was trickier. He should have paid more attention when watching Silvia and Mindy do this, but he managed to replace his natural pink hue with a richer red. Anthony leaned back to get a better look at himself. Then he snorted.

"It's not even my color!" he said in disbelief while laughing, because after all the anticipation and dread, the stupid lipstick didn't even suit him. Anthony rolled his eyes and tried to wipe it off, most of it ending up as a red smear that marred the corner of his mouth. He stopped and did a double take, because it almost looked like blood. And he kind of liked it. He met his own gaze in the mirror.

"You're such a freak," he said.

Anthony felt a swell of affection. For himself. Whatever this was inside of him couldn't be suppressed so easily. The assholes of the world hadn't managed to beat it out of him. But they had, for a brief moment, almost tricked him into thinking that he was weak. He'd nearly handed the sword to them, so they could use it as a weapon against him, when in truth it was his alone to wield.

Anthony leaned back and considered his own reflection. "Maybe a different color next time." He already knew there would be other opportunities, because he wasn't giving up. Instead he would embrace his inner strength—the sparkling diamond core of his true self. He still didn't understand the full implications, but he'd never get there if he stopped now.

Remembering that practice makes perfect, he reapplied the lipstick, leaving the weird smear intact. Anthony didn't pick up the washcloth again. Instead he returned to his room, turned up the music, and stretched out on the bed while wearing a smile. Then he closed his eyes and danced with the twin sister in his heart.

Dear Reader,

You are powerful! Reviews and word-of-mouth are what truly make a book successful, and I need your help more than ever. I'm an independent author, which means I don't have the backing of a publisher. That's by choice. My stories are unabashedly queer. I don't want to compromise my vision in the name of marketability. Providing you with an authentic experience is too important to me, especially as a gay man who writes from the heart. So if you enjoyed spending time with Anthony, Omar, Ricky, and the others, please consider writing a review, sharing a link to the book on social media, or contacting a friend to express your excitement. You can also become a patron to the arts by joining me on Patreon where I offer exclusive content and early access to my latest stories long before they are published. Thank you for the support you've already shown when buying this book!

With love,

-Jay Bell

Listen on the go with audiobooks!

Many of Jay Bell's books are available on audio too. Fall in love while you commute to work or ignore that annoying relative while losing yourself in an adventure. Find out which books are available and listen to free chapters at:

www.jaybellbooks.com

-=Books by Jay Bell=-

The Something Like… series
#1 Something Like Summer
#2 Something Like Autumn
#3 Something Like Winter
#4 Something Like Spring
#5 Something Like Lightning
#6 Something Like Thunder
#7 Something Like Stories - Volume One
#8 Something Like Hail
#9 Something Like Rain
#10 Something Like Stories - Volume Two
#11 Something Like Forever
#12 Something Like Stories - Volume Three

The Pride series
#1 Pride High: Book 1 - Red
#2 Pride High: Book 2 - Orange
#3 Pride High: Book 3 - Yellow
#4 Pride High: Book 4 - Green

The Loka Legends series
#1 The Cat in the Cradle
#2 From Darkness to Darkness

Other Novels
When Ben Loved Tim
Kamikaze Boys
Hell's Pawn
Straight Boy
Out of Time, Into You
Switch!

Who the hell is Jay Bell?

Jay Bell is a proud gay man and the award-winning author behind dozens of emotional and yet hopelessly optimistic stories. His best-selling book, Something Like Summer, spawned a series of heart-wrenching novels, a musically driven movie, and a lovingly drawn comic. When not crafting imaginary worlds, he occupies his free time with animals, art, action figures, and—most passionately—his husband Andreas. Jay is always dreaming up new stories about boys in love. If that sounds like your cup of tea, you can get the kettle boiling at:

www.jaybellbooks.com